Finntown of the Soul

3 ⁰⁰

Also by Pat Eilola:

The Fabulous Family Holomolaiset

A Finntown of the Heart

Finntown of the Soul

Patricia Eilola

NORTH STAR PRESS OF ST. CLOUD, INC.

St. Cloud, Minnesota

ISBN: 0-87839-278-5
ISBN-13: 978-0-87839-278-0

First Edition: July 2008

Printed in the United States of America

Published by
North Star Press of St. Cloud, Inc.
P.O. Box 451
St. Cloud, Minnesota 56302
northstarpress.com

Dedication

To the memory of my mother, Ilmi Marianna Brosi, known through out her life as "Marion Johnson," loving wife and mother, dedicated and creative teacher, and principal. My mother was a woman who so influenced other's lives that, at her memorial service, almost everyone there spoke up with a wonderful memory of her, and the financial contributions we received enabled us to give a thousand-dollar scholarship to a student at the high school in Cook, Minnesota, where she completed her teaching career.

She gave unstintingly as a teacher and as a mother, grandmother, and great-grandmother, whom her great-granddaughter Katy called "Gum-Gum," probably the term she most enjoyed being called.

It is also dedicated to our daughter, Mary, and her husband, Chuck Kimball, who have inculcated Mary's grandmother's love of learning into their children's lives. We hope that this book will help them to value even more the education they received as they read about what their great-grandmother went through in order to achieve what she did.

Acklowledgements

Many thanks to Mara Kirk Hart of Duluth, who read and reacted to every single page of this book, offering comments and suggestions that were invaluable. I chose to follow some of her suggestions, but not all; therefore, all errors in the book are attributable to me and to me alone.

Many thanks, too to Kara Darling of Williamson Music, a division of The Rogers & Hammerstein Organization, on behalf of Irving Berlin Music Company, for arranging to grant me permission to use the words of Irving Berlin's song "Always" in this book. ("Always" by Irving Berlin, © Copyright 1925 by Irving Berlin. © Copyright renewed. International Copyright secured. All rights reserved. Reprinted with permission.)

CHAPTER ONE
Farewells

P*oor Ma.* I stood in front of her with my back against the front door of our rented house in Kinney begging, "Please, Ma, do we have to leave?"

Standing behind her, holding tight to her long skirts and pushing against her back, my little sister Margie screamed, "Let's go! Let's go!"

One bone of contention between my sister and me had always been school. Whereas I could not bear to leave the school in Kinney behind, Margie didn't care if she ever learned English. She insisted on speaking Finnish and staying at home if it were at all possible. Since this time she considered herself on the side of the just, her urgings rose in volume as her clutch on Ma's skirt tightened. "Mr. Salin's waiting. The wagon's loaded. Let's go!" she howled.

On the gravel road just beyond the picket fence Ma had so lovingly built and painted, stood Mr. Salin patiently holding his horses, who were *whooshing* their tails and stomping, ready to go. The wagon was filled with all of our worldly belongings—our black cook stove, Ma's White treadle sewing machine, a chair and two tables, the davenport that turned into a bed, and boxes of cookery, clothing, and essentials.

All we needed to do was to lock the house, climb onto the wagon, and join the exodus of Finnish families who had decided to leave the iron mines behind and set out for homesteads in Zim.

But even at this last second, I pleaded, "Please, Ma, isn't there some other way?"

Ma's shoulders slumped. She handed Margie to Mr. Salin, who set her on the tailgate with a blanket over her, and faced me for one final time. "Ilmi." She sighed and tried hard to contain her impatience. "We have no other choice. We cannot pay the rent here. In Zim at least we will have our own place."

1

"But we have no *place*," I cried in desperate rebuttal. "Everyone else has raised some kind of dwelling, but we have nothing but the land. How are we going to live?"

Ma's lips firmed up. "We'll find a way. Now move."

This time the tone of her voice brooked absolutely no more argument. "Go and sit on the tailgate with Margie and give me the key so that we can lock the door and leave."

We had been over those same arguments again and again, but I had to give it one last try. "Ma, there is no school in Zim."

"There'll be a one-room school as soon as the men can get it built."

"So I'll be back with the babies again. Miss Loney had promised to double promote me into the upper grade room so that if I worked hard enough there was a chance that I could take the eighth grade state boards and graduate this year."

"Perhaps the teacher there will help you, too. I know this is hard for you," Ma concluded with unusual forbearance, "but we have no choice."

In an unusual gesture of affection, she drew me to her and patted my back and wiped away my tears. But in the process, she procured the key and locked the door.

"We have to make it, Ilmi," she said, fiercely, with all the force of the Old Ma, the Ma we knew before the difficulties of this pregnancy. "Now, climb onto the tailgate with Margie so we can be on our way."

Finally, with that same shade of her old spirit, she grabbed me by the arms and said, "At least we are together."

Since it would not serve for me to throw myself down on the steps like a heroines in the movies we had watched in Salins' garage, I finally accepted what I could not change and climbed up on the tailgate next to Margie.

Mr. Salin, aware of the fragility that had accompanied Ma's "delicate condition," helped her onto the front seat, wrapped a lap robe about her, whistled to the horses, and off we went with Margie bouncing up and down, anxious for the adventure to begin, and me sobbing quietly into the blanket.

In truth the only part of Kinney I was truly glad to leave was the chicken wire fence which divided the end of Main Street from the beginning of the Oliver Iron Mine and the cave where the good and bad gangs had brought me when they joined together to make me well again at the end of that incredible summer. When starvation had loomed, Pa gone, of course, and Ma ill with the first stages of pregnancy, I had found a way to Ely to search for Uncle Charles, who had promised to take his money from the bank, to quit his job at the mining company, and to rescue our family, buying a farm where we would all live in paradise.

We had never heard from him again. My precarious voyage to the metropolis of Ely on the Vermilion Iron Range, the ensuing discovery of Uncle Charles's death, the intercession of my guardian angel and the gypsies, and my hard-won battle with influenza had acquainted me with those things in the world I could not change. Try as I might, the move to Zim was another one of them.

Uncle Charles's insurance money had been just enough for us to buy a small plot of land and the minimum essentials for a dwelling.

I was crying first for the loss of my dreams of finishing school so that I could join the educated world, the English world, working toward a better, happier future where I could get a real job to support Ma and Margie.

Tears were flowing also because we were closing the door on everything I had come to love—for my teacher Miss Loney and her belief in me, for the supportive solidarity of the "good gang," though most of them were moving, too, for the growing friendship with the members of the "Bad Gang," mostly Italians and Slovenians, especially Kabe, whose full name— Diodado Carmen Joseph Vanucci—was saved for times of extreme dereliction.

As I was recovering, Kabe had begun to read the novel *Ivanhoe* by Sir Walter Scott aloud, and our audience had grown to include most everyone within listening range. We had planned to reenact the final scene as a play with Kabe as the evil Knight Templar Brian de Bois Guilbert, me as Rebecca (in danger of being burned at stake) and Eino Salin as the hero Ivanhoe.

The lines between gangs had dissolved that summer, and more than any place we had lived, following Pa as he got one job and either quit or was fired and sought another, Kinney had become home.

And finally, perhaps worst of all, I cried for the decision I had made just the night before, a decision which had severed our close relationship with Mr. and Mrs. Alex Savolainen of Virginia beyond repair. It had been the correct decision. I knew that. But it still hurt.

Ma, a creative and skilled seamstress, had been Mrs. Savolainen's dressmaker since her husband had brought her home from an expedition to the East to find a wife of culture and grace. In his eyes, Anna Savolainen was perfection. But no ready-made garment fit her stout form, and Ma had been able to make her look to the public the way he had always seen her.

When I disappeared from home to begin my quest to reach Ely and Uncle Charles, it was to save my family, which was approaching starvation. Margie had even begun to eat the ashes from the wood stove. Ma had appealed to Mr. Savolainen for help. Owning stores in Virginia, Duluth, and Ely, he was familiar with the route, circuitous as it was from Kinney to Ely, and it had been he, with the aid of the gypsies, who had fulfilled my quest including my need for retribution. In the process we had become fast friends.

Thus it had been no surprise the night before to see their roadster whirl up to the road in front of our rented house, to say good-bye we thought. We greeted them at the door, dusting off their outer coats and leading them into the kitchen.

Mr. Salin was coming later to load everything into his wagon so we still had furniture in place though everything was laden with boxes.

Unlike their usual visits, however, it was not I with whom they wished to speak. (Oh, how I blessed Miss Loney's class in rhetoric. I had even begun to think in correct though somewhat stilted English). They sat down but did not settle back. They accepted coffee, but did not drink it. They chatted about the Penguin Club dance and the lovely the frock Ma had made for Mrs. Savolainen. I never could call her "Anna."

Then they had surprised us all by asking Margie and me to leave.

"We have something very important to discuss with your mother, and we have reached the point where it cannot be postponed," said Mr. Alex with a twinkle in his eye for me. "Will you take Margareta Seraphina outside so that we may talk privately?" He and Mrs. Savolainen were among the very few to call Margie by her full name, the rest of us abbreviating it to a version that seemed to fit her better.

Most of this conversation took place in Finnish, of course, since Ma was not fluent in English.

Bewildered, for I was usually the focus of their visits, I had taken Margie by the hand and slipped out the back door leading to a lean-to porch. Although I knew I shouldn't, I left the door ajar, whispered to Margie to be still, and fastened my ear to the opening.

"We have come here this evening," Mr. Savolainen began, patting his wife's hand, for even though the door I could sense her nervousness, "both of us, to offer . . ." At that he paused as if searching for the correct words, then gave up the search and simply said, "to offer . . . to ask you to consider . . . to allow us to adopt your daughter Ilmi, whom we call 'Marion.'"

I gasped, hurriedly clamped a quick hand over Margie's mouth, and used a strong arm to hold her back from charging into the grownups' discussion. She turned and clung to me as I did to her.

Dimly I understood that this was one of those life-affecting moments, a time when two roads diverged, and I could not travel both.

I squeezed the door open a bit more. Just at the edge of our view, Ma sat like a statue, immobile, her face frozen as a porcelain doll's with the smile still there, but it not reaching her eyes, which looked from Mr. to Mrs. Savolainen again. Her only movement was to raise a hand to her throat.

Mr. Savolainen took her silence as permission to continue. "You must know that all the time that she and I spent together in Ely first searching for her Uncle Charles then for those who had murdered him and finally seeking restitution, my affection and respect for her grew. Her insight and intelligence, her composure and creativity, her ability to see beyond the boundaries of prejudice to turn to the gypsies, so much reviled, impressed me. Above all, I admired her insistence on putting herself at risk, on bearing the symptoms and finally the pain of the influenza, to go willingly into the pest house in Ely to draw the truth from the young Mr. Smith, who was a minor accomplice to what had been a nefarious plot. Her fortitude in that and in all circumstances increased my feeling of affection for her."

Ma, hands, now clasped in her lap, sat unmoving. Just a few months ago she would have thrown a frying pan at anyone making such a suggestion.

There was a long pause.

Then Anna Savolainen added, "I had heard all of Mr. Savolainen's remarks and understood the strength of his feeling. But not until the night of the retribution ball at the Forest Hotel in Ely did I see the potential in this child. Her grace in the face of the cream of Finnish society, her overall demeanor were all that I would ask from a daughter."

Her voice dropped to a whisper, "The daughter we will never have."

Alex continued with Mrs. Savolainen breaking in to add a word here and there. "Since we have visited her during her convalescence, our feelings for her have grown even stronger." He floundered.

Mrs. Savolainen concluded simply in her soft gentle way, "We have learned to love her and would like to adopt her, giving her the English name we used that night at the Forest Hotel. She would become Marion Brosi Savolainen."

Ma bent her head. Such arrangements were not uncommon among the Finnish community. When there were two many children in a family, one or more were often informally "adopted" by another family which was childless or needed the help.

I clung to Margie, and she clung to me, and we held onto the door with all of our might. I knew full well what the Savolainens offered—an education at the very best schools, inclusion into the highest rung of Finnish society, travel to Mrs. Savolainen's home on the East Coast and beyond. It was impossible not to yearn for such things.

Moreover, I had come to love the Savolainens, too, Alex as my guardian angel and Anna for all she had done for Ma.

Ma swallowed hard, and we could see her wringing her hands in her lap. She, too, understood all of the ramifications of what the Savolainens offered to me. And she also understood that the offer had been suffused with love.

Mrs. Savolainen, sensing in her silence that Ma was at least considering the offer, assured her. "We would not try to separate her from you and her sister. We could easily arrange to spend holidays together. I have even considering offering you the post of housekeeper in our home and allowing you to bring Margareta Seraphina along."

Ma's eyes flashed. and Mrs. Savolainen quickly amended, "But all of that would, of course, have to be worked out to your satisfaction."

"For a time," Alex continued, "we would like to take her with us to Mrs. Savolainen's home on the East Coast. Of course we would outfit her appropriately. Quick as she is, she would have no trouble picking up nuances of language and style appropriate to one of her age in that setting."

Faced by Ma's silence, he added, "I am sure she will continue her education past high school," he said, quickly, because Ma was beginning to stir, "for which we would bear the cost."

Then he added rapidly, as if he knew he had little more time, "In return we would also promise to make life more comfortable for you and for Margie. A house in Virginia or in Kinney, if you prefer; a monthly stipend so you would not have to work."

Ma still did not speak, though she uncrossed her legs so that she was facing the Savolainens more squarely. She quit wringing her hands and simply clasped them in her lap.

On the porch, Margie and I held each other fiercely. Tears were running down Margie's face. I simply stood and thought about what my life would be like if Ma said, "Yes."

I did love the Savolainens. Had it not been for Alex Savolainen's guidance and support, I would never have found Uncle Charles's grave. We would never have received the insurance money or the restitution money, little as it was. He had cared for me and guided me every step of the way, once he had found me, trusting me to lead him into the gypsy camp when gypsies were considered pariahs, following their suggestions, providing a room for me above the jewelry store he owned in Ely, whether his managers, the Stembers wanted to or not, even finding Pa at a lumber camp in the mist of the northern forest when it was not clear whether or not I would live.

It was Mr. and Mrs. Savolainen who had arranged the grand ball at the Forest Hotel in Ely, which unveiled Mr. and Mrs. Smith as the criminals and upstarts they were. I knew full well all I owned these two good, good friends and how deeply my feelings for them went.

A part of me wanted to be a part of their lives in a world where Margie and Ma would never be hungry again and need never again depend upon Pa's desultory visits and meager contributions to our family's survival. That part of me yearned for security.

I knew that Ma's unusual quietude meant that she too was considering all of those factors and weighing them against the reality of our lives— hers and mine and Margie's. She had closed her eyes, and tears ran down her cheeks. Ma never cried. Suddenly I was terribly afraid that she would think of me first and all that the Savolainens were offering.

But in the final analysis the decision was mine. During that past summer I had lost the innocence of girlhood where all is black or white and begun my passage into the adult world and its many shades of gray.

Ma did not need to call me in to make my wishes known. Of one accord, Margie and I burst through the door. Margie ran sobbing into Ma's arms. I stood with my hands clasped behind my back so tightly that my knuckles were white.

I stiffened myself until my back hurt, looked squarely at Mr. and Mrs. Savolainen, and thought again of how dear they were to me.

"Please do not think that I do not love you," I said, my voice breaking. "Next to Ma and Margie, you are the nearest to my heart. But my heart has responded unequivocally. No matter what, I could never leave Ma and Margie."

Mr. and Mrs. Savolainen had risen when we came in. They hugged and kissed me but had the good sense to don their driving coats, pat Ma, murmur their love and understanding and leave.

Ma had still not risen. "You are very sure, Ilmi Marianna? We are leaving behind everything you want, even here in Kinney, small town that it is. Our homestead in Zim has nothing, not even a house. We will have to start from scratch and eke out our living as we can."

"But we will be together, Ma."

Only then did she, who was so loath to show emotion, rise, holding Margie, and we stood together. "Like Three Musketeers," I averred.

I had been strong last night. I had helped Mr. Salin load our few belongings into the back of his wagon, grateful for his help, for most all of the houses around us were dark, the Finnish families long since settled in Zim.

Now I huddled under the blanket, still crying as we passed the chicken wire fence, ashamed that I had lost my strength this morning and made things even harder for Ma.

I had known in my heart that we had to leave Kinney. It was the child in me who had cried and held back the key to the house.

A hint of pink tinged the edge of the horizon as we headed up Highway 25 toward Little Swan then east toward McDavitt township and the small spot on the map marked with a dot and the word "Zim." But instead of watching the beginning of a new day, I cuddled next to Margie and fell soundly asleep, worn out by a vague, dreamlike mixture of grief at the thought of all we had left behind mixed with fear of where our journey would lead us.

CHAPTER TWO
The Journey

If we had had an automobile, we could easily have made the trip from Kinney to Zim in a day. But Mr. Salin, no doubt aware of the way Ma bit her lips and hung on tightly to the seat to minimize the jouncing and bouncing declared that the horses were tired, a fallacious remark if I had ever heard one, and decided that we stop in the late afternoon close to the banks of a branch of the St. Louis River to spend the night.

We dined on Mrs. Salin's inedible bread, which at least gave us exercise in chewing, drank fresh water from the stream and carefully divided up the strips of smoked salmon, cut down to the skin so we could savor every bit. It sufficed. Mr. Salin made us a bed of pine boughs under the wagon. Ma threw blankets over it. We washed as best we could and settled down under the lap robe for the night.

Maybe because she had been outdoors all day, Margie fell asleep almost right away, curled against Ma's back. As soon as she was completely comatose, Ma turned over. I rubbed her back as best I could. She said it helped. And we whispered almost all the night long, sharing as we rarely had before. I don't know whether it was the strangeness of the place or the simple closeness (I could say contiguity, but Eino Salin did not know I had gotten that far in copying his vocabulary notebook, and I didn't want to cheat.)

Ma whispered, "Are you sure you were right to say no to the Savolainens? They are such good people, and I know they meant well."

I paused long enough to make clear to her that I had thought about it and thought about it and thought about it all day. "I was right to say no. I don't doubt that at all. I could never leave you and Margie no matter how much I care for them, and I do. I love them both, and I hated to hurt them. But they were asking too much. They wanted me to become Marion when most of me is still Ilmi Marianna."

9

It was hard to find words to justify a decision that didn't need justifying so for a while we just lay there in silence.

Ma unbraided my hair and sat up to brush it free of twigs and bits and pieces of gravel and leaves. And then she just kept on brushing it, soothingly, brushing it down and back and smoothing it with her hand until I was so relaxed I could have fallen asleep. But I didn't want to miss out on this private time with Ma.

"Do you want to be Marion?" Ma asked, but quietly, as if she really wanted to know the answer.

I thought about that question for a long time, too.

"Yes. I think so. Someday. Maybe when I go to high school or college and am more English than Finnish. 'Ilmi Marianna' is a mouthful for anyone who isn't Finnish."

"And what will happen to Margie and me when you become Marion?" she asked, a tremble in her voice.

"I think," I said, after another long pause, "that by then it will just be natural—sometimes I'll be Ilmi Marianna, especially when you're angry with me." I giggled, holding my hand over my mouth so I didn't wake up Margie. Not that anything ever did. I'd often thought she'd sleep through an avalanche or an earthquake.

Even in the dark I know Ma smiled, too.

"You are determined to finish eighth grade and go to high school and maybe college?"

Ma knew the answer. I wondered why she asked. Then I knew.

"I will graduate from the eighth grade as soon as I can. This year if it's at all possible. The sooner I do, the sooner I can to high school and if I work hard enough to college, and then I can take care of you and Margie, and we'll never have to go through times like this again."

"I'm so sorry." Ma hugged me to her. "I should never have let this baby come to be. I knew after Margie's birth that another one would be . . . very difficult."

"Oh, no, Ma, don't say that! Margie and I want a baby brother. Just think. We'll have a man around the house that we can trust!"

"My dearest girl, you must know how many years from now that will be."

"We don't care. From the very beginning we wanted Baby Teddy. And once he's born, you'll be back to yourself again. It's just right now that you have to be careful and have extra rest and not overdo. One thing we have to do once we get settled is to make baby things. I know I'm not good at sewing, but I want to help.

"And as far as high school goes, I know I'll have to work for my board and room. I'll have to live with the family I work for. Maybe they'll let me come home for weekends. Or holidays." There was a long silence. "But that's at least a year away, maybe more."

Ma said, "I promise I'll do everything I can to get a school built in Zim, or at least a teacher hired, even if she has to stay at someone's house. I know Miss Loney sent boxes of books for you to study, and we'll make time so that you can work on your own or maybe with Eino Salin. Remember what Miss Loney said, 'If you can read, you can learn.'"

We lay quietly again for a while, thinking our own thoughts. I turned Ma over so that I could reach her braid, undid it, and brushed it slowly, gently.

I wanted to ask one more question, but I wasn't sure I dared, even during such a time of special closeness. But it was dark and I decided to take a chance. Ma could always refuse to answer.

"Why," I asked, "is Pa the way he is?" That was all I had intended to say, but the rest of my feelings just spilled out.

"Why does he leave us without food or money or wood for the stove? And why does he get so angry?"

I thought about it for a while. Ma waited and let me think and let me say what I felt. "It's as if he's two people. One is gentle with animals and plays the fiddle and makes up songs and verses and sings with the choir. The other is a . . . demon. I'm afraid of him. He yells and throws things and stomps out, grabbing his shaving things and some clothes and sometimes his fiddle. He gets so angry I'm afraid he'll hurt . . . me . . . or . . . you . . . or even Margie, though he never seems to get quite so mad at her. We don't know if he's coming back or not.

"Sometimes," I admitted, "I miss him because there's no one to do the heavy work like chopping wood and digging a well and plowing so we would have crops and animals to raise."

I waited a long time before adding in a whisper, "And sometimes I'm so afraid of him I wish he'd never come back."

Ma held me tightly against her as if I, not Margie, were the younger, and brushed back my hair and said, "Shhh, shhh, shhh" until I was too sleepy to remember that she hadn' t answered my question.

11

"I think,' she finally whispered, "that he was never meant to be a husband or a father. It's . . . just not in him. And I'm at fault, too, Ilmi."

"Oh, no, you aren't!" I sat up so fast I almost woke Margie.

"Yes, I am. I get angry with him, and when we're both angry with each other we do and say things we don't mean. I try to hold my temper, but when he quits a job when we need the money so desperately, I am just as guilty as he is of throwing things and screaming."

Stubbornly, I insisted, "He deserves it."

"Ah, well, who knows who is right?" Ma sighed, tired now.

"When will Baby Teddy be born?" I murmured just before she fell asleep. I believed in my heart that Baby Teddy had come into being during that happy time when Uncle Charles had chosen a beautiful spot for us to buy with his savings from his work with the Oliver Iron Mining Company in Ely. We had gone there together, Uncle Charles and Ma and Pa and Margie and I found a pathway to paradise with a hillock and a brook and arable land. Pa had played his fiddle and sung happy songs. Ma planned where her kitchen window would be. Margie and I played, believing in the certainty of the dream. Oh, we had been so happy that day and even the next. I dreamed of how Baby Teddy would look and imagined what it would be like to hold him in my arms. I did not really sleep that night. It was a night given to thought and conjecture, to reminiscence and tears, carefully covered by the lap robe.

I worried about Ma. Living as we did, then, close to the earth, with animals—cows, horses, pigs, chickens—part of every family's life, we kids grew up knowing how animals procreated. It was not much of a leap in understanding to liken the process to humans. Houses were small, walls thin, privacy rare.

The whole process seemed ugly. My mind replayed over and over the stories I had heard of women who had died in childbirth, bearing too many children, their bodies simply wearing out from the strain of caring for one baby while they were carrying another under their aprons. It was not uncommon for there to be more than ten children, sixteen even, though that was rare unless the first wife died and the second added to the number. Rare was the family that could afford a bedroom for each child and a separate one for the parents.

Except for the Salins. Somehow they had managed to limit the number of children to two. I thought to myself that if I had had a daughter like Sara, I wouldn't want another child either.

12

Her brother, Eino, was all right, though. He had been kind to me, especially when he realized that going to school and learning were as important to me as they were to him. In Kinney, though he had been in the upper grade room and I still in the lower grade, he had loaned me his vocabulary notebook. In fact, the idea of keeping a list of new English words with punctuation and definitions marked had been his idea in the first place. For years he had been the undisputed king of the Kinney School vocabulary contests.

When I had asked him what we would find in Zim, he had turned his head and said, "You don't want to know." And on that note I must have fallen sleep, for before I knew it, Mr. Salin was hitching up the horses, telling us it was morning and time to go.

All that next day Margie chattered. She recited again the names of the families who had already moved to Zim and built houses or shelters that were in some stage of construction—the Kolanders, the Ikolas, the Spinas, the Salins and the Aros will all be waiting for us, she counted with a bounce for each name. It was not the families that she looked forward to seeing, of course; it was all the children there to be to play with.

"I'll have to walk to most of the houses," she admitted with a pout and a grimace.

I forbore from comment. She was right. Only the Kolanders had built close to the St. Louis River; the other houses were spread out between Zim and that other spot called "Little Swan."

Salin's was the closest house to our land.

I could put up with Eino. In fact, he and I had started our own Speak English campaign. But Sara, Margie's bosom buddy was the bane of my existence. My vocabulary failed when I attempted to describe her. Or perhaps the truth of the matter was that I tried hard not to cast aspersions or make derogatory comments. Ma refused to allow them anyway. "If you can't say something nice, don't say anything at all," she lectured me, in Finnish, of course.

Sara Salin was equally obnoxious whether she was speaking Finnish or English, for the joy of her life was the degree of difference between her family life and ours, theirs being superior in every way.

And worst of all, Margie absorbed Sara's bragging and passed it on as if Sara's prominence redounded upon Margie. That day, because we were on our way to Zim where the Salins had already built their house, Margie got going on what Sara had provided in scrupulous detail.

"They have two stairways," Margie gloated, as if they were hers, "one leading from the large side porch upstairs and a second one with newel post and balusters leading upstairs from the living room. Sara said we could play on the back one because it's all dark."

I sighed.

Ma interrupted to ask if I knew where the family Bible had been put. I located it on the treadle of the sewing machine.

"Will you hold it, please, Ilmi? I started worrying about it and couldn't remember where we had put it."

I climbed up and clasped the Bible, keeping it carefully closed. Therein lay a secret that I was not supposed to know, a secret that I wanted to forget. Had I dared I would have dropped that Bible onto the gravel path behind us, and the fact that it contained would have been lost forever. But the book was so beautiful with its maroon, padded cover and leather bindings, the pages illuminated with gilt edges, the pictures so lovely, so like what my teacher in school called "great art" that I could not bring myself to deface it. Books were sacred to me. Even that one. So I held it carefully closed, the latch pointed toward my tummy so that it would not open by accident and reveal the dreadful secret which, if known, would wreak havoc with our lives even beyond that which Pa's absences constantly created.

"Hold it tightly, Ilmi," Ma warned, as though she could read my mind.

I hoped that interchange would have set Margie on a different track, for she was constantly talking, but it did not. Margie barely skimmed the surface of her eulogy to the Salins' abode.

"The side porch," she continued, as if she had not been interrupted, "is large enough so the men can change from their barn clothes there, and Mrs. Salin can do the washing without having to mess up the kitchen. The kitchen has not only—can you believe this?" She forced me to look at her and I looked up at the sky and put one knee over the other and bounced it in an effort to seem to be listening. "Not *only*," she repeated with emphasis "a black iron cook stove like ours that's used for cooking and heating but *also* a modern *separate* kerosene stove for heating the living room and the rest of the house."

It's a good thing that Mr. Salin was sitting so far in the front and that Margie's voice was offset by the sound of the horses' hoofs. I think he would have switched Sara if he had known she bragged this way.

But there was no stopping Margie. She went on about the pantry built under the back stairs and the living room with triple windows facing south and double ones facing west. The sun porch on the north side of the house had windows all around "so we can play there even on the hottest summer days, " Margie eulogized. It was hard not to be envious.

"And on her mother's dresser scarf there's an ivory comb and brush set with a matching covered dish with a hole in the center for her mother to keep the hair when she cleans her combs and brushes. When she goes out, that hair can be rolled into a 'rat' to make her pompadour higher and fuller."

I bit my tongue from commenting on Ma's hair, which hung in luxuriant waves down her back almost to her knees. She had no need of a "rat."

"*And*," Margie concluded, "the dresser set is made of *ivory* with small flowers as decorations, not of celluloid."

Ma's comb and brush and mirror, which I had packed, had been made of celluloid, which, over the years, had cracked, and the mirror had blackened.

"Sara has her own room, and Eino has his own room and Mr. and Mrs. Salin have their own rooms with registers so that the air from the living room stove will keep them warm in the winter, and every room has its own closet with a round piece of wood upon which they could hang the clothes which they ordered from the *Chicago Mail Order Catalog* or from Sears Roebuck."

She could have added "so there."

I could not top that, nor could I criticize the outside of that house as we approached it late that afternoon. How nice it looked with narrow siding boards painted white and window frames painted red! Mr. Salin had had workmen there all summer so the Salins had already moved in and begun to harvest the vegetables—potatoes, carrots, and rutabaga—from the fields Mr. Salin had cleared, plowed, and cultivated over the summer, while I had spent that time finding a way to Ely and recovering from the devastating illness which had wracked me body and soul when I found out that Charles was dead, our dreams of paradise an illusion, and Ma and Margie and I hardly better off than when I had left them.

I knew, of course, that our land would not be like the Salins. But when Mr. Salin put the brake on and yelled, "Whoa!" to the horses, Ma and Margie and I sat stupefied. Especially Margie. In her mind she had gotten things all twisted up and believed that we, too, would walk into a house, perhaps not as grand as Salins' but a shelter at any rate1, ready for us to move in.

"Here's your place," he told Ma.

We had driven alongside of the railroad tracks for much of the day, and nothing had changed during those miles, not even the uniformity of the bumps on the road.

Except for a few trees and underbrush and tall grass, we had passed nothing else—no hillocks, no houses, no plantations of trees, no nothing, except alderbrush, bleak stands of birch trees, dead-looking tamarack, and acres of swamp from which spruce and balsam trunks, lacking branches and needles, stuck out like the arms of dead and dying things, flailing for something to grasp before they too sank in the mire. I counted a few scrawny popple trees and a few Norway pines, but not much else.

Our acreage that evening looked like nothing more than peat bog. Sometimes later in the spring the ground actually reeked, as if it had been formed of decomposed, odorous layers of murky, mucky globs that could hardly be termed soil.

The absence of a good tree lot meant we would have to search for a supply of wood for the winter, though we had hauled as much as we could fit in the wagon from the house in Kinney. "No sense leaving it for the next renters," Ma had said with firm practicality when Margie and I demurred about moving what we had so carefully piled not even a year before.

Mr. Salin looked at the land, looked at Ma, and said, "Why don't you and the girls come to our house to spend the night? Tomorrow morning we can get a crew together to put up a shelter for you, and then we'll unpack the wagon." It was an honest invitation, genuinely meant.

But Ma's chin rose, her back stiffened, and she refused—as she always refused—what she perceived as charity of any kind. "Thank you, Mr. Salin, but we are already too much in your debt. If you will leave us the blankets, perhaps the lap robe, the clothes line, that iron pot under the chair there— can you see it?—and some wood, we will make do."

Poor Mr. Salin. Probably he had received strict orders from his wife that we were to be brought to their house for the night. But I understood how Ma felt. This was what we had to face, and the sooner we took charge of our own lives and quit relying on others to help, the better we would feel.

I knew then what Eino had meant when I had asked about our homestead and he had said, "You don't want to know."

When Margie said she wanted to go to Salins' to play with Sara, I stuffed her skirt in her mouth and held her so tightly she hadn't the breath to argue while Mr. Salin followed Ma's simple instructions, stringing the clothes line between trees and fastening the blankets on it with clothes pins that looked like small dolls with legs. They squeaked when he pushed them down as if they, like Margie, would rather have gone to Salins'.

Then Ma thanked him again for his help and indicated politely but firmly that we would now manage on our own.

"A crew of men will be here in the morning to empty the wagon and to begin to put up a shelter," he said, shaking Ma's hand and patting it gently. He really was a kind man. Then he nodded to Margie and me, climbed onto the front seat, clicked to the horses, and headed off toward home.

For a minute Ma stood still and looked around. Then she sat down on a fallen log and pulled Margie onto her lap. I sat as close to her as I could get, drawing strength from her, though heaven knows where she could find enough to face what seemed to us a monumental task.

"I'm hungry. I'm thirsty. My *pempu* is sore. I want . . ." Margie began her usual litany, in Finnish of course.

Although Ma was trying hard to make her quit sucking her thumb, Ma shut her up by the simple expedient of moving Margie's thumb toward her mouth. Surprised, Margie finished the movement, and settled back down, her right thumb in her mouth, her left hand twirling the small hairs that escaped her braids. I bit back tears.

Then Ma took a deep breath and said, "First things first."

She carried Margie away from the shelter Mr. Salin had made, held her with her pants and skirts up, and told her in no uncertain terms to go potty. Margie, who preferred to wait until it was too late, amazingly did her jobs, and Ma wiped her clean with leaves.

"Now," she told Margie, looking her firmly," I want you to walk around our camp and pick up every single twig and branch you can hold and bring it to me. We need to build a fire and have some *puurua* for supper."

"Ilmi," she continued, "You will help me build a tripod so that we can cook the oatmeal, and then I want you to go down to the river and bring back as much water as you can carry." She gave me a pot.

"At least we can eat something and rinse our faces and hands before we go to sleep. While you're down there, you wash yourself. That will save some steps."

17

Amazingly, Margie listened and did as she was told, and I was glad to have something productive to do. Ma hummed a Finnish song as she worked, and, as the sun began to set, we ate from the pot, enough to make our tummies full. I took the pot down to the water, washed it, and brought it back filled with water without being told. Ma and I identified a spot, then used it as an outhouse. Leaves worked as well as the pages of a catalog for wiping. Then we snuggled down on branches we arranged, as Mr. Salin had fixed the night before into a sweet-smelling mattress, covered ourselves fully clothed with the lap robe, and asked Ma to sing to us before we fell asleep.

I could hear the brush wolves off in the distance yipping and growling at their pursued quarry, a rabbit perhaps. We heard the scream of the rabbit and then the silence, which spoke as loudly as the cries of the wolves and the rabbit, for we knew why they were silent. They were feasting.

Off in the distance we could see the Salins' house lit with kerosene lamps in the windows. It looked as if they had put up a pole barn and a sauna as well as the regular barn and the house. Mr. Salin was a go-getter, Ma had always said.

But somehow that night with my head on one of Ma's shoulders and Margie's on the other, our arms intertwined, the horrible feeling of being bereft almost disappeared. We had survived the worst possible moment. We had arrived. We had each other. And Ma's soft soprano warded off the terrors of the night.

For then, it was enough.

CHAPTER THREE
Build

We awoke next morning to a pink, orange, and blue sunrise that started at the horizon and rose turning the dark sky into a palette of soft tones reaching tentative waves into the dark as if the day was not quite ready, like us, to get up. It peeked through the branches as we looked, still nestled together in our warm spot under the lap robe in our tent of blankets. The world was absolutely quiet, and Ma pointed with her finger quickly moving to her lips for us to be still to see a family of deer—the doe, and a pair of nearly grown fawns—come to the river to drink.

Then Ma, considering us to have lolly-gaggled long enough, hurriedly carried Margie to the designated toilet spot with me close behind. While she built up the fire to make our breakfast gruel, which in Finnish we called *puurua*, Margie and I dismantled the tent. I folded the lap robe neatly and removed the bed of brush. After we ate, Ma insisted that we all go down to the river to wash our faces and hands in the icy water, which was flat at the edges with a night scum of frost and thin ice. It boded an early winter.

By the time we heard horses being harnessed at the Salins and at houses at greater distances away that we glimpsed as the sun rose, Ma had tramped out the area where she wanted our shelter to be and set Margie and me to clear it of twigs and branches while she hacked at the underbrush with the hatchet she always had on hand.

Help we might need, and charity we must expect, but no one would catch us sitting or sleeping or awaiting help. We were on the job when Mr. Salin drove up with his wagon, rubbing his hands and blowing on them to warm them against the cold, ready to begin the unloading so he could get to the boards. First came the stove with its flat cooking surface and four removable burners with lids and black iron lifters, all intact. Then the water boiler was unloaded, fire box, pots, pans, even the copper kettle with a ring around the bottom so that it fit perfectly into the cooking burners.

Ma dickered with Mr. Aro, the second to arrive, to exchange our lumpy davenport for an iron bed with a tuck-under trundle, which he would bring that afternoon. She promised to work on a woolen outfit for each of his five children as soon as the shelter was finished and she had time to sew. The white rectangular table and matching chairs came off next. Ma made sure the boxes were not laid on the ground but on the stove or the table so that they would not get damp. One of them was full of the books Miss Loney had sent. I yearned to delve into that box, but by then the rest of the men had come by horseback or wagon. Mr. Aro took the davenport that had been the source of my glee when I wreaked my revenge on Wilho Field, who beat me in the spelling bee long ago in Kinney. I had closed the davenport with him inside of it screaming when the Fields came to visit one Sunday afternoon. I watched it go with some regret. My punishment had been more than worth the crime. I still smiled to myself when I thought of poor Wilho, caught not only within the confines of the davenport but later in school having plagiarized a poem for the Mothers' Day program. I was not unhappy to leave him behind.

But I had little time to reminisce. Despite her condition, Ma had set the younger children to gathering wood. The lot was not quite as bad as it had seemed the evening before. There were some scraggly jack pine and popple. She told them not to go too near the river or out of sight of each other, warnings we had all heard before since we were in a sense alone in the wilderness, far from the relative civilization of the close-packed houses and stores of Kinney. While red-faced Mr. Spina, the butcher; Mr. Kolander, Mr. Ikola, and Mr. Saarinen conferred with Mr. Salin about the base for our shelter, Ma should have rested and talked with the women who gradually joined in the house-raising party, every one bringing at least one item of food so that there would be a sumptuous lunch.

But while the men scratched their heads and talked about ways and means and measured the boards and discussed the height of the walls, Ma brushed the whole area with a scythe. She was good with the scythe, so good that we were warned explicitly not to get near her because she sharpened the edge to razor sharpness so all of the small brush went down as if would under a thresher's wheel.

But Ma didn't stop there. We had spent insurance money to buy two windows, a door, and enough boards to make a half-house.

"We can finish the other half next spring," Mr. Salin offered.

Ma refrained from comment and instead showed him the sketch she had made based on what we had been able to buy. She wanted the door and the window facing east so we would get morning sun and the second window facing south for afternoon sun. The west and north wall, she said, were to be the tightest, for that was the direction of the winter winds, and we had nothing but the boards to keep them out.

The men divided themselves into crews with Mr. Salin and Mr. Aro supervising the laying of the base, making sure it was square and not too large for the number of boards. Mr. Kolander and Mr. Ikola began on one wall; Mr. Saarinen and Mr. Spina on the other. They were all skilled carpenters, whose work, though rough, was square and tight.

While the ladies gossiped, they laid out the larder—venison stew and roast partridge, fresh boiled potatoes in their skins, and rutabaga, boiled and mashed, berries of every sort. These berries were fresh and canned and made into pies and cakes, and the ladies had brought more loaves of bread than we could count and creamy butter and buttermilk.

Ma took care to rest when she needed to, for we were able to see Baby Teddy kick, and sometimes when he was really active, all the children wanted to touch him. Margie was possessive, making everyone stand in line and take a turn and not tire Ma out needlessly. I was proud of her.

My job was to help Ma make stairs and a wood box. Mostly, I tried to help her saw left-over boards into equal lengths and hand her the nails.

Mrs. Aro exclaimed over Ma's tripod and made a big pot of strong coffee. When the sun reached its height and the men's shirts were wet from sweat and they were taking their caps off to wipe their foreheads with their sleeves and putting their caps back on to keep their hair out of their eyes, she rang the dinner bell, and everyone found a place to sit.

Everyone knew, including Mrs. Salin herself, that she was not a good cook, but she had brought pickles from their pickle barrel and canned goods, some of which we had never tasted—like peaches and pears—and sticks of penny candy for us kids.

Toivo Aro and Eino Salin and I debated about foregoing the penny candy, for we were the oldest, but Mrs. Salin insisted that we enjoy some too.

While the men drank a second cup of coffee, some of them slurping it from the saucer through sugar lumps held between their teeth, they picked up the theme that had brought all of us here.

"Here we are together in Little Kinney," Mr. Spina joked, his face even redder, not all from exertion. I suspected he was sipping something stronger from a bottle outlined by his pants pocket.

Ma asked, "Does anyone have a Hoosier cupboard for sale? There wasn't room for ours in the wagon?"

"We have an extra one on the side porch," Mrs. Spina answered, adding, knowing Ma, "perhaps we could exchange that for a suit for Eino? I swear that boy grows out of everything I order before it comes from the catalog!"

Ma nodded.

Eino blushed and disappeared. He was at that awkward stage where his voice ranged from high to low and he was painfully conscious of participating in any conversation. I don't know how it had happened, but he seemed to be a head taller than he had been last time we had talked, which had not been a very long time ago.

"At least the land is flat," Mr. Saarinen stated the obvious. "And the soil is . . ." He struggled to say something positive. ". . . not too bad."

Maybe it is good at your place, but it certainly isn't here, I thought, keeping my mouth shut as good girls should.

"It's going to be good to do our buying at your store instead of the company store," Mr. Aro said to Mr. Salin, who nodded. "I could never keep up. On payday I always owed the store most of what I had earned."

"You know we'll never get a job in a mine again," Mr. Kolander said. "They know why we left. They knew about the plans for a union."

The men nodded. They knew. They knew the company knew.

There was a moment of silence among the women. They too knew that with this move they had indeed put their names on the black list, where Pa's name had been ever since he had tried to start a union in Virginia.

We didn't have any choice. Perhaps that was one reason they had come to Ma's aide. It was all for one. We were forming a community, and we had to help each other.

No one said it. No one had to. The little ones were screaming and running around with their penny candies. The women began clearing the board table and carrying the dishes down to the river to wash, setting a kettle on the tripod to heat. Their conversation turned to the need for a school and the problems with children and all the work to be done before winter.

But not Ma. As soon as the men had the walls up and braced, up she went on a makeshift ladder to help pound the boards for the roof.

"Ma," I protested, "please, please get down. What if you fall?"

In the only English she ever used, she said, "The hell I will."

"Ma," I shook my head in despair, "please don't swear."

"The hell I am," she said, pounding as expertly as the men. It was the strangest thing. Ma struggled so hard with the transition from Finnish to English, except for the swearing. Her friend, who was named Maija or Mary also, when we lived in Virginia taught her some very effective words to use when she was angry.

I spent the rest of the afternoon handing up tarpaper and nails, holding walls straight, settling Margie for a nap when the mothers decreed it was time, and worrying.

As the shape of the half-house assumed form, two of the men—I think it was Mr. Spina, whom I thought would have a heart attack if he exerted himself any more—and Mr. Kolander, a teetotaler if there ever was one set about digging a well not far from the house. They only had to go down about ten or twelve feet before they hit water. Although they agreed that this was not sandy loam soil, nonetheless the water was drinkable. By that time I was so tired, I don't even now know who gave us a pump and built a wooden stand for it so I could draw water.

Somehow, by a magic as rich as alchemy, by nightfall, we had a house—well, half a house, it's true—but a four-walled shelter nonetheless.

Mr. Spina had called his crew over to rig up a chimney so we could build a fire in our wood stove. The bed was set up against the west wall so we could see the sun rise through the window. The women and children had gradually all gone home. Mr. Spina promised to bring the cupboard over next day and pound some pegs so we could unpack the boxes and hang our clothes.

I was so exhausted by the time the men left, having moved the stairs into place and accepted Ma's thanks and her offers of serving as seamstress for every family in return for all that they had done to help, I could have fallen into bed fully clothed.

"You take Margie to the river, strip her down, dunk her in, no matter how she screams, soap her head to toe, and dunk her in again until she's clean!" Ma ordered.

My back breaking, I almost argued that I was too tired. Then Ma gave me *that look*, and I grabbed Margie, a clean towel, and a heavy woolen nightdress, and dragged her down to the river kicking and screaming all the way. One of the women—I don't know who—left us a gallon of sweet milk, which the men had set in a shelf they had built about a foot down into the well. By the time I got through with Margie, rubbed her down, pulled the nightgown over her head, and carried her back, she was half asleep. Ma let her tangled hair curl for the night as she drank a cup of warm milk. She looked like a pink angel as she reached her arms up for a bedtime kiss from me, and I forgave her trespasses with all my heart.

Then I turned to Ma, who pointed us toward the river, too. I shuddered, but, remembering how good Margie felt, I forbore from argument. We walked down together as the sun set, stripped, waded in, shivering, soaped ourselves as quickly as we could, dunked down, dunked again, came up sputtering, grabbed our towels and ran for the house. Ma's hair, loosened from its braid, streamed behind her. I could see her tummy moving: Baby Teddy was kicking up a storm. Holding glasses of warm milk, we sat in front of the fire. I combed Ma's hair free of tangles and braided it in one long braid. She did the same with mine, and we both climbed into bed, one on either side of Margie.

I should have fallen fast asleep, but I lay there looking at the flames in the firebox of the wood stove remembering all that had been done for us that day.

Tomorrow, I thought, *I will unpack my books and ask about a school.*

"Tomorrow," Ma whispered, "I have to build an outhouse."

Just as I was falling asleep, Ma reached for my hand and put it on her tummy. "Say good night to Baby Teddy," she whispered. I felt him kick.

For the first time in a long time, I turned on my back and thought of Pa and of all he was missing and of how kind the men of Little Kinney had been to us that day.

Six families formed the backbone of our community. The Kolanders had settled along Highway 7, which ran from Zim to Little Swan. They were the farthest away. Among the families were over twenty children—Kolanders had three, Ikolas eight, Saarinens three, Salins two, Aros five, not to mention we two and some a bit farther away toward Little Swan. All of the children had fathers; all the women had husbands to till the soil and build the houses and saunas and barns and plant and reap the crops.

Where, I wondered, *is Pa? Why is he so different?* Ma was beautiful. Margie was too and lovable when she chose. I was ugly with my black hair and green eyes. I was skinny and small for my age. But the gypsies had liked me, and the Savolainens had loved me. Was I the reason Pa stayed away so long? The dates in the Bible crept into my mind like canker sores, festering. But I pushed those thoughts away and cuddled close to Margie, warmed myself from her warmth and fell asleep, pushing the questions so deep down into my soul that I vowed not to think of them again.

Ah, Ma, I should have been older or wiser or strong enough to say, "how can we move to Zim when you're pregnant and I'm barely twelve and Margie's such a baby, no matter her age?"

But Ma, it seemed had been right. And on that comforting note, I fell asleep.

CHAPTER FOUR
A Surprise

Dawn that second morning of our home in Zim rose opalescent, pearly, like the stone in the engagement ring Miss Loney had received from her fiancé just before we left.

I woke as from a dream slowly, looking longingly at the box of books, wanting, above all things, to take them out one by one, and, as I did, to remember her instructions to me should Zim not have a school.

Then the sounds of hammering and nailing sent me scurrying. I quickly took off my nightdress under the sheets, and reached for my work dress, thinking it would be on the chair where I had left it. When I looked up, however, there was Mrs. Aro, holding it up for me to slip into.

She had her finger to her lips, pointing to Ma and Margie, and motioned me out of bed, indicating swiftness and quiet. I looked outside to the place where our short-term outhouse had been and found that Mr. Aro and Mr. Saarinen had already dug the hole and were in the process of building a two-hole outhouse. Mrs. Aro motioned for me to use the pee pot she had put in the corner and covered with a cloth for the time being, then set me up at the table with a fork, knife, cup, and plate.

The aroma from the oven suggested she had a pan of *kropsua* ready to come out, and she served me one of the middle slices just the way I liked it, slathered with butter and sugar. My coffee was more milk than coffee, but I didn't mind. She had generously shared her larder with us that morning, and I had to admit she was as good a cook as Ma. The butter did not have even a tinge of the rancid taste lazier cooks allowed to form if they didn't work out all of the cream with their ladles in the big flat butter bowl, both made of wood just for that purpose.

Pouring herself a generous slice and what looked like a second cup of coffee, she sat down and whispered, "Your ma way overdid herself yesterday and we have to make her rest today. Mr. Salin will be here to get Margie in a little while, and we'll bundle her up even if she's half asleep and send her over to Salins. Mrs. Salin will take her for the day."

I knew that Mr. Saarinen was the best finishing carpenter in the community, and the rough outside work was really wasted on him. She said so in no uncertain terms.

"My Urho is good with the outside building, but it's a waste to have Mr. Saarinen doing that kind of work. When your ma wakes up and has a chance to freshen up so she's comfortable having him in the house, you and she can tell him what kind of shelves you want built and where, and he'll get that done in no time flat.

"He's already roughed out the boards, but he needs the exact length in order to do the final sanding. Mr. Kolander said he'll help finish up the outhouse. It won't take them long. I'd guess they'll be through by noon. Oh, by the way, I asked them to make one low seat for Margie."

I leaned back, still tired from yesterday. "That's a great idea. But I don't know how Ma will take all of this, Mrs. Aro. She is already feeling way too much in debt to all of you, and that's not good for her either because she stews about it and that makes her even more upset."

Mrs. Aro's hair usually hung half askew, and though her housedress and apron were clean, they were rarely ironed, but she made me feel as if she knew the priorities in life and had them clearly set in her mind and was not about to deviate from them. I think her will was even stronger than Ma's.

"Right now," she said firmly, "your ma's first priority is that baby. She needs your pa, but he's not here. She needs a family to step in to help her. She hasn't any. So, what do we do? Right now, I mean. Right now, we help her. I think that once it's put to her that way, she'll see the sense of it. And I mean to put it to her pretty strongly. Will you help me?"

I was flabbergasted. No one had ever addressed a problem to me like this before. Ma and Pa tended to talk around things and then get mad when the other didn't understand, and what could have been arranged in an ordinary manner wound up in a fight. I liked this way of doing things.

"Yes." I looked her straight in the eyes and said, "I'll take over the morning chores that Ma will want done. If you make another pan of *krop-sua* for the men and another pot of coffee, I can do all of the cleaning up and take charge of Margie until Mr. Salin comes. I have some ideas about the shelves, too, because I have boxes of books to use for studying. If I take them out and set them side by side, Mr. Saarinen can see how much space they'll need. He can guess how many shelves we need for clothes and dowels for hanging things, but Ma will feel better if she can tell him where she wants them."

"Ma can what?" came the sleepy question from the bed.

"Oh, nothing for you to worry about right now. Perfect timing." Mrs. Aro bustled over to the bed, rolling Margie into her arms and into a blanket. Outside, we heard the clanking of the harness and the plodding hoofbeats that heralded the arrival of Mr. Salin. He knocked on the door, said "Good morning" to Ma and "I'll be seeing you later," took hold of the sleeping bundle that was Margie, nodded to Mrs. Aro and me, and left.

Ma sat up, brushing her hair back from her face, looking tired and bewildered.

I pretended I wasn't there, finished my breakfast, and began cleaning up Mrs. Aro's and my dishes.

All the while the pounding went on outside.

Mrs. Aro sat down on the bed by Ma. "Now, this is what's going to happen today. I'm going to spend the day here kind of being the assistant general, making sure the men do things the way you want them done. My Urho and Alfred Ikola about have the outhouse ready. They've been working with Mr. Saarinen since before dawn—one high hole, one low hole. They've built so many of them this summer, they've got it down to an art. This is what we've all been doing for each other. Every time someone new moves in, the rest of us chip in to help them. In return, they help us when we need it. The first of us who got here—that's the Salins and us—well, we decided that since none of us has got family here, we're going to be family for each other, and that's the way it's worked ever since. You just happen to be the last one to move in, so the men are pretty used to doing what they've been doing all along."

"But," Ma began to protest, "there's no way we can pay them back the way you've been able to help each other."

"Well, my dearie, I'll tell you a secret that you already know."

I got such a kick out of Mrs. Aro's voice because she was speaking so matter-of-factly to Ma that it was going to be hard for Ma to argue or to talk around her.

"There's a lot of us in this community that's got a lot of talents. Me, for example. I'm a good one to have around when there's a baby on the way because I know a lot about birthing, thanks to my mother and my grandmother in Finland who taught me. And I'm learning more and more about herbs and healing and such. My Urho doesn't have a kitchen floor he can eat off of, but he knows if somebody is sick, they'll send for me. Urho is an unusually good man with a crosscut saw and an ax and can figure in his mind how many boards you might need if you want to build, say a sauna that so big by so big."

"But . . ." Ma tried to continue, "I . . ."

Mrs. Aro finished the sentence, ". . . can sew clothes that look better than the ones we order from the catalog. And if we buy the yard goods, why, when you're feeling better, maybe you'll take that White sewing machine and have it hauled over to, say, our house, and make some winter clothes for our kids who grow out of them faster than we can buy them."

I hadn't moved a muscle during this discussion because I wasn't sure how it was going to turn out, but when Mrs. Aro leaned over to give Ma a hug and say, "Now it's my turn to do a little extra," and hear Ma's barely suppressed tears and whispered "thank you," I unfroze and went about my work again.

And so the morning went. We weren't using the trundle bed so while Mrs. Aro helped Ma get dressed and freshen up, I made up the bed and started washing the dishes. The next pan of *kropsua* was ready just about the time the men were ready for a morning break and a cup of coffee.

Mr. Saarinen sat down, then, with Ma and they sketched out where the shelves should go and how long and wide they should be.

It took a lot of gumption for Ma to admit that we needed an extra shelf for Pa's shaving things—his single-blade razor and his soap dish with the compartment for soap on the top and the scoop for the brush on the side of the spout and the pink roses decorating the edges. His razor strap, the ultimate threat for punishment, a good two feet long and two inches wide, was made of leather fastened to a nail on one end. Pa held on to the other, stropping the razor back and forth to keep the edge flawless. Spanks on the rear with the razor strap hurt harder than anything. I'd gotten my share, especially when I didn't watch Margie.

Ma also indicated the placement for the dowels where we would hang our workaday dresses, aprons, coats, and good dresses. Mr. Saarinen even figured out a way or running a curtain across that area so it looked as if we had a closet.

But no one spoke up when Ma asked if we would help arrange the furniture. The night before, everything had been brought in helter-skelter and put down. The bed was on the north wall. The stove had to be under the chimney. Other than that, it didn't look finished. I bustled around washing windows and hanging the lace curtains Ma had washed and starched before we left Kinney. Otherwise it was as if everyone were waiting for something. Mr. Saarinen had virtually finished sanding the shelves and was waiting to put them into place. The floor needed to be swept two or three times at least and then scrubbed. Mrs. Aro swept and swept again. Mr. Kolander and Mr. Aro had finished the outhouse, building stairs and making a little half-moon in the door. They sat down outside and drank more coffee. Ma was getting fidgety. She needed to rest, but with all of those people there, she felt she should be making some kind of coffee cake. Mrs. Aro got her talking about baby clothes, and they took out the material Ma had already set aside.

And then we heard a wagon again, Mr. Salins' from the sound of it, but coming from the railroad depot rather than from the Salins' house. We heard Margie jabbering to Mr. Salin. She must have been sitting on the high seat.

It was as if everyone took a deep breath and sprang into action.

Suddenly a noise from the door, an "Oh, no, we can't accept this!" came clearly from Ma. She and Mr. Salin were standing by the wagon, which held a large crated box.

Ma repeated, "I can't accept this. I had mentioned to Mrs. Salin that I would do some extra sewing for the Hoosier cupboard Margie says you have in your side porch, but this isn't any extra cupboard. This is brand new. I can't . . . we can't . . .”

Margie danced around singing, "Yes, we can! Yes, we can! And it didn't come from Mr. and Mrs. Salin's back porch. It came in the baggage car of the railroad train, and Mr. Salin took me along so I could see them unload it, and it took four men to get it into the wagon, and I got to sit on the high front seat because there wasn't any room for me in the back with the box, and I don't know what's in it, though I can guess, but Mr. Salin won't tell me, and if we don't open it up and find out *right now*, I'm going to *explode!*”

By then the reason for the men hanging around was clear: the box was on the ground, and they were carefully dismantling the wooden crate.

Ma repeated over and over, "It must be some mistake. We haven't ordered anything. I haven't the money to pay for it." She turned, distraught, to Mr. Salin, "You'll have to bring it back!"

And then it was unwrapped, in all its glory, dusty from the trip and still packed in parts, heavily shrouded, but clearly a Hoosier cupboard made of golden oak with a top and a bottom and an enamel center board which could be drawn out or pushed back in, depending on its need.

We had seen cupboards like that in the catalogs. This was the top-of-the-line special with three long shelves on the right and three narrow ones to the left on the top with doors that closed. A wire clamp held a recipe book open, and two golden glass panels enclosed the top with a clasp. The bottom section had three drawers to the left, a narrow wide drawer on the right, and wide shelving below that with another door and a matching hinge.

"We cannot accept that," Ma repeated over and over again, still not comprehending. "That is surely not the one you have on your porch. I would have been happy with any cabinet you had on your side porch."

Mr. Salin paid no attention at all, looking at our house and figuring where to put it. It would be a tight squeeze, but if he moved the table under the window that faced south, he could put the cupboard on the west wall.

He ignored Ma, who was making futile gestures to hold him back.

I didn't care what Ma thought. We needed a cupboard like that desperately to hold dishes, pots and pans, extra clothing, and canned goods. Oh, the list of uses went on and on.

"Let us help you," the men told Mr. Salin, taking his side without a glance at Ma. Together they maneuvered in the bottom, then the top, which was attached with a rounded heavy gold piece of metal screwed top and bottom to allow room for the inch-high enamel piece to slide right in where it belonged.

"It could use a good dusting," Mr. Salin opined. "There's nothing dirtier than new furniture that's been sitting in the box for days."

Ma collapsed on a chair, beaten. "How can we ever begin to repay you?" Ma never cried, but she was crying so hard that Mrs. Aro grew concerned and shooed the men out.

Mr. Salin stayed long enough to explain that it was "all bought and paid for. And a good deal it was, if I do say so myself. Not bought from any store neither, but ordered straight from the company to be sent to me by railroad arriving this morning, packed in the largest box I've ever seen."

31

"You and Sara can make that box into a playhouse, yes, you can," he said, "if yer Ma'll let you come and play."

He looked at Ma. "Might be a good idea to let the little one wear off a bit of steam and have some fun while you and Ilmi and Mrs. Aro get some work done here. Might be that you two will find time to walk over this afternoon to get some of the staple goods set aside for you, too. Or maybe I can bring them with the wagon when I bring Margie home tonight. Could be you'll even take time to rest a bit between your chores. Want to come with me to play in the box?" he asked Margie and lifted her up to sit inside of it during the ride home.

Flabbergasted at the length of this speech from so taciturn and laconic a man, Ma was left with "HOW? WHO?"

"I reckon if you think on it, you'll guess" was all he said. Then he clicked to the horses, leaving Ma and Mrs. Aro and me to wash and clean the cupboard, to give Mr. Saarinen final directions for the placement of the shelves for the books, which had been contingent on the size of the cupboard, and to empty the boxes. With the three of us working, we might even be able to mop the floor with a strong lye solution, wiping off the stairs, too, and when it was dry lay down the braided rugs Ma had made from scraps of old clothing. Some of the rugs she had sold, but the ones that matched the quilt, we kept. Two of them would almost cover the entire walking space of the floor.

I ran my hands over the cupboard, feeling the strength and beauty of the wood.

"Oh, Ma, there's even a flour sifter built into to the left hand top!"

Sometimes I think we get just as tired when good things happen unexpectedly as when bad things do. Ma was white as one of our sun-bleached sheets as she joined me, pulling the enamel drawer out, murmuring, "It's just the height for me to knead bread and *pulla.*"

Much as I wanted to delve into the book boxes, I helped her mix a mild soap solution, and we washed every inch of the cupboard. I carefully stood on a chair to wipe the top and slid it out from the wall to make sure the back was clean, too.

"Ma." My voice was muffled from my position and from shock. "There's a shipping label on the back."

We could not move the cupboard out far enough for Ma to see it, and Baby Teddy precluded her squeezing in back. I read it aloud:

Glued on the top were the letters "B C 516

    Ship to Mrs. Knute (Mary) Brosi

    Zim, Minnesota

    care of Mr. Joseph Salin, who will deliver and set up this cabinet."

Glued to the bottom:

    "Helpful Information."

"These are just paragraphs of warning that the boards may seem to shrink or grow depending on the atmospheric changes."

"Oh, Ma, here's the shipping label. 'This cabinet was manufactured by Larkin Factory #19, Buffalo, New York, and shipped to the Ketola Dry Goods and Furniture Store in Virginia, Minnesota, where it was purchased and marked 'paid in full.' I can barely decipher the last name. But, oh, Ma, I know who sent it. It's signed 'Alex Savolainen.'"

Tears streaming down my face, I finished wiping the back, squeezed myself out, and hugged Ma, who was shaking her head.

"He knows we haven't the money to send it back," she said.

"We shouldn't even try," I remonstrated. I wiped my face, bit my lip and then took a chance and said what I believed: "It's not charity, Ma. It's a gift of love."

As the days went by, we found there was more. An account had been set up for us at Salins' store, not so large as to be embarrassing, but large enough for us to replenish our meager supply of necessities before winter came on.

Mrs. Aro stayed long enough to fix us a light supper and to tuck Ma into bed with a warning about taking an easy day tomorrow.

Suddenly "tomorrow" had new meaning.

Whether she wanted it or not, I hugged and kissed Mrs. Aro, and with no prompting at all, so did Margie.

We had been reminded of and found family of which we had not known. Our "God Blesses" were fervently voiced and gratefully heartfelt that night. We felt singularly blessed.

CHAPTER FIVE
School

hen the word spread like wildfire that the St. Louis County Unorganized Territory was going to build a one-room school to serve the twenty-five or so children in the Little Swan-Zim area, I was so excited I was beside myself. So was Eino Salin. His dad contracted to haul some of the building materials to the school site, which was centrally located, about two miles from our house. Anyway, Eino and I asked permission to ride on the wagon so we could see where the school was to be and managed to spend a part of every day there, making ourselves helpful, we thought, but probably just getting in the way. We handed boards up when it looked as if they were needed, ran around with nails, and often just sat and watched.

Thank goodness wintry September had turned into a milder October. The building crew sent from the Unorganized Territory was well-versed in the building of one-room schools, so the men from our community, though their help was welcome, were not needed. They took upon themselves responsibility for adding two outhouses—one for the boys, one for the girls—and for providing a woodshed well stocked with wood for the big black pot-bellied stove that was delivered the same day as the school bell was raised in the cupola atop the front entry. The inside was very simple. The teacher's desk was set on a small dais in the front with a blackboard running all across behind it. Desks of varying sizes were nailed down in rows, and windows were set into the west and east walls and on either side of the double-entry door. Double steps and a railing finished off the front, and the crew from the Unorganized Territory said the teacher would be ready to start school the following Monday at nine o'clock. She would ring the bell when she was ready.

I was so excited that weekend I virtually counted the hours. Margie pouted, but that was to be expected. We took especially thorough saunas at

Salins' on Saturday night, and Ma made sure our clothes were washed, starched, and ironed from undergarments all the way out. Either I had grown or my school dress had shrunk because Ma had to do some fast adjusting, taking down the hem and the waistband. But by seven-thirty that morning we were ready with metal lard pails, carefully washed, filled with bread and butter and jam and a piece of cake for this special occasion.

I had looked over the books from Miss Loney and decided not to take any of them until the teacher—Miss Heino—placed me according to her wishes. I did, however, tuck the letter from Miss Loney carefully into my pocket, ready to give it to Miss Heino as soon as the opportunity presented itself.

"Now mind you stay neat and don't play in the dirt on the way to school," Ma warned Margie. She looked at me and said, "You watch her."

She softened somewhat, then, knowing what this meant to me. I was not going to have to study alone! We were going to a real school! And today was especially important to me because I did not want to be put with the little kids, even though I was no bigger. I prayed that Miss Loney's letter would weigh into the teacher's decision so that I could join the upper graders.

"If I am not put with them today," I told myself, "I'll work so hard that I'll earn a promotion."

It felt as if my whole future weighed on what happened today, though good sense told me that I had a whole term to prove myself.

We could see in the distance that Sara and Eino were waiting for us. Ma gave us each a hug and a kiss and said, "Be good and do the very best you can."

When I looked back, she was still standing outside the house waving her handkerchief.

As we approached the school, we greeted all of the others coming from different directions. Everyone had a lunch pail. Everyone was dressed in what looked like their very best. We all had that look of fearful, excited expectancy. All except Toivo Aro. I didn't like the look on his face at all. He looked as if he had played a good trick on someone and was just waiting to see the results.

Even though it was well before nine o'clock, the front doors opened for us to see our teacher for the first time. Dressed in a cotton dress with a frilled apron, she did not look any older than we were. But her hair was wound in a braid around her hair, and she held a school bell in her hand, and she was smiling. She didn't need to say a thing. We had all been to school enough to know that we were supposed to line up by size before we went in. So we did. Except for me. I stood with the bigger kids even though I wasn't the right size to be there.

When she had counted roughly the twenty-five students she had been led to expect, she rang the school bell as if to announce the official beginning of the year. She didn't need it to keep us quiet. Except for some shuffling of feet from Toivo, we stood quietly, waiting to hear what she had to say.

"My name is Miss Heino," she began. "I am to be your teacher for this term." Even though she wasn't tall, she held that position of prominence at the head of the stairs while she looked every one of us directly in the eyes. Some looked down shyly, but most of us smiled back. "I shall expect a lot of you. But I shall be there to help you every step of the way. The School Board of the Unorganized Territory debated long and hard about building this school. It was the Assistant Superintendent George Bakalayer who convinced the superintendent that you deserved an education just as if you still lived in Kinney."

She had clearly heard the story of our mass exodus and disassociation from the mining town and the mining companies.

"Together, we can prove the superintendent wrong. We can convince him and the School Board that it is not the size of the school but the quality of the student that makes the difference. So, let us begin today to be the very best we can be."

Tears came into my eyes as I took that vow from the bottom of my heart.

"Come in now, taking your seats by size. I know we shall have to do some juggling of places even today, but leave those decisions to me. I am the teacher. It is I who will make the decisions. Please sit down at whatever is the next desk, whether or not it ends up being the right one, fold your hands, and refrain from talking. In a few minutes I want to see a roomful of students who are ready to take a placement test, one which will enable me to rearrange you more accurately. Each desk has a pencil and a piece of paper on it. Do not lift the pencil or touch the paper until I tell you to." There was a pause. "At that moment, school will begin."

Behind me, I heard Toivo snicker, and I felt a qualm. Had Miss Heino been warned about him? Then, I tried to relax. Whatever happened or didn't was not under my control. Taking a deep breath, I followed Hilma Saarinen into the building and gasped.

Miss Heino had prepared herself and the room well for this opening day. Multi-colored gingham curtains hung on the lower halves of all of the windows. The front bulletin board above the blackboard was covered with matching material and fall pictures, cut from a magazine and framed in orange and brown construction paper.

A line perhaps four inches down on the blackboard held the ABC's in print and in exquisite cursive white chalk writing. A milk can painted brown and filled with cat-tails filled one corner of the front of the room, and the other corner held a podium with a huge dictionary perhaps a foot or more in width and length. I checked later. It had 3,194 pages. A richness of words! Centered in front of the class on a low dais, the teachers' desk held a vase full of chrysanthemums, a cup of pencils, a box of erasers and rulers, and against the blackboard lay erasers and a five-fingered wooden holder for chalk to draw a musical scale.

I was relieved to see that everyone did exactly what we were told. Some of the seats were too big, some too small, but no one complained. We did not touch the pencils or the paper.

Then Miss Heino opened the narrow middle drawer of her desk. For a second she gasped and recoiled. Then she gathered herself together, straightened her back, and lifted a writhing snake from the drawer. I gave Toivo a scathing glance.

"Whose is this?" she asked calmly.

Without hesitation, everyone looked at Toivo, who began to bluster, "Hey, that's not mine."

"Bring it outside, please," Miss Heino continued, without a quiver in her voice.

When Toivo came back in, she lifted out a dead mouse.

"And to whom does this belong?"

Toivo didn't even lift his head or go back to his seat. He just took the mouse and went outside.

"You need not return to class until school has been dismissed, Mr. Aro," Miss Heino said, her voice and eyes as cold as I imagine that snake had been. "I shall see you then *with* your father."

"Aw, I'm not afraid of you," Toivo blustered, getting ready to slam the door behind him.

But there was Miss Heino, half his size, looking up with no trace of fear. "That is good, Mr. Aro. I am not afraid of you either." And she closed the door behind him.

Taking a deep breath, she returned to the front of the room, smiled a rather tremulous smile, and asked, "Should I expect any more surprises?"

We answered in a chorus, "No, Miss Heino."

Toivo was there before us the next day, hat in hand. Word had been passed around that Mr. Aro had told Miss Heino in no uncertain terms that whatever punishment she found it necessary to give him in school, he would get double at home.

But for the time being, we could all relax. None of us liked what Toivo had done. Then it was as if we started the day all over again.

"Take up your pencils," Miss Heino began, "and write or print your names on the left side of the paper. On the right side write or print today's date. Please note that I have it written and printed on the front board."

Starting from the back of the room, then, she handed out last year's state board examinations. Eino and I were given the ones for eighth grade.

Eino protested, "But in Kinney, Ilmi Marianna was just in the lower grade room."

Miss Heino simply looked at him, and he apologized.

"Remember, young Mr. Salin, I am the teacher here."

While those of us who could read wrote answers to the examinations, she called the others up to the front of the room one by one to read aloud to her softly.

Although I had tried hard to entice Margie into learning by making flash cards of simple words, she had never progressed beyond the words that named foods. She just shook her head when Miss Heino gave her the Elson-Gray basic primer. Margie landed in the front row, which was good because Miss Heino could keep an eye on her.

I was not moved down, in spite of Eino's protests. As we left that day, she took him aside and said, "Miss Brosi read the first page of 'The Legend of Sleepy Hollow' from *Prose and Poetry Adventures, Grade Eight*, without a single error except in pronunciation."

It was true. "Sometimes when I understand the meaning of a word from the context, though, I fudge about looking it up to check the pronunciation and I add it to my vocabulary notebook anyway."

"What is a vocabulary notebook?" she asked.

38

Eino showed her his. It was probably his tenth. "I started doing this in Kinney," he explained, "so I wouldn't forget the word."

"He was the king at Kinney School when we had vocabulary competition," I added, proudly. "And he has shared his notebooks with me."

"I'll give you some good paper so that you can practice your penmanship at the same time," Miss Heino said, smiling and nodding. "What a wonderful idea to keep a notebook! No wonder your English is so good!"

I was less enthusiastic about the idea of practicing penmanship on good paper. I hated penmanship. It was the only class I really struggled with, though often I needed a word or two from Eino to set me up in arithmetic. What difference did it make whether the letters looked like the letters in the Palmer method book or had some individuality, as mine did?

Before we left school that night, Miss Heino kept Eino and me after the others and brought out her Palmer Method certificate in its black frame. "I'm going to hang it on the wall next to my eighth grade diploma," she said. That was all it took. I vowed I would get that kind of certificate, too. My minor mutiny ended without a word being said.

Miss Heino was amazing. Most days she radiated happiness. She was barely eighteen and had just graduated from high school herself. She had had no special training. She did not, as teachers in the bigger schools were required to, have a teaching certificate. But she knew more than we did and she never let us forget it, but always in the gentlest way.

Only against Toivo Aro was she forced to take stronger steps, and he very nearly cost himself his entire eighth grade year. He adamantly refused to learn from his mistakes, and therein lay his second mutiny. Not that he cared, but his parents desperately wanted him to finish eighth grade. To them it was a benchmark in their Americanization.

Miss Heino's stamina received its final and most frustrating test when she trusted us with real ink in our inkwells. While we were out for recess, Toivo walked from desk to desk, dipping his fingers into the inkwells and dribbling ink on the desks. Catching him in the act, Miss Heino shook with fury. She took him by the ear, though she was barely half as big as he was, and made him scrub every vestige of the mess he had created. Some of the ink, which even his strong fingers could not eradicate, served as an excellent reminder of the strength of her character and of the power those little fingers could exert on what my mother called the "*niskaan kaavat*," hair she too pulled behind our ears when we misbehaved.

Mr. Aro, true to his word, seconded Miss Heino's punishment with a barber strap on Toivo's rear end. After that, Toivo behaved himself whenever he condescended to grace the schoolroom with his presence. He was wont to get lost between the Aros' homestead and the school. We blessed the days when he did because then Miss Heino could give the rest of us all of her energy and attention.

I loved the hours spent in school and adored Miss Heino as I had Miss Loney. She, too, became my guide toward that better world into which the Savolainens would have whisked me. I never second-guessed my choice. It was my task in life to work my way up, and I approached every lesson with a willing heart. By some magical alchemy, everything in the world but the books, books, books dropped away once I walked into school. I loved learning. And I loved the recognition it brought me. Every time I earned a hundred per cent on an assignment, I felt better about myself. Somehow it vindicated me, made life worthwhile, and seemed worth any amount of effort.

For a while that fall, school was everything to me. I was happy. Miss Heino had not only read the letter from Miss Loney but had written back to her about my progress. I had two guides, helping me toward my goal.

And Eino Salin was a good friend. He never took advantage or presumed that there was anything between us but friendship. We worked together, helping each other when we needed help.

Miss Heino suggested that we make flash cards so we could quiz ourselves on the words.

That was a wonderful idea. I used it with Margie at home, too, asking Ma to go over the same list of words with her every night, adding a few every week. It was a devious method of getting Ma to speak more English, too.

I wish I could have been as comfortable and happy with things at home. But that was a downhill battle.

Ma continued to insist that washing be done on Monday and hung to dry on the clothes lines. She continued to insist that our aprons, pillowcases, napkins, tablecloths, and cotton dresses be starched and ironed as soon as the flatirons were unpacked even though the flatirons weighed so much that Margie could not handle them at all, and it was a struggle for me. They weighed just as much for Ma, and she was carrying Baby Teddy, who, it seemed, consumed all of the food she ate, leaving her thin and wan.

Increasingly, the baby seemed to suck everything from her, leaving her arms and legs and face ever thinner, drawing her into herself, centering there, leaving us outside.

At first, she refused to listen when I said I would scrub the floors. She insisted upon carrying the water in the pail by the door where we washed our hands and into the reservoir on the right of the stove. We did have a roof over our heads, but the walls supporting it lacked insulation. Since they were made of boards rather than logs, the wind actually sifted snow in through the cracks.

Miss Heino must have guessed that things were not right because all of the other parents came to our school's Christmas program except Ma and Pa. Pa had not followed us to Zim, though Ma had left word with our neighbors for him in case he appeared. Ma was too weak to manage the trip, though the Salins offered to bundle her into blankets and bring her in their sleigh. Ma was too proud to ask for help. She rested, reserving her strength for our own family Christmas.

The other families gathered at the school dressed in their best, sleigh bells singing for those who, like the Salins, had horses and buggies or cutter sleighs. Margie and I were both in the Christmas program.

"How do I look?" Margie asked me anxiously, as we stood on the dais behind the curtain dividing the teacher's desk and the front of the school from the audience, who squeezed into the student desks or stood along the walls and across the back.

"Like an angel," I said without qualification, giving her a big hug. She did. The teacher had made white crepe-paper gowns for the angels to wear with gold tinsel belts and halos. Margie's hair, released from its braids, curled in ringlets around her face and the halo. Her cheeks were pink with excitement, her eyes a sparkling blue. She was the perfect Christmas angel, so filled with glory it was as if she could fly.

When Eino read the verse in which the angels appear to the shepherds tending their sheep, all of the angels flocked out to join the shepherds with their crooks, sitting on bales of hay. Their high piping voices sang, and I could hear Ma's bell-like tones in Margie's high soprano.

We had had no trouble getting her to sing. The problem was getting her to stop singing. Eino had foreseen the problem and handed out sticks of peppermint candy. It didn't fit into the pageant, but the shepherds lifted the angels up beside them, and they forgot the audience in their delight at the candy.

I had no trouble being a silent, somber Mary, my black hair well covered by a draping of blue. Miss Heino had arranged that the center section of the stage "curtain" be lifted in two places so that Toivo and I were framed as Joseph and Mary. Saarinens' baby, barely a month old, slept in a manger Mr. Saarinen had contrived with hay beneath its blankets.

The kings—chosen from the next biggest boys—Fatso Spina, Billy Ikola, and Nestor Kolander—wore crowns made of construction paper bright with glitter, brought their gifts and said their lines with only a little prompting from Eino.

Miss Heino had explained in detail the meanings of "frankincense" and "myrrh," but the boys were not impressed though they tried to seem as if they were.

At the end we all sang "Silent Night" first in English and then in Finnish. Because the school board had decreed that the schools of the Unorganized Territory were to present their programs only in English, the story was told as much in pantomime as in words, for few of the adults spoke English. But I will never forget the sense of belonging as the curtains were pulled back and we all drank hot coffee, ate homemade Finnish *limpaa*, lighted the tallow candles on the balsam tree, and sang the Christmas carols Miss Heino had taught us. When we left to go home, she tucked an orange into every waiting mitten. Margie had almost finished hers by the time we got home, rind and all, and she cried, so to keep the peace I gave her and Ma some of mine, too.

I tried to bring Christmas home by making little gifts for Ma and Margie, and we made six-pointed stars of white paper to hang in the windows and paper chains from red and green construction paper with messages of love inside of the circles.

Ma had knit matching scarves and mittens for Margie and me—blue for Margie, red for me. And she had managed to put together a small table, chairs, and cupboard for Margie to play house with. They were painted bright red and had been hidden at the Salins awaiting Christmas Eve when Mr. Salin, pretending to be Santa Claus, delivered them in his sleigh, bells a jingling.

She had used some of the money left by the Savolainens to buy me a beautiful padded journal, filled with lined blank pages for me to fill with my own thoughts and dreams and feelings. It even had a tiny lock with a secret combination that only I would know. For me, it was the perfect gift.

At school we had made Ma round clay circles with hangars on the back and our handprints with our names and the date on the front. Ma cried when she opened the presents we had wrapped in leftover bits of cloth, and she hung them right away and made us stand back with her to look at how much they enhanced the wall between the window and the stove.

Altogether, that Christmas gave us a night and a day to remember. Mr. Salin brought a partridge for our Christmas dinner, and Ma explained to me just how to fix it and the potatoes and the rutabaga. We even had pumpkin pie made from canned pumpkin. I made the crust all by myself with lard and flour and ice water. We ate the whole thing.

I had hacked down a small balsam tree and set it into a pail of water in the corner. It stood upright because the water froze.

Perhaps that was the omen of things to come, for the wheel of fate had turned indeed. It was as if Ma had garnered all of the strength she had to make Christmas happy for us. When the celebration was over, slowly and insidiously she seemed to give up, lying in bed, barely talking, eating very little. Margie was frightened into good behavior, singing songs and brushing and combing Ma's hair.

My first morning job was to carry wood from the woodshed into the woodbox by the door. I fed the stove's firebox with its cast iron grates and fire all day. It ate voraciously, but it kept our breakfast *puuroa* warm in a double boiler set on one of the back lids. The white enamel coffee pot perked on the other. I kept the water reservoir full, just as Ma had, with trips back and forth to the pump. After washing the breakfast dishes, I swept the floor, dusted the table and chairs and the iron bed head and ends, peeled potatoes and carrots or rutabaga for our dinner *mojakka*, and spent every extra minute I could find during the two-week Christmas break studying the books Miss Loney had sent—from early morning until Ma insisted I blow out the kerosene light and come to bed.

Sometimes I walked Margie over to Sara Salins' to play because Ma was so weak that she could not bear the noise of the children's play at home. Margie did help, though. She tried to dry the dishes and managed the flatware without dropping it. She set the table and put the dried dishes away. When I studied, she took out her Elson-Gray primer and read aloud to Ma, often making up words to match the pictures. I had to smile when she did that. She was surprisingly inventive.

43

On warmer days I made time to take Margie out to make snow angels and snowballs. Every trip to the outhouse was a major production, involving a change from our boiled-wool house slippers into boots, coats, scarves, and mittens.

Ma had always been deathly against having a "peepot" in the house, considering them slovenly. "For heaven sake, anyone can walk to the outhouse," she said when one was suggested.

But one unusually cold late December morning, I came back from bringing Margie to visit Sara with a white enamel pot with a red edge and a white cover also edged in red. I placed it carefully on top of a towel in the corner and helped Ma to get there.

Neither of us mentioned it again. She gratefully accepted my offer to empty it. Most of the time I got to the outhouse, gagging all the way. Sometimes as soon as I got outside the door, I threw up.

She was able to sit up to eat with us, but otherwise she slept a lot. I gave her sponge baths. On Saturday nights, Margie and I bathed in a washtub I filled with hot water from a boiler and the reservoir on the stove. Even boiling water cooled off very fast.

Thus we survived December. When school began again in January, we made it there on most days, though often we arrived late.

It was January that almost did us in.

CHAPTER SIX
Help!

I was so worried about Ma that I could not bear to keep on the way we were going. So, I took two steps without consulting her. First, I wrote a letter explaining the situation to Mr. and Mrs. Savolainen. It came back, unopened, stamped "forwarded." I knew by the time they got it, the time for action would be long past.

Secondly, I decided to see if there were a doctor in Virginia who could help. I begged a ride from Mr. Salin, who drove the milk wagon from our area, either to the railroad tracks or, once in a great while when there were other errands, directly to the Virginia Co-op Creamery. I asked him if I could go with him on a day when he went to the creamery in Virginia.

"You'll have to get up before the crack of dawn, young lady," he warned me.

"Just tell me when to be waiting outside, and I'll be ready."

"Tomorrow by 5:50. No later."

"I'll be there."

Difficult as it was to leave Ma for the day, Margie promised that she would not touch the stove except for filling the wood box, and in the last analysis she didn't even have to do that. Mrs. Salin offered to sit with Ma while Sara and Margie played with Margie's small kitchen and Sara's porcelain doll with its wardrobe of clothes. After all, it would be just for the morning. Mr. Salin had to be home early enough to do the rest of the chores, and Margie had proved herself remarkably responsible during this dreadful time. Thus, early one January morning before the start of the school session, I plotted my morning, praying that this quest would be more successful than last summer's had been.

How I hated lying! But early that morning, while Ma was still half asleep, I helped her to the pee pot, emptied it, tucked her back into bed, and leaned over to whisper. "Ma, I am going to school to help Miss Heino get ready for our next term. I'll stay there until we have everything cleaned and organized. Don't worry. Mrs. Salin is coming for a short visit, and Sara and Margie want to play with their Christmas gifts."

Ma lifted a soft hand, so limp and different from her usual firm clasp that it broke my heart as it reinforced my decision, and said, "That'll be good, Ilmi. You deserve to have a little break . . . (she waved her arm around the house) from all of this."

Not that it all looked any different. I had stayed up late to blacken the stove, scrub a floor that did not need scrubbing, wash windows that were perfectly clean, set the table neatly, and ready the *puurua* for Margie's breakfast.

When I heard the stomping of Mr. Salin's wagon, I wrapped Ma's heaviest shawl over my very best woolen dress, put on my woolen stockings and winter shoes, which were almost too small, and ran outside to climb up on the wagon so quickly that Ma would hardly hear it stop.

On the way, I asked Mr. Salin once again the question I had asked Mrs. Aro, who was a healer, an old-fashioned *hieroija* with knowledge she had brought with her from Finland and more she was learning all the time: "Who is the very best doctor in Virginia?"

Lifting his woolen cap to scratch his head, he pondered the question and answered in a roundabout way that he and Mrs. Salin had discussed that very question and both had come up with the same answer—Dr. Raihala. He was obviously a Finnish doctor. I wasn't sure that I wanted a Finnish doctor. I wanted to talk to one who was young and new and really up-to-date on problems and procedures with birthing. It was a lot to ask of a very short morning.

Mr. Salin dropped me off under the Depot clock at the Silver Lake end of Chestnut Street, Virginia's main thoroughfare.

"It's a long walk to the other end of the street," he warned me, "so don't stop to window shop. Once I've dropped off the milk and cream and done my errands, I'll have to get home. There are two small hospitals. That I know. I'd just walk into one of them, look at the names of the doctors on the doors, hope that one is in this early, knock on the door, go in, and hope they'll give you time to tell your story. Don't go into Dr. Aysta's office. He's a dentist. I'd look for Dr. Raihala or the new man. I don't know if he talks Finn, but you do damn—excuse me, Ilmi—*well* with English. He's

Malmstromi or some such. Good luck now. And don't waste time looking in store windows."

I almost interrupted him to say that I had come on too important an errand to waste time window shopping, but that would waste time talking, so I shut my mouth and waited politely for Mr. Salin to finish.

"Anyway, I'd go to both of the offices and see which one has time to see you. They usually see patients by appointment only," he concluded, "so don't be disappointed if you don't get in."

I set my jaw, straightened my back, and vowed to get in even if I had to lie and say I thought I was getting diphtheria. Or something equally bad. Maybe an onset of typhoid fever.

"Thank you, Mr. Salin."

"Mind you, girl, you don't have all day. I have some errands to run for Mrs. Salin and some stock to pick up for the store. I will meet you here under the clock when I get through. I won't wait long."

I wanted to tell him that he had wasted a good part of the small amount of time I had telling me not to waste any, but I didn't. I just jumped down, threw the words "I'll be here. Thank you, Mr. Spina" over my shoulder and set myself on my way. I didn't allow myself to glance in one single shop windows, except the one that said "Ketola's Dry Goods and Furniture," which seemed to cover a whole block.

"I am here on a mission," I kept telling myself, hurrying as fast as I could without running, which would give me a stitch in the side and take even longer.

There they were at the end of the street, two buildings that looked imposing enough to be schools or community buildings or hospitals. As I got closer I saw the words "Virginia City Health Department." I took a deep breath. It didn't *say* hospital, but it certainly implied it.

Walking up the stairs, I felt like the heroine Rowena in *Ivanhoe*, quaking with fear. But I had also played the part of the courageous Rebecca and adopted that mien as I approached the lobby. Inside, benches lined the long hall with doorways labeled with doctors' names. The benches outside of the sign "Dr. Raihala" were full of grown-ups hacking and coughing and children with snotty noses sitting on their grandmothers' laps, and I crossed that part of the hall quickly. I did not need to bring any germs back to Ma.

I turned to the door marked "Dr. Malmstrom." There were only two women sitting there, both very well-dressed, both obviously wealthy, and I worried about what he would charge. But there were only two people in front of me so I knocked on the door politely.

"Come in," said a pleasant voice. "What can I do for you, young lady?" a lady in white with a white cap asked me in a kind voice. She was sitting at a desk in front of another door. Her desk was neatly arranged with stacks of papers and file folders. It had a name plate: "Francis Callahan Malmstrom."

"Are you a nurse?" I asked, though that fact seemed obvious.

"Yes," she answered, still patiently, as if I were her only concern. "And I am Dr. Malmstrom's wife. Now, what may we do for you? Are you ill?"

To my dismay and utter bewilderment, for I had thought myself strong enough to complete this errand without crying or making a dismal scene that would make me sound pitiful, tears began to run down my cheeks. I hated pity just as Ma and even Pa did. But I couldn't help myself. Once the tears started, they simply refused to stop. I just stood there and sobbed.

The nurse got up, put her arm around me, and led me through another door into an inner office.

A lovely young woman dressed in what must be the height of fashion because I had peeked into the windows of Ketola's and seen the mannikans was on her way out. The nurse handed me very gently to an enormous man in a white coat with an instrument of some kind hanging around his neck. He must have been six feet tall of more, and he was twice the size of Pa. Not fat. Just ample. There was a lot of him, topped by a head full of black curly hair, which looked as if it needed a good brushing.

Turning to the nurse, he said, "I'd like to see Mrs. Reid next week. Fit her in, preferably in the afternoon." Then, enfolding me in those enormous arms, he sat down on a big chair that twirled back when it held his weight, and set me on his lap. From his back pocket he produced a neatly ironed white handkerchief, gave it to me to blow my nose, and waited. Gradually the sobs dwindled to tears, and I managed to regain some control of myself. I was absolutely mortified, but he didn't seem to notice that or to mind at all. "And what is wrong with you, child?"

His English was a bit difficult to understand. It had some of the same lilt as Anna Savolainen's Finnish, but it was much more bluff and hearty. I concluded they had both come originally from or studied somewhere out East.

Sharp eyes looked kindly but steadily into mine, now red and puffy. "I take it you are ill and want an appointment?"

"No," I wailed. "It's Ma." Taking off his stethoscope (I learned later what to call it), he set me on the chair next to his desk, leaned back in his own chair, and, acting as if he had all the time in the world, simply waited.

I knew I had very little time, so I took a deep breath and hiccuped. He brought me a glass of water from a sink in the corner. I looked down at the floor deeply ashamed of the puddle my boots were making. I had been too nervous to remember to wipe them clean.

"Now," he gave me a keen look, "whatever it is, let's have it."

I blurted it all out with no remembrance of the speech I had been planning ever since I decided to take this momentous step. "Ma is going to have a baby any minute now, but I think probably in January because the last time she and Pa were together and not fighting was last May. At first she was throwing up all the time. Even now she just picks at her food. She is too weak even to go to the outhouse. She has to use the peepot, and she hates that, and she can't bathe because she doesn't have the strength to get up except for when I change the bed—putting the top sheet on the bottom and a fresh top sheet and pillow case and change her night gown and brush her hair. There's too much of her hair to wash unless I filled the wash tub." I took a deep breath, and the rest burst out, "And even before we moved from Kinney to Zim, Pa left us, and now Ma can't make any money sewing because . . ."

The doctor unbuttoned his white coat, took the handkerchief from me, held it to my nose, told me to blow just as if I were Margie, and finally, holding my hand, explained, "She must be suffering what is called 'hyperemesis gravidarum.'"

My eyes widened, and tears threatened.

"The bad thing about it is that there is no cure."

I closed my eyes, but he held my hand harder, forcing me to look at him, "But the good news is that it will end when the baby is born."

"What can I do?" I whispered.

"Could you bring her into the hospital in Virginia?"

"No." There was no sense beating around the bush. Even had she been strong enough, we had no money to pay for a hospital stay.

"Then I can't suggest much more than I think you seem to be doing already," he said, thinking aloud, his eyes not on me but on a page of a medical book and something he remembered from medical school. I could see his diploma hanging on the wall. He had graduated from the University of Minnesota and was an accredited doctor of internal medicine.

That was infinitely reassuring. He really looked too young to be a doctor, in spite of the contents of the white room—a high narrow bed, a cupboard obviously full of medicines, a table with an immaculate white cloth holding a variety of evil-looking instruments, a bookcase full of medical books and magazines, a small desk built into the wall with the seat for him and the chair next to it where he had put me. And, of course, his white coat.

"She should eat whatever seems to appeal to her, lightly cooked fruit or vegetables, soup broth made from meat to give her protein, crackers when she feels nauseated."

My shoulders slumped. Mr. Salin's stock of fresh vegetables and fruit was meager to say the least, and everything cost more than we could afford.

He dug in a drawer in front of him and handed me a packet of white pills. "If she were a child, I would call what she has a form of pernicious anemia. She needs iron to build up her blood. Give her one of these pills three times a day. If she gags on them, mix them with—do you have applesauce?"

"Oh, yes!" I exclaimed, "Quarts and quarts that Ma put up herself before we left Kinney. We had an apple tree in our backyard."

"That's good, then," he said and thought for a moment, pondering.

"How old are you, child?" he asked.

I wanted to lie and say I was older, but given my size and shape, not to mention Ma's adjurations against lying, I answered, "Twelve." Then added quickly, "And a half."

"Do you live alone with your Ma?"

"There are three of us—Ma and me and my little sister Margie."

"Have you neighbors to give you any help?"

That reminded me of Mr. Salin, and I looked frantically at the clock hung on the wall between two windows overlooking Chestnut Street. It read nine-thirty. I hoped it was in time with the Depot clock. "Yes, but you see everyone is very busy because we all moved to Zim to get away from the mining companies and the men couldn't get work because they were trying to organize a strike, and anyway we all wanted to live on our own land so we moved, all of us, to Zim and Little Swan."

"Is that on the Duluth & Mesabi railroad line?"

"Yes. Our house is between the railroad tracks and the St. Louis River, closer to the river. Salins are our nearest neighbors. But, oh, I must hurry. Mr. Salin is leaving for Zim with his wagon as soon as he gets his milk delivered and his errands done, and I need to be at the depot by the time he comes to get a ride home."

Leaning back in his chair, Dr. Malmstrom rubbed his face, then set himself and the chair straight and looked into my eyes directly. "Since there is rail service to Zim, it is possible that I could come to deliver the baby. If there were a way to let me know . . ."

I opened my purse and, with all the dignity I could muster, asked how much it would cost for him to come. I knew we couldn't afford it.

He brushed the money aside and added, "We could discuss your payment then—perhaps spreading it over a series of months." He grinned. "I'm not that much in demand yet because I haven't mastered all of the languages spoken here, so my rates are relatively low."

When I continued to dig for money, he said, "There is no charge for today either," adding hastily, "there is never a charge for an initial consultation."

"Do you know anyone who could come to get me when your Ma's time comes?"

"Well, perhaps Mr. Salin. I'd have to ask him." I dared not make promises that other people had to keep.

Rising to his full height, he towered over me as he accompanied me out of the inner office. He told his nurse to prepare his next patient for a complete examination and continued out into the hall holding my elbow as if I were a great lady.

"And what is your name, my small friend?"

"In Finnish I am called 'Ilmi Marianna' Brosi. But my friends Alex and Anna Savolainen and my teacher in Kinney, Miss Loney, preferred to call me by an English version—'Marion.'"

"Twelve years old, eh?" He shook his head then left me flabbergasted by giving me a big hug. "Good luck, kid. I wish there were more I could do to help."

I wished that too, of course, but there was reassurance in Dr. Malmstrom's affirmation that I had been doing all I could. Then I raced down the stairs and across every street, ignoring cars and horses and wagon and made it just in time.

Mr. Salin was waiting patiently, the back of his wagon filled and carefully covered with a tarpaulin against the snow that threatened to inundate us.

"Get any help, Ilmi?" he asked.

"I'm not sure. Look. He gave me this packet of pills. He listened. He didn't charge anything. He said the first consultation is always free."

"Well, that's good," Mr. Salin said, maneuvering the horses along the city streets and out toward Zim. By and large the road followed the path of the railroad tracks.

But most of all, I said to myself, he helped me believe that I'm doing the right things, the very best I can. More than anything, I had needed to hear that.

"Otherwise, I guess he mostly just confirmed what I already knew— that this is an unusually difficult pregnancy," I concluded bluntly. Then I blushed and wished I could take the words back. I embarrassed Mr. Salin by using the word "pregnancy." His ears turned bright red, and he pulled his hat even lower to hide a very red face.

I should have said that Ma was "in a very delicate condition" or some such socially correct euphemism. Trust me to put my foot in it, I thought, and remained mute for the rest of the journey home.

It had begun as a dark, cloudy, foggy day, fraught with the threat of storms, so it was wonderful to see a kerosene lamp in the window, lighting our way. Everything seemed quiet. Mrs. Salin slipped out the door, carrying a sleeping Sara, wrapped in a blanket in her arms. Mr. Salin reached down to hold her as Mrs. Salin climbed up to the front seat of the wagon.

"Shhh," she told me. "Your ma and Margie are asleep, for the afternoon I think. There's some soup on the back burner of the stove. I'm sorry I didn't make it. It came from a can, but if you add a bit of salt it tastes quite good."

"Thank you so much, Mrs. Salin, and," waving over her, "Mr. Salin, for the ride. I'll tell you what the doctor said tomorrow or as soon as I can," I cried softly.

There was no sense to asking Mr. Salin to bring Ma to the hospital. We could not afford it in the first place, and in the second place, as I learned before the night was over, it was already too late.

CHAPTER SEVEN
First

The new session of school began in the frigid midst of unceasing January blizzards, one following the next. Winds blew from the arctic north, attacking us with pellets of snow that hurt when they fell, like mini-white stones.

By the time the new session began, I had already set up a routine that we followed morning and night. I refused to listen to Margie's screams of frustration, sleepiness, anger, or the temper tantrums which she threw with obdurate stubbornness whenever she did not get her own way. I simply dragged her along with me, brooking no form of resistance. I was bigger and strong enough to force her to do as I said.

Under my breath, I hissed, "DO NOT DISTURB MA, OR I WILL TAKE YOU OUTSIDE AND WHIP YOUR BARE BUTT WITH PA'S RAZOR STRAP UNTIL IT HURTS FOR YOU TO SIT DOWN."

I only had to do that once. After that, she pouted and fussed under her breath, but she did what she was told and did not disturb Ma, who barely awoke to eat the breakfast *puurua* I put on a chair by her bed. After that and a cup of strong coffee, she used the pee pot, gratefully assisted me in washing her face and hands and rebraiding her hair, and sank back under the covers.

I got up before sunrise to put wood into the woodbox just inside the door then fed the woodstove's firebox as full as I dared. It ate voraciously, but I stocked it so thoroughly that by the time we left for school, we were almost sweating, and a low fire still burned when we hurried home in the afternoon. The school days were shortened by the length of the sun, which helped a great deal. Our own breakfast *puurua* stayed warm in a double boiler set on one of the two back lids and the white enamel coffee pot perked gently on another. If Ma felt up to it, she could help herself to another serving at lunch-time.

I ate on the run and urged Margie to do the same.

When I went out of the house, I used the outhouse and carried out the peepot. When I came in, I carried in water or wood. I ordered Margie to do the same thing. Even if she could carry in only pieces of kindling, it helped. After washing the breakfast dishes, I swept, dusted the table and chairs and the head and footboards of the bed and the beautiful oak on our cabinet, all of which crowded our meager floor space. Margie expanded her wiping ability to include the dishes without breaking them and to put them away where they belonged. Finally, I peeled potatoes and carrots for dinner *mojakka* and, pulling boots and mitts and a coat on both Margie and me, hauled her to the outhouse and back one more time before we left for school.

Sometimes the temperature dipped so far below freezing it was really difficult to get the ice in the well-box broken so the pump could draw water, and our windows grew thick furry designs of frost. Then Mr. Salin drove us to school, picking up everyone who lived on our side of the schoolhouse. But cold weather meant he had extra work, too, with the cows inside and the floors to muck out.

I gagged when I first went into a barn and vowed to quit drinking milk forever, a vow that for all practical purposes was impossible to keep. When we used to have a cow, Ma used a separator to skim the cream off, leaving the milk for us to drink. She cleaned the separator so religiously that none of the milk products, butter, cream, or milk held any rancid taste. Now, we had to be grateful for whatever neighbor sent us milk or butter or a bit of cream, no matter how it smelled or tasted.

After supper, I studied my lessons, added to my vocabulary notebook, made sure that Margie had finished her assignments and read aloud to Ma, got both of them ready for bed and collapsed myself.

All the while, I worried about Ma though typically she never complained. Never, ever.

So, when, in the middle of a January night in a snowstorm that threatened to bury our half-house (I actually had to go outside periodically to sweep the snow away from outside the door so we would not get closed in), I heard her groan. I woke up right away.

Margie and I had long since left the trundle bed, which sat too near the icy floor and joined Ma each night in the big bed, with Ma by the wall where it was the coldest, Margie in the middle where it was the warmest, and me on the inside so I could get up to refuel the woodstove.

Ma groaned again. She had curled into a ball around herself.

"Ma, are you all right?" I asked, quietly so as not to awaken Margie. I don't know why I bothered. Margie could sleep through a tornado, be swept into another county, and wake up never knowing the difference.

"I . . . I . . . think something's wrong," Ma whispered between gasps. "Will you light the kerosene lamp and check . . ." The words trailed off.

Grateful for the felted shoe packs that kept my feet warm even that freezing night, I hurried to the table, found a match, turned the wick high enough for me to see, and squeezed myself between Ma's side of the bed and the wall, pushing the bed far enough out so that I could get to her.

Wordlessly, she pulled back the quilt and the white flannel sheet. Her nightgown should have matched the sheet. It did not, not along the bottom anyway. The bottom looked pink and wet.

Ma groaned then tightened into herself still more.

I swallowed hard. Biting my lower lip, I pulled the covers up with my free hand, leaned over to touch my cheek to hers, carefully so as not to tip the lamp and thought hard. What should I do? Should I try to go to Salins? Should Mr. Salin and I try to get Ma to the hospital in Virginia?

Ma whimpered and bit back a cry which rose precariously close to the level of a scream.

There was no time. Hurrying, I set the lamp back on the table, turned the wick down, and as quickly as I could pulled off my nightgown and pulled on my woolen everyday dress, which I had left to hang over the back of a chair to stay warm in the heat from the stove. The dress was too small for me, but I appreciated the wool and tried to ignore the short arms and hem and waistband. Although Ma usually considered it slovenly not to hang up our clothes and under normal circumstances would have taken umbrage at our going to sleep in our underwear, she had not demurred when I had only partially undressed Margie and me before we went to bed. I don't think she even noticed my laxity with regard to the clothing I took off but left as close to the fire box of the wood stove as was safe.

Dressed, I considered taking my hair out of its nighttime braids to brush and rebraid it, the normal second step in my early morning routine. But, I told myself, it was not morning. And anyway, I always had trouble rebraiding my hair. There was just too much of it. It was another of the faults Pa carefully repeated when I did something wrong. Ma had to use a wet iron brush to repress the curls. Sometimes they escaped even though she made the braids so tight that my eyes slanted.

Standing there irresolutely, wondering what to do next, I saw Ma thrash convulsively and struggle to swallow an accompanying scream.

Margie half woke up, and I made up my mind. I hauled her out of bed, in spite of her protesting, even when I propped her standing up against the Hoosier cupboard. Pushing and pulling, I prodded her into her coat and mittens, boots, hat, and scarf.

"You're going to Salins' for the night," I told her, ignoring her sputters and mutters of protest. I didn't try too hard to wake her up more fully. She'd ask too many questions. I could sleep-walk her the mile or so to Salins'.

In no time, I threw on boots, mittens, hat, coat, Ma's woolen scarf, and, yanking the door open and closing it firmly behind us, half carried, half pushed Margie in the direction of the Salins.

The heavy snowfall had obliterated the path, but someone had left a kerosene lamp on in Salins' house, and I followed that small light as a beacon, falling and getting up and falling again, sometimes dragging Margie behind me, sometimes shaking her, screaming "Move! Move! Move! Walk! Walk! Walk!" in her ear, pulling her braids, doing anything I could to keep her going.

When we reached the Salins' side porch, I pounded on the door. No one heard me. They did not have to get up in the middle of the night to stoke the fire in the kitchen stove. Mr. Salin had bought a heating stove made of cast iron with steel plates around a middle fire chamber decorated with nickel plated trimming. Sara Salin had pointed out all of the details to Margie, and Eino had explained the principal of air circulation that drew cold air in from near the floor and passed that air up through the stove until it rose very hot from a air collar, thus, in his words—and I'm sure the words of the Sears & Roebuck catalog—"furnishing a steady circulation of heated air" that would warm "not only the downstairs but the upstairs of a Big House" even on the "Coldest Winter Days."

Even then I had not appreciated the verbal capital letters that had emphasized the efficiency of this very expensive ($34.75) new addition to the Salins' already well-equipped home.

That night I cursed the damn stove. Because of it, all of the Salins were no doubt upstairs asleep in warm beds, in their own rooms.

Screaming, I pounded on the door again and again, yelling until my voice was hoarse, "Help! Help! Help! I think the baby is coming, but something is horribly wrong! PLEASE, PLEASE, PLEASE, PLEASE, COME AND HELP!"

I leaned a recumbent Margie against the door, which, to my utter astonishment swung open, and there stood Mr. Salin, pants obviously pulled over his long underwear, suspenders dangling, front unbuttoned. Margie fell into his arms, and he reached out to pull me in, yelling at the same time, "Irma! Ilmi Marianna and Margie are here, half-frozen. Hurry!"

"Tell me again what you were shouting outside. I heard the screams but not the words." Patting me on the head, he set me on a chair, pulling off my mittens and boots and rubbing my hands and feet, then doing the same for Margie.

My teeth were chattering so I could hardly get the words out. "Ma . . . it's Ma . . . I think the baby is coming . . . she's in awful pain . . . and she's bleeding . . . Something is terribly wrong . . . I didn't know where to go to ask for help . . ." I choked back a sob and every vestige of my pride and begged, "Please, will you help us?"

Before I had a chance to finish repeating the sentence, Mrs. Salin was there, dressed and taking charge. No matter that her baked goods even exceeded mine in dryness and hardness, Irma Salin was a kind, thoughtful, and perspicacious woman. Reading my expression as clearly as my words, she took control.

"Eino," she began to yell, but he appeared in the doorway to the upstairs, buttoning a woolen shirt and hopping into heavy pants and socks, "you run to the Aros. Tell Mrs. Aro to get her things together. Your pa will come to pick her up as soon as he can. Better that she be ready."

Eino nodded, finished dressing, and ran.

Mrs. Aro's mother in Finland had been a well-known *kuppari* and healer. She had passed along what she knew to her daughter, our neighbor Mrs. Aro, who had retained a goodly amount of old country wisdom and natural medicine, even though her practices tended to be scoffed at by the medical community of this new land. It did not matter. She had served as a midwife, and she was all we had.

As Mr. Salin donned his outerwear, Mrs. Salin saw to it that Margie was disrobed and dispatched into Sara's bed. I'm not sure that Margie ever really woke up.

Refusing to take off any of my outer clothing, I stood as close to that magical stove as I dared, felt guilty for dripping snow water on the floor, and waited while Mrs. Salin disappeared upstairs only to reappear minutes later even more heavily clothed with a pillow case in her hand. The folds and creases showing through the cotton looked like bed linens. Sheets? Towels?

Without grumbling, Mr. Salin went outside to hitch up the horses.

Neither he nor she argued when I trailed Mrs. Salin out toward the wagon. He boosted both of us up to the wagon seat, covered us with a heavy lap robe, and jumped up himself. Off in the distance I heard those brush wolves howl again. A small animal—a rabbit?—cornered, screamed. Then the stomp of hooves on the snow and the creak of wheels and traces and the whoof of the horses' breath covered the sound. In minutes we had traversed the mile that had taken Margie and me what had seemed like hours to walk.

For a minute, Mr. and Mrs. Salin sat unmoving with me between them, frozen like the air, I thought until I realized that they were doing their best to offer the comfort of body heat and Mrs. Salin's comforting arm.

Ma's scream split the stillness, then, drawing a line between the two worlds—the Salins' world of warmth and safety and ours of peril.

"Why don't you go back to our house with my husband? Leave your Ma to me and to Mrs. Aro," Mrs. Salin told me, reaching to hold me in what was for her an unusual embrace. The Salins were not an outwardly affectionate family, though we all knew the children were well-loved.

"No," I said, squirming away, following her as she turned and slid, and found the wooden step, and jumped down. "No. I can't leave Ma again."

Mrs. Salin started to argue, but Mr. Salin overrode her. "Let her stay," he said. "Sometimes not knowing is worse than knowing."

I didn't understand what he meant, but Mrs. Salin obviously did, for she turned toward the door, pillow cases in hand. "You'll go to get Mrs. Aro?" she threw back over her shoulder. "Eino should have gotten her up by now. She'll be waiting."

"I will." He clucked the horses on, and we hurried inside.

CHAPTER EIGHT
Baby Teddy

Even during the brief time that I was gone, the fire in the wood stove had burned down. Leaving coats and boots on, we rushed to Ma, who was writhing and twisting under the covers, crying indecipherable words, making animal sounds not unlike the cries of the rabbit, she, too, cornered by fear and pain.

Mrs. Salin checked the boiler on the stove. "Good. You have hot water on," Mrs. Salin told me, looking around as if to assess the meager weapons in her arsenal. "Now. Since you have insisted upon staying, you must sit down and stay out of my way. Do what I tell you to do but do not ask questions. If you get sick, go outside to throw up."

I nodded, turned up the wick on the kerosene lamp, lighted another for Mrs. Salin to carry to the bed, swept out the snow that had blown in with us, as best I could, for every time I opened the door, more blew in, and in general did as I was told.

I cannot clearly describe all that happened that night. Much of it I spent in shadows darker than those inhabiting the corners of the shack. But in the flickering light from the wood stove and the lamps, I saw Mrs. Salin bending over the bed, shaking her head, lifting the quilt and sheets to push towels under Ma's legs and buttocks. I smelled blood and saw blotches on the sheets and quilt, turning the towels dark. I heard Ma's screams and saw her hands clenching the quilts, grabbing the white iron spokes of the headboard, reaching out for Mrs. Salin's hands, which held hers tightly for a minute.

"Come here, Ilmi," Mrs. Salin said. "If you can, put a chair by your ma and hold her hands. Even if it hurts. If you can," she added frankly, throwing me a hard glance.

I caught that look straight on and made my actions prove that I could. Biting down on my lower lip to hold back the gags and retches, closing my eyes against reality, I clutched Ma's hands as hard as she did mine, so hard it seemed as if my bones would shatter, and there I sat until I heard the door open just a narrow slit.

Mr. Salin asked, "Should I go for a doctor?"

The door opened wider, and I sensed Mrs. Aro's presence. She usually smelled good, like balsam boughs. Ma said it was something she put into her soap. But that night she smelled like a combination of concern and . . . was it rubbing alcohol?

"No," she told Mr. Salin as she doffed her coat and scarf and leaned over Ma. "It's too late. The baby is coming now. Right now."

Ma screamed again and held my hands so tightly I thought I too would scream from the pain. But it was the last scream.

The room reeked of fresh blood, like the yard at butchering time, right after the pig's throat was cut. But stronger.

"Here." Mrs. Salin held a basin in front of me, and I threw up into it. But I didn't open my eyes.

"It was a boy," Mrs. Aro said.

"Yes." I could hear the sorrow in Mrs. Salin's voice. "He was perfect . . . beautiful."

So. We did have a Baby Teddy. Then I caught the tense of their verbs. Past tense. Opening my eyes, I saw Mrs. Salin wrapping the baby in a towel and, laying him on the table, wiping off blood and mucus with a washing cloth, untying a cord from around his neck.

I had barely heard Mrs. Aro ask for a sterilized knife, Mrs. Salin open the knife drawer and her ejaculation of "Oh, my! Mr. Brosi could have made a living making knives!"

"Could have" was the right expression when it came to Pa, I thought.

Getting up, I stood close to Mrs. Salin. The baby's face looked grayish in the lamplight. She unwrapped the towel for me to see him. He was perfect. Beautiful. Cleaned, his hair, so blond it was almost red, formed a soft fuzz. I knew without question that his eyes were blue, like Margie's.

I studied Baby Teddy. His hands had tiny fingers. Even fingernails. He had long, dark eyelashes. Like mine.

"I am so sorry," Mrs. Salin said. "When this happens, when the cord wraps wrongly, when the mother hemorrhages like that, the child always dies." Her voice was as soft as the hands that continued to clean him gently, soothingly, lovingly. "Would you like to help with him?"

"Come here," Mrs. Aro interrupted, her voice urgent. "Not you, Ilmi. Irma. Now."

Mrs. Salin ran. Even those few steps, she ran.

I dipped the wet washcloth in the warm water and washed Baby Teddy. In the background, I could hear Mrs. Aro's muttering, "I can't stop the bleeding. More towels."

Mrs. Salin was crying, sobbing out loud, unashamedly, she who was the soul of Finnish containment.

I wrapped Teddy into another clean towel, sat down near the stove, and held him, crooning, toughing his head and his cheeks, smoothing the downy skin, trying to warm him, though even I knew how fruitless that was.

He would never know that the world, too, could be warm.

"There's one thing. My mother told me . . . in the old country . . . it worked sometimes. I brought the . . . . Get me a cup. Fill it with rubbing alcohol. And a match." Mrs. Aro's voice sounded different, harder, more authoritive.

About that time, everything began to slow down for me as if the world were coming to a halt. In that jerky half-world, I watched Mrs. Salin take a stoneware cup, open Mrs. Aro's purse, take out a bottle and pour.

I knew from the smell that it was rubbing alcohol.

Mrs. Aro took the cup, lighted a match, held it to the surface. As the liquid flamed and burned, she hurried to the bed, threw back the covers, pulled up the blood-soaked gown, and—turning the cup upside down— laid it on Ma's belly.

"Pray," she ordered us.

Mrs. Salin busied herself emptying the basin into the slop pail, wash-ing it with soap, refilling it with hot water. She moved like a character in the Saturday movies we had watched in the Salins' garage in Kinney, as if the frames of the film moved too slowly, lacking grace, soundlessly.

Mrs. Aro packed fresh towels between Ma's legs, slit the gown, pulled it down and off, changed the cup, then covered Ma with clean linens.

A knock at the door meant Mr. Salin had come back. I had not heard the horse or wagon. In times of sorrow, men were known to muffle the horses' hoofs and remove the sleigh bells. His arm slipped through the door which he had barely cracked open.

"I thought you might need these." He handed quilts to his wife. A hammer. Nails.

"Yo. Yes. *Kiitos*. Thank you," Mrs. Aro said. She and Mrs. Salin moved the bed so they could nail one up on the north wall. It cut the draft considerably. They changed the cup then covered Ma with the other quilt.

The door opened again, this time wide enough to admit two buckets of water. Mrs. Salin put them on the stove to heat.

The next two times it was armloads of wood, carefully emptied into the woodbox, one stick at a time.

There wasn't a sound from the bed.

The night slipped away as Teddy had, quietly, without cry or fuss, as if he had not cared to fight to be a part of this world of pain.

I held him and forced myself to keep on breathing even though I hated the invasive effluvia of blood and death.

"Is Ma dying?" I asked, understanding completely now why knowing could be no worse than not knowing.

"I'm not sure." Mrs. Aro sounded abstract. "I don't know why. But sometimes . . ." She poured another cupful of alcohol, lighted it, carried it toward the bed.

"Is she burning Ma?" I finally asked Mrs. Salin, the words having taken shape slowly, unwilling, too, to be born.

"No." Mrs. Salin gathered all of the bloody linens together and thrown them out the door for Mr. Salin to load into the wagon and take home. She scrubbed the floor. The sharpness of lye soap beat back the smell of blood.

Mrs. Aro lifted the quilts again, repacked Ma with towels, reapplied another hot cup, recovered her with the quilts and blankets, laid a well-wrapped hot lid from the wood stove near her feet.

Just when it would seem that the lid and cup would be cool, she was there repeating the sequence over and over again, each time, leaning over to lay her fingers on Ma's neck and her ear on Ma's chest.

"She's still breathing."

I breathed, too. So did Mrs. Salin. So did Mrs. Aro. They were deep breaths, as if our own lungs, full, could help Ma's.

I wanted desperately to ask what Mrs. Aro was doing. But the ministrations, carried on with a cyclical rhythm had taken on an almost magical aura, one I dared not disturb. Whatever she was doing, it was not hurting Ma. She was lying back restfully, using all of her energy to breathe.

I was proud of Ma. Ill as she was, it was not in her nature to accept help. She was the doer, the giver; from the earliest time that I could remember, she had been the source of strength and courage, whatever the situation.

I remembered pictures of her as a young woman and as a bride. She was so slender and fragile that Pa's hands could have spanned her waist. Dressed in white lawn with lace inserts, her hair piled high into a pompadour, she had been the epitome of a lady.

It was difficult to equate that image with the Ma I had always known—a strong, stocky woman with little regard for the cotton and woolen dresses that she threw on, leaving her shapeless. Her hair, loosened only when I brushed it or when she washed it in the sauna, she braided tightly and wound into a bun fastened with hairpins atop her head. Easily the equal of Pa in verbal battles, she learned to swear in English as fluently as in Finn, and I remembered well their last battle when Pa quit his secure, well-paying job with the streetcar line and left in a huff, iron pots and pans accompanied by screams of fury following him out the door.

We had not seen him since although the spectral figure that visited my bed when I was so ill in Ely that past summer may have been he or perhaps only a figment of my imagination.

To watch the change in Ma as Baby Teddy grew within her and even more during these last two months of her increasing debilitation would have been terrifying beyond belief if I'd had time to think. I'd been too busy to dwell on a situation I simply had to face. Now with time to think, I felt the strength draining out of me, and a fragment of a poem passed through my mind. I could not recall the whole. It was something like "when something . . . duty? says 'thou must' then youth replies, 'I can.'"

"I can't!" I wanted to wail. The rock upon which I had built my life had turned to sand, and I didn't know where to turn. Tears ran down my face, and I hadn't the strength to wipe them away.

And so the hours passed. Eventually dawn sneaked in through the kitchen window, a gray listless dawn, carrying morning along.

Ma continued to breathe.

The smell of blood was almost gone by then, Mrs. Salin having washed Ma, too, and changed the bedclothes. The last pack of toweling had not been removed. Mrs. Aro had not even continued to check it, for it wasn't all red as the earlier ones had been.

Has all of her blood emptied out? I wondered. Is there any left? Can her body make more?

I do not know how time passed after that, for I fell into a deep sleep, still sitting straight up, only my chin drooping onto my chest. When I awoke, Baby Teddy had disappeared from my arms.

Mrs. Aro was spooning a vile smelling concoction into Ma's mouth. Most of it ran down into a waiting towel, but gradually some went in. Then some more. Ma was swallowing.

When Mrs. Salin and Mrs. Aro told Mr. Salin—through the door— "God be praised, I think she'll live," he came in to get me and took me to their house. Someone, I think it was Margie, undressed me and helped me sink into a bed so soft and warm that I floated away into a timeless world I was loathe to leave.

They told me later that Ma and I both awoke at about the same time. I felt as if I had slept forever and yet not slept at all.

Both Mrs. Aro and Mrs. Salin stayed at our house all that day and the following night and day. Mr. Salin explained to me that Ma needed to rest and that the best thing I could do for her was to allow her time to do that. They would feed her warm broth whenever she awoke and keep her warm and clean and comfortable. My job was not to worry.

Eino helped. He quizzed me on the new words in his vocabulary notebook and set me to copying the ones I didn't have. We worked ahead on arithmetic, and he explained to me, much more clearly than the teacher had, the complexities of long division and the fascinating equations of algebra. They had a globe in their living room so the geography chapters made more sense than they had at home. And I had already completed the history and literature books, since they were always pure pleasure.

We made up contests of memorization, timed ourselves, and recited to each other. Mr. Salin excused Eino from many of the barn chores and hours in the store which, Eino explained, were intended to help him learn the business "from the ground up."

Margie, of course, was in heaven. Sara had several books of paper dolls, real ones, not the ones I cut out of the catalog for Margie, and the two soon had Sara's room turned into a city with houses for the dolls and cupboards for their clothes. Both girls had promised, cross their hearts, to be careful with the scissors, so they were allowed to do some of the cutting upstairs. When they were called down to eat, they cried, "But we just started playing!"

I wanted to see Ma, but Mrs. Salin came home late the following afternoon with Mrs. Aro's adjuration that I was to stay away one more night.

"My own family is perfectly capable of taking care of itself," Mrs. Aro had said. That was probably true. Mrs. Aro was not the housekeeper Ma was. But she ruled her household with an iron hand, her husband included. In addition to her renown as a healer and midwife, she had won prizes at the county fair for her jams, jellies, preserves, and canned meats. Her family would not starve.

It was fortunate that I listened to Mrs. Salin instead of giving way to that urge to see Ma. The next morning when Mr. Salin returned from the Zim railroad depot, he brought with him a package wrapped in brown paper and addressed in an elegant hand to "Miss Ilmi Marianna Brosi, Zim, Minnesota." The return address read "From Mrs. Francis Callahan Malmstrom, Virginia, Minnesota."

Everyone clustered around me, asking who she was. I knew she was Dr. Malmstrom's wife. Everyone had known of my trip to Virginia and of Dr. Malmstrom's kindness.

Inside the brown twine and wrapping paper lay a box with a note affixed to the top.

"Dear Miss Brosi,

"My husband, Dr. Malmstrom, was deeply moved and impressed by your courage in coming to see him on behalf of your mother. He expressed his wish that he could have done more. Please accept this small token of our concern for you and your family and our most sincere wish that you and your mother will enjoy dressing your baby in this outfit, one our son John wore briefly and outgrew too soon. It gives us great pleasure to think of its being worn by another well-loved child. With our best wishes that all is well and your fears have been allayed, Francis Callahan Malmstrom."

Inside of the box lay an exquisitely crocheted gown of fine white wool with a matching cap, booties, sweater, and shawl.

I had tried my best, until then, to do my crying in private. But by the time I had passed the note around and we had all read it and touched the gift that had been a part of the kind of layette even a catalog could not offer, we were all in tears.

Mr. Salin harumphed and blew his nose several times before telling me that Mr. Saarinen was putting the finishing touches on a small mahogany coffin. "I just happened to have the boards," he said, as if mahogany lay ready for use in everyone's barn. "And Mr. Saarinen had joined and sanded it to a perfect sheen."

Mrs. Aro had a small length of white satin set aside. Once Mr. Saarinen had completed his work to his satisfaction, she would pad and line the inside with satin, even forming a small pillow for Teddy's head.

"Should Ma see this?" I asked.

"Out of the Mouths of Children cometh wisdom" had been the topic of a talk given at a women's club meeting in Kinney. I didn't remember any other part of the lecture or the discussion, but Margie and Sara both said, "She has to, doesn't she, Ilmi?" as if I knew the answer to the question. "Won't she feel better knowing how much other people have cared and shared their feelings with us?" It was the first sensible sentence I had heard come from Margie's mouth. Then, as if to controvert that fledgling step into adulthood, she burst into tears, stuck her thumb in her mouth, and buried herself in my skirts.

Mr. Salin and Mr. Spina, whose eyes were suspiciously red ("This damn cold—excuse me, Miss Ilmi—just won't go away"), whose handkerchiefs suspiciously damp, managed to break through the snow and hack far enough into the ground to open a grave. They draped the pile of earth with green cloth.

As soon as Ma was able to stand, Mr. Saarinen brought her the coffin, and we left her alone to dress Baby Teddy in the beautiful cap and gown and booties and wrap him lightly in the shawl. When she was ready, I helped Ma dress, and the men carried her to a chair set near the gravesite near the edge of our property, which the community had designated as the beginning of a cemetery plot.

We had no ordained minister. But Mr. Aro, who no doubt had had some experience in working with his wife in these circumstances, read a passage from the Bible, in Finnish of course, and related the simple facts of Teddy's name, birth and death dates, and survivors. We were hard put to include "Knute Pietari Brosi," but Ma insisted and so we did.

Mr. Saarinen had also carved a cross and engraved it "Baby Teddy Brosi"—with the birth and death dates underneath. Ma dropped the first handful of dirt onto the coffin. I followed her as did Margie, and then we went home.

There should have been coffee and *pulla* served afterwards to all who attended, but by common consent, though we had a constant stream of visitors that afternoon, no one stayed to eat or drink. They pressed Ma's hand, hugged or kissed Margie and me, and left quietly.

As soon as possible, Mrs. Aro took charge, indicating that it was time for Ma to rest. I helped her get Ma into a nightgown and into bed. Margie, too, was exhausted, from the effort of having to be good for so many days in a row.

At the last I was left alone to sit at the table with the kerosene lamp turned low trying to come to terms with all that had happened in such a short time. Why, it was still January!

I knew the floor needed sweeping, but Mrs. Aro had filled the stove with wood and the boiler with water and Mr. Salin had loaded the woodbox so full that some of the logs were leaning against the side. The lamp chimney needed an ammonia washing. I was still a bit behind in my school work. There were things I should do, especially cover and care for the food that every family had donated, enough, if I cared for it as I should, to last us weeks. But I couldn't seem to move.

I awoke sometime during the night, cold, my head lying on my arms. Getting up actually hurt, I was so stiff. I reloaded the firebox, turned out the kerosene lamp, and climbed into bed beside Margie. Neither she nor Ma stirred.

I knew that winter would pass and spring would come. But right then that was little solace.

I fell asleep composing in my mind a thank you note to Mrs. Malmstrom. But I did not have the energy to write it down.

CHAPTER NINE
Escape

For weeks, it seemed, we waited, Margie and I. We waited for Pa, who did not return. We waited for Ma, who, strange as it may seem, came and went. Sometimes she seemed her old self, washing, ironing, cooking, baking, and cleaning. Often she slipped away into a world we couldn't reach, sleeping or simply sitting there, but far away.

So it went on until it seemed there would be no end.

What I would have done had there been no school I can't imagine, but there was, and it was everything to me. To the other students, studying and school may have been work. To me, they offered a mental and physical haven.

Although Miss Heino was barely older than we were, she was an excellent teacher. The younger students, including Margie, adored her. The older boys respected and obeyed her, and I considered her a friend as well as a teacher. She understood my need to help my family survive and did everything she could do, just as Miss Loney had, to help me. That meant she made me work harder than any other student in the school. And she had a reason.

School offered wondrous times of joy and excitement. It was the source of learning, yes, but it was also the source of inner change so that I who took every word of my class work seriously was gradually turning into an American. Becoming an American, speaking English, doing what Americans do had always been immeasurably important to me. Miss Heino did not demean our Finnish heritage. But regardless of the extent to which that permeated our home lives, she gently led us—well, me, anyway—along the path toward becoming educated American citizens, with all of the privileges and opportunities that opened up for us.

We didn't know what other school rooms looked like, but ours was as homey as Miss Heino could make it. The larger schools had separate cloak rooms with hooks and a shelf above them. Some of the larger consolidated schools springing up to replace the smaller one-room schools supposedly had electricity or gas lighting, furnaces to heat the whole building, separate rooms for separate grades, a library, and amenities which we could barely imagine. But no consolidated school could have been more comfortable or offer an atmosphere more conducive to learning, except for the heat, than ours.

Around the pot bellied stove was a fender where we could put our lunches. Sometimes they froze anyway. Sometimes I spent the day in coat and boots. Like my beloved Miss Loney, Miss Heino rarely used her desk except for holding answer books and lesson plans. She moved among us, helping, answering questions, posing problems for us to consider. One group would be reading silently while another was reading quietly aloud while another was working arithmetic problems on the board.

Our desks were nailed to slats on the floor in long sections and varied in sizes from the small to the large. But somehow Miss Heino had managed to get extra chairs which she arranged so that we could sit in a semi-circle when we worked together and when she read aloud. That way we all heard a story appropriate to the season. In October, it had been "The Legend of Sleepy Hollow." "The Landing of the Pilgrims" and "The Courtship of Miles Standish" had filled November, and we had heard the entire *Christmas Carol* in December. Of course, a lot of it went by the little ones, but they grasped the story if not all the words.

She encouraged her older students to make flash cards of any unfamiliar words, and we met as a group at least once a week to offer our cards for the others to share. She allowed us to use the big dictionary to fill out the cards. We approached that book with such reverence that it was almost like touching and using the Bible.

She trusted us in many ways, especially in relation to an alternative to Eino Salin's notebook. We made flash cards with the word on one side with its pronunciation, the definition and part of speech and sometimes the sentence in which the word appeared on the other side. When we had made ten or twenty of these, we were allowed to test each other or test ourselves. Eino and I had a running competition for the number of words, but we also studied together during the week. How we looked forward both to hearing the new chapter and to adding new words to our English vocabu-laries! We tried hard not to speak Finnish in school, and Miss Heino polite-ly corrected us when we lapsed.

Toivo was not at all interested in vocabulary. Instead he prided him-self on being at least one week ahead of Miss Heino's lesson plans in arith-metic or mathematics. Naturally, I had to enter into that competition, too. That cost me double duty because Toivo tried to be much friendlier than he needed to be. I had to stay clear of his "Russian fingers and Roman hands," as he put it, thinking that so clever.

Our school had been carefully allotted the number of books that there were students in the classes, but Miss Heino somehow managed to wangle extras as students advanced. She fought for lined paper so we could practice our penmanship and extra foolscap to use for arithmetic. I'm sure the cost of flashcards came from her own pocket, slim as that was, because she made barely enough to live on. It's a good thing that those families with enough rooms or with extra food allowed her to live in or visit and not make her pay board.

With joy we decorated the front bulletin boards, matching the color and the kind of display based on the season. In September Miss Heino made gold and brown leaves, using the first ones to fall as patterns. In November, we tried to make the turkeys with different colored construc-tion paper tails. December dictated snowmen with carrot ears and scarves and funny colored hats.

But Miss Heino hit her stride when we came back from Christmas vacation. That first day, instead of going right back to studying, she said she had seen enough snow flakes in the windows of homes and stores that had four or five points to last her a lifetime.

"Snowflakes," she told us, "have six sides. Always. And no two are ever alike." She had written out and dittoed off directions and given us several sheets of paper because, as she said, it was a tricky business to get a snowflake just right. During Christmas vacation, she had also gone to the St. Louis County office and gotten sharp scissors for all of us. We were paired, then, each one of the older kids with a younger one who would have difficulty with the scissors. She had already made exquisite white snowflakes and hung them from the every possible spot in the room, so we had abundant samples. As we worked, folding and snipping, she complet-ed the steps with us so we were able to watch her. She watched us, too, and

70

if we made a mistake, she simply gave us another sheet of paper so we could start again.

"First," she said, "square a sheet of white paper to eight and one-half inches."

We measured and cut and continued to follow her directions in folding and cutting through nine steps.

"I have found," Miss Heino said, "I must have cut out at least a hundred snowflakes before I got the hang of it, and the lady who taught me said it takes good scissors. So, if your first tries don't work, borrow the scissors from someone who made one successfully, and keep trying." And finally, she said, "I have an iron set up in front of the room to make the edges sharp." And sure enough, there it was.

"Once you've made one, you'll want to keep making another and another. Any time you have a minute from your lessons, come up to borrow the scissors. I'd like to see a whole ceiling of snowflakes and many to take home by the end of January. Store them closed with the edges together. Oh, and note that on step one all three folds come to the edge together."

We sat stupefied. "Can we really do this?" we asked almost in unison.

I certainly had no faith in my ability to recreate these fragile, delicate beauties.

"I'll tell you a secret if you promise not to tell," Miss Heino whispered. "I didn't know either until I visited an old friend of my mother's during vacation. We got to talking about snowflakes, and I expressed my frustration about the ones I had seen with four or five points, and her house was full of the right kind, hanging in the windows, on dark walls, just everywhere. I asked if she would teach me, and she said yes. It took one whole afternoon!"

"I want you to write a 'thank you' note to her when we're all finished. She's a very special lady."

"Does she live in Zim?" we asked, thinking about inviting her to visit us so we could thank her in person.

"No, she lives in the country, in Idington, near Angora. I took the train to visit her, and her husband met me with his horse and sleigh."

We went to work. It did take most of us all day, but, oh, what beautiful creations emerged! We actually cheered the first one made, incredibly enough by Toivo, who, of course, made a crude remark about his hands.

71

I helped Margie make one to take home to Ma, and I managed two, though they were not nearly as lovely as Miss Heino's.

All in all, it was a perfect January day. By afternoon, those of us who had mastered the technique, got going on the assignments written on the board, and by late afternoon, went homeward with our proud new creations and our homework for the next day.

I don't know which excited me more. But the excitement dwindled as we approached our house. The house was dark, the kerosene lamp unlit. We started to run, sure that the fire, too, must be out.

The minute we walked in the door, we entered our second life, one where the intricacies of making snowflakes properly was supplanted by making sure Ma was warm and fed. I worked ten times harder at home, but without the pure satisfaction and delight of school.

CHAPTER TEN
Valentine's Day

Miss Heino offered us another joyful challenge on Valentine's Day. Again, she managed to get enough red construction paper and, probably from her own pocket again, lacy doilies.

"Ask your mother if she has any red or white yarn that she can spare," she suggested to us.

Ma never had enough and to spare, but next day Sara Salin raised her hand after the opening exercises ("The Pledge of Allegiance," "The Star Spangled Banner" and sometimes "America, the Beautiful").

"My family is contributing a whole skein of white yarn," she announced. We tried to look grateful. We made valentines to tape to the wall and to hang as mobiles from the ceiling. We made valentines of every size and shape for the windows, and finally we each made our own valentine boxes decorated for the valentines we would receive. Magically, a box for each student appeared (And Miss Heino had us send Mr. Salin another "thank you" note). We devoted an entire afternoon to cutting and pasting our mailboxes and another to copying verses Miss Heino put on the blackboard or writing our own.

"I have only two rules," Miss Heino said firmly. "Each student must receive one valentine from every other student, and none of them may be cruel."

Since Valentines had to be written in our best penmanship, it was an afternoon of WORK. Oh, how I wished that Ma had been able to send cookies or some treat to share on Valentines' Day, and I did ask her if she would.

Tears ran down her face as she shook her head, and I found myself holding her and assuring her that it was all right. She became so distraught that I tucked her into bed early with a hot stove lid by her feet, and she lay in bed and cried, "I cannot. I simply cannot. I am so sorry, Ilmi, but I cannot."

I felt awful.

"Oh, Ma, what's wrong?" I asked, sitting next to her on the bed holding her hand.

But she just cried and said over and over, "I do love you and Margie so much, and I'm so sorry."

Margie and I held her closely and said, "We know that, Ma. We know," soothing her until she fell asleep.

It took me a long while to catch on, but that fall, before the birth of Baby Teddy, Margie began taking an invidious delight in wreaking vengeance upon Sara Salin for her incessant bragging. Since both of them were in the same grades—first and second grouped together—Margie had ample opportunity for revenge.

One day handfuls of snow were lodged at the end of Sara's coat sleeves and were still frozen when the day was over and she went to put her coat on. That night Sara had a very cold walk home.

Looking suspiciously at Margie, I was led astray by blue eyes expressing absolute innocence.

Another day ink just happened to spill on a dress that Sara acclaimed loudly was "not homemade but ordered from the catalog." Margie was assiduous in helping to clean up the spill, which completely ruined the dress, since only lye soap would remove it, and that application would also remove the pattern.

A surreptitious unbuttoning of buttons on the back of one of Sara's dresses left a clear view of her underwear. Margie commiserated instead of joining in the pointing of fingers and laughter Miss Heino put an abrupt end to.

A dipper full of water dropped "by accident" onto ringlets Mrs. Salin set in rag curls every night so Sara's hair would curl as Margie's did naturally. Water or humidity made Margie's hair bounce. Water or humidity made Sara's hair lank as a horse's tail. Again I suspected Margie, but felt a secret pleasure in these incidents. Sara's bragging was very hard to swallow.

Each time one of these incidents occurred, however, I gave Margie the look, an imitation of Ma's unspoken warning that dire consequences would follow if we continued.

After Baby's Teddy's birth and the kindnesses shown us by every family in the community, those incidents abruptly ceased. We never discussed them openly. They were, perhaps, the first of many "sister secrets" we found ourselves sharing as we came to rely more and more on each other.

During January, especially, we became accomplices in the serious struggle to hide from everyone else, grown-ups and children alike, the true state of affairs in our household. There were three bodies living in our house, but only two of us showed any evidence of life.

The old Ma popped out of bed before us every day. On Mondays she had the dirty clothes sorted into piles and the white clothes soaking before we got up. When we got home from school, the dried clothes smelled sweet and clean and lay neatly where they belonged.

Tuesday was ironing day, and she had a good part of the work done before we were up.

And oh! for Wednesdays! Bread dough was rising in one bowl and biscuit dough in another as we left for school. We knew we'd come home to freshly baked treats. In that normal world I would have invited our teacher for coffee and freshly baked goods after school. Although we never came home to a dirty or messy house, Wednesday night was a good night for company. The house sparkled.

After school in that other world, Ma wanted to see our assignments and praised us. She laughed at the funny things that had happened, and shook her head over Toivo's antics. And always we worked on trying to improve her English, using words and phrases she repeated and absorbed.

Although that Ma had disappeared even before we left Kinney, she reappeared sporadically, especially when we were trying to get settled in our "half-house." Thus our lives became divided into two parts—then and now.

Now she slept or sat on a chair by the window, brooding all day and most of the night. Sometimes she simply stayed in bed. She ate if I fixed food and fed her. She struggled to answer "yes" or "no" if we asked a question. She used the pee pot even during the day. When we got home from school, the house smelled. She never went out.

Margie may have been a trial to me once, but she became my accomplice during that interminable time when Ma's soul slipped away from us, though her body remained in the house.

Now washing clothes took two days and ironing, three. We left cleaning for weekends. I tried to develop a schedule, putting the white clothes to soak on Sunday night and memorizing poetry and studying theorums while I ironed. But there were limits to what I could do.

Our problems extended past the things in the house that Ma simply could not do. I didn't want to walk home with the Salins, even though Eino was never anything but kind, because sometimes I had to go there to ask for food, and I had no money to pay. Other families helped us when they could, with a chicken or some potatoes, or a cut of ham for some bacon if they had something leftover from butchering of a pig. Ma could have killed a partridge with a rock on a good day. But now we had no good days.

To top it off, my Valentine card from Toivo said, "Roses are red, and violets are blue. Sugar is sweet, and so am I. Let's get together and you'll find out. Love, Toivo."

It took all my forbearance not to throw it into the stove.

In spite of Toivo, school was my life. Shortly after Valentines' Day, Miss Heino officially promoted me to the eighth grade, which gave me the right to take the State Board Examinations and to graduate with the other eighth graders of the St. Louis County Unorganized Territory that spring. She did it with no ceremony but with a simple re-seating and a new set of books, especially for literature and arithmetic. I smiled when I saw the literature book. I had already read it and memorized most of the poetry. But the arithmetic book would take a good deal of work and concentration. Otherwise, I had been doing eighth grade work all fall term in Zim and as much of it as I could overhear in Kinney, simply by getting my hands on the books and doing the assignments the bigger kids were doing, answering the questions at the ends of the chapters, memorizing the spelling words, and of course, continuing to add to Eino's and my separate vocabulary notebooks. Margie had even begun to enjoy at least the special days and the stories.

Moreover, Margie had actually become a great help to me. Without Ma's expertise, washing clothes took so long because they had to be hung on clothes lines in the house to dry. What a mess! There was little ironing, yet it took me at least two days. I tried to develop a schedule which got the cooking done before I messed the floor with flour as I tried to do the baking. It took a long time because Ma had no recipes written down. It was "a handful" or "a pinch" or "a couple of small spoons." I tried to follow her advice step by step, but the bread burned, the biscuits refused to rise, and I gave up on *pulla* or cakes or cookies.

It was amazing how much Margie could do without coaching when she set her mind to it. She turned out to be a much better cook than I. One morning she got so disgusted with drinking burned coffee and eating lumpy cereal that she threw both into the slop pail and started all over again. She made fresh coffee and smooth cereal, told me to sit down and eat, and fed Ma herself. She had Ma's knack of knowing just how much flour should go into a bread or biscuit dough. I always added too much and my end product was always dry. Either that or I baked it a bit too long, considering the longer the better. Margie could tap the loaf and sense the exact moment when the bread or biscuit was neither under nor over done.

"How did you do that, Margie? Will you teach me?" I asked in great consternation when another of my attempts failed.

"I can't," she said. "You either can tell or you can't. I'm sorry." In the humidity, because I had been scrubbing and putting potatoes to boil, her hair had curled even more tightly, and she was pink cheeked from the effort of kneading the breads and *pulla*, her eyes sparkled. She looked good enough to eat.

For the first time in my life, I truly appreciated having a sister. And when I reached out to give her a hug, she returned it hard, then teased me about leaving the floor half washed.

We took another step together as soon as I scrubbed the rest of the floor, washing us onto the bed instead of heading out the door.

"Please, please answer us, Ma," we begged, settling down on each side of her. "What's wrong? What can we do to make you happy?"

She tried to turn away from us, but one of us was in the way all the time. "Here, Ma, let's plump up the pillow. Ma, I'll straighten your nightgown. We really, really want to help. Please, please answer us, Ma," Margie and I begged. "What's wrong? What can we do to make you more comfortable?"

"Nothing," she whispered. "There is no help." She looked at Margie and me and said, "I'm so afraid."

"Of what, Ma?"

"We will starve."

"No, Ma. Mr. Salin is giving us credit until Pa comes back."

"He'll never come back," she cried, despairingly. "Never. I can't . . ."

With me holding one hand and Margie the other, I said, "We can, WE CAN make it. Even if we have to eat lard sandwiches."

Ma gave me a look that spoke volumes, and she lay back into the pillows, exhausted by the horror of having to send us to school with lard sandwiches.

I wondered how little she ate when we were not home. Probably nothing.

"We can," Margie and I insisted. "And as soon as spring comes, we'll borrow Mr. Salin's horse and plow and plant . . ."

She interrupted. "Charity. We can*not* live on charity. We will not live on charity."

"Just enough to get us through the winter, Ma, and we'll make do until spring."

"Winter," her voice trailed off, her eyes turning from my face to Margie's to the hoarfrost windows . . . it will never end."

I had read somewhere a line that said "there was in me an invincible summer." We could not find it in Ma, no matter how we tried.

CHAPTER ELEVEN
Pa

At that exact moment we heard a noise at the door. It opened with a strong kick, and there stood Pa, a bag over his shoulder, stamping his feet to get the snow off his shoes.

He set his battered fiddle case on the bed. Unwrapping a knitted scarf, he also shed a jacket, opening the door briefly to shake the snow off and hung it on one of the hooks as close to the stove as was safe.

Ma had put up four hooks. She had had some hope left.

Then, unbelievably, he raised me from the bed to give me a hug. Pa was tall, six feet at least. By comparison I shocked myself into awareness that I had grown.

Turning to Margie, he told her, "Stoke that stove up. We're going to have venison steak for supper, and it has to thaw."

Then he reached down gently as if he were picking a flower, took Ma's hands, and lifted her up to hold her, making soothing, crooning sounds as if she were a child.

It was obvious from her slender form and the lack of any childish accouterments that she had lost the baby. Pa must have heard that from somewhere because his sounds were accompanied by a pat on her tummy.

I did not know whether to laugh or cry, to throw a frying pan in his direction, or to pour him a cup of coffee. I didn't know what to do or say so I did nothing at all.

But this was a Pa I had seen only a few times before in Virginia and when we were happy in Kinney and especially that day when Uncle Charles drove us to Zim where we spent a day in Paradise and named the land that was to be our own "Happy Corner." That day Ma placed the imaginary kitchen table where she knew it would go, paced out the rooms,

79

and overlooked Margie's usual indiscretions, even when she got caught on a tree limb.

However, these episodes had been of short duration with Pa more likely to get mad at his boss or because of some slight he felt had besmirched the Brosi family identity, either left us to fend for ourselves or spent days with his pencil or fiddle, caring not one whit that our larder was virtually empty of even the necessities of flour and sugar, crackers, lard, meat, vegetables—everything we needed in order to live.

But I had rarely seen the father who appeared that day. He was another man—different from himself in every way.

Taking Ma's hands, he turned her to face him. "All is well," he said in Finnish, enfolding her in his arms and then in his lap.

Pa was a big man, not fat, not stocky, but tall and lean, as if he were made of tensile steel. He lifted Ma's chin and kissed her on the lips.

I watched, aghast, certain that Ma would give him a good smack against his face, a slap made ineffectual by her own weakness but filled with all the anger she could garner. Instead, she leaned her head against his chest and began to cry. I did not need to be a grown-up or to have anyone tell me that the tears were for his leaving us, for her loneliness, for the effort it had taken to get us to Zim, for the loss of Baby Teddy. They were the tears she had willed herself to hold in, the tears that had kept her from living, wanting nothing but the oblivion of the hoarfrost winter, the tears she could not share with us.

Suddenly I realized why Ma had married him. He was a handsome man, spare, with prominent cheekbones, deep-set incisive eyes that looked right into my soul, understanding what I couldn't find words to say.

Gently, he moved Ma to one knee and motioned me onto the other, and hugged us both. Then he laid Ma on the bed, drew the quilt over her, and soothed her cheek. I'd seen his hand calm a horse. I had seen a chickadee rest on his finger.

That hand touched Ma's eyes so she closed them and fell into a restful sleep. The worry and pain seemed erased by that hand, and I felt a sign of relief. Then he, who usually spanked and disciplined me and pulled my hair or my *"niskaan karvat,"* the small hairs behind my ears, drew me to his lap with a tentative movement, giving me leave to back away if I needed to. But he exuded such warmth, I leaned gratefully into his hug and surrendered my worries with a deep sense of gratitude.

"Why don't you put some potatoes on to boil, and I'll take care of the meat," he said. Margie, now riding on Pa's shoulders, said, "I'll set the table."

"We need to get some potatoes from Salins and . . ." he looked around, "some coffee. Ilmi, will you make a list. Margie can help."

Pa walked over to the shelf which held his shaving things and smiled. "She did not completely lock me out."

Ma must have prayed or hoped at least that Pa would return, for she had made that shelf for his shaving things and there was room on our top shelf for extra underwear, socks, a shirt, and pants.

"We probably need to get you a new winter coat," he told me and asked, "Is there any yeast?"

Not knowing whether to nod or shake my head I simply put the extra potatoes away and ventured on a trial run. "We're almost out of coffee, too."

While we ate, we made plans. Pa said he would get us some fresh meat tomorrow. He opened the unmade trundle bed for us, gave Ma the equivalent of a sponge bath, and tucked her in with a kiss then turned to me.

"Ilmi," he said, "please make a list including the length of sleeves a new coat would need. Tomorrow we'll get caught up."

I fell asleep that night feeling as if I were living in a dream world. What, I wondered, would life be like when I woke up? I didn't know what to answer Eino when we walked to school the next morning.

"So, your pa's home again," Eino commented, urging me to lag along behind the group that included the Aros and Margie and Sara—those of us who lived on the west side of the St. Louis River and usually walked to school together. Babbling in Finnish, they rarely listened to our conversations, always carried on in English. "For good?" he asked.

"Who knows?" My response had a bitter edge. Wonderful as last night had been, there had been good times before, and they all ended the same way.

"Has that helped your ma? Don't worry," he raised his hands, school bag and all to fend off an explosion. "No one knows but me. I just happened to be awake this morning when your pa came in before my pa opened the store."

He paused, giving me time to decide whether or not I wanted to talk about this. Then asked, "How's it going?"

I shrugged, "For Ma and Margie heaven. I don't know how I feel." I stopped for a moment both to set my book bag down and to let the rest of our group go a bit more ahead. "It won't last. He'll be here and then gone again. In all the years I can remember, it's always been that way. They can't live with each other, but they can't live without each other either. When all is well, it's . . . wonderful. Then something sets them off, and they quit talking to each other, or Ma loses her temper at Pa because he quit another job, and he leaves, and we start all over again. But having him here now seems to be a blessing. We were losing Ma."

"I guessed that. My ma was worried. So was Mrs. Aro. They didn't know whether to offer help or not. It could have been resented."

"Things were pretty bad. Worse than you know. Ma . . . just slept . . . and . . . looked out the window. Some days she didn't even get dressed. It's been . . . awful . . . since Baby Teddy's birth . . . and death."

"My ma would have been right to come."

"No. Ma is adamant about our not accepting any more charity. It's about the only thing she says over and over again. Otherwise, she . . . just isn't there."

"Let me know if I can help."

I knew he meant it and was sensitive enough not to push.

"I will. It helped . . . just to talk about it. I'm also wondering where Pa goes when he leaves. What's he doing to earn money? He said he was going to buy me a winter coat. The ones your dad has in stock are way more expensive than we can afford. I made a list of all the food we need, and it was a page long. He can't work in the mines, and he quit his job with the streetcar line. It's the wrong time of the year for him to leave a lumber camp. Where is the money coming from? That scares me. If you find out . . ."

We needed to hurry. The group was waiting for us. The school bell was ringing.

"Wait for me after school. I have an idea of what he might be doing. But you have to promise not to tell anyone, especially not your ma."

"What . . . ?" I wanted to beg him to stop right then and tell me, but we had reached the school yard, and everyone else was in line. Miss Heino gave us a strange look, the kind that said she had never expected us to be tardy.

"I apologize," Eino said, taking the blame. "We were talking about . . . things. We didn't mean to be late."

"I accept your apology," Miss Heino nodded, still giving us a quizzical look.

That day was endless. Because it rained, we couldn't go outside during lunch time or recess.

I couldn't stop wondering about Pa and where he got the money. I knew how expensive the coat that fit me would be. He couldn't support himself with his fiddle and his pencil alone any more than those two things alone helped to support us. I knew he liked making knives, but that was something he did at home. He never tried to sell them. It haunted me all day, causing me to make so many simple errors that Miss Heino finally asked me if I were ill.

"I do have a dreadful headache," I admitted, which was true. The bad part of Pa's return was the fear that began when he walked in the door and made me feel as if I must watch everything I said and did while he was there, setting off a battle that would cause him to leave.

"Would you like to go in the back of the room and lie down on the bench?" Miss Heino asked.

I shook my head. The last thing I wanted was to be alone with my thoughts. Then I asked if I were very careful if I could read her new poetry book. She had brought it back with her to school the last time she went home. It had been sent to her as a birthday gift from a wealthy aunt who lived in England and loved poetry as much as Miss Heino and I did. Miss Heino's aunt had gone to hear several readings done by a young expatriot from New England and had bought several copies of a slender volume of his poetry. She believed he would one day be heralded at home in the United States as he was already being recognized there as a new, fresh voice. His name was Robert Frost.

"Of course, you may. That always helps me, too, when things look bleak," she answered, bringing it to me.

I excused myself from the double desk I shared with either Eino or Toivo, depending on the subject we were studying, and moved a chair into a shaded back corner of the room, where I curled up with my head leaning on the window sill. I opened the book with great care so as not to harm the binding, allowed it to open where it would and found a poem that I memorized.

In the poem entitled, "Fire and Ice," Frost foresaw the end of the world—destruction—as happening because of either the fire of desire or the ice of hatred.

I certainly understood the icy quality of hatred. When Ma and Pa fought, they treated each other with an icy cold shoulder, refusing even to talk to one another, enlisting me as go-between, telling me what they wanted the other to hear, forcing me to try to help them toward a middle ground and peace.

The fire of desire seemed banked, although having Pa come home just now seemed to make a world of difference to Ma, gently pulling her out of herself and her sorrows and guilt into almost her normal self.

But the author did not mention the kind of fire hatred can engender. I had heard Ma swear and seen the dents in the walls and door made by the pots and pans she threw at Pa when he quit his job with the streetcar line. There was destruction in that act and in her screams at him, a fiery anger that sent him away, even though we desperately needed his job and the money he made in order to stay alive.

Frost's poem made me think of Ma and Pa. It made me see them, not just as Ma and Pa, but as human beings who were not unlike others. Oh, I am doing a poor job of explaining why, but "Fire and Ice" helped me grasp the totality of strong emotion, and in some ways made me fear it. I didn't ever want to fall in love if it were to become the whole world, as it was for Ma and Pa during the good times, and the source of near desctruction during the bad.

I had awakened before to find his shelf empty of shaving cup, shaving brush, his razor strap, his sharp-edged razor, his extra clothing, his mirror, and depending upon the depth of his anger, his fiddle, too.

Until Baby Teddy was conceived, Ma's strength kept us going and held us together. Her fragility forced me to seek help the previous summer, not from those in Finntown, but from those who gave me what others found in a place—a sense of caring and a willingness to help from within them, from their hearts.

Now Pa was with us again for the first time since last May. This time with money. I counted the minutes of that school day, recited the poem to myself, and waited through the endless minutes, wondering what Eino knew. Finally the bell rang signaling the end of the school day. I hardly even waited to say good-bye to Miss Heino, but stayed close to Eino until, on the way home, lagging again behind the others, he asked me if I had ever heard of the name "Harjun Kassu."

"No. Not really. I've heard the name whispered, but whenever one of us kids comes within earshot, everyone changes the subject. Why? Who is he?"

"He's a bootlegger. Lives somewhere near Lake Leander. Makes some of his own moonshine but imports more of it when he can get it across the border from Canada without getting caught. He buys it cheaply there, sells it for maybe double the price here. He gets guys who are down and out or sometimes hooked on alcohol or daredevils who like to thumb their noses at the revenue agents to drive the trucks and to do the delivery to men who stash it away and sell it, usually adding on a commission of their own. Harjun Kassu pockets the money, but he pays his drivers well. He has to. If they get caught . . . it's all up for them."

"Are you telling me that Pa works for this man this . . . what did you call him?"

"Harjun Kassu. I'm not sure, but there's a good chance that he might. It's an on-again-off-again job. He lays off—or is it lies still?—well, anyway, when the agents are sniffing around, he works his farm, innocent as can be, hides his still in the woods, doesn't sell or deal at all. Then, when the agents back off, thinking they had the wrong man, he gets the word out that he's open for drivers and open for business, and everyone makes some fast money until things get tight again."

"But Pa doesn't drink. At least I've never seen him drink."

"That would make him ideal. He could be trusted to keep his head and think fast if things got tight. There was a run just a few nights ago. I heard the truck make its usual stop, heard some activity, saw the lights go on and off again, like a signal, heard the truck start up, the gears grind, and then it was quiet again."

"But who, around here . . . certainly not your pa!"

"No. He doesn't dare get into that business. We do all right with the farm and the store. But the revenue agents have checked him out thoroughly, walking around the store and the house and the outbuildings, looking for hiding places. Pa knows he doesn't have any booze, but he still breaths a sigh of relief when they're gone."

"The last time they visited, they had the description of one of the drivers. It fit your pa to a 'T.' I wouldn't be surprised if he was gone when you got home. None of us would mention him. I don't know whether it would be better for you to tell Margie to keep still or just to let her be. She prattles on in Finn most of the time, anyway, and the revenuers speak English mostly. Once in a while they'll bring someone along to translate, but someone in every house can talk some English, enough to be understood."

85

"But . . . who?" I wanted to know who took the delivery. Their farm was not far from Salins'. But if someone were driving a truck, they were so noisy it could be any of the families we had known from Kinney, and there were others, now, moving in, some of whom had not come from Kinney—the Korpis, the Ikolas, the Makis, and some others whose names I didn't know who lived in Little Swan.

"It's better not to know. I didn't look out of the window, and I kept my head under the pillow. It's a lot easier to tell the truth, than to trump up a lie. The revenue agents are quick to catch on. At least they seem as if they'd be."

"So . . . whether Ma needs him desperately or not, he might have to go either to haul more liquor or to escape the revenue officers. He might not be there when I get home."

I wasn't sure whether to be relieved or unhappy when we got home, and he wasn't there. But everything I had written on the list was. Including a new winter coat that fit me to perfection. Ma was up making supper, wearing a new dress, her face flushed from the fire, we were supposed to think. She didn't quite meet our eyes when she explained that Pa had a new job and would be back as soon as he could. In the meantime he had left us with food and enough money to replenish our larder as we needed.

I thought of fire and ice and forced myself to be happy that for Ma the world had not ended. I would never allow myself to love that deeply, so deeply that to be apart could be a kind of death. Ma had always seemed so strong that I had never thought of her needing Pa or loving him so deeply that his very appearance made her come alive again.

CHAPTER TWELVE
Fear

Ironically, that was March, the month of my birthday, a day which we never had really observed, though I had never thought about why. Sometimes Ma made a special dinner or asked me to choose what I would like best that night. But, as I came to surmise after balancing the dates in the Bible, perhaps because of the dates in the Bible, March nineteenth had never been made especially significant. I was not surprised that morning to see that Pa had left. He usually managed not to be home for my birthday. But that year, the year I turned thirteen, March nineteenth was especially significant in that I became absolutely sure that life was ending for me. I awoke early, feeling my stomach cramping as if I were experiencing a recurrence of the influenza with nausea and dizziness and a wetness between my legs that felt like urine. A quick groping under the sheets for the crotch of my snuggies, the knee-length woolen pants that Ma insisted we wear from the first snowstorm until the trees were in full leaf, confirmed the damp feeling.

"Oh, God," I thought, "what next?" I had not lost control of what Ma called my "small poddies" or my "big poddies" since way before Margie was born.

Ma's training method for both body functions was quick and thorough. I surmised that she had used the same technique on me as she had on Margie, although it took Margie longer to give in. Ma had brought her into the outside toilet, lifted her up, showing her how to balance over the hole, and told her clearly in Finn that there were to be no more wet or dirty pants.

"I don't have time to be washing underpants every single day. We will change on Wednesdays and Saturdays after sauna. In between, your underpants are to remain clean. Do you understand?" She had held Margie's chin hard and made her meet her eyes. "Do you understand?"

Margie had nodded, frightened by the threat in Ma's voice.

I had warned her as soon as Ma went inside that she meant business. Any accidents would be punished with a spanking. We even had to pick the tree branch so that it was long enough for Ma to handle and strong enough to withstand a firm application to our buttocks and thighs.

I shivered, remembering the feel of the switch. I had tried with all my might to hold it, but even I had had accidents. Sometimes when I was playing hard, I just forgot. Sometimes at night, the poddy just came, and I couldn't stop it. That meant Ma had to wash the bedding, too.

"It is dirty," Ma had told me. "Dirty. Dirty. Do you understand?"

I had nodded. I had understood. I just couldn't always make my body behave.

By the time we had moved to Kinney, Ma had won the battle of the outhouse even with Margie. It helped a lot that our rented house there had a relatively new outhouse with two seats—one high for grownups, one low for children.

All of that had taken place long before our move to Zim, of course. Because of the switches, and as we grew older, the razor strap, Ma's technique succeeded completely.

She always said that any woman with a child over a year old still in diapers was just too lazy herself to do the training. It was as if we were horses. But poddy training was probably the worst, and here I was, thirteen years old on that very day, committing the unforgiveable: I had wet the bed. Quickly and quietly so as not to waken either Margie or Ma, I slid up and, holding my nightgown tightly against the wet spots, I duck-walked across the kitchen floor. I looked back as I neared the door, hoping no wet spots darkened the pine planking and saw, to my horror, that I had left a red trail behind me. A line of dots. Blood.

I stifled a scream, ran to the dishpan, hanging above the warming oven, wet it in the pail of water that stood on a stool by the door, and dabbed at the marks. Some of them came away completely, but in some places they had already sunk into the porous wood. The more I dabbed, the more drops came. Giving up, I pulled more of my nightgown around my bottom and ran out toward the outhouse. The gravel path hurt my bare feet, and small stones stuck to them. I ran as fast as I could, and shivering with cold and fear, made it to the outhouse. Closing the door behind me, I pulled off my nightgown and my snuggies. They were bright red. I sat down, positioning myself over the hole carefully, and looked down between my legs. I had not wet the bed. It was not urine that I saw on my clothing and on the page of the catalog that I used to wipe myself. It was blood. I was bleeding. Bleeding to death, I was sure.

Terrified, I sat there as long as I could. But the shivering and shaking grew worse and worse, and the bleeding didn't stop.

Cautiously, I scurried back to the house, the dry part of my snuggies pushed between my legs, held front to back with the driest part of my nightgown. I opened the door a crack. Nor a sound. Ma was still asleep. Margie hadn't moved.

I found a clean pair of underpants on a shelf. Far at the end of the shelf, almost hidden, lay a pile of white flannel squares. I didn't remember Ma's hemming them. She must have done that late at night while we were asleep or perhaps during a brief respite in the days long ago when Baby Teddy was still a prayer in her heart as well as a baby growing within her womb. Folding two of the squares into narrow rectangles, I made a pad for the blood and took two extra squares with me. I dressed hurriedly in my heaviest woolen dress, which had been set aside to be brushed and hung on the line and then laid carefully into a wooden box with moth balls to preserve it for next winter. Or for the winter after that. Whenever Margie grew into it. I didn't bother with my hair but pulled on my old winter coat left hanging near the new one—Pa had not forgotten—my mittens and matching tam, and crept out the door.

I did not know where to go, but I knew I could not stay in the house to die. Death had visited already that winter. I don't think Margie really understood what had happened, but Ma's actions during the ensuing months had certainly underlined the need to remove her from the additional pain of another loss. I couldn't remove her from pain. But I could remove myself.

"She might worry for a little while," I told myself. "But most days she's not here enough to know or care. If worse comes to worse, Margie will run to Salins'."

And so I opened the door just wide enough to edge through it and closed it behind me without a squeak.

"Where should I go to die?"

My self answered fiercely, "You don't know for sure that you're going to die. First you need to get the bleeding to stop."

I remembered how much blood had stained the bedding and towels when Baby Teddy had come into the world, but Ma had lived. Surely, there was hope for me.

"Should I walk to see Mrs. Aro and see what she would do?"

"Oh, sure," my self scoffed, "you're going to walk into the Aros' kitchen dripping blood all over the floor? The boys will all see it. Toivo will see it. And he'll never let me forget it. If he saw it, I would be better off dead."

When we cut ourselves, Ma ran cold water over the cut, pressed a clean cloth hard on the wound, then bound it when the bleeding stopped.

"Okay." Taking a deep breath, I headed for an endless supply of cold water—the St. Louis River. Running in spate still washing over the road and walking path, it had slithered up to the high point where, during some previous flood, rocks had been carried high and dropped when the river reached its crest and started lapping its way back into its usual channel. I found a rock large enough to serve as a seat just at the edge of the river's reach. Curls of frothy waves cleaned that rock every now and again, and, I thought, it might make me feel clean too.

I looked carefully in every direction, but it was barely sunrise, the sky dark grey and lowering, without even the promise of pink to the east.

Of course, it was important to keep my shoes dry. I left them and my stockings up high on the bank and, holding on to bushes and branches, worked my way down to the rock. I wondered about the pad. It felt so dirty that I took it off. Blotches had already discolored the two squares and seeped onto the sides of my underpants. Pulling my skirt and coat up around my waist, happy for once that the coat was too short, I sat down on the rock, eased myself out of the pants, held them and the squares with my left hand so that the water could rinse them clean, and waited.

Without the pads to serve as a measure, I could not tell how much blood I was losing, but every time the waves splashed my bottom, they came away tinged pink.

Slumping into myself, I sat and waited to die. Waited eons, it seemed. My back hurt like fury, but the knots in my lower tummy grew numb from the cold, and I weighed the pros and cons of waiting there like patience on a monument, smiling at grief, or undressing completely and slipping into the water, to be numb all over quickly. To have this end.

I mused about "patience on a monument, smiling at grief," wondering where the line came from and why I had remembered it just then.

The flannel squares and my underpants, washed clean, I laid them upon a higher rock. They'd never dry there, but I knew it was important that none of my things wash away.

And finally, like a deluge, heavy as the river but salty and warm, the tears came. I cried because of the disparity in the Bible between my birthdate, March 10, 1910, and the date of Ma's and Pa's wedding, May 4, 1910. I cried becuase that disparity made me a bastard.

I cried because I was cold, because my back hurt, because I was afraid. I cried because Baby Teddy had died. I cried because if I died, Ma and Margie would cry, even if Pa didn't. I cried for our house in Kinney and for Uncle Charles. I cried for the Savolainens, whom I missed with an ache that never stopped. I wept for the gaping void of loss—of Pa and the gypsies, of the dreams of a paradise in Zim, of the hopes and promises that, barely a year ago, had seemed within my grasp.

"A man's reach should exceed his grasp or what's a heaven for?" slipped into my mind, and I remembered that it was Robert Browning's line, and I cried for all of the poems I would never read or memorize or recite.

The bleeding did not stop. But the tears did, eventually. Or rather they subsided from sobs into rasping gulps.

Leaning forward, I let go of my coat and dress and splashed my face with water over and over again.

Then, sodden and utterly weary, I got up, folded the wet squares of flannel to size, placed them carefully between my legs, picked up everything else, and, with a deep sigh, started for home.

I had cried myself out. I had bled. But I was still able to think and walk. Whether I wanted to be or not, I was still alive.

It was good that the river had been high. Margie and I had a good excuse not to go to school. I hung the clean flannel cloths and my snuggies on the small drying rack Ma had set near the stove. Two clean dish towels covered them completely.

I wish I could say that Ma had awakened and, finding me gone, was dressing to go to look for me, but she was still asleep. Margie had changed position and used the pee pot instead of going to the outhouse. The smell permeated the house, but it did serve to mask any residual smell of blood.

My coat and dress, though wet, were not dirty. Hanging from the designated hooks, they looked heavier than usual, but not all that different. I tore a strip from one of the floor rags to form a make-shift harness around my waist and fastened the flannel strips to it front and back. Then, as if it were just any ordinary day, I set the peepot outside the door, shredded Fels Naphtha soap into a pail, ladled in hot water from the boiler on the wood stove, and set about to clean my nightgown and then the floor.

One nightgown looked much like another nightgown. Neither Ma nor Margie would notice that I had gone to bed in one and gotten up in another.

By the time they got up, I had made coffee and *puuroa*, eaten a small bowl myself, and set myself down at the table with my school books and a cup of coffee. Even though Ma had strict rules against using the kerosene lamps during the daytime hours, I lighted the one that sat in the middle of the table, and dropped two sugar lumps into my white stoneware cup.

Usually I forced myself to do arithmetic, science, and geography first, leaving the beloved history and literature as a reward. That morning I set everything aside except the literature book and allowed it to open wherever it would.

Sometimes when I did that, it seemed to open at just the right place, to something I needed, something to help me understand why things were the way they were. Or I was able to fit my own meanings into the words on the page. But that morning even more than usual, the lines seemed etched there just for me: "Invictus" by William Ernest Henley:

> Out of the night that covers me
> Black as the pit from pole to pole.
> I thank whatever gods there be
> For my unconquerable soul.
>
> In the fell clutch of circumstance,
> I have not winced nor cried aloud.
> Beneath the bludgonings of chance
> My head is bloody, but unbowed.
>
> Beyond this place of wrath and tears
> Looms but the horror of the shade,
> And yet the menace of the years
> Finds and shall find me unafraid.
>
> It matters not how straight the gate,
> How charged with punishments the scroll.
> I am the master of my fate.
> I am the captain of my soul.

A deep sense of peace washed over me when I read those words. I had endured. I would survive.

Two days later the bleeding stopped as if by accident. It had lessened bit by bit. I had washed my flannel cloths and reused them.

Three days later, when the river had dropped so that the bridge and walkway were safe, Margie and I went back to school.

I had scrubbed myself clean all over, using a basin of hot water, rubbing every spot on my body, rinsing it, drying it. I had washed my hair in the basin and carried in pailful after pailful of water to rinse it, using vinegar with the last rinse. It was hard, still, not to feel dirty. I wanted to pull my shoulders in around my chest and hide my face behind my braids.

Instead, I marched Margie along with me, ignoring her protests, reciting to myself over and over again the words from the poem, memorized to be mine for all of my life.

Forcing my chin up and my shoulders back, I got in line with the rest of the pupils and waited for the teacher to ring the school bell.

I ignored Eino, who looked hurt. But I felt as if everyone were looking at me, as if everyone knew, as if I still smelled vile, as if the blood blotched not only the flannels but my deepest, innermost self. Certain that God had singled me out to be punished in this ugly, hateful way, I checked the back of my dress every time I got out of my seat. Praying that I would not bleed again, I stumbled through the day, again making so many errors that Miss Heino called me aside at lunch time to ask what was wrong.

"Nothing," I told her.

"Are you sure there isn't anything you'd like to . . . talk about . . . or ask me?" she offered, touching my shoulders lightly with the palms of her hands, then lifting my face with her gentle fingers, forcing me to raise my eyes to hers.

"No." I clenched my teeth to hold back tears. "Thank you," I whispered.

In April it happened again. But I kept my own counsel, washing the flannels as needed, watching the sheets, too, for the telltale signs of first blood.

CHAPTER THIRTEEN
Halcyon Days

t the end of the next day of classes after the April episode of bleeding, I lagged behind the group, waving everyone to go ahead home and, when the last shape had disappeared, turned back into the school room where Miss Heino was sitting quietly at her desk correcting papers and recording assignments. We had talked about graduation in a general way that day, and I had to share my fears with someone I could trust. Miss Heino was the only one I could think of. Standing with my hands behind me, I bit my lips and then said, "I may not be alive by graduation."

Shocked, she asked, "Why? What's wrong, Ilmi Marianna . . . whom I would like to start calling 'Marion'?"

There was no room for jokes in my heart, and I said it flat and straight. "I am slowly bleeding to death."

She set her record book aside, stood up, and drawing me toward the biggest desks, poured me a glass of water. Gently she asked, "Is it happening once a month?"

"Yes."

"And the flow of blood, is it heavy?"

"Yes, always for at least a day or two. Then it gradually decreases until it's gone, and I pray it won't come back, but it does." I drank the water and looked away, feeling dirty and horrid for sharing such ugly and intimate details.

"Oh, my dear, this is perfectly natural."

My head shot up as my eyes met hers.

"Have you talked to your mother about it?"

"No. Ma has had too much to deal with as it is. I mean, Baby Teddy died last winter. She's still grieving. I can't add the fact that she's going to lose another child."

"Trust me, Ilmi . . . Marion . . . she isn't. You have simply become a woman."

Taking hold of my hands, which felt like ice, she explained, slowly and carefully, "This is a perfectly natural and important sign that you are growing up. You are thirteen now, are you not?"

I nodded, not trusting myself to speak.

"Once a month, a woman's body prepares itself to accept a man's sperm to create a child. If no sperm come to meet the eggs in her uterus, the uterus sheds its bloody surface, the nesting place for the baby. This is a perfectly normal and natural event, especially when you are old enough to love someone and marry and are ready to create a child. Until then, each month the body prepares itself, then lets it go. Here . . ."

She got up, went to her private bookcase, picked up a book, opened it to a chapter on reproduction, and told me to read that chapter. I did as I was told, while she went back to correcting papers. I read it twice, studying all of the pictures and answering the questions to my own satisfaction. If it was written in a book, I thought, it must be true. But I had to ask for sure. "Is this true for sure, Miss Heino?"

She came back down from the small dais to put her arm around me and confirm my conclusion incontrovertibly. "It is absolutely true for every woman who lives upon this earth. It means, my dear, that you are growing up. You are no longer a child. You have become a woman."

"Oh, my!" The relief was so enormous I had to bite back the tears. "Thank you, Miss Heino. I think I do understand now. But before . . . I was awfully frightened."

"But that's not the only reason you have come to school with your eyes all swollen and red, is it?"

"No. But I can't talk about it." The tears began again. I thought of how Ma had been and of how hard we had to struggle to make ends meet and of how afraid I was that Pa would never come back, and the fear and privation would begin again.

"Remember I'm here when you need me. By the way, how have you handled the flow of blood?" she asked.

"I've used the flannel squares Ma cut to use for diapers for Baby Teddy. I've folded them to fit inside of my underpants and pinned them there. At night I washed them and hung them on the drying rack or put them in the warming oven to dry."

"I think I can make the process a bit easier for you. Check with me on Monday. Are you aware that it will happen every twenty-eight to thirty days?"

"I can measure it on the calendar, thank goodness," I answered. "It would help to count the days so I could be ready a little ahead of time." My world had come alive again. "Thank you, Miss Heino." I ended the conversation with all my heart and fled.

The following Monday Miss Heino very unobtrusively gave me a small bag which contained a cotton circle about the size of my waist with a flap in the front and one in the back and two big pins. It kept the flannel pads in place much better than my underpants had.

I did not know how to thank her without divulging the contents of the bag, but she simply said she had found some things of hers that she thought might be of use to me.

No one seemed to find it unusual or extraordinary. She often sent one or another of us home with a small bag of something she had found that we might like.

It was heaven to have this huge worry allayed.

Soon after that talk, she kept Toivo, Eino, a new girl named Sara Ikola, and me after school to take what she called a penmanship examination. "It is," she explained, "a part of the new graduation requirements." She gave us some time to practice and then provided us with paper upon which we were to do all of our penmanship exercises, ending in a letter to be replicated in our very best Palmer Method penmanship. I was glad she hadn't warned us ahead of time because I would have worried myself into a frazzle. That way, I simply had to do what was asked of me in the best way that I could. And, with much encouragement from Miss Heino and the competition from Toivo and Eino, both of whom wrote a beautiful hand, I had made great strides that year, though I never enjoyed it. After that we were tacitly excused from penmanship when the little ones practiced around, around, around and push, pull, up, down. I continued to practice, however, to perfect my own ability. But it felt different, heavenly to practice for my own pleasure, not to please anyone else.

It was heavenly also to have the windows open and smell the fresh spring air.

But it was not heavenly to think about graduation. I consciously refrained from letting myself deal with that worry when it wasn't yet May.

And then suddenly Miss Heino was walking toward the calendar to turn it around, and it almost was.

The next morning she surprised us again. "There will be no regular classes tomorrow," she said as she pointed toward the calendar and May. "I turned the calendar just a bit early. Tomorrow is the first official day of May. May Day. And it is a day of celebration."

She picked up a book lying open on her desk and read aloud this passage:

"Ever on the first of May did magic walk—the legends say—
Maidens rose at early dawn to find a dew-sequined lawn,
And she who humbly bathed her face in dewdrops in the magic place,
She, they say, need never fear the curse of freckles for a year,
And, did she add a certain rune—lo! she would wed a lover soon!"

Laying the book down, she continued, "Long before the Christian era there were May Day festivals in honor of Flora, Goddess of Flowers. Through many centuries people have continued to adapt these celebrations even unto the present day. It seems a custom particularly identified with feminity."

The boys looked at us and laughed.

"Little girls make May baskets which, filled with flowers, they hang on the doors of their playmates' homes. Older girls in schools and colleges dedicate the day to spring sports. Wellesley has its hoop-rolling contest, Vassar's crowning of the May queen is a tradition, and Bryn Mawr raises a tall Maypole around which its students dance. Those are very famous girls' colleges."

"We won't be hoop-rolling," she laughed and looked at Toivo, "but we are going to do something special that will involve all of us, not just the girls. Be sure to be here!"

Everyone was. Even the weather cooperated. It was just warm enough to go without a coat, and we left hats, scarves, and mittens at home.

When Miss Heino stood on the top step ringing the bell, she was smiling. That is not to say she didn't usually smile, but that morning she was smiling with all of her being, and I'm sure they could hear the bell on the other side of the St. Louis River.

We filed in, little ones first as always, shedding any overshoes, setting lunches on the fender around the pot-bellied stove, and turning to see a sheet of bright springy construction paper on every desk. Not September orange or October black or brown, not Christmas green and red, but pink and yellow, summer green and violet, every color of the spectrum that cried "spring!" Also on each desk we found a small container of paste and a pair of scissors.

After the regular morning ceremony, Miss Heino, from under her desk, produced two baskets. One was a solid pink; the other, a combination of spring tones. Both were formed of strips of construction paper cut and pasted together to make baskets with handles.

"When you go home tonight," she explained, "you will bring a basket as pretty or prettier than these." (We gasped. Nothing could be prettier than those.) "But we need to set some rules first. Any suggestions?"

Sara Salin, looking avariciously at the pink on my desk and the yellow on hers said, "We should be able to exchange colors."

Toivo Aro had blue and liked it. Moreover he did not like Sara Salin. "But only if both people agree."

"No grabbing," commented Eino, typically.

Jenni Aro, who was usually so quiet we forgot she was there, added, "Maybe we could exchange just one or two pieces."

"I think we should help each other," I suggested.

"I have three more guidelines," Miss Heino said. "Give a basket to someone you love, to someone who has been kind to you, to someone who has been nasty to you as an apology, to someone to whom you owe an apology, and last and mostly importantly, no one may receive more than one basket."

We all nodded our agreement.

With his usual ability to make something ugly of something beautiful, Toivo whispered to me, "Yay, yay, it's the first of May. Outdoor screwing starts today. Wanna screw?"

I hadn't the vaguest idea what he meant. No. That's a fib. I did. But I pretended I didn't and vowed not to speak to him all day. The prevailing mood of the classroom was too happy to pay any attention to his coarseness. We set ourselves to following Miss Heino's explanations and tried some experiments of our own. By noon all of us had baskets pasted firmly together.

Miss Heino said they should sit for a bit now, and we trooped outside to find that one of the fathers had raised a pole in the back of the building where we wouldn't see it. Miss Heino had obviously given him directions about how to attach ribbons, and after we had eaten our lunch-es—gulped them down, that is—she showed us how to dance around the Maypole, boys and girls together, girls alone. It was really a compliment to her enthusiasm to see the big boys holding a ribbon and dancing to the old familiar songs we all knew.

When we were tired and the bell rang, we all took deep drinks of water from the dipper and the pail, our energy well-channeled.

"And now what?" asked Toivo, but not belligerently.

Miss Heino drew two similar baskets out from under her desk, or perhaps they were the same ones, finished as she wanted us to finish ours. Anyway, they were both filled with natural ornaments—bits of birch bark with poems copied in perfect Palmer Method, green plants like princess pine or spruce or balsam bits, unusually shaped rocks—all things we could find if we looked. Most lovely were the primroses, the tiny yellow May flowers with their pansy faces, and the sweet and delicate white and pink arbutus.

Miss Heino warned us about that loveliest and most fragrant of flow-ers. "If arbutus is picked roughly and the roots are disturbed, it will not grow again, so be very careful if you can find some. I found some but left most of it for you to seek."

That afternoon we looked and looked and looked and ran back to the classroom with our treasures and looked some more. I found among the moss a nosegay of arbutus and actually went for scissors to cut the flowers so that their root system remained untouched. I found a clump of princess pine and some soft green moss.

Almost all of us wrote poems or messages on birch bark or on a sheet of foolscap, using our very best Palmer Method and copying poems that made us think of spring. I chose lines by William Wordsworth:

> A violet by a mossy stone
> Half-hidden from the eye!
> Fair as a star when only one
> Is shining in the sky.
>
> "Up! up! my Friend, and quit your books
> Or surely you'll grow double,
> Up! Up! My Friend and clear your looks;
> Why all this toil and trouble?

The sun, above the mountain's head,
A freshening luster mellow
Through all the long green fields has spread
His first sweet evening yellow...

And hark! How blithe the throstle sings
He, too, is no mean preacher
Come forth into the light of things,
Let Nature be your teacher...

One impulse from a vernal wood
May teach you more of man,
Of moral evil and of good
Than all the sages can. . . .

Enough of Science and of Art;
Close up those barren leaves,
Come forth, and bring with you a heart
That watches and receives.

I tried to do all of "Lines Written in Early Spring."

Oh, I could have filled a basket with poems by Wordsworth!

It was a beautiful day because we all worked together, the big kids helping the little ones so that everyone would have a basket to bring home.

And wonder of wonders, Pa was back and Ma and Pa weren't fighting! The house was quiet as we approached, and I held my breath. A venison stew bubbled on one of the back burners. The washing had been done and was drying on clothes lines Pa had tightened and restrung from tree to tree and even found a pole with a fork to lift them to catch the breeze. Ma had washed the windows and washed and ironed the curtains. The table was set for dinner. After some discussion, we decided that I would give my basket to Pa, and Margie would give hers to Ma because so often we paired off differently.

They exclaimed with pleasure, had us read the poetry aloud and translate it, and set the baskets on the table in the middle as centerpieces.

That night Pa did not leave. He and Ma shooed us to Salins' to buy a candy treat, and when we got home Ma was already in her prettiest white nightgown with white tatting on the collar and tucking to the waist.

Oh, how well I remember that evening! It gave us a glimpse of paradise, of the way families could live. Pa even hauled in enough water so that we could wash each other then slide into the trundle bed between clean sheets just off the line.

Then Pa took out his fiddle and played songs we recognized from Finland—folklore and songs he had brought with him and then songs he had made up himself, and we went to bed looking at our beautiful May baskets.

"Oh, my," I remember Ma saying as I fell asleep, "aren't they lovely?"

And she wasn't just looking at the baskets.

Next morning she and Pa studied the baskets more thoroughly, noticing all of the little touches we had added—a perfectly smooth oval rock, the poems written on birch bark, the bits of princess pine and yellow May flowers, the arbutus.

I was old enough to know that such halcyon moments never lasted, but not old enough to prepare myself to have them end.

And end they would. There were two challenges ahead of us—Mothers' Day and graduation, and each posed its own problems, none of which could be ignored.

CHAPTER FOURTEEN
Silence

t home, no sooner had the pleasure of May Day ebbed than it was time to plan for Mother's Day. Miss Heino had written it in her lesson plans, but regardless of that fact and regardless of what the calendar said, we had a late season snowstorm and were released from school early.

It was clear the minute we walked in the door that Ma and Pa had been arguing all day, but they seemed to be silent arguments. I think Ma had guessed how Pa was getting his money.

Ma was a devout member of the Women's Christian Temperance Union. She had been ever since we lived in Virginia and saw what drinking had done to the Wirtanen family and to her friend Maija, whose husband stopped to gamble and drink when he got his paycheck, and usually came home with nothing left. Finally he quit going to work. He'd take his lunchbox to the Northern Club or to someone's garage, wherever men met to gamble and drink.

One day Maija Wirtanen followed him there, and that was the end of their marriage. She took the children and left him, moved to Duluth and opened a small restaurant. Ironically, the restaurant was on the bowery. She and Ma wrote letters back and forth regularly. Ma couldn't help but share them with us, even if it meant just leaving them lying around. I read everything in sight. One letter was about a drunk named Michigan Stiff, who insisted that women were trying to come in the open transom window above his door. He had delirium tremens and saw snakes and elephants chasing him. Another character named Apple Annie was a rag-picker, who pushed a wagon up and down the streets, selling apples and picking up rags, but rumor had it that she had lots of money hidden in some secret place. I didn't think we should move there, no matter how Maija Wirtanen urged Ma to join her.

Maija and Ma had become good friends the first day they met in Virginia, long ago when we finally found Pa after a long trip from Canada through Malcolm and thence to the Mesabi Iron Range. Ma and Margie and I went to see the upstairs apartment of the house Mrs. Wirtanen was showing. She rented the downstairs. Ma said, in Finnish of course, that the apartment was filthy. Ma said she would take it because she could scrub away the urine and shovel out the shit. Maija Wirtanen rented to her on the spot. Her own downstairs apartment was immaculate. So was ours, as soon as Ma was through, and when they found out that Ma's first name was also "Maija,"—both "Mary" in English—it was as if they had found soul-mates.

When Maija Wirtanen left for Duluth, she wanted Ma to come too and help run the restaurant, but Pa had gotten a job with the streetcar line, and the future looked . . . full of happy possibilities. And so it had been for quite a long time. Most of the years in Kinney had been wonderful, with Pa bringing in regular paychecks and Ma tending the house, sewing to earn extra money, and us finally enrolling in school.

Under no circumstances would Ma condone Pa's earning money by rum-running or bootlegging or whatever anyone called it. If she had found out, there would have been no bounds to her anger, and I fully expected Pa to hear about her feelings in no uncertain terms.

But this time I think his punishment for Ma was that, instead of leaving, he stayed. He insisted on acting as if everything were normal, forcing her to keep up a facade for Margie and me. Underneath, Ma was as furious as I had ever seen her. It was a seething anger which, mixed with the pain and depression wrought by the loss of Baby Teddy, began as silence. Then, as the days went on, deepened. I don't have the words to describe what we saw happening to her that May. She didn't seem physically ill. But emanating from her was a deep-seated soul-searing pain. Day by day, she withdrew again, from Pa and from us and from the world. Again, we came home from school to unmade beds, to unwashed dishes and clothing, to cold food left to spoil on the stove.

Often Pa would be sitting on the front stoop doing something useless, anything he liked to do—making knives, playing the fiddle, ignoring Ma, ignoring us.

Pa liked to make knives. He had borrowed a whetstone from Mr. Salin and bought some lengths of steel about the width he wanted. Years ago he had made me what he called a "lady's knife," about six inches long, with a thin curved blade set into a black leather scabbard, oiled until it was firm and hard, curved like the knife with a steel band across the top, my initial on the leather and an eight-piece link with a clasp so I could carry it on my belt as, he said, wealthy women did in Finland. The one he made for Margie was identical, though the leather was brown.

Ma had carefully set them on a shelf too high for us to reach.

Sometimes when Toivo Aro got to be too much for me, I wished I could carry that knife, though what I would do with it remained unclear.

Pa was not an artist like men in Finland, whose *puukkos*, were given as gifts or passed on from generation to generation as the sons reached their eighth birthdays, a tradition especially among the Sami people, for whom the knives meant survival. Their *puukkos* would be strong enough to cut branches to build a shelter, to gut and hold a rabbit for cooking, to use as a weapon when necessary. Those were made by master artisans who signed the blade, which would never fall from the scabbard, even if the scabbard were turned upside down.

Pa made utilitarian knives, ones Ma could use in the kitchen. That May he was working on a virtual machete with a blade a foot and a half long, tapering to a point and an elaborate handle with criss-cross strands of alternately cream-colored and maroon leather, fastened to the blade with iron and a small iron handle for the first finger. Ma could chop a chicken or a pig or a partridge or even a deer into sections with a knife that big and that sharp.

"Here, Ilmi," he told me, "see how sharp it is."

I shuddered, aware of all of the potential such a knife offered.

Margie, however, exclaimed over it, cut her finger so it bled and she cried, and Ma said, "Now look what you've done."

He showed us that it was as sharp as a razor blade, using it to shave one morning.

When he gave it to Ma, I know he expected appreciation. Her mouth closed tighter, and she put it up too high for Margie to reach. I never saw her use it.

But I could not waste my worries on bootleggers or knives or even on the state of our family's stilted existence. My sole objective continued to be to study and study and study some more.

Ironically, as if nothing more could happen to interfere with that studying, as if nothing more could be added to what I was already bearing, one more problem arose, involving a new student at our school named Sara Ikola.

The day she enrolled in school, she had been the only one from her very large family to do so and, based on the level of her reading and writing skills, had been seated with Toivo and Eino and me.

All that day my head itched, and I told Ma before I went into the house that I was terribly afraid that I had caught something from her. No matter how sick Ma was, the thought of one of us bringing home hair lice was an abomination Ma refused to abide.

"You stay outside," she told me as she checked Margie's hair, which was free and clear. "Get me the pail, a thin comb and some kerosene," she ordered Margie. Then she made me lie down on the top step with my head on a clean dish towel while she unwove my braids, clucking and shaking her head and bawling me out for not being more careful.

It did no good to try to explain that Miss Heino had made me sit by the new girl and that she had scratched her head all day. It was my fault for not being more careful.

Oh, that was awful! "MA!" I screamed. "THAT HURTS!"

Regardless of my protests, after she had pulled and yanked my braids apart, she poured undiluted kerosene on every speck of my hair. I held my hands to keep it from my face. It smelled worse than it felt. Then she used a thin comb to catch whatever bugs had not died in the kerosene bath, and finally took the dish cloth, wrapped it up tight, and threw it into the firebox of the woodstove, which she had stoked to roaring, regardless of the fact that it was May and the day warm. With the kerosene in it, it *whooshed* loudly. Then began the washings with lye soap, the strong kind she used on the floor, and finally a wash and rinse with the more gentle soap she usually used for shampooing.

The last dishtowel she wound around my head was free of lice, but I felt as if my head had been shorn of hair, also.

That night she marched over to the Ikolas' home and told Mrs. Ikola that if she sent another child to school with lice, Ma would report her to the County Health Department as an unfit mother.

I don't know if there even was a County Health Department. Neither did Ma. But she managed to put the fear of the Lord into the Ikolas. That must have been the reason that they dribbled into school one by one. Free of lice.

Since those of us who lived in Zim were all Finnish and took saunas on Wednesday and Saturday nights, those having even an old fashioned *savu-sauna*, built so quickly it did not have a chimney, and we came out coughing from the smoke, but clean, head lice had never been a problem.

Miss Heino had mentioned that at the first Parent-Teacher Meeting held the previous fall night. "I am so grateful," she told the mothers and fathers, "that your children come to school clean and free of illness or infection. I have heard stories from some of the other teachers . . ." she shuddered. "Anyway, I do thank you from the bottom of my heart that I can concentrate on teaching my class work, rather than on teaching basic health habits."

That was somewhat of an exaggeration, but it had just the effect she wished, for even those who tended to be slovenly at home made sure their children came to school clean.

At any rate, Sara and I never became kindred spirits, although we worked together and helped each other when we could. I think her mother was afraid of my ma. Little did Sara Ikola know that that forceful spirit, that strength of character, that insistence on fighting for what she believed in lay latent in Ma these days. Like the fire in the firebox, it had been banked, awaiting the blow-up that was bound to happen. In the meantime, episodes like the trip to Ikolas were isolated instances in an overall downhill slide. Whatever it was—her anger with Pa, her disappointment that he had once again brought her to believe in him only to find out that the truth was only the cause of more pain—perhaps the sum-total of all that had happened during the last year that had been filled with trial and tribulation—was leeching her of the strength I especially needed and wanted.

Rumor had it that I was approaching the high point of all of my school years thus far. I still had many challenges to conquer before I reached that peak, but it was there, within my grasp, and more than anything, I wanted to share the possibility with Ma and Pa. I wanted to share it with the world! But it was too early to celebrate.

I tried hard not to waste energy on being angry or on focusing on what was happening at home. At this point I had to be selfish. I did what I had to do at home to keep myself fed and clean and to help Ma. Margie helped too. And we ignored Pa, treating him as if he weren't there, which he often wasn't. But then, he ignored us, too. I knew that Ma was slipping away and that we had to act. But not now. Even that had to wait. The end of May was coming and with it . . . deliverance and fulfillment.

CHAPTER FIFTEEN
Rumors

ne night *Miss Heino kept* Eino and Toivo and Sara
Ikola and me after school. Margie had permission to go to Sara
Salin's to play, and I was to pick her up on my way home.

"State Boards are coming the day after tomorrow, and I think we can
be comfortable with all of you in spelling and orthography," Miss Heino
told us.

That night she showed us again her Palmer Method Certificate. Although it had been hanging on the wall in a black frame behind her desk
since the beginning of school, we had never studied it closely.

It was beautifully done, of course in Palmer Method:

The Palmer Method of Business Writing
A.N. Palmer
Originator and Author
Teacher's Certificate
This certifies that Miss Isadora Heino has completed
the prescribed method
of Muscular Movement Business Writing
in a satisfactory manner and is thoroughly qualified to execute and
teach successfully this system of Business Penmanship
in Testimony Whereof this Award is given at
Chicago
BOARD OF AWARDS

S. W. PALMER   C. J. NEWCOMB
W. L. NOLAN   A. A. DAVIES
GOLD MEDALLION

"WOW!" Toivo was actually impressed. Eino nodded. I knew mine would look the same because Miss Heino had already told me that my score was high enough to enable me to teach, and little shivers ran up and down my spine. Eino, Sara, and Toivo would not be granted the ability to teach, but otherwise their certificates would look just the same.

"And now," Miss Heino sighed, "for the last two requirements. The day after tomorrow I shall ask all of the students but you four to stay at home. The State Boards have not arrived yet. I shall not see them until they are delivered either on the train or by special messenger tomorrow night. To ensure that I offer no special favors, I shall ask Mr. Salin to keep them locked in his safe and put them into my hands at school in front of you that morning so that everyone will know that I shall not see them either until I hand them out that morning. I'll be sure to structure the day so that you have some breaks, and Mr. Salin and I have some special treats to give you in between sections.

"Thanks to Toivo, I believe you are all well prepared in mathematics."

Toivo actually blushed.

"And, Ilmi, between you and Eino and your vocabulary notebooks, you have helped all of the children gain a truly amazing English vocabulary. I believe a good part of the test is based upon your ability to identify a synonym or antonym for a given word, and of course there will be passages for you to read and then respond to questions relevant to the passage."

She paused. "It was only a year ago for me, and I'm trying to remember what else we had to do. Those areas have stuck in my mind as being of major importance. But each year the examinations change. Of course, there will be questions delving into your knowledge of American history, world history, and world geography." She frowned. "I hope we have devoted enough time to those areas. If you have a chance, do some special reviewing of the names and dates of the presidents, the major rivers of the world, the continents, the countries, the capitols of the states. Oh, dear, there is just so much."

At first we looked at her abashed, and then Eino broke the ice. Patting Miss Heino on the shoulder, in a gesture totally foreign to him, he said, "If we are not well enough prepared, it is not because you haven't worked hard enough to prepare us. The fault, if there is any, will be ours."

She reached a hand up to pat his, as we nodded and smiled. I thought for a moment that she was going to cry.

"You know," she said, "when I thought last summer of coming here to teach, I was so hesitant, so afraid. I was sure I would be happy when the year was over. Now I find that the year is almost over, and I shall miss all of you, you four especially so very much."

Toivo blushed an even deeper scarlet. I fought to keep from crying. The next few minutes were a jumble of "thank you's" all mixed together. How much we would miss her and our little school . . . and each other!

"Well, now," she said briskly, bringing us back to the topic at hand, "get a good night's sleep tonight and tomorrow night. I don't think that last minute cramming will do any good. Eat well, and that morning, come to school at the regular time. Ilmi, would you wait for a minute and walk with me? I'm going to Salins' for supper tonight, and you have an important decision to make."

My eyes widened, and I felt afraid.

"Oh, it's not that bad. It's just something we need to discuss, you and I. As for the rest of you, I'll see you in the morning as usual. The examinations will arrive one day early, so in case they are late, we will all know to postpone our nervousness! Remember to eat and rest. Try to keep from worrying. I'll provide you with brand new pencils so all you need to bring is a substantial lunch and your selves. Wear something you feel comfortable in, even if it's not something you usually wear to school. Eino, tell your mother I shall be there post haste."

And so we were left alone, Miss Heino and I. "All year, my dear," she said, taking my hand, "I have called you 'Ilmi' or 'Ilmi Marianna.' Is that the name you would like printed on your diploma? Or are you ready to step out into the great world as 'Marion'? I have to send in the list of names for diplomas tomorrow, so I need to know by morning."

We walked along in comradely silence for a while, and then I said, "When I go to high school, I shall enroll as 'Marion Brosi.' But if I'm introduced on graduation night here by that name, everyone will turn around wondering who that is!" I giggled. "I think, because it is the name I've used all this year in school and at home, I'll stay as 'Ilmi Marianna Brosi' even though in after years I might have to explain who that was!"

She laughed. "You can't imagine the number of times I have wished I could change from 'Isadora!' I can't imagine what my mother and father were thinking. You can imagine the nickname I had when I was in school."

It came to my mind instantly, but I hated to say it.

"Yes," she grimaced. "Izzy. What heaven it has been this year to be 'Miss Heino'!"

I was so grateful to go home laughing that I went about doing my jobs with a willing heart. It wasn't a Wednesday or a Saturday, sauna days, so I fixed myself a big basin of hot water and gave myself a good sponge bath before I went to sleep.

Ma and Pa were still in their silent stage, but Margie prattled on about my having to stay after school and got me to tell what happened. When I told them about "Izzy" even Ma and Pa laughed. I went to sleep with a light heart and a prayer that I would not let Miss Heino down but would find myself able to do the very best I could the day of the examinations.

Thanks to her good advice and solid preparation, it wasn't a bad day at all. The sections of the test were timed, and we were provided with special treats—candy and soda pop—to keep us going.

When I hit the last and theoretically the most difficult mathematics problem, I couldn't resist giving Toivo a mouthed "Thank you!"

He must have been at about the same point because he mouthed back, "You're welcome."

The examination done, we walked home exhausted, comparing questions and answers.

As we left, even Miss Heino breathed a sigh of relief. "Now we have only the recitation to complete the graduation requirements. I should find out who will come to hear you and when very soon."

In the meantime, she admonished us to review the pieces we had memorized during the year and to keep working on our regular school work, "for you will be going on to high school next year, you know."

The Recitation was an additional requirement only of the Board of Education of the Unorganized Territory. Superintendent Lampi liked to listen to memorization, and he believed it to be an excellent educational tool. Thus candidates for honors in graduation were also called upon to recite memorization for a member of the administration. It could be the superintendent, the assistant superintendent, or one of the supervisors. It depended, said Miss Heino, on the luck of the draw.

In the meantime, since the state boards were scored by experts in the county office, or perhaps by the state board of education—I never did find out where—the results came back quickly. Miss Heino received them by special delivery, sent to Mr. Salin, who had acted as chairman of our unofficial board of education, and delivered to her by hand near the end of one of the school days when we were reviewing for our day of recitation.

Miss Heino read the list of scores compiled by all of the graduates of our three one-room schools, for we would graduate as one unit in the largest of the three buildings. She read it to herself without changing expression or making any comment.

We completed the school day as usual, but we felt within her an air of suppressed excitement, as if she were working hard to contain herself and having a hard time succeeding.

At the end of the school day, with absolutely no change of expression, she said, "Ilmi Marianna, would you stay please for a moment when the rest of the students are excused? Margie, you may wait with your sister if you wish."

Eino and Toivo gave me quizzical glances as they walked by, and Eino gave me a pat on the shoulder as if for good luck.

I thought to myself, "Oh, please, God, don't let something else have gone wrong. I truly cannot bear to have one more burden upon my shoulders or bring one more burden to Ma."

At first, I didn't dare stand up, for fear I'd wet my pants. Then Miss Heino beckoned me to the front of the room and pointed down at the sheet of paper on her desk. It was a list of all of the eighth grade students who had taken the state board examinations, in order of rank, from highest score to lowest.

For a second, my eyes blurred, and I couldn't read what was written on the paper. Then I could, but I didn't believe it.

But I had to believe it because Miss Heino gave out a completely unladylike "*WHOOP!*" and grabbed me by the waist and danced me down the middle aisle of the school and twirled me around until we both were dizzy.

My name was at the top of the list. I had earned the unbelievable score of one hundred per cent. I had not made one single error in the entire state board examination.

Margie started to cry because she didn't understand.

Miss Heino lifted her up to hug her and whirl her around and said, "Your big sister is the smartest student in all of the three schools in Little Swan and Zim and all of the schools in the Unorganized Territory! On graduation night, she will be the valedictorian of the eighth grade class and give the valedictory speech!"

Margie squirmed down and asked anxiously, "Is that good?"

"Oh, Margie," I told her, tears of joy and excitement streaming down my face, "it's better than good. It's wonderful! It's all I have ever hoped and dreamed of!"

I turned to Miss Heino, who was crying, too, and tried to say, "Thank you so much. I don't know how to thank you."

"Oh, my dear child, you have earned it a million times over. All I did was supply you with the materials. You are the one who did all of the work. I had secretly hoped, but I never dreamed that you would do this well. I knew you would score high, higher than the others, but to earn one hundred per cent . . ."

It was as if the starch just went out of her. "Oh, my" was all she could say after that.

I, too, collapsed, overwhelmed.

"Of course, there's still the memorization," she reminded me.

"Yes. I have to do well on the memorization."

But we both knew I had always loved to memorize whether it was required or not. If I could just keep my head about me and not freeze, that would be sheer joy, not work at all.

"Well, then," said my practical Margie, "let's go home and tell Ma and Pa."

Instantly, my balloon deflated.

As Miss Loney had predicted in Kinney an eternity ago, Mr. George Bakalayer had been named the representative of the central office of the schools in the St. Louis County Unorganized Territory.

Oh, how I wanted to share the possibility with Ma and Pa!

Before we left, Miss Heino got down to practicalities. On graduation night I would receive the scroll that proved I had achieved not just a student Palmer Method certificate but one that would allow me to teach it. That was also a singular honor for one so young, she repeated.

Secondly, we discussed the ceremony itself. Because there was a newer, larger school than ours, close enough for our students to reach, the graduation would be held there and would include graduates from all three area schools.

I marveled at how quickly the area was growing. Marked just by the number of schools, it was growing very fast. Rumor said that yet another new school would be built this summer. When completed, the building would hold four classrooms. Moreover, those students would enjoy indoor plumbing, separate for boys and girls, and on the second floor, a teacherage with three bedrooms, a living room, a dining room, and a kitchen.

But that was all in the future. In the here and now, at the end of this school year I realized I might be—would probably be—a key speaker—the student with the highest grades on the state examinations and recitations. I would be the valedictorian and give the farewell; the second high would be the salutatorian and give the welcome.

Before Margie and I left, I asked Miss Heino what I should wear.

She had no idea what her answer did to me—"white shoes and stockings," she said, "a pastel-colored dress with a matching hat, if you wish. There won't be special robes of any kind."

My heart plummeted. Had there been graduation robes, whatever I wore would have been covered. I would have been dressed just like everyone else.

But if I were to be on stage giving a speech, I desperately needed some clothes that would be appropriate. I prayed that Ma and Pa and Margie would be there to clap, and I prayed they would understand the need for a new dress and all that went with it.

And I hoped all the way home that they would be excited.

Oh, how I wanted share an ecstasy of joy! I had incredible news that Ma and Pa would want to share. Miss Heino and I had jumped up and down. Margie and I had jumped up and down. I wanted to come home bursting with news that would break through Ma's silence and Pa's indifference, for this was not ordinary news. It was extraordinary—the kind of once-in-a-lifetime celebratory news that would make a family share a rare moment of true happiness. I prayed as we ran home that I could somehow make them understand.

And then if it came true, there would be the matter of my clothing, and that would create more excitement and planning of a sort we had never experienced.

But when I told him, Pa said repressively, "I'd expect nothing less of a Brosi."

Ma said nothing at all. Later, she listlessly commented, "Well, I guess you've worked hard enough."

I'd have to face the problem of clothes myself. But how? That was the question.

Chapter Sixteen
Recitation

I continued to steel myself as May went along, never knowing whether I was going to come home to fire or ice. Sometimes Ma and Pa weren't talking to each other. Sometimes Margie and I walked into an out-and-out battle. I tried to put their problems out of my mind, to eat whatever was served for dinner, to do my chores, and then to study and study and study some more. I had one challenge to work on—the recitation—which was a requirement only of the Board of Education of the Unorganized School District. Miss Heino had warned us over and over again that one of the members of the central office or one of the members of the school board would ask us for three examples. "I've asked every teacher I know who has been through this before," she said. "Usually the board's representative offers some latitude on an abridgement of a longer work, but he will request one full short poem and one medium-length piece of prose or poetry of his own choice."

It's a good thing I like to memorize! I thought. I memorized all the time, while I scrubbed floors or washed dishes or ironed, when I was supposed to be asleep at night and in the morning, while I sat in the outhouse, when I walked anywhere alone.

When Pa wasn't there, Ma liked to listen to the rhythm of English words even if she didn't understand the meaning.

"The superintendent of the Unorganized Territory schools considers memorization another method of bringing English not only into school but into the home. The school district wants immigrants to speak English rather than their native languages. Does that make sense to you?"

Miss Heino also warned us that we might receive little or no warning when the day came for us to do our recitation. Sometimes the representative of the board sent a letter in advance. Sometimes he didn't.

Sure enough, two days after her warning, when we got to school, one of the school district supervisors was already sitting at Miss Heino's desk, ready to hear our recitations.

Miss Heino barely had time to whisper to the little ones, who sent the whisper back down the line that *he* was there. It was too late to send the rest of the children home.

When we got settled, extra quietly, Miss Heino introduced herself to him, just in case he didn't remember her name, and he introduced himself to her and to us as "George Bakalayer, Supervisor of Academic Studies, particularly English and American Literature." He was not a tall man, but he exuded an air of kindly confidence, looking us straight in the eye and seeing us as students and as people.

"How many candidates for honors does this school have?" he asked.

Miss Loney answered, "Three, sir." (Sara Ikola had joined our class too late to have done the amount of memorization Miss Heino considered needful, and Sara had asked to be excused rather than to embarrass herself.)

"Who is to begin?" he asked in a kindly way.

I looked at Toivo, and he looked at Eino, and they both shook their heads so I raised my hand. "My name is Ilmi Marianna Brosi, Mr. Bakalayer, and I will attempt to recite a poem of your choice."

When he asked me to recite "Abou Ben Adhem," my heart fluttered and for a minute I closed my eyes and shook. It was one of my favorite poems.

"Please walk to the front of the room and face me and the other students," he directed.

I folded my hands behind me, set my feet apart so I wouldn't fall, and began. I tried hard to change my voice when I spoke as Ben Adhem and when I was the Angel. Since the poem was not well-known and since it told a story, the children enjoyed it and clapped when I finished. Mr. Bakalayer nodded and said, "Very nice."

Then it was Toivo, who recited "In Flanders Fields," and Eino, who recited Lincoln's "Gettysburg Address" just as well as Lincoln had, I thought. Both received a round of applause and a complimentary comment from Mr. Bakalayer.

Miss Heino had taken up a position in the back of the room, and I could see from the drawn look on her face and her stiff posture that she was as nervous as we.

She relaxed a bit as each of us returned to our seats and gave us a nod of encouragement.

"Miss Brosi," Mr. Bakalayer continued, after writing some lines in a notebook laid open on Miss Heino's desk. "Next, I should like to hear 'Paul Revere's Ride' in its entirety, if you please."

I almost jumped with joy. It was another of my favorites. I had "performed" this poem for Ma and for Margie and her friends so often that it had become less a recitation than a dramatic reading. I gave it all my heart and soul, speaking to the children as I always did, moving around and using gestures when they were appropriate. I tried to use different voices for the narrator and for Paul Revere and spoke to my whole audience. I could feel it went well, and I loved it.

The ending almost brought me to tears. When I finished, Mr. Bakalayer cried, "Hear! Hear!" Then I wondered if I had overdone it and should have stuck to the straight recitation format. But it was too late. I couldn't have done it any other way.

Again Toivo and Eino were given poems of relatively the same length. Toivo stumbled through his. He had never liked memorization. Eino finished his, but his Finnish accent was so pronounced that I'm not sure whether Mr. Bakalayer understood him or not. That was typical of Eino. I wanted to tell Mr. Bakalayar that Eino was simply nervous and that he could speak very good English when he was not under pressure, but Miss Heino took care of that.

Then she suggested that we all take a half an hour break. Sending the lower grades outside, she mothered us, making sure we had a chance to go to the outside toilet, that we had each ate something, and that we had all took some deep breaths of the sweet May zephyrs (Eino's word) blowing outside. As a special treat, once we had a chance to get our breaths, she brought out bottles of soda pop and a choice of candy or something salty for us to nibble on.

She and Mr. Bakalayar stayed inside drinking soda pop and eating licorice candy. Imagine! I could hardly believe this man who held my future in his hands actually drank soda pop and ate licorice candy just like us.

Half an hour later on the dot, after Mr. Bakalayer had also had a chance to go outside to refresh himself, Miss Heino rang the school bell again, but she needn't have. Everyone was already seated and ready. The excitement in the room was almost palpable.

"Miss Brosi, we shall continue the same order. Please indicate the poem you have chosen for your longer piece and begin as soon as you are ready."

I tried to exude an aura of calm, walked to the front of the room, turned, put my hands behind my back, waited for a few minutes, as if to indicate that this was to be a serious reading and said, "I have chosen a slightly abridged version of Henry Wadsworth Longfellow's 'Evangeline.'" I took them through the beginning, "The Marriage Betrothal" of Evangeline and Gabriel, touched on "The Decree of the English," and accented Part I "The Beginning of the Long Search"—their separation, the irony of their missing each other by passing on two sides of an island, and the wandering over the prairie until the ending. When Gabriel died in Evangeline's arms, half of the class was crying openly. I saw Mr. Bakalayer surreptitiously dab at his eyes. In the back of the room, Miss Heino stood leaning against the wall, as spent as I.

Toivo and Eino waited for a while. Then Toivo said, "I have nothing prepared to match the quality of Ilmi Marianna's performance. Eino said, "Neither do I. But I'll give it a try." He did plausibly well with "The Courtship of Miles Standish."

When he was through, the whole class clapped, and Mr. Bakalayar stood up and clapped and so did Miss Heino, who was also crying, and then we all went home.

I felt drained as if I couldn't walk even one step. Eino grabbed my book bag and carried it and timed his walk to mine.

It looked as if all four of us, even probably Sara and Toivo, who lagged along, too, would graduate from the eighth grade into the wide world. It was exhilarating and daunting.

This world had felt very safe, thanks to Miss Heino. In order to get our high school diplomas, we would have to go to one of the town schools in Mt. Iron or Virginia. None of the schools of the Unorganized Territory offered high school yet. But we weren't thinking of that right then. We were spent and happy and humble and grateful, for we knew how wonderfully Miss Heino had prepared us for whatever our future would bring.

When we got to Salins', Margie, Sara, and Jenni Aro had obviously been playing outside.

"Ilmi! Ilmi!" They had been playing in the mud so hard that even Margie's blonde curls were brown, but I hadn't the heart to bawl her out though I know I was supposed to because I was the older.

"It's Jenni's birthday today and her mother has invited Sara and me to go there for supper! Can I go? Please! Please! If you think it's all right, Ma and Pa will, too!"

Under normal circumstances I would have demanded that she come home first to wash off and change clothes, but Sara and Jenni looked as muddy as she, and I didn't think it would matter to Mrs. Aro one way or another.

Mrs. Aro had grown up learning her special skills from her mother in the old country and was honing her knowledge here. In fact, one room of their house was like a doctor's office because it was filled with dried herbs and a separate fireplace so that she could concoct her experiments and complete her remedies. But except for that one room, their house . . . it's unkind to say it . . . but it's true . . . it was a mess. It wasn't exactly dirty. It just served as an adjunct to her real concern. There were places to sit, to eat, to sleep, to talk. But given two tasks, one of which involved her healing skills and the other a kitchen floor that needed scrubbing, she'd not pause in making a choice. She cared about people.

Margie did not need to be neat to be welcome there. Mrs. Aro's abilities did not end with her heartfelt caring for others or her healing skills. She could have had work as a cook for any family with the money to pay. She didn't need recipes. She was so creative that she could put the most unlikely combinations of ingredients together—a handful of this and a pinch of that—and, like Ma on her good days, wind up with something delicious. Margie was guaranteed a warm welcome and a delicious supper.

"Go ahead, Margie."

For that I received a hug which made me brush off my new coat and a "I'm so proud because my sister is the smartest girl in school!"

Trust Margie to manage to make a compliment sound like bragging. But that night I was too relieved and happy to care.

Only one problem stood between perfection and disaster on graduation night—that same simple yet unsolvable matter: what would I wear?

CHAPTER SEVENTEEN
Graduation Plans

The county office had been wise in designating School 159 as our graduation site. It was about five miles, perhaps a bit more, from our house, but it had a real cloakroom, a dais large enough to hold the graduates, and plenty of room for the families and guests to sit.

The eighth graders from 159 offered to make a picket fence to separate the graduates from the audience and an arched trellis within which we would stand as we received our diplomas. Prospective graduates from School 98 contracted to make crepe-paper roses to trim the fence and trellis and for us to wear as corsages or boutonnieres. And Miss Heino and I, with the desultory and rather left-handed help of Sara, Toivo, and Eino, took it upon ourselves to provide letters to be pinned to a navy blue curtained backdrop. We were ordered to make a sun with radiating waves of light out of heavy gold oak tag paper with the motto "Sunrise, not Sunset" in letters made of the same material encircling the sun.

I should have been delighted with those plans. But they barely moved me to smile.

As Miss Heino and I worked on the sun and the letters, carefully tracing them first on graph paper, trying them out for size, and, once we were satisfied, redoing them on the precious gold oak-tag, she was at first very quiet.

I took that to mean that she was taking this task very seriously as I was so I was quiet, too.

Then she set her scissors down, grasped both of my hands, and asked, "Can you keep a very big secret, one I am not supposed to divulge, but if I don't, it will just come blurting out past my lips no matter how hard I try to keep them closed?"

I closed my eyes. She had found out about Pa's rum-running. She had heard about Ma's depression. Those were the only two secrets I knew that were never to be spoken outside of the family.

"How did you guess?" I asked dully.

"Oh, Ilmi, it's nothing bad! It's . . . it's . . . I can't keep from telling you! Your scores were the highest not only for our three schools but for *every single school in the whole unorganized territory!* If you want to, you could be granted a temporary certificate to go out to teach *next year*, even without a high school diploma. They were that good!

"Mr. Bakalayer wrote me himself. He'll be the speaker the night of our graduation, and he'll hand out the diplomas. He intends to speak to you about that possibility then! It's virtually unheard of! Oh, Ilmi, I am just *bursting with pride!* Of course, it would be a small school, one with only lower grade students, but it would pay you something, a little bit anyway."

The thought was so tempting that I had to shut my mind against it. It felt as if I were Eve being offered the apple by the serpent.

"That is a very great honor," I responded very slowly. "But I'm absolutely committed to going on to high school. I shall have to work for my room and board to do it. But if I stop next year, I may never go back, and the door to the future will close with me left on the other side. It'll help, won't it," I asked her anxiously, "when I apply for my room and board, to show how seriously I take my education? Certainly the family will understand that I'll take my commitment to work for them equally seriously."

"Yes, of course they will." Miss Heino looked at me with her head turned sideways, slightly askew. "You do know what you want out of life, don't you, Ilmi?"

I sighed, closing my eyes as if in prayer. "I am absolutely committed to furthering my education."

Then I shared with her my ultimate dream. "I hope to finish high school and go on to college and become an interpreter. That way I can make use of my Finnish background and use it to help others become Americanized." It sounded high-flown and ridiculous coming from someone who was barely thirteen.

"Well, all I can say is that I wish you luck from the bottom of my heart," she said with a heartfelt smile and hug. "Now, it's back to work for us."

After a time of quiet, she posed another question. "I can't help but sense that there's something wrong, Ilmi. Could you find it in your heart to share it with me? You know we have shared other secrets that I've kept between us."

I was not able to risk a mention of Pa—his anger and the way he was lately attacking whetstone, shaping and turning the steel. The look on his face sometimes frightened me. Pa was always telling me that I might be smart but that I had no common sense. He was right. I was inept with many of the basic womanly tasks, especially cooking and baking, and I asked questions instead of keeping still as a woman should.

And Ma, who drifted in and out of reality, was completely beyond my ability to help, beyond my comprehension.

"She's grieving," Mrs. Aro had told me. "She lost the baby she wanted so desperately, and having your pa at home right now . . . in the state he's in . . . is no help at all." In our small community, nothing went unnoticed, but most of what was noticed was left unspoken. The fact that they took me aside to try to explain meant that they were treating me as an adult.

"I am not!" I wanted to cry, desiring nothing more than to crawl into Ma's lap and have her hold me and be herself again, washing on Monday and ironing on Tuesday, and cleaning and baking on Wednesday, and mending on Thursday, and visiting or entertaining on Friday and going to Kahvi Kekkeri, our informal religious services on Sunday.

Half of me wanted to shake her when I saw her looking out the window or lying in bed in the middle of the day. The other half sensed that she was ill but in a different way from the night Baby Teddy was born. This seemed to be a sickness of the soul, made worse by Pa's irritability and indifference and sometimes downright cruelty.

"We all have choices," Pa told Margie and me. "If your ma chooses to be sick and do nothing, there's nothing we can do for her except wait until she chooses to get well."

That seemed on the surface to be what Mrs. Aro and Mrs. Salin were saying, but it did not sound understanding. It sounded critical. Mean. I did not raise the topic again.

Margie took to spending more and more time with the Salins and the Aros.

I tried to keep up with the housework and continued to be plagued by my new worry. Graduation night I would take center stage twice—once to give my talk on the assigned topic—"The Value of a Rural Education"—and again when I received my diploma.

What a scarecrow figure I would make if I went in the clothes I had to choose from! My shoes were black and so small they cramped my feet. Miss Heino allowed me to go barefoot to school, though that was really against the rules. The stockings I owned were made of wool from toes to waist. They tended to sag down around my buttocks because I had grown so much. Such was the case with my "good" cotton summer dress: the sleeves were too short, the waist and length too high, the neck too tight. The only dress I had that fit me was dark wool, meant to be worn during the coldest winter days.

Instead of answering Miss Heino, I stood up straight and spread my arms. "This is the best I can do. It is the only summery dress I own."

"Oh, dear. We shall have to do something about that."

"But what?" I asked in despair. "I have looked at every single dress at Salins' store. The ones that would be suitable we cannot afford. It's too late to send for one from the catalog, and there isn't enough money to do that anyway."

"Your mother is an excellent seamstress. Couldn't she . . . ?"

The question came too close to reality, and despite my very best efforts, my eyes filled with tears.

"Now, then," Miss Heino said, "let's set that aside for a time. We have a long walk to get the sun and these letters to 159. Why don't you practice your speech on me as we walk? I imagine you have it pretty well in mind already?"

I smiled. I had been working on it ever since the day of our recitations. "Just in case," I had told myself.

"Dear family and friends, teachers, and Mr. Bakalayer, representative of the school board," I began, and talked about how rural schools were often set up by people with few English skills, how a generation of immigrants had provided education to a generation of Americans, that rag-tag to start, the rural schools were providing an education to match city schools. I said that rural schools helped its students round out their education.

I gave Miss Heino a side-ways glance then, for she knew that I had no intention of rounding out my own education with this graduation. But since very few of the eighth-grade graduates did intend to go on to school, the quote was apt. Then I went on to say how rural education had also benefited the immigrant parents who had helped set the schools up, how students came home and taught those parents, improving more citizens.

"That's not altogether true," I admitted to Miss Heino when we sat down to rest for a while in a quiet meadow under the trees, sheltered from the sun. "Pa refuses to learn English. He reads and writes, even writes poems, but he insists on doing it in Finnish. Ma's willing, but she has so little time now. When we were in Kinney . . ." My voice trailed off. So much had changed since we left Kinney, most of it the kind of change I had to keep to myself.

Taking a deep breath, I pushed on to the conclusion:

"School is an important place, at times even a magic place, for many of our families." I thought of our Christmas program and remembered how crowded the one-room school had been, how it had smelled of wet wool, and the noise when babies cried. Thought of that made me gulp, but I swallowed the tears and rushed on. "But at Christmas, someone served coffee and lighted tallow candles were clipped on a tree, and every child in our school participated in singing or reciting poetry. And as the fire died in the pot-bellied stove and the children were wrapped to go home, at least one kind teacher, "and I knew I would look at Miss Heino as I said this, "handed each of her pupils a bit of candy and a real present to cherish over a season when, among our farm families, such presents were few."

I was glad I had another chance to practice that paragraph because it often caused a wellspring of tears. The more I said it, the more it came out to be less emotional and more rational. Factual. As a valedictory address should be, I thought, and concluded, "The years to come will see the beginning of the end of the one-room school as newer, larger consolidated State Graded schools open. But beautiful big buildings can do no better a job than have our small buildings. For the soul of the school is its teacher, and the heart is the desire of the pupils to learn. With glad hearts we thank our school administrators (I would nod at Mr. Bakalayer) for the opportunities they have given us. We have truly valued our rural education."

By the end, I was standing, emoting even, though to no one but Miss Heino and the blueberry bushes that lined the trail.

She wiped her eyes and clapped hard enough for a whole audience.

And then we went to trim the stage and review the program.

The program had been typed at the St. Louis County office in Virginia, and copies had been mimeographed to be handed out to guests.

Inside of the cover, the full names of the graduates were listed in alphabetical order. Mine was still written as "Ilmi Marianna Brosi." It had two stars after it with the word "Valedictorian." I did not recognize the Salutatorian's name. She was from another school.

Soon after we had our sun and the letters fastened to the curtain, Toivo, Eino, and Sara burst in the door. It seemed as if everyone from the other schools came at once, and we began to rehearse.

We practiced walking in as Sara Salin played "Pomp and Circumstance" on the piano, practiced sitting down and standing up in unison, practiced singing the national anthem and made sure we all had our hands on our hearts for the Pledge of Allegiance.

Stiflying giggles, we practiced standing up one by one to walk through the archway, taking the scrolled diploma with our left hands and shaking hands with Miss Heino, who played the part of Mr. Bakalayer by putting on a fake moustache, with our right hands.

We practiced standing until the last diploma had been handed out and listening to the class will and the class prophecy, which had been written by the teachers and were supposed to be funny.

We sat down in unison as if to listen to the final speeches and rose together as we would at the end of the ceremony and marched out to the rhythm of "Priests' March."

All the while I worried about what I would wear.

I had twenty-four hours to solve the problem, for the next night was graduation night at School 159. I could not hide or refuse to attend. My name was already on the program.

What, oh, what shall I wear?

It was a good thing that the long walk to School 159 and back and the practice left me so exhausted that I could hardly put one foot in front of the other as I neared the bridge over the St. Louis River, always the signal to me that I was almost home.

When we had left Miss Heino at the school, her last words had been, "Don't despair, Ilmi. Come to see me here in the morning first thing, and we'll deal with the problem of your dress and shoes and all." She looked as exhausted as I felt.

I could see Margie sitting on the stoop, messy from a day's play, her hair tangled, her face blotched with tears, still hiccupping from what must have been a massive onslaught. I sighed. Knowing Margie, even on the best of days it took almost an hour to get her cleaned up and ready for bed. Clearly, this had not been one of her better days.

Then my stomach twisted into a knot as she ran to me, clinging like a limpet, the sobs beginning again, punctuating the words: "Ma . . . and Pa . . . they're . . . hurting . . . each . . . other!"

Although she really was too big to carry, I leaned over to lift her, and she jumped up, her legs encircling my waist, her arms strangling my neck, her face pushed into my shoulder like the head of a turtle, hiding.

I had no free hand to open the door, so instead, I called through the screen door, "Ma, are you all right?"

Neither of them heard me. Nor could I make any sense of the shouting. But I guessed what the fight was about. Baby Teddy again.

I had hoped and prayed that time would heal the wounds that bruised their marriage. But there were so many wounds, old ones brought up anew, new ones thrown into the fray. Like Margie, Ma was crying hysterically. Not crying, really. Not weeping. Not howling. The sounds she made rent the air in hoarse animal sounds. I heard dishes shatter, wood crack, fabric tear. I heard her pounding her head against the wall harder and harder, as if she were intent upon destroying everything, including herself.

Pa was swearing, shouting, bawling, and roaring accusations. I could imagine him leaning over her, pointing his finger at her as he did, yelling the same accusations that surfaced every time they fought. "Why do you make me stay working at jobs I hate? All you care about is money! You're just like Maija Wirtanen, turning your husband over to the police! She was the reason he couldn't stand to be home, her and her endless pushing, pushing, blaming him for everything. Did she think she was perfect? Did she? And then she went off, taking the kids, and they were his kids, too! No wonder he drank. She drove him to drink with her holier-than-thou ways. Everything had to be perfect. He couldn't walk into the fucking house with his fucking boots on. His own house! And you're just like her!

"And why didn't you tell me about being pregnant? Why did you take it upon yourself to move to this godforsaken hole without leaving me any notice? Can you imagine how humiliating it is for a husband not even to know where his wife is? And you're such a Goddamn hard head, I bet you were up there on the roof working with the men when they were building this house."

I could imagine Ma flinch.

"You were, weren't you? You never learn. You didn't take care of yourself, and the baby died. That was my son, too. And he died. Died. Did you take care of yourself? Did you rest? Did you eat? No. You just went ahead and did whatever you wanted to do just like you always have, without thinking about anybody but yourself."

I could hear him take her by her shoulders and shake her. "You Goddmn bitch." He stormed past us out the door and disappeared into the gathering darkness.

Soon afterward, I heard footsteps. Obviously the fight had been overheard. Mr. Salin and Eino were walking toward us. Mr. Salin was carrying a bull whip. He'd won contests at the county fair using that whip.

"Let us take Margie home for the night," he said. At first Margie clung to me. But when Eino held out his arms, she went to him willingly. "Will you and your ma be safe here tonight, or would you feel better coming to our house, too?"

All we could hear from inside the house was Ma crying, saying over and over again, "It's my fault. I know. It's all my fault. If I had rested more. If we had stayed in Kinney."

Mrs. Salin appeared behind her husband. She was breathing hard, but she opened the door and went in without knocking, murmuring, "No, it was not your fault, Maija. Mrs. Aro has said that over and over again. No one knows why the cord wraps itself around the baby's neck, but when it does, there is nothing that can be done about it. It is no one's fault. Certainly, not yours. You are a wonderful woman. Why, all of us marvel at how beautiful you have made your half-house. Sara and Eino have called it 'Happy Corner' because they so enjoy coming here. We care about you." I don't know how much of what she said connected with Ma, but slowly the sobs ebbed, and she clung to Mrs. Salin's hand and thanked her over and over again.

Not knowing what else to do, I served some coffee and left-over bread to Ma and Mrs. Salin, who fed Ma and soothed her as if she were a child.

I had not been aware that I had been crying, but it felt good to wash my face. Mrs. Salin whispered, "Our sauna is warm. Why don't you walk over and take a nice quiet sauna just by yourself? Sara and Margie will have splashed each other somewhat clean by now. For tonight, that'll suffice. I'll sit with your ma for a while yet. Is there a hook on the door in case your pa should come back?"

"He never does after one of these fights." I was pretty sure of that.

After the sauna, I met Mrs. Salin on the way home. She said Ma was asleep.

I had always been aware that she was a perspicacious woman. She held me to her long enough for me to relax against her strong, kindly shoulders and said, "Tomorrow, we need to get together to see about what you will wear for graduation."

My mouth gaped open like a fish, but I was too tired to find words to hook onto hers. The next thing I knew, it was morning. I was in bed beside Ma, who was waking up, too.

Her face was so swollen she could hardly see, but she pulled herself out of bed, took the pail by the door, went outside to fill it full of water, poured some into a basin, and rinsed her eyes again and again, then washed herself, sponge-bathing, setting fresh coffee to perk at the same time.

I could tell it hurt her to move. When she had poured herself some coffee, she sat down at the table, and I knew the tears were flowing again.

Selfish as it was, and I knew I was being terribly selfish, I knew I was going to graduate that night. I would appear on stage in front of the families and friends of three school communities. What would be on my body? On my feet?

I poured myself a cup of coffee and went outside on the stoop to drink it. Except for Mrs. Aro, no one in the community had Ma's skill as a seamstress. And Ma had no strength left. None at all.

Had Pa come back at that moment, I don't know what I would have done. I wanted to kill him.

CHAPTER EIGHTEEN
Graduation

Mrs. *Aro visited me that morning* early. She said there was professional help available for people who suffered as Ma did. She called it a disease that as yet had no formal name. Most people would have said she was having a "nervous breakdown." Mrs. Aro said it was more than that. She explained to me that sometimes, especially when the baby died, women fell into a depression from which they could not extricate themselves. It was not their fault. It was not something they could talk or think themselves out of, no matter what Pa said. It was a disease, like chicken pox or measles or mumps or a bad cold. Those things happened, unplanned and unheralded, and we needed to accept them and see them through. I wish I could quote what she said that morning, but all I could think of was "What am I going to wear tonight?" Selfish though it was, it overrode all other concerns.

Finally, I blurted out, "What is Toivo wearing to graduation?"

"Why, we bought him a new suit with a white shirt, black shoes, and a bow tie from Reid's Dry Goods in Virginia. Is that what's worrying you now, Ilmi?"

I waved my hand at the hooks on the wall. Obviously, no graduation dress hung there.

"Well," said Mrs. Aro, taking me by the hand, "we're doing ourselves no good in that department by staying here. Let's see what the Salins have available."

We got there even before the store opened, but Mrs. Salin was waiting all the same. Miss Heino was there, too. Briskly, she addressed the question from the bottom up.

"I know you ordered extra pairs of white shoes with the graduates in mind, Mrs. Salin. Are there any left that might fit Ilmi?"

I demurred, insisting that we couldn't afford new shoes. None of the women paid me a speck of attention. Before I knew it, I was seated on a chair drawing a pair of white silk stockings up over my foot and slipping on a pair of white shoes with small heels and a strap across the ankle. Buttoned, they fit perfectly. I tried to look at the price tag, but Miss Heino whisked them away. "I ordered them especially for you, Ilmi, so let's have no arguments about it." Mrs. Salin was equally adamant.

Eino entered the store, but she whisked him away so that I could draw the white silk stockings up to see if they fit. I was glad I had cut my fingernails in preparation for the ceremony so they didn't snag. Like the shoes, the stockings were exactly my size, and like the shoes, they disappeared into a pile.

"I don't suppose your mother would allow us to cut your hair," Miss Heino said, knowing the answer.

"Never! And Pa would have a conniption."

"Then we shall make two braids and loop them in the back so that they are the same length as a bob." Mrs. Salin studied not only the catalogs but Godey's *Ladies' Book*. Although Sara's hair tended to hang straight like a horse's tail, she set it in rag curls every night so, unless it rained or was very humid, Sara had curls that seemed as natural as Margie's.

"Did you wash your hair in the sauna last night?" she asked.

"Oh, yes. And thank you for keeping it warm. I washed it twice and rinsed it with lemon water. Had you put that there for me?"

"For you and for Eino. Don't tell anyone, but he's vain about his hair."

He had a right to be. It was brown with copper highlights. Mrs. Salin knew just how to cut it so that he looked like one of the boys in a magazine. "I gave him a trim last night with the graduation exercises in mind so there would be one less thing to do today."

She set me onto a higher stool so she could match the sides perfectly from a middle part and began what she called a "French braid." I had never seen one, but it began almost from the outset of the separation of hair, drawing in sections not just at the neck but one finger full at a time. I sat absolutely still and crossed my fingers.

While Mrs. Salin was doing my hair, Mrs. Aro and Miss Heino went through the racks of dresses, skirts—long and short, blouses and the longer waisted "blousson," which were much more in style. They put two pieces together, shook their heads, tried other pieces, shook their heads, studied every dress, my size or not and finally brought out a soft cream-colored chambray pleated skirt with a scalloped edge stitched in peach and a matching blouse of chambray with a rounded collar and scalloped sleeves, also stitched in peach. It was exquisite, but I had looked at it before and passed it by because it was way too big for me and we could never afford it even if it did fit.

Miss Heino said, "If I could use your mother's sewing machine, I could take out the buttons in the back, take a wide tuck, and replace the buttons. The back of the collar would overlap some, but not unattractively."

Nodding, Mrs. Salin suggested making a plait in the front. "That might be better hand-stitched. I can do that. If I hurry, I might be able to edge each side with peach embroidery floss. Check to see if we can match the color."

Miss Heino did. I almost turned my head, but Mrs. Salin jerked me back. "Ilmi, do not move your head one more time, or I will not answer for the consequences."

"The skirt will be even easier to take in," Mrs. Aro announced. "Since the top will cover the waistband, I can make neat pleats on each side and on the front and back if necessary. Now, all we need to worry about is the length."

"I'm through, except for the ribbons," Mrs. Salin handed me to Mrs. Aro and Miss Heino without giving me a chance to look into the mirror. Rummaging through her ribbon drawer, she compared colors with the peach trim, almost giving up until, "Aha! Here's a perfect match." Dragging me back to the stool, she tied the French braids from one side to the other just over my ears. When she showed me myself in the mirror, I said, "I can't believe this is me. Or I," I corrected, smiling at Miss Heino. The ribbons gave the effect of a cloche hat. I loved it.

Then, skirt and top in hand, we trooped the mile across the field to our house. Ma was sitting on the bed, holding her head as if she had a headache. Mrs. Aro took Ma to the outhouse, dunked her head, even her hair, into the ice-cold water pail until she cried out, "I'm awake!"

"Good," said Mrs. Aro. "We need your help."

Ma was so fragile from not having eaten well for so many weeks that it took all her energy to get herself dressed and her hair brushed and braided.

Margie had followed us instead of staying at the Salins' to play. For once what was going on at home seemed much more interesting. They were pinning the blouse and skirt as they planned to stitch them.

"If I stay still as a mouse in the corner, may I please stay?" asked Margie in her prettiest manner.

"Yes," Mrs. Aro said. "But don't interrupt us unless we ask for help."

On her own, proof that she could do it if she wanted to, Margie changed, washed, brushed and braided her own hair, and sat down on the far corner of the bed, her eyes as big as saucers.

"Oh, Ilmi, you look beautiful. Like Rapunzel before she let down her hair."

Bemused, I felt like a doll, turning and standing still on the floor and on a chair and on the floor again as the three women pinned and stood back and pinned again. But they couldn't seem to get it right.

Suddenly, it was as if Ma woke up. "No, no, no. You're forcing the material too much," she said firmly and shooed them away. "Open the sewing machine. Do you know how to thread it? Have you brought cream-colored thread?"

Mrs. Salin made it clear that she could, at least, fulfill that minor requirement.

"Now," said Ma. "The skirt is too long. Give me the scissors."
She ruthlessly cut away the whole waistband, then asking advice from those who had recently seen models at Reid's in Virginia or in catalogs or on the street, she adjusted the length until all three chorused, "Yes! Yes!" To that new waistline she pinned the belt, forming neat pleats until the sides met with just enough overlap.

"Now," she ordered, " I could stitch this on the machine, but the top is going to take more work, and this could easily be done by hand with one holding and another making neat, even stitches."

We noted that she had thought ahead so that the button hole and the end of the waistband remained intact. So did the pleat down the side. We just had to re-sew the buttons.

By then, we were sweating, as much from nervousness as from heat. It was an ordinary May day, neither hot nor cold. Ma opened our two windows as wide as she could and propped the door open.

About that time Mr. Aro appeared on horseback, carrying a basket.

"Ah," said Mrs. Aro, "just in time." She thanked him with her eyes, took the basket from his grasp, and laid out our noon-time collage: fresh bread and raspberry jam, hard-boiled eggs with salt and pepper, grounds to make fresh coffee for everyone but Ma, who drank an herbal concoction which smelled . . . like medicine. She made a face but drank it down, every bit. Margie got some fresh butter from our well box and milk for the two of us.

I ate sitting in underpants, not snuggies, with a towel tied around my breasts to make them fashionably flat. While we were eating, Miss Heino disappeared for a while, coming back with a bag of underclothes. Her own, I guessed. They were not only made of the finest lawn but had been exquisitely tatted and embroidered. The workmanship reminded me of the box of clothing we had received from Dr. Malmstrom's wife, and I wondered about Miss Heino's background, about her family and why she had accepted such a humble teaching job. Thinking back over the year, I realized that though she did not have a large wardrobe, what she had worn had been fashionable, though not extreme. She had neither bobbed her hair nor shortened her skirts as the newest styles dictated. Instead, she had dressed . . . like a teacher. I wondered how she dressed when she was at home.

The afternoon's task was to make the "blousson" top long enough to be stylish but short enough so that it didn't engulf me.

Using a small pair of scissors, Ma completely cut the sleeves away from the bodice and used the machine to make a larger seam. By then she had set the ironing board up, and step by step, she ironed all the way.

Miss Heino murmured a line from Macbeth, "When shall we three witches meet again,/In thunder, lightning or in rain?"

"When the hurly-burly's done, when the battle's lost and won," I said, adding the next line to the quotation as best I could.

That afternoon was a fight against the clock. The graduation exercises were to begin at eight, allowing farm folk to finish their barn chores and clean up before coming to the ceremony. That meant Mrs. Salin and Mrs. Aro had to leave in plenty of time to get themselves and their families ready on time.

During her dash for the correct undergarments, Miss Heino had brought along the clothing she would wear that night. This dress, a dream of pink chiffon, owed nothing to her job as schoolteacher. It was exquisite. "Will you do my hair as you did Ilmi's?" she asked Mrs. Salin, but without the ribbons? I have a hat to match the dress." Her hose also matched her dress, and so did her shoes. *Oh, my,* I thought. But when I looked at myself in the mirror I had to murmur the same thing. "Oh, my." I was no longer the simple "Ilmi Marianna Brosi." I looked from top to toe like a graduate, like a valedictorian.

Somehow, in some way, I would have to find time and method to pay my good fairies back. But they seemed to find the way I looked when they were finished all the recompense they needed.

Mrs. Salin said they would be by in about an hour to give us a ride to School 159.

Miss Heino went home with Mrs. Salin, leaving me with the final task, one only I could do—get Ma and Margie to come to the graduation exercises.

Margie helped. "I'll behave. I promise I will, Ma. I'll iron my new summer dress and polish my shoes and sit quietly so I don't get wrinkled. I won't make a sound except to clap for Ilmi when she finishes her speech and when she gets her diploma."

But it was as if when the women left, they took all of Ma's energy with them. She didn't close up the machine. She didn't even sweep up the clippings or pick up the pins. She just lay down on the bed, clasped my hand, drew me to her to give me a kiss, and said, "I am so sorry, Ilmi. If there were any way, but I cannot. Perhaps if I rest now, Margie and I can make it there for your speech and the handing out of diplomas. But please forgive me. I'm so very tired."

With every breath of my being, I wanted to tell her that she need not walk, that Mr. and Mrs. Salin would give her a ride in their buggy. They would help her find a seat and bring her home as soon as the ceremony was over. But Mrs. Salin had said all of that, and it had fallen on deaf ears.

Finally, I just gave up. I couldn't bear to ride with those families, who would be all together, and I knew I could be on time even walking if I left right away. So I put on my old shoes, carried my new ones, kissed Ma and Margie, tried to make sounds that said I understood, and set off alone for School 159.

I was the first one there so I helped set up the table in the back where parents and friends would be served coffee or punch and cake after the ceremony. The Salins and Aros and Miss Heino arrived, without Ma and Margie. They found seats together, but I had no chance to talk to them, for by then we were being lined up according to height, ready to march in as soon as the clock turned to eight.

All through the graduation exercises, I watched the door, hoping that Pa and Ma and Margie would slip in, even late, no matter how they were dressed, so that they could hear my speech, so that they could hear Mr. Bakalayer's announcement.

After we had all risen for the Pledge of Allegiance to the flag and sung the National Anthem, Miss Heino rose and walked to the podium set on the other side of the picket fence, opposite the flag.

"Ladies and gentlemen, it is with great pleasure that we recognize as our special guest tonight, as representative of the School Board of the Schools of the Unorganized Territory of St. Louis County, Mr. George Bakalayar. Mr. Bakalayer."

She waited until he reached the lectern, where they shook hands, and he turned to the audience.

"Parents, friends, members of our staff, and graduates, it is with great pleasure that on behalf of the Superintendent of the Schools of the Unorganized Territory of St. Louis County, Mr. C.H. Barnes, that we recognize tonight that student who, of all of those graduating, all across the county tonight, has achieved the highest academic rating. I emphasize, with considerable pride, that her academic achievement ranks first not only at this graduation site but over all other graduates of all schools in the county this May. Truly, the valedictorian of the entire Unorganized Territory, she has earned the highest commendation our school system can proffer and our most sincere congratulations. I have the singular honor of introducing to you this year's valedictorian, Miss Ilmi Marianna Brosi."

He stepped back as I rose to meet him at the podium. He surprised me by shaking my hand and then giving me a warm and heartfelt hug. "We are very proud of you, young lady," he said for my ears only.

Everyone clapped, of course, and Miss Heino wiped away happy tears.

But no one I loved walked through the door of that school building before, during, or after my speech. I addressed it to a blank wall, to the emptiness in the back of the room, to the heads of the families of the other graduates, to the ceiling, to the floor, fighting back tears that threatened to overwhelm me at any minute. I think the words were audible. Miss Heino nodded, and the Salins and the Aros especially clapped when I was through. I couldn't remember a word of what I had said and hoped the speech I had practiced so thoroughly had come out of its own accord. Sitting down again, I followed the rest of the ceremony as if it were a blur, envying Hilma Hiltunen's straw hat, still glancing toward the door, but infrequently now.

Crossing the stage, the first to receive my diploma, I remembered to grasp the diploma with my left hand and shake Mr. Bakalayer's hand with my right hand. Standing and waiting for the others to receive theirs, I glanced inside.

The flame of knowledge topped the words which ran centered as follows:

The Schools of the Unorganized Territory
This certifies that
Ilmi Marianna Brosi
has completed the County Course of Study and
has passed the County Superintendent's examination
in Orthography, Reading, Writing, Arithmetic, English Grammar,
Geography, Hygiene, American History and Elementary Citizenship and
is awarded this
DIPLOMA
And when this instrument bears the seal of the County Superintendent
it further certifies that the holder had State High School Certificates
in Arithmetic, Geography, Grammar, American History.
Witness our signatures:
Given at School 159 in the County of St. Louis, State of
Minnesota, this twenty-fifth day of May, 1923

It had a gold seal. It was spectacular in its padded moiré maroon case. I had gone through the ceremony like the robot Miss Heino said science would one day create. Then I marched off the stage and out the door, heading toward home.

"Please, Ilmi," Miss Heino begged, "stay long enough for people to congratulate you. We're serving punch and cookies. Everyone wants to see you . . ." Her voice trailed off.

The only ones I had wanted to see had not come, and she knew it.

Holding my speech in one hand and my diploma in the other, I began the long trek home along a moonlit path. But the world was dark around me. When I came to the walkway by the bridge, I stopped to watch the moon's reflection on the water, the rippling sparkle of starshine. For a long time I looked down at that water and considered seriously how good it would feel, how cool, how smooth. Like the "Lady of Shalott, I am more than half sick of shadows."

Were I to be in that position, I thought, ironically, who would there be to listen? Taking the sheaf of pages of my speech, the full text of the words I had written and memorized with such care, I tore them in half and the halves in quarters and the quarters in eighths and the eighths in six-teenths until my hands were not strong enough to tear them again, and I threw them down on the water where they lay, snowy white, falling light, floating, silently sighing.

They drifted like bits of broken moonlight into the water, floating along the river of crystal light into a sea of dew.

I thought of Wynckin, Blynkin, and Nod, sailing off in a wooden shoe, and I watched the pieces of my dreams riding the spring freshet.

Had I the courage, I would have chosen to sail off on that river of crystal light, away from all of the ugliness I knew awaited me at home. I looked into the swirling water and considered that alternative—I thought seriously about making an end to my life, which seemed so pointless in the larger scheme of things.

For what seemed like forever, I stared into that water, trying to under-stand what I should do. Of the two considerations, neither seemed an easy road. But in the scope of the universe, one seemed to draw me on. I still wanted my education. Perhaps that was the turning point for me. At that moment, it was life that I knew I would choose.

At the same time, I vowed with a force so strong that it shook my entire being, "I shall never live like this. Whatever it takes for me to get there, I shall make it to that English land, the land of the literate, where there are jobs that pay good money, and no one and nothing will stop me."

CHAPTER NINETEEN
Repercussions

My *body fell asleep the minute* I lay down next to Margie that night. I had barely taken time to wash my face and hands.

But my mind refused to let go of the pain in my heart. All of the other graduates had had someone there to clap for them when the diplomas were awarded. I wouldn't have wanted the whistles and yells that the Aros gave Toivo. That seemed vulgar and out of place. But when my name was called, there was absolute dead silence. Then, Miss Heino stood up and clapped and when Salins and Aros, Spinas, too, and Saarinens and the rest of the families of "Little Kinney" realized Ma and Pa were not there, they joined her with a spurt of polite clapping. But I had been Valedictorian! Ma and Pa should have been there to stand and clap just as the Salutatorian's family had! I knew I was "nursing my wrath to keep it warm," but I could not get rid of the hurt.

All during that long walk home alone, I felt worse and worse. I knew it would have been better for me to have stayed for punch and cake. Miss Heino would have made me feel included. So would the Salins and the other families. But they were not *my* family. I'm not sure why that had been so important to me, but it just was. Perhaps the Salins had asked Margie to go with them, but who would have been there to wash and dress her? I had thought, when Ma roused herself that afternoon to help with my dress, just hours before the ceremony, she had finally understood how important it was. It had been important enough to warrant the hasty restyling of the clothing I was going to wear. It had been important enough for my hair to be done in a special way and for me to wear white hose and white shoes.

"Please don't be late," I had begged. "I'll even save seats for you." And I had saved three seats until the latecomers took them.

I awoke next morning to Margie squatting on the bed next to me, her eyes red and swollen. She had obviously rubbed her nose and her eyes with the back of her hand, and that had mixed with the inevitable dirt that matted her hair and streaked her face and the dress she had been wearing yesterday afternoon. No one had helped her into pajamas. It looked as if she had been alternately sleeping and crying all night.

"Oh, Ilmi," she continued to sob, "I did try so hard to get to your graduation, but by the time I was ready, the Salins and the Aros had gone, and I didn't know how to find the school five miles away, and I was afraid to go all alone. So I just sat here and felt awful and thought of you all alone there and was so, so sorry not just for that but for all the naughty things I have done. I have not been a good sister, and I am truly, truly sorry."

She burrowed down into me, like a small animal seeking solace, and I held her closely and said, "Shhhh . . . shhhh," as Ma used to do. When she finally hiccupped herself into silence, I wiped her face and hands and hair as best I could.

"I know you wanted to come, Margie. Remember yesterday afternoon? You sat and watched Mrs. Aro and Mrs. Salin get me all ready. I knew you cared about how I looked and about all of the plans. If I had been thinking clearly, I could have just taken you with me. So you see it was my fault, too. Now let's just kiss each other and know that we both meant to do our best."

We kissed, Margie's a fat slobbery smooch, and exchanged hugs. Then she cuddled down beside me and asked me to tell her what happened. I told her all about it, anyway as much as would have meaning to her, leaving out the parts that would hurt her even more. It was like a story, and she fell asleep to the rhythm of it.

All that time Ma was sitting in a chair in the corner staring vacantly out of the window, as if her soul had fled somewhere far away. I knew she had a right to be tired. She had done more work, spent more time outside of herself, and returned to the world more fully yesterday when we were working on my dress than she had in months.

Maybe she was feeling the way I felt last night there on the bridge, seriously considering the virtues of oblivion, the end of pain. For years I had put all I had to give into my schoolwork. And the people who were closest to me, my own family, had not seemed to care at all. That had hurt almost beyond bearing. For years Ma had put everything she had into making us into a family, into keeping us together, into helping us survive. Perhaps it now hurt beyond bearing that she felt she had failed. Perhaps she believed Pa's awful words about this all being her fault.

I can't say I understood, but there was a glimmer, a tiny crack in the wall I had built of anger and resentment . . . and love.

Miss Heino had given us a little speech on our last day of school the day before graduation, hoping to make us think seriously about our lives and our education.

"I know," she said, "that some of you will not continue your formal education after the graduation exercises. But not going to school does not mean you should quit learning. I have seen your homes and met your parents. Many are voracious readers of magazines and books and newspapers, but most were Finnish. The leap from Finnish to English, from considering Finland their homeland instead of America, always seems to come 'someday.' Maybe you can help them make that 'someday' come sooner.

"Many of you have developed a kind of Finn-glish as your primary language. You can work at home at dividing the Finnish from the English, keeping the best of both languages. Some of you have Anglicized your family names or your own names. I've seen some of your families at my night school classes. I commend them and you for encouraging them to continue.

"Girls, the years ahead are harder for you. If you can attend high school and earn a diploma, you'll be eligible to teach in small one-room schools. Some might even go on to college. If we are fortunate, by the time our first graders and second graders," and she looked down at Margie and Sara especially, "graduate from the eighth grade, they may be able to complete their high school courses in the county schools."

"I know how hard it will be to move to Mt. Iron or Virginia or Chisholm and work for your room and board so that you can go to school because that is what I did. You won't be paid. But you'll have a bed to sleep in, food to eat and the right to attend school in exchange for cooking, cleaning, and caring for children, in short, acting as a live-in maid. It won't be easy. But I've worked with you all for a year, and I know you have the will and strength and power to do it. Perhaps my most important gift when we say farewell is to say 'fare thee well' as you move into the future."

Although she had clearly tried to direct her words to all of the children, I caught her looking back to me again and again, willing me to find the strength to achieve my goal. I knew she believed in me.

Sitting there on the edge of the bed, remembering all she had done for me, I was very close to tears again. But they were healing tears. At least one person whose opinion I valued, perhaps above all others, believed in me. I got up, put my hand on the Bible, which always lay on its own stand atop a doily on a small round table Ma had made especially for it, I vowed to myself that I would continue to work to deserve Miss Heino's belief in me. No matter what I had to do, I would earn that high school diploma.

My feelings that morning were in turmoil—loss mixed with anger and determination. Once I got Margie freshened up, I got mad, so mad I understood why and how Ma threw things when she felt like this—before she gave up. I decided not to mention my diploma or the graduation ceremony at all unless someone—like Ma—asked a direct question.

I made up the bed, washed my face and hands, combed my hair, and redid it into the everyday easy plait down my back. I poured myself a cup of coffee, dunked a piece of *korppua* into the coffee and set myself up to iron. The basket was full.

When I went to use the outhouse, I could not see Margie anywhere. Pa sat outside, working on a knife.

Had Ma been herself, she would have chided me for sleeping so late. The sun had almost reached its zenith, and it was hot and buggy outside.

Hurrying back in, I latched the screen door Ma had built of scraps of left-over lumber, and opened the windows as high as they would go, grateful for the screens Ma had rigged up so the house was largely free of the insects that permeated a May morning in Minnesota.

They not only kept the bugs out but made conversations easy to follow. Sara and Margie should spend more time playing here. Margie's table and chairs and cupboard could be taken outside, and they could make plates out of birch bark and food from moss and rocks. I did that when we lived in Virginia and I had a good friend, Amalia Barone, the closest girl friend other than Java I had ever had.

While I was sprinkling the tablecloth, aprons, Pa's shirts, and Ma's and Margie's good dresses that had been starched or put in the starching pile, I thought about my good friend Java and wondered if she would spend this summer with her Aunt Mary in Kinney and if there would be some way we could see each other.

As I was beginning to iron the flat pieces that hadn't been starched—dish towels, sheets and pillowcases, underwear, work-a-day dresses, and shirts—I heard Pa outside. Oh, how I wished we had a hook so I could prevent him from coming in! But he was sitting down, probably on the chopping block, talking to someone. I slipped over to the doorway to listen. More than anyone in Zim, Mr. Aro had maintained his insistence on speaking Finnish. He seemed to think that if he spoke loudly enough and slowly enough even those of us speaking English would follow him, and of course we understood Finnish just as well as we always had.

Mr. Aro was a strange man. He seemed to exist in his wife's shadow. Yet he had always been there to help when needed, and he had always treated me kindly. What on earth could he want of Pa this morning?

"Knute," he began, as if this were the continuation of a previous discussion, "I come to ask again if your Ilmi Marianna will marry my boy Toivo once they are of age. I'll give them forty acres of land and a cow," he said, slapping his hat against his neck to kill mosquitoes.

The bugs—mosquitoes, black flies, gnats, and no-see-ums—were out full-force, precursors of a storm in the afternoon. The air was so heavy that the moisture didn't need to fall as rain. Everything felt sodden already. Even the ironing that hadn't been starched and sprinkled looked as if it had been. No matter how hot the flat irons got, every piece I ironed tended to feel a little damp when I got through. I laid them on the drying rack before I put them away. Oh, my, but it was hot work. I had to keep a fire in the stove to keep the bottom part of the iron hot. I clamped the top part onto a new hot bottom as the one I was using cooled. The irons were heavy, the clamps with the handles hard to maneuver, the ironing board propped between a chair and the table wobbly. It was not a good task to approach when I was not in the best of humors. But in this weather, if I didn't do the ironing, the clothes would mold.

I had not been listening seriously to the conversation going on outside, until I caught the gist of it. Then it connected. Me? Marry Toivo Aro? *You have got to be kidding*, I said to myself, switching the handle to a new hot base.

"My Toivo, he's a good worker," Mr. Aro continued. "And that cow, she's a good milker and a good breeder. There'll be at least one calf if she took when we put her out with old Bull. Can't get much of a better start than that."

"Sure can't," agreed Pa, and sat down on the chopping block, using his hat in the same way. "Come on into the house for coffee."

"Ilmi!" he yelled, as if a yell were necessary.

Taking a deep breath myself, I set the flatiron back on the wood stove to keep it warm, re-rolled the tablecloth I had sprinkled so it wouldn't dry, and drank a dipperful of water—lukewarm already—from the dry sink as I passed.

Pa could fix his own coffee. I pretended not to hear a word he said.

More provident husbands built summer kitchens, sometimes as an adjunct to the sauna, sometimes as a completely separate building, with screens all around a shaded porch and the stove in a well-ventilated separate room. Washing, ironing, and cooking could all be done there, leaving the house cool for eating meals or entertaining company or sleeping.

Some families, like the Salins, even had gas stoves in their summer kitchens so they didn't have to keep a fire going to keep the flatirons hot. The catalogs advertised gas irons, too. But that seemed too good to be true.

"We're lucky to have a pot to pee in and a window to throw it out of," Ma often said. In English yet.

There had been a time when she would not have let me hear her talking that coarsely. But everything had changed, none of it for the better since we left Kinney for an uncleared, untilled, brush-filled corner of Zim.

I sighed as I wiped my hands on my apron, an act of rebellion of which Ma would not have approved had she been alert. "Towels are for wiping hands," she had lectured, more than once, frowning at the sloth that all too often kept me from taking the extra steps to the commode with its back towel holder and a round towel, changed daily.

I stepped outside long enough to let the screen door bang behind me as I took a firm stance on the stoop, my arms folded in front of me, my mouth in a tight line, my jaw so clenched my ears hurt.

"We got your future planned for you, girl," said Mr. Aro. "We got you a good arrangement."

I met Mr. Aro's gaze squarely and shook my head. "No, Mr. Aro, you do not. I already have my future planned, thank you very much. I'm going on to high school."

Pa hooted, "How you gonna go to high school, girl, when we got no high school in Zim?" His English, which could be as good or bad as he wished it to be, reinforced his contempt for my decision.

Having spent months weighing alternatives even before I heard Miss Heino's lecture, I was ready. "I'm going to high school in Virginia. I'm going to stay with a family there and get a job working for my room and board."

"And who's going to hire a runt like you?" Pa knew that hurt. In spite of beet greens and cod liver oil, I was still small for my age, underfed, undernourished, frail, and slight. All my body's strength, if seemed, went to my hair, which was long, black, thick, and curly, and to my eyes, which could turn so green that it was as if they had yellow lights inside them. They sparked like a firefly's tail or a ball of sap from a poplar log.

I swallowed hard. At that point I really didn't know.

"So," Mr. Aro continued, "you really haven't made your plans then, have you? So you can think hard about my Toivo."

Even from ten feet away, I could smell the manure on his boots and pants. He hadn't changed out of his barn clothes before he came to propose for his son. As a matter of fact, Toivo hadn't been enough of a gentleman to propose for himself something for the future.

"No. I shall not marry your son Toivo. Or anybody. I'm never going to get married. I'm going to Northwestern College in Chicago, Illinois, where I shall earn a degree in foreign languages and become an interpreter."

"You got to think, girl, and get your head out of the clouds and your nose out of the air or a book," Pa said, rather mildly for him. "You don't need no high school education to wash diapers."

"I certainly don't because I shall never wash diapers. I need a high school education so that I can get away from here and from you and from barn smells and manure piles and cows and boys like Toivo, who think that just because they have forty acres and a cow they can get you out in a haystack and do what they please."

Pa was quiet for a while, considering. "Has Toivo made a pass at you?"

I snorted. "Try passes plural. Every time he gets a chance. And he brags about it. 'I got Russian fingers and Roman hands,' he says, as if that's clever. If he's not trying to get extra friendly, he's making sick jokes about it. I wouldn't have Toivo Aro if he came with two-hundred acres and four-hundred cows."

"Say," Pa turned to Mr. Aro, "I don't want your boy pushing himself on my Ilmi."

The worm had turned.

"You tell him to keep his fingers and his hands to home and his jokes in the outhouse where they belong."

Mr. Aro began to bluster, but at least for then the issue was closed.

I worked on the ironing all day, fixing myself some biscuit and an apple for lunch but too angry to fix anything for Pa.

"What's for lunch?" he came in and asked.

"Whatever you want to fix yourself," I answered, in what Ma would have called a 'smart-aleck' tone. Ma would never have brooked it.

"So you graduated from eighth grade last night."

"Yes, I did. My diploma is on the table."

"You come home with Salins?"

"No. I walked."

That caught his attention. "Alone? At night?"

"It's the way I have to face the world," I said, the tears just ready to come. I blinked them back very, very hard.

"That bridge over the St. Louis River is not too firm after the spring freshets. You didn't cross on that."

"Yes, I did. I even stood on that bridge for a long, long time. I thought it might be better if I just flowed away with the current. I was the only graduate there without some family in attendance."

"Even Mrs. Aro, who was hours away from having a baby?"

"Even Mrs. Aro. She didn't look good, and she left right afterward, but she came."

The silence lasted until late afternoon when Pa came in again. I had just finished the ironing, hung the ironing board and pads away, and put all of the things I had ironed back where they belonged.

"You know there isn't a chance of your going to high school, Ilmi," he began.

"Don't even start that." I flung the last sheet back on the bed and left it unmade. "I'm not asking for help from you. I'll do it myself."

Then I finished making the beds neatly, pulling the top sheets down hard, making square corners and tucking the freshly washed and aired and ironed sheets on top with their corners also squared. A light blanket was adequate, but Ma insisted that we have a bedspread on top to finish off the look of the bed so I added them to the bed and the trundle bed even though we would be going to sleep soon.

I stalked out of the house, slamming the door behind me.

Halfway to Salins I met Margie. Margie was really too big to be carried, but she had played outside all day and lived through the big fight and needed to be loved, so she jumped into my arms clinging like a limpet.

"We have to go home to Pa again," she said. "I hope they don't argue tonight."

"Was it bad after I left?" I asked, holding her close.

"Ma fell . . . well . . . no . . . Pa pushed her against the bed, and she hit herself on the head of the bed. I thought she was dying because she went all white and limp. I bet if you looked, her arms would be all black and blue. It took a long time for her to come to. I was afraid. But there was nowhere to go for help. Everyone was at the graduation. Pa kept yelling and pointing his finger at Ma. I don't remember anything more until this morning. I was crying too hard."

"I'm so sorry that we didn't get to your graduation. Sara said there was a golden sun with the letters 'Sunrise Not Sunset' on the background and a picket fence with flowers on the top. She said you gave the best speech she had ever heard when you gave the val—val—well, you know. And she was sorry that she didn't stand up right away to clap when you got your diploma the way they did when Eino got his. Were you very, very disappointed, Ilmi?" she asked, burrowing into the curve of my throat and patting my cheek.

"Yes, I was. But I'm better now. Thank you for telling me . . . about what happened."

"I'm honestly very, very sorry, Ilmi." She clung tighter until I finally sat down and held her on my lap and kissed her and said I understood.

"I love you, Ilmi," she said, her eyes bright with tears.

"And I love you, my one and only sister," I answered, kissing her tears.

The bugs were so bad, I picked her up again, and she swatted them while I hurried as fast as I could. Margie was no light-weight anymore, but I knew she needed to be carried.

"Ilmi, can I ask you a question?"

"Anything."

"Why does Ma keep letting him come home? He just hurts us. He spanks me even when I don't deserve it. He hits Ma and yells at her."

"Did he spank you last night?"

"No, because I crawled way in the back of the big bed behind Ma and under the covers. It was hot, but when it got dark, he didn't see me."

"Why does Ma keep taking it? We manage to get along when he isn't there, and we're a lot happier than when he is."

When Ma got up, Pa having left again, I refused to let her take that chair in the corner. I turned it around to face her and sat down on it myself.

"Margie asked me last night, and I am asking you today, Ma. Why do you allow Pa to abuse you? He flails you with cruelty, blaming you for things, for decisions, for . . . well, for example Baby Teddy's death. It was not your fault that he died. Mrs. Aro made it very clear that it was just one of those awful accidents that happen sometimes that no one understands."

"No one understands or remembers all he's done that was good," Ma shook her head. "He married me when no one else would marry me. You remember how awful it was for That Child in Virginia that horrible summer day in August when we found her in the swamp crawling with leeches? I would do anything to keep you from having that kind of life.

"It's not the same, of course. But nonetheless, you were born before I was married, and in the Finnish Evangelical Lutheran Churches, that's a sin. I would have been ostracized. You would have been ridiculed.

"Your pa may not be the kind of man I wanted as a father for you and Margie, but he does accept you as his daughter, and that's important in this society. Do you understand at all? He's terribly jealous of the man he knows I loved and still love. But his anger does not change my feeling. I have rarely been able to love him the way he wants to be loved. At least I think that's the core of his anger, and when his anger explodes, it destroys everything in his path. That's why he has had such a hard time keeping a job. I have to endure it in order to have a father of some kind for you and for Margie."

"So you allow him to continue to hurt you and Margie and me. Last night, for example," I fought back the tears. "I gave the valedictory address, and there was no one of my family to hear me or to clap or to be proud. No one . . . except Miss Heino. I was the only graduate without family there. I walked home without stopping to have punch and cookies and stood by the river and thought I would be better off in the river than in this body, which hurt so hard I couldn't stop crying."

Margie grabbed me hard around the waist. "You wouldn't fall into the river, would you, Ilmi? I'll walk with you and hold your hand so you don't fall in."

I leaned down and picked her up, her legs around my waist and her head on my shoulder. "Thank you, Margie. It's a great help to know that someone cares for me that much. I love you." I wondered if I had said those words often enough or clearly enough before.

"I love you, too. You are my only sister and the most special one I'll ever have."

Ma's hand dropped, and she looked ill and white. "Ilmi, Mrs. Aro asked yesterday if you would come to see her. She's worried about us, too. I'm sorry with all my heart that we missed hearing your speech and being there for you. Would you read it for us tonight?"

With venom in my glance, I answered, "I tore it up and threw it into the river. You have no idea what last night meant to me. What it did to me, not having you there. I can't explain it. But I won't ever mention it again. It's over. I faced it alone, and if I have to, that's the way I'll face the rest of my life. But I won't give up the way you have."

I had no idea how cruel those words were. All I know is that they did hit home.

CHAPTER TWENTY
Help for Ma

*I*___*was at my wit's end*___ as I walked to the Aros' the next morning. Mrs. Aro had been delivered of another baby, a girl this time. She wanted to see me as soon as possible.

"They're going to name the baby 'Marianna,' kind of after you," Margie explained, "because she can change it to 'Marion' if she wants to as she grows up."

"Can I come with you, Ilmi?" Margie begged. "I wouldn't bother anyone. And maybe Jenni could play."

I doubted it. In all likelihood, Jenni would be busy helping with the baby. I kissed Margie and said, "No, not this time. But I promise to take you another time, especially when the baby is a little bigger so you can hold her."

That pacified Margie for the time being, and I gave her a pair of school scissors, which Miss Heino had sent home with me and an old catalog so she could cut paper dolls. "Why don't you sit on the bed by Ma so you can show her how well you are doing with cutting?" I suggested.

I made sure my face and hands were clean, smoothed out the wrinkles on my dress and set off for a longish walk.

Sighing deeply and reliving Mr. Aro's proposal and my response along the way, I felt awful. Mrs. Aro was such a special lady. If she too asked me to marry Toivo, it would be more difficult than to refuse Mr. Aro.

When I knocked on the door, I heard the call, "Come in, Ilmi Marianna. I'm in the first bedroom at the top of the stairs. Please pour yourself a cup of coffee and come upstairs so we can talk."

Otherwise the house seemed remarkably silent.

I was loathe to eat or drink anything there. The kitchen needed a good cleaning. But Mr. Aro certainly had provided her with ample room for their

148

growing family. There were two rooms downstairs—a kitchen and a living room or parlor and three rooms upstairs, one for the boys, one for the girls, and one for Mr. and Mrs. Aro. Her special "hospital room" was separate though linked into the house with a doorway that opened into the kitchen.

"I'm tired so I'm not going to mince any words, Ilmi," she began. "Would you prop a few more pillows behind me so I can sit a little higher?"

I tried to arrange them to her satisfaction. She looked so healthy and strong, the only evidence she had given birth was the baby, wrapped in a flannel blanket, lying on the bed sleeping.

I said, "I'm sorry, Mrs. Aro. I know we owe Ma's life to you. But I cannot marry Toivo, even for forty acres and a cow."

She laughed so heartily that she had to hold herself still because she said it hurt.

"Oh, child, I have no intention of trying to persuade you to marry my Toivo. He is a good boy, but he is not the boy for you. I know you will go to high school somehow and probably college, too. In no time at all you will out-distance him intellectually, and no man likes to have a wife who is smarter and earns more money than he does, though I think Toivo would very much like to have you in his bed."

I blushed scarlet.

"But that is neither here nor there. I am very concerned about what's happening at your house."

I wanted to ask what she meant, but she knew that I knew exactly.

"First of all, let's consider your Pa. Rumor has it that he's back. Mr. Aro believes he's started to imbibe the product he's importing. Do you understand what I am saying?"

"That he is drinking strong spirits? I think that might be true."

"It may be just too easy to get a hold of now. Or it may be his pay is a jug or two of liquor. I'm speaking plainly to you, Ilmi, as if you were an adult."

"Yes," I mumbled, ashamed for Pa.

"How quickly life is forcing you to grow up." She paused, shaking her head. "But for heavens sake, don't be ashamed. What your pa does or doesn't do has nothing to do with you except for making it more dangerous to have him at home. Knute Brosi has a vicious temper. That not a secret. And it is no secret that alcohol always makes a bad temper worse."

"Be very careful when he is home. If you can, get you and your Ma and Margie out of the house and to Salins' on any pretext."

She sighed deeply, repeating herself. "How old are you again, child?"

"Thirteen in March," I repeated, feeling sick to my stomach.

"It breaks my heart to have to put so important a matter in your hands. But your ma is in no condition to act. She's grieving not only the loss of her baby but the loss of a husband she has stood by through thick and thin. God knows why. I'd have left him long ago." She paused. "But that's not for me to say."

"Staying at home in bed or sitting on a chair is obviously not the answer for her. How long has this been going on? Since the baby died?"

I nodded, miserably. "Except when Pa first came home with money to buy me a new coat and us some food. Then he left again, and Ma . . . just couldn't manage."

"I thought so, but I was hesitant to interfere. I have some answers when the sickness is of the body. I do not know what can cure a sickness of the mind. Let's face facts. She needs help. No one here can give it to her. So we must look elsewhere. There's a hospital in Fergus Falls that specializes in mental illnesses."

My eyes must have doubled in size. I started to shake uncontrollably.

"There, there. I know this is almost impossible to bear. I don't know if that's the place for her. I don't like what I have heard of the hospital there. But I have a suggestion. Why don't you ride along with Mr. Salin when he next makes a milk run and talk to that young Dr. Malmstrom, who was so kind to you before. Tell him how your ma acts, what she does each day. I will pray for all that he does. Perhaps he will say that you do need to send her to a doctor in Virginia or Duluth or even to Fergus Falls. Tell him about the difficulty of the baby's birth and death. Tell him she's still grieving about that loss. Tell him she feels she has to keep her marriage going when a woman with any sense would have kicked your pa out years ago. You may not be aware of how worried she is about you and how terrible she feels because she did not go to see your graduation exercises. Congratulations, by the way. Your speech was the best part of the ceremony."

"You're welcome. But if Ma were sent somewhere to recuperate, what would happen to Margie and to me?"

"You need to leave. You're going to go to high school, I know. As soon as I'm able, I'll see what kinds of jobs are available in Virginia. Salins would take Margie for the month or two if your ma's hospitalized. She's there half the time anyway. If that doesn't work, Margie could come here. She's a good influence on my Jenni, who's growing up too fast. Jenni needs to learn how to play and get dirty and be a little girl, not a small mother. Then if Knute chooses to return to your house, there would be no one for him to hurt."

I sat quietly on the chair by Mrs. Aro's bed and thought for a long time.

"Wouldn't it be better to tell Pa to never come back? I'm big enough to take care of Margie. I could help the mothers by taking their children for a few hours every day for a kind of playschool. Maybe we could even use the school building. It would be a good experience. Miss Heino would help me, I know.

"Mr. Bakalayer said the school district is seriously considering moving our school building onto the site of School 159 and remodeling it to serve as a teacherage until the upper level is completed."

"Let's take this step by step. First, ask Mr. Salin for a ride and go to visit Dr. Malmstrom. He may even know of a family that needs a helper. The sooner you get used to what you need to do, the easier it will be to add school-work to the household chores."

"In the meantime, I'll do what I can. It's not that I want you to leave home. Nor do I want to break up your family. But right now, each one of you needs something different. We care about you, Ilmi," she said, reaching over to pat my hand and draw it up to touch her cheek. "We all do. Not just the Salins and us."

Mrs. Aro was a wise woman in many ways, and I tried to approach what we had discussed with Ma while I was doing the dishes that night— without mentioning Pa or Fergus Falls or anything except the suggestion for me to see Dr. Malmstrom about a job and perhaps to find some help for her.

Ma didn't react. Later as we were lying in bed, during that time when we used to exchange confidences, she whispered to me, "Oh, Ilmi, I know I need help. I try so hard, but I cannot seem to find the energy to do the things I need to do."

Thus, everything arranged itself very nicely. Mr. Salin was his usual kind and helpful self. This time he did not even warn me to hurry. He said that he would come to pick me up at the hospital. "Just come out when you're ready, Ilmi," he said, patting my hand.

Dr. Malmstrom greeted me at the door when it was my turn to go into his inner office. He remembered my name, put his arm around me, and asked, "And how are things with you, young lady? Am I to continue to call you 'Miss Ilmi Marianna'?"

Shyly, I told him that now that I had graduated from the eighth grade, I would like to begin using my grown-up American name, 'Marion' Brosi. At that he whooped and twirled me around the office and said, "I'll bet you were the valedictorian!"

I blushed and nodded.

"Why am I not surprised?" he teased.

I started off with the easy question. "Do you know of a family in Virginia that might need a maid . . . right now?"

He sat down on his round stool, twirled around a few times, and said, "The person to consult is my wife. She knows most everyone on South Side, both those people she visits socially and those she helps as best she can." He was thinking aloud. "I think it would be good for you to work for a family that doesn't speak Finnish. That would improve your English, not that it needs any improvement, but the more you speak it, the more natural it will become, until you even dream in English. Then you'll really have mastered the language."

I nodded, agreeing wholeheartedly.

"But that's not the real reason I came." I bit my lip and twisted around. It was not easy to talk about this.

"It's your mother, isn't it?"

"Yes. She is not better at all. The baby, we called him Baby Teddy, was born with the cord wrapped around his neck."

"Oh, I am so sorry," he said, reaching over to grasp my shoulder. "I have wondered what happened and worried that I could have been of help."

"She almost died, too. Mrs. Aro, a woman from our community who knows the old ways of healing, saved her life in what will sound to you like the strangest way. She filled a stoneware cup with alcohol, lighted the alcohol, and, turning the cup upside down, laid it on Ma's belly. Then she covered her up and kept changing the towels that packed her . . . where the baby came. She did that all night and the bleeding stopped. Then Mrs. Aro gave her herbs to drink, and very slowly she kind of came back to life."

"I shall have to meet your Mrs. Aro. I think she may be able to teach me a thing or two. But what do you mean by 'kind of came back to life'?"

"She . . . hasn't, except for a short time when Pa came home. And one day when she helped remake a dress for me for graduation. Otherwise, she just lies in bed or sits in a chair and looks out the window."

"Who does the washing and ironing and makes the meals?"

"I do the best I can. My sister Margie has tried, too."

"And as for your Ma . . . I have an idea there, too. Underneath, she must be a strong lady, or she'd never have produced a child like you."

I blushed.

"I'd hate to see her sent to a place like Fergus Falls." He was quiet for a long while.

"I would like to meet with your mother. Is she strong enough to dress and come here?"

"Would that be considered an 'initial consultation'?" I asked, fearful of the charge.

He laughed, a big booming hearty laugh that shook the walls and gave me a big hug. "For you, my dear Miss Marion Brosi, all rules of payment are suspended. Someday I will be in a position to ask a favor of you and then you won't charge me for an 'initial consultation.'"

I couldn't guess what I could ever do for him or for his wife, but I knew he meant well, so I smiled and nodded and went into the waiting room where he made an appointment for me to bring Ma in.

There was no one else there so he sat down beside me and continued, as if there had been no interruption, "There's a Finnish lady on North Side named Hilma Maki, who's worked with me on cases just like this one. She's taken women into her home who have borne more than their spirits can carry. She gives them rooms of their own, three good meals a day, and a chance to walk or read or think. She will not, however, allow them to sit and ruminate over their problems. She has the gift of listening without judging and encouraging others to share whatever they feel comfortable talking about . . . always at their own speed . . . always with the knowledge that what they say will go no farther. I call her an 'Earth Mother.' She never takes more than one visitor at a time, and her house is open now.

"When things overwhelm me, I spend a morning with her. Sometimes we walk. Sometimes I don't say anything at all. Sometimes I talk. But I always feel better when I leave. Do you understand, Marion?"

"I think so. Ma used to be kind of like that before. And Mrs. Aro is, in some ways. Does it cost a lot? For Ma to stay there, I mean?"

"Never more than the visitor can pay. My friend doesn't do this for the money. She's comfortably settled, financially. She does it . . . for the love she has to share, and—to be honest—for the companionship. She says without a guest to share her life, it would be very empty."

And so, it was arranged. Margie moved to Aros' to spend at least a month teaching Jenni to play.

Looking her straight in the eye, I emphasized, "Margie, it is also your responsibility to have Jenni teach you to work. Mrs. Aro can use all the help she can get with a new baby and all. You know how to wash and wipe dishes, and you know how to scrub a floor and when it needs it. You know how to hang clothes on the line and how to sort them for washing. I expect you to earn your keep."

"I will," she promised solemnly, and I believe she took those words to heart.

The next day I dressed Ma as if she were a doll and brought her to Dr. Malmstrom's office. I was frightened by how thin she was. Her very best dresses just hung on her. I did her hair in its usual pompadour, but it too had lost its gloss and fullness. She had to lean on me very hard just to get out the door, and Mr. Salin had made a bed of lap robes and blankets in the bed of the truck so she did not have to sit up during the drive. I sat beside her and held her hand.

Mr. Salin helped her up the steps of the hospital and into Dr. Malmstrom's waiting room. The room was empty, thank goodness, and he came out right away.

"Dr. Malmstrom," I began, very formally, "I am very proud to introduce you to my mother, Mary Rajamaki Brosi, Mrs. Knute Pietari Brosi.

"Ma, this is the doctor I told you so much about. His wife sent us that beautiful outfit for Baby Teddy."

At that Ma's eyes filled with tears. Dr. Malmstrom motioned me out of the room, drew Ma to a comfortable seat by his desk, and said, loudly enough for me to hear, "I am proud to meet you, Mrs. Brosi. You have certainly raised an extraordinary daughter."

He closed the door, and I waited, trying to read Thackeray's *Vanity Fair,* which Miss Heino had suggested for my summer reading project. But I had a difficult time keeping my mind on the text. Every time I heard movement or sound from the inner office, I tried to think of what was going on in there.

Dr. Malmstrom spent a long time with Ma. His nurse came in later to take her place at her desk. At one point he asked her to come in for a while. She did for a long while. When she came out, she said my mother seemed very healthy physically, a bit undernourished, perhaps, and in need of rest, but not in need of hospitalization.

"Thank you," I said, fervently. "That's good news, isn't it?"

"Very good news," she affirmed. "But Dr. Malmstrom would like a second opinion. He has asked me to get Dr. Raihala from just down the hall." She left and returned with the other doctor.

"*Katsutaan, sanu Raihala,*" he twinkled at me, walking by into the inner office.

He looked just like Miss Heino's pictures of Santa Claus with a fat round tummy and a red nose and a big smile.

Again, I waited a long, long time.

When they invited me in, Ma was talking in Finnish to both of the doctors. I had not realized Dr. Malmstrom also spoke Finnish.

She was speaking lyrically, as if she were reciting the runes of a poem. "It's the loneliness," she said. "I live . . . like a maple tree in winter, bereft of leaves, alive but dormant, pared to a skeleton of gray, my whole world reduced to a wintry bleakness."

My mouth dropped open. I had always thought of Pa as the poet of the family. Here was Ma speaking in similes and metaphors that I understood better than literal speech.

"Moments fall or rise in fragmented pieces." Her voice rose and fell in rhythms, too. I wondered if she had read the *Kalevala*. "Shards of the past rework themselves into windows of brilliant color, but they are fragile, so fraught with the danger of breaking that even leaded molds cannot hold them firm. I remember those moments with Knute, but the pain of his leaving and the equal hope and fear that he will or will not return have cracked the lead so that the windows shatter, and the beauty is lost even in dreams."

"At home I have done nothing but rest, but the pieces refuse to reform. I myself feel . . . broken . . . and I awake in the night to feel the edges of the shards reformed into ugliness so that I cannot sleep and yet I want to sleep without the fear of awakening."

Was Ma warning us that she was thinking of suicide? Or was she just talking of it as a thought without an action?

Dr. Raihala took over. "I have heard Dr. Malmstrom's suggestion. I want you to hear the other alternatives. We could send your mother to Duluth. I'm not in favor of that alternative. Neither of us would agree to put your mother into one of those concentrated centers for the treatment of the insane. She's far from insane. If your friend Mrs. Aro would like to come in to discuss our decision, we would be delighted to share our reasons with her. We believe that your mother is simply exhausted. Bone-deep tired, physically, mentally and emotionally. So, these are the options."

Dr. Malmstrom put a file folder in front of me. Both doctors sat down to give me time to read. I scanned it, picking up important points:

"There is no differentiation between those who overuse drugs and alcohol, those with epilepsy, and those who are criminally insane. In some cases a single untrained aide is responsible for up to fifty-five patients at night. Patients are strapped to beds and chairs."

Dr. Raihala interposed, "I read a recent report presented to the governor which told about a nude girl locked in a narrow 'seclusion room.' Her wrists and ankles were tied to the side of a metal cot; the cot had no mattress, a thin blanket between her body and springs and folded over her; window wide open with outside temperature sub-zero. The nurse stated that she was without clothing or mattress because she was destructive."

He shook his head. "The sheer monotony of the hospital's routine contributes to the number of disturbed patients. Normal men and women are nervous upon entering the hospital. Inside they find nothing to keep them occupied. There are no clocks or calendar; even soap and toilet paper and toothpaste are rarely found. All the material which would allow the patient to continue normal habits are missing.

"Eventually," he continued, pacing, "many simply blow up, wanting to escape, to find some privacy, their clothes, and scream to go outside. The answer for the hospital is to tie the patient into a camisole—a straight jacket—and strap him or her to a base—a bench, a chair, or a bed. Worst of all, a popular treatment is electric shock or drugs to induce convulsions to shock the patient out of his or her dream world. Right now I'd call many of the state hospitals cruel, outmoded excuses for treatment.

"I'm sorry for getting carried away like this, but many of your neighbors will ask you why your mother has not been hospitalized. They may criticize you and us for not sending her to a center designed to treat the 'mentally ill.' Neither of us can bear to think of your mother in such surroundings.

156

And we do not apologize for our choice. We have visited these hospitals. We speak from experience. We have written about the conditions in existence and found we speak to deaf ears. Only when the conditions are brought to the forefront, to the public, perhaps through newspaper articles or books will there be a change.

"Right now, we advocate the approach Dr. Malmstrom already described to you. A walk outside with someone to listen if she wishes to talk. Every woman who has gone through this program has evidenced a marked change for the better, a renewal of spirit so that she can return to living with the kind of love and enjoyment she once felt."

"Oh, yes," I agreed.

And even Ma closed her eyes, and the tears ran down her cheeks and she said, in Finnish and in English, "Please let it begin today."

Finally, we all filed out.

"We have agreed," Dr. Malmstrom said, quietly but firmly, "that your mother will not go back home with you tonight. I'll drive her to see the lady I talked with you about. It's just a short drive to Mrs. Maki's house.

"Perhaps you could drive back to Zim with your friend Mr. Salin and pack a suitcase to bring here tomorrow morning. I'll make sure that your mother receives it.

"For the next few weeks, we'll leave her to rest and recuperate. She knows that you and Margie will be well taken care of and that her only responsibility is to heed Mrs. Maki's advice and to take the mild sedative I will prescribe and bring along for her. It'll help her not to dwell on the past but to enjoy the present—the beginning of summer. The chokecherry trees are in blossom, and Mrs. Maki is planting her garden.

"Your mother won't have to do anything, not even make her bed, if she doesn' feel up to it. She may read, but only books or magazines designed to help her see the world in a positive, happy way. Mrs. Maki has a sauna, which is heated every night. As soon as your mother's strong enough, I'd like to have her walk to look at gardens, eventually at the gardens in the North Side Park and the greenhouse.

"You and Margie may come to see her after a time. But not before she's ready. When you visit her, there must be no dissension. Walk with her. Speak of happy things. Make sure your sister understands that she must behave herself, or leave her home. Bring along no negative gossip. Accept no discussion of Knute.

"At the beginning, one of us will visit her each day. We'll encourage her to talk, but if she doesn't want to, we'll just sit with her or walk with her, talking lightly of nothing at all or even not talking.

"We don't know how long this will take. She has a lot of guilt and pain to work through. We'll encourage her to sit down with a pen or pencil and paper every day and write about those feelings. Good feelings and bad feelings. Then I'll encourage her to wipe out the unhappy feelings in any way that feels right to her. The good feelings we'll build on and make into . . . oh . . . commandments that she can fall back on when she goes home.

"Is there anything she really likes to do?"

"Oh, yes. She loves to work with wood. She made a table and chairs and a cupboard out of scrap lumber for Margie last Christmas."

"Then we'll make some scrap lumber available to her as she improves.

"As for you, young lady," Dr. Malmstrom said, "you may also pack a suitcase. My wife has found you a challenging first job. I'll have the name and address ready for you. You'll begin as soon as you get there tomorrow morning."

Dr. Raihala left after giving both Ma and me a good solid Finnish hug. Dr. Malmstrom replaced his white office coat with a suit coat that matched his slacks, gave Ma and me a chance to hug and kiss each other and murmur warnings about not overdoing and being careful.

"I love you so much," we both said at the same time, which made us laugh, and on that note Dr. Malmstrom led Ma out the door. I had to hurry after them to meet Mr. Salin and tell him what had happened . . . but not all. So much had happened to change my life I could barely hang on to it all myself.

CHAPTER TWENTY-ONE
First Job

When I reached Dr. Malmstrom's office the next morning, having ridden to Virginia with Mr. Salin, I quailed.

It was my word of the day, chosen at random from the dictionary, but it perfectly described my feelings. I understood exactly what it felt like to be a partridge faced with Ma's inexorable approach, deadly rock and slingshot at the ready. Like the grouse whose body would supply our supper needs, I too shrank with fear, freezing into physical immobility.

No one I knew—not even the Huhtalas or Ketolas, cream of Finnish society—now lived on Virginia's South Side in the area that ran south of Chestnut Street, the main business thoroughfare. Finns chose the upper South Side, round the Finnish Temperance Hall north of Chestnut Street, up to and a bit past Bailey's Lake.

Virginia's North Side—where my one-time best friend, Amalia Barone, lived and where Ma and I had chased the gangs marauding a misbegotten child in the summer's heat of my childhood—was a land apart. There truckloads of grapes were delivered to Italian families for wine-making, and Slovenian mothers packed cabbages into crocks of sauerkraut that reeked noxious fumes out of open windows. Picket fences bracketed front yards. Backyards were meticulously tilled and planted with vegetables that seemed exotic to me, not just the Finnish plots of onions, potatoes, carrots, and rutabaga but eggplant, kohlrabi, tomatoes, peppers, and garlic.

Appropriately enough, we were expatriates of a sort, partly because of Ma's and Pa's liberal religious beliefs, partly because of Pa's reserved nature, partly because of Ma's work ethic. If she needed to, she'd spend twenty-four hours a day in a desperate attempt to keep Margie and me and our house immaculate, to fill our pantry with produce, canned in times of plenty in preparation for the inevitable times of need that followed Pa's quitting another job. We had rented an apartment in between Finntown and what Finns called "Italia vitsi." I had always been aware that we didn't fit well into either designation. I, especially, didn't fit.

Margie, on the other hand, was growing from a roly-poly pink and golden baby, into the epitome of Finnish—a lovely Finnish child with wide-set blue eyes and softly curling blonde hair. I remained dark and skinny with black hair too heavy for my head, green eyes that tended to slant when I got mad—("Cat eyes," neighbor kids taunted.)—and skin tones so olive that when I had sat around the Barone's kitchen table, sharing supper with Amalia and her abundant family, I fit right in.

Or, to be more accurate, I *had* fit right in.

Sighing deeply, I resolutely turned my back not only on the neighborhoods that were familiar to me but on the past and the tendrils of memory that pulled and tugged me into the past and held me there.

Sometimes I was able to wrench myself loose. But too often I felt as if, like That Child, whom Ma and I had found prosecuted for her mother's wrongdoing, writhing with leeches, I too was doomed.

Had the rich promise of a future in which I nestled under the wings of my guardian angels, the Savolainens, Alex and Anna, come to pass, everything would have been different.

They had taken one step too far, and Ma and I had no choice but . . .

I shook myself.

This was neither the time nor the place for recriminations. It was time for me to make my own way, I told myself, as I had on that day not so long ago when I began my search for Uncle Charles. "One step at a time." I proceeded to set my feet to moving ahead, past the library (which was still closed; it was a good thing, too, for I loved libraries), past the imposing pillars of Roosevelt High School, toward forbidden ground, where spacious lawns surrounded mansions, two- and-three stories high, set well back from the broad thoroughfare so mundanely termed "Fifth Avenue."

Dr. Malmstrom had written the address down for me. "You'll be working for the Reid family. And be sure to let us know if it gets to be too much," he added, clearly uncomfortable about the annotation but also considering it necessary. "I don't want you working yourself to death. Keep in touch. Do you hear me?" He fixed those eyes on me, and I knew he was speaking of concern.

I had concerns, too, looking down at the floor, at my cotton dress, at least a size too small, at my shoes, which hurt. I had thought of the meager contents of my carpet bag and, taking a deep breath, I had asked, "Are you sure they want me?"

"I'm positive," he had answered, smiling. "My wife spoke to Mrs. Reid at length last night, and they not only want but desperately need someone just like you. YOU, to be exact."

"But . . . but . . . he owns the big department store on Chestnut Street. How can I possibly fit in?"

"Just by being yourself. The minute you walk into that house, you'll see how desperately you're needed. It doesn't matter what you look like or what kind of clothes you wear. Trust me." He had turned my head gently so that I had to look into his eyes. "Do I care for you and for your family?"

I had gulped. "Yes." Then I had to laugh and make the answer more affirmative.

And so I walked and gawked, feeling a bit like Christian approaching the gates to the Celestial City. I clasped the slip of foolscap with the address and directions as if it were my scroll. I checked house numbers, and tried to pretend that I belonged there, too, just as did the men and women I met, mostly heading in the opposite direction toward the noise and businesses of downtown Virginia.

Farther into South Side, a quiet serenity reigned. I heard the sound of a piano from the open window of a gingerbread house, the curlicues and arabesques of the trim on the porch and moldings and stairs painted (I stopped to count) at least five different colors, ranging from a dove gray through soft shades of azure to a deep navy, almost as purple as an iris.

Wrong notes. A child practicing, I guessed.

Although I couldn't sing a note, I had inherited some of Pa's sense of pitch. He never needed a pitch pipe to tune his fiddle. How ironic that he had never been able to tune in to us the same way, I thought, not for the first time.

On the corner of Fifth Avenue and Fourth Street, a vine-covered loggia led to a sprawling beige stucco house with a red tiled roof, shuttered windows, and—I stopped to listen to the water—a small fountain—or was it a birdbath?—centering a rose garden. It looked like a picture in my last year's geography book, the chapter entitled "How Children Live in Spain."

I couldn't see any house number, but the numbers of the street and avenue told me I was there. Some inner sense told me not to go to the front door, but if there were a back door, it wasn't visible from the street. Nor was there a walkway or sidewalk.

And then, I saw the house number painted a deep maroon with green trim. Painted in complementary shades, the house looked huge. On my left, a sun porch had windows on the front and sides. On the right, broad steps led to an open porch, pillared and gated. Three floors up, the roof peak framed double windows. "My room?"

The windows and gate were closed, but a gravel driveway led along the side to a small building in the back. The square door and hay lift near the high roof suggested it had once been a stable, but a car was just barely visible through the windows on the large ground-level double doors.

I turned onto the cobblestone walkway leading to a back entry, gathering my courage as I approached the door, and knocked.

Although my character left a lot to be desired (Ma reeled off my list of vices with disturbing regularity, headed, of course, by pride and a tendency to daydream), timidity was not usually among them. But no one could have heard my first knock, even had the house been silent.

It wasn't. Even through the door, which led to an enclosed entry porch where the icebox sat, and another door leading probably to the kitchen, I heard babies crying. Yelling, actually. Screaming with a degree of pitch and volume even Margie had never achieved, gifted though she was at tantrums.

I knocked harder.

Again, there was no response other than the wailing, which, as I listened, unsure of what to do, seemed to follow a wavering pattern, dipping almost to a *diminuendo* before accelerating again and rising into a crescendo.

Timing my next assault on the door to the brief moment of lessened volume, I pounded. Again, to no avail.

"Well," I told myself, "there's really only one other option." Turning the knob carefully, I opened the back door, skirted the icebox, which, I noted, had overflowed the drip pan, flooding the entry floor, and knocked on the kitchen door. Hard.

When that failed, I let myself into the kitchen.

Dirty dishes hid the top of the table. Pots and pans smoldered on the stove, exuding noxious fumes and overpowering even the smell of burned bacon and solidified cereal. The room reeked sour milk.

I blew my breath out with a whoosh, set my carpet bag down on an empty chair, gritted my teeth, and yelled, "Is anyone home?"

A ridiculous question, rhetorical to say the least, but what else was I to say?

From somewhere far away, a desperate voice cried, "Yes! Is it Marion Brosi?"

"It is." Thank goodness my lungs had never been "weak" as the doctors had described my blood. Either that or years of dealing with Margie had given me voice power far exceeding my size.

"Come straight upstairs, please!"

Heading toward the noise, which was, praise be, in its diminishing stage, I picked my way around a massive dining room table flanked by oversized matching chairs and sideboard. Heavy draperies, closed above a window seat, emphasized the darkness of the ceiling, a green that verged on black. Above mahogany wainscoting, the walls had been papered with dark green and maroon stripes. The table had been cleared, but the cloth, stained and wrinkled, had not, and table, chairs, crystal chandelier, drapes, and the heavy rug running almost wall to wall were covered by a layer of dust which lifted and fell as I walked by. I sneezed.

Hurrying on through the formal parlor, where overstuffed furniture flanked a brick fireplace, I finally located the front foyer from which a wide, dark staircase led up to a landing before angling back over itself. Upstairs four doors opened from a central hallway the size of our whole house in Zim. One led into an inside bathroom—I could see a toilet and sink—and the others to bedrooms, one of which had been decorated in pastel colors.

In that doorway stood Mrs. Reid, though she did not look much older than I. Sighing deeply when she saw me, she motioned with her free hand for me to take off my coat and hat, and nodded toward the crib.

The baby had spit up on her house dress, and its twin was thrashing around, disarranging an already overloaded diaper.

Yesterday's vocabulary word had been "sinecure." This certainly won't be one, I thought, rolling up my sleeves and digging in.

It took every waking minute of my first two weeks there for me to make some order of the chaos. Mrs. Reid, though she was, in fact, much older than I, was far younger in experience. Before she had married, she confided to me during the days that followed, she had never had to cook or keep house. She had never cared for a baby.

"Mr. Reid is so busy. And help is so hard to get. Or to keep," she added.

I could certainly understand why.

Many times during those long days I was tempted to trek back to Zim, even if I had to walk every step of the way. I had to remind myself over and over again as each day progressed that this is not the way life would always be. This was an interim time, a means to an end, a necessity were I ever to achieve my goal of a high school education.

I kept plugging along. Gradually order began to emerge out of chaos.

Given the magnitude of the tasks awaiting us, I was relieved to find that even Mrs. Reid could see we had to divide the work. That first day I took one twin; she took the other. Between us we managed to get them fed, bathed, and tucked in for a nap.

Then I attacked the kitchen. Had I opened the door to the basement stairs, I probably would have started there, but that little surprise didn't emerge until Day Two.

By the end of Day One, I had emptied the ice box pan, wiped down the inside, and scrubbed the back porch and stoop and stairs. Soaking the dishes, cutlery, pots, and pans in washbasins and scouring when necessary, I gradually managed to get everything back into the pantry. Thankfully, I had examined the pantry before I began putting things away. Since the shelves were virtually empty, I washed them first.

Opening the windows helped air the room out, and by attacking the floor a section at a time, changing water ruthlessly, I managed clean walk paths and finally, piling chairs on table, a linoleum free of spills, stains, tracked-in dirt, and baby messes.

But it took all day, with stops in between to do my half of the twins' care.

Mrs. Reid cleaned herself up and went grocery shopping. Mother Hubbard's cupboard had nothing on theirs, but I think she was frantic to escape even for a few minutes from the mass confusion even if it was just to a grocery store.

Thank goodness, Mr. Reid did not come home for dinner. He had a meeting, Mrs. Reid said. I made a pan of *kropsua*—a mixture of eggs and milk poured into hot pans and set into the oven to rise and bake. Slathering the flat popovers with butter and sugar, we ate every bit, sitting rather companionably at the kitchen table.

Unfortunately, I admitted during that brief time of communion, when Mrs. Reid praised my cooking skills, fixing eggs and/or cereal and setting potatoes to bake constituted the limit of my culinary ability.

"I'd actually like to learn to cook," she admitted with a slight smile. "I got a cookbook for a wedding present."

She rummaged through some drawers and came back with a brand new copy of *The Household Searchlight*. "I'll do the cooking," she offered triumphantly. "After all," she added with naive confidence, "anyone who can read a recipe can certainly cook."

It was slow going, but she eventually managed to come up with three simple meals a day for the two of us.

Mr. Reid left before breakfast, took lunch at a downtown cafeteria, and dined with other businessmen at what he called "The Club." Rarely did he get home before I went to bed, no matter how late that was. As far as I was concerned, he existed merely as a source of clothes which needed washing and/or ironing. He changed his worsted suits every day, though they all looked the same to me, whether they were dark brown or blue, diamond weave with the jacket lined in alpaca or single-breasted pin stripe. Once worn, every suit required brushing and pressing before he wore it again. He changed his cotton broadcloth dress shirts every day. Every one needed to be starched, sprinkled, and pressed. Mrs. Reid added, rather nervously, that he liked all of his clothing pressed, including undergarments and stockings.

Although at first it felt unseemly for me to be ironing his shirts and drawers, union suits and short sleeved, short legged Nansook suits, I finally decided that since I washed them, ironing them was not much more indelicate. Still, it was an act of intimacy that I would have preferred to leave for Mrs. Reid.

One evening Mr. Reid invited Mrs. Reid to join him for a "Ladies Night at the Club." Oh, I did love seeing them off, for she wore the most elegant frock I had ever seen. I did not have the words to describe it. She pretended to be modeling it for me, pointing out the "dainty silk georgette crepe with a softly bloused bodice, clusters of narrow folds on front and back, and inverted pleats on the skirt, which is draped over a matching georgette drop slip."

"Oh, my," I said, for the first time understanding why Mr. Reid had chosen her, in spite of her obvious failings as a housewife.

Mrs. Reid learned to cook, but she never got the hang of washing or cleaning up, and the kitchen messes continued to be left for me.

Mr. and Mrs. Reid did not return until long after I had settled the twins down for a third and final time and crawled up the back stairs and into my small, hot third-floor bedroom.

There were two sets of stairs leading to the central staircase landing, one for my lord and lady and their guests and one for the servant girl. Me. Mine was narrow, dark, enclosed, and pointless, I thought, because once I opened the door on the landing, I had to traverse the second floor, use the toilet there if that was permitted, as it was when Mr. Reid wasn't home, then take a second small dark enclosed stairway up to the third floor servants' quarters, two airless rooms.

"Eventually," Mrs. Reid told me the next morning, "Mr. Reid had said they would be able to afford full-time, paid, live-in help. But for now," she explained somewhat apologetically, "we have to settle for someone like you willing to work in exchange for room and board. After school starts in the fall, if you stay with us, we'll have to make allowances for your school schedule. And, of course, that means that I'll have no help available during the school day." I could tell as she sat mulling it over that if it were up to her, Mr. Reid would be persuaded to act expeditiously.

After their night out, Mr. Reid agreed to hire a lady to come in to do what Mrs. Reid called "the heavy work," washing walls and floors and windows.

All that left for me then were the dusting, sweeping, dust-mopping, bed-making, picking-up, washing and wiping dishes, helping with the twins . . . and washing clothes and the ironing.

It was a good thing I didn't have time to open the basement door to check on the state of the washing that first day. When I felt I could cope with one more job and did open the door leading from the kitchen down into what we would have called a cellar but what was, because of the rock foundation and finished floor, a lower, underground level, I almost threw up. And I came close to falling down the stairs, though nothing would have happened to me had I tripped and gone down because the stairs, every single step, and the floor all around the base of the stairs and most of the rest of the open area, not counting the enclosed storage closets and shelving, every single inch of space was covered with dirty clothing, all mixed up— sheets and towels and washcloths, his underwear and hers, the twins' soiled bedding and diapers and soiled garments . . . I still gag when I think of that moment when I met my nemesis.

I felt defeated before I even began.

But Mrs. Reid, standing behind me, holding her nose, offered a bit of good news. The city of Virginia had recently put to use a city-wide (well, South Side at least) system of steam heating with a huge central plant near Silver Lake not far from the railroad depot. Underground piping would, eventually, lead to every home and business in the city. It already led to the Reid's house. Thus, I had hot water aplenty at the turn of a faucet. In addition, Mr. Reid had purchased for his wife "The Best Hand-Power Washer" Sears, Roebuck & Co. made. I did not have to wash by hand. I just had to sort the clothing into piles, load the machine, get it going, put the wet clothes through the wringer and rinse them in side-by-side stationary tubs. If it were a nice day, I could hang the wet clothes on lines behind the garage. If not, lines had been hung from one end to the other of the basement.

Still, even with those conveniences, during the weeks that I lived with the Reids, I never got caught up with either the washing or the ironing. I did convince Mrs. Reid to put the diapers into a separate covered pail for me to rinse. I did make order of the initial chaos, filling the clothes lines outside and using the additional ones strung from wall to wall in the basement every single day until the piles diminished to the cycle of daily additions. Thanks to Ma's good example, I managed to get the white clothes almost white by generous additions of bluing. I knew how to make starch, adding cold water first to the correct amount of dry ingredient to form a smooth mixture, then adding boiling water to achieve the correct amount of stiffness, more for Mr. Reid's collars and the antimacassars that lined the backs of the chairs in the parlor and covered the side tables and the lace curtains that I fastened to the needle-like edges of curtain stretchers so that they dried so stiff and taut it was almost hard to re-hang them. More boiling water made a lighter starch for aprons, tablecloths, napkins, and housedresses. I carefully sorted the whites from the colored clothes, the heavily soiled from the pieces that just needed freshening, the hardy from the delicates, and ended with the rag throw-rugs.

But oh, the work!

It wasn't that I resented it or that Mrs. Reid was difficult to work for. The work was overwhelming by its sheer magnitude. The house was huge, the babies needy, the housekeeping process totally lacking the kind of system that had always enabled Ma to keep our home immaculately clean, tidy, and sweet-smelling. Except for those times when Pa was gone, our pantry overflowed with foodstuffs—crates of crackers and apples, canned venison and whitefish and berries of all kinds, staple items like flour and sugar purchased in bulk, and weekly replenished shelves of homemade bread, sweet Finnish *pulla*, cookies, pies, and cakes.

How Ma had managed, up until the last, I truly did not know, but I did know it took every ounce of energy I had to keep going during those weeks between my arrival at the Reid's and the time Mr. Reid finally hired full-time help. The woman he hired was Ma's age. When she asked me how much work there would be, I just shook my head, thankful that my time was up. When I filled my carpet bag for the last time, kissed the twins, who howled at the thought of my leaving, and gratefully accepted the paper money Mr. Reid forced upon me, I felt like a convict released from prison. For a good two months, I had not had one day off. I had not heard from Ma or from Margie. I had been worried sick about both of them . . . when I'd had the time. Mostly, I had been too much on the run to think about anything except what I had to do next.

"How are we going to manage without you?" Mrs. Reid lamented at the moment of my departure.

"How indeed," I thought with asperity, knowing one thing for sure. It wouldn't be easy.

CHAPTER TWENTY-TWO
Truth

Upstairs in my garret, I had daydreamed that a tall, dark, handsome stranger would throw pebbles at my window, ask me to throw down my hair so he could climb up, rescue me from serfdom, and carry me to his kingdom where we would live in love and peace and plenty for all of our lives. I would pay our servants extravagant salaries and house them in cottages with thatched roofs and window boxes and picket fences and gardens of flowers and all modern conveniences.

Of course, the window didn't open, and my hair was not blonde like Rapunzel's, and I was too young to marry anyone, but someday . . .

Just before I left, Mrs. Reid climbed the narrow flight of stairs to the third floor to give me an envelope that had just been delivered.

"Whew," she exclaimed. "I didn't realize how steep those steps are or how airless this room is. Why didn't you tell me the window didn't open? I'd have hired someone to make sure it did. You poor, dear child."

She looked at me as if she were seeing me for the first time. "You really have been a treasure to me, and I have truly appreciated it. I hope you know that." She joined me where I was sitting and gave me a real hug, not the kind an employer gives a servant. "Please keep in touch with me so I know how you're doing in school, where you decide to go, and let me know if you need a reference to get another job. I'll have Mr. Reid's secretary type one that will put you on top of any list of applicants!"

Then she remembered the note. "This just came from Dr. Malmstrom's office. The messenger said you should read it before you left Virginia." She rose quickly. "Oh, dear, I think I hear the twins stirring. I'll have to go." Then she looked around again. "We'll definitely have to do something about this room if we expect to keep any permanent help."

169

I bit my tongue, took the note, uttered a polite but not overly enthusiastic "thank you," took my carpetbag full of clean clothes, and left, walking right by the twins' door.

I skipped down the stairs and out the door, breathing an enormous sigh of relief. Even though I knew my next job would be at least as challenging because I would have schoolwork to fit into a twenty-four hour day, right then I felt as if I were five years old and could race down the sidewalk doing somersaults, skipping and hopping and playing hopscotch on the cracks and smelling the fresh air and seeing how much the flower gardens had grown and hugging the trees. I was free! Free! Free! Whirling in a circle, I called out to the obvious displeasure of two elderly ladies taking sedentary stroll, "Whee!"

Then I read the note.

"Dear Miss Marion," it began. "Please come to see me at my office as soon as you leave the Reids. I have a proposition, which I think will offer you great joy and satisfaction, and, your mother a peace of mind she has not known for more than thirteen years." It was signed "Sincerely, J. Arnold Malmstrom, M.D."

I read it twice and turned my footsteps from the Co-op Creamery where I had planned to meet Mr. Salin toward the hospital where Dr. Malmstrom had his offices.

It was very early in the day, partly because I had been anxious to go, and partly because I knew Mr. Salin began to pick up the huge containers of milk set by the roadside almost before the sun was up and completed his route to Virginia while the milk and cream were still warm from the cows.

Dr. Malmstrom's outer office was dark, and his nurse had not yet arrived, but there was a light on in his inner office so I knocked, but quietly in case he didn't want to be disturbed. Evidently he didn't, for a rather growly Papa-Bear voice asked, "Who's there?"

"It's me. I mean it is I," I corrected, remembering Miss Heino's lecture on narrative case for a predicate nominative following a linking verb, "Marion Brosi. Do you want . . ."

That was as far as I got before the door opened and I was enveloped in a "Papa Bear" hug. "And how are you, my small friend?" he asked, looking at me a bit anxiously. "I have . . . well, rather, my wife has . . . heard that you had quite a job with the Reid house and that you did very well creating organization out of chaos. People notice, you know. The iceman said that after you got there, the back steps were scrubbed as was the floor. The ice box had been wiped down and the pan cleaned of any drippings. All he had to do was put in the fresh ice. He told the iceman who delivers ice to our house that he felt he should take his shoes off because the entry rug was so clean. How about that, my small friend?"

Then he stood back. "I do not like the look of you, however. You are all eyes and hair. Didn't they feed you?"

My mouth twisted and so did my legs, and my hands drifted behind my back, and I answered honestly, "I'm afraid Mrs. Reid is still in the learning stages when it comes to cooking, and that has never been my strong suit, though Ma has tried to teach me. My cookies burn, my cakes fall, my *kropsua* usually doesn't rise. My bread is dry or has holes in it." I looked at him apologetically. "Ma and Margie have the knack. It just skipped right over me."

He laughed then said, "We need to do something about that."

Replacing his white coat with a suit jacket, he took my hand and walked me toward a restaurant. He made me order whatever I wanted, and I wanted everything but settled for crisp bacon—lots of it—and an omelet (because I didn't know what it was, and it sounded elegant) with cheese, and whole wheat toast with jam, which sounded healthy.

"Bring me coffee, lots of it. And for you, Marion?"

"Oh, yes, coffee, please."

The waiter put his pencil behind his ear, nodded pleasantly, said he would bring the coffee right away, and disappeared.

"Now, I must begin to call you 'Marion.' My 'Ilmi Marianna' has grown up."

I smiled. "I'm trying."

"But not too hard, I hope." He grew serious. "I didn't mean to be mysterious." Playing with his white cloth napkin, he folded and unfolded it while he talked, as if he wasn't quite sure how much to say. "But what I want you to do when you have eaten a good breakfast is to see your mother."

"Oh!" was all I could manage. Books always say "And her eyes were shining." I'm not sure if eyes can shine, but if they can, I know mine did.

"She's come a long way, a very long way. I'm extremely proud of her. She's followed our suggestions to the letter, even when it was difficult. We kept her informed about where Margie was and where you were and assured her that you were both safe and well. But we did not encourage her to delve further into your situations. This was her time. These were days set apart for her to concentrate on regaining her own strength, physically, mentally, and emotionally.

"Deep down, I think you know your mother has a tremendous well of strength of character, strength of purpose, and faith in herself. Our emphasis, Dr. Raihala's and mine was to help her to believe in a very simple statement: whatever life holds for her, she can face it. We have encouraged Mrs. Maki to help her remember times when she made decisions on her own, with no one to lean on, and to bring back to the surface of her mind all of the things she did to make those decisions workable and effective.

"In addition, Dr. Raihala and I urged her to grieve for the loss of Baby Teddy in every way. To cry. To scream at God for His cruelty. To explain over and over again that she was not at fault. She did nothing wrong. Had she been in the hospital with both of us handling the birthing process, we could have done no more than what Mrs. Aro did. Someday, I pray," he said somberly, "that medical science will progress to the point where these accidents can be prevented. We as physicians are not there yet.

"We talked about grief as a natural outgrowth of great love, for only those who love deeply are capable of grieving, of feeling the pain, and of growing so that the pain is accepted as a part of life, ever present, but no longer all-consuming. "Do you understand what I'm saying, Marion?"

"Yes. I think I do."

"But there's something else your mother needs to share with you. She is ready to do that now. So, after you eat well, I'll give you another address. Walk there slowly, thinking of your mother, seeking within yourself the strength you'll need to hear all that she has to say. I . . . wish that she . . . perhaps would wait . . . until you are a little older. But in many ways you are already 'grown up.' After she talks with you, if you need to, come to see me . . . or Dr. Raihala . . ."

"I'd rather see you."

"Thank you for your faith in me. You know, we doctors have doubts, too. We don't always have all the right answers, no matter how we try.

"But I know we could talk, as we are right now. No, *as* we are right now."

He grinned. "What did you say your teacher's name was?"

"Miss Heino."

"Remind me to send her a letter of commendation."

I had been eating while we had been talking, in between sentences and during pauses as we thought about what to say.

"Your plate is empty. I hope your tummy is full. It's time for us to be on our way. I'm late for work, and my poor nurse—the boss—will be beside herself. Here's the address. See me afterward if you need to. Otherwise, you could stay with Mrs. Maki and your mother overnight if you wish, or here"—he dug in his pocket and pulled out some paper money—"is enough, I think, for you to catch the Duluth & Missabi back to Zim if you are anxious to get home. Give your mother my best." He left more paper money and some change on the table, and we walked outside. "And try not to take on the world, Miss Marion."

I waved good-bye as I read the address. It was, as I had known it would be, on North Side. "Thank you for the breakfast!" I called after him.

Waving an arm, he hollered back a "You're welcome!"

"Silver Lake" must have been named at this time of the day, I thought, rejoicing in the freedom to cross the bridge I had crossed more than a year ago to enter a gypsy camp in search of help. I had needed courage then. Deep inside, I sensed I needed as much or more now as I headed for the slight hill that marked the beginning of North Side, not Finntown, but what Ma called "Italia vitsi"—the place where the Italians lived. But this address was just barely within the confines of "town." The house lay on the border, facing a park with trees and swings and a fountain. I had heard that at night when the fountain threw rainbows around a broad central circle, the water was colored—red and green and blue. How beautiful that must be! I was thinking. And as I looked up, I saw Ma sitting in a swing on the porch of a large white Victorian house with a wrap-around porch filled with plants and flowers.

She looked as if she belonged there, rested and restful, waiting for me to join her.

When she saw me coming around the corner of the house, she jumped up and ran to meet me, half laughing and half crying, "Ilmi, Ilmi, Ilmi," she repeated over and over, as I stammered, "Oh, Ma, it's so good to see you!"

Stepping back, I looked at her. "You look . . . like Ma!" I exclaimed.

"I am Ma, back again from . . . somewhere else," she said simply, "and almost ready to go home."

She told me to sit down while she got us each lemonade from the kitchen.

I was hot and sweaty, and a glass of something cool sounded just right, just what Ma would think of to help me cool off and relax. When she came back, we sat still for a while and sipped. She asked if I had had breakfast. "Oh, yes, Dr. Malmstrom made sure of that. I ate so much I could hardly walk the first few blocks. Now I feel good."

"He's a good man." Those were the words, but they sounded like no more than a lead-in to what she wanted to tell me.

"I have felt for the last several weeks that this is the time for me to share with you the true story of your conception and birth, and he, of course, listened and honored my judgment and my feelings. He agreed that, although you are still very young, that very youth might help you to come to terms with this."

Finishing my lemonade, I set the glass down and turned to give her my full attention.

She took my hand and held it, patting it now and then and looking at me and then away. "This is so very difficult," she finally said, "but I will not be at peace until it is done."

CHAPTER TWENTY-THREE
Ma's Story

It all began when we were aboard ship, coming to America, our hopes and dreams keeping us steadfast in spite of the abominable conditions we faced aboard. We tried to keep clean, but there were so many of us in such a small space that it was impossible. Can you imagine living for five weeks with only sponge baths, saunas, no clean water, not washing your hair in all that time, never having a chance to clean your good clothes, watching them get all wrinkled and moldy?"

I shook my head. I could imagine it. It sounded horrible, especially for Ma, who strove for cleanliness in her person and in her surroundings.

"Ma, when I asked Pa directly if I were his daughter, and if he were my pa and he said 'yes.' I don't think he would lie. Does what you need to tell me have something to do with that? Is he my father, or was he lying because it was what I wanted to hear?"

"Oh, he'd lie all right if it suited his purpose. Maybe he thought you were too ill to hear the truth. He wouldn't hesitate to lie when it's something to do with the sacred Brosi name. The dates he put into the Bible, however, are correct. He could not lie there. You were born on March 19, 1910. We were married on May 4th, 1910. It would have been possible for him to be your father. But he isn't. He doesn't know the whole story. No one does, except me. And now you. You deserve the truth."

That shook me to my core. Gritting my teeth, I said, "Please, then, Ma, tell me the whole of it. I'm strong enough to stand whatever it is."

She smiled ruefully as she shook her head. "I shall start at the beginning. When I got off the boat and went through the registration lines, believe it or not I got the job because I looked so awful. After I registered as Mary Rajamaki, a gentleman came to talk to me. He asked if I had a family or plans or if I were looking for work."

"I tried as we crossed the ocean from Liverpool, England, to study English the best I could so I had picked up a few words. 'Work, I work hard,' I told him.

"He spoke to me in a loud, slow voice, the kind one uses with someone who is short of wit. He told me that he was the senior assistant to Mr. Charles Young of Boston and had been assigned to come there to hire an upstairs maid. I understood that I would have my own room or share with one other woman servant. My task would be to clean the upstairs bedrooms. There were three on the second floor and two with a sitting room and nursery on the third floor. 'Would you be interested?' he asked. 'Is there something of yours that we need to get?'

"I told him that I had a trunk with the name Mary Rajamaki. I remember telling him that I would work hard. I would scrub and keep everything very clean. Then I asked him if I would get paid.

"'Yes, of course,' he began to sound impatient. He motioned to a young man who by magic had my trunk in front of us. We drove from New York to Boston in an automobile. It was called a Ford. Oh, how fast it went!

"When we got there, I was brought in to see Mrs. Young. She shuddered, told me to take a bath and clean myself thoroughly and then ring for Mrs. Christopherson, the housekeeper. She told me that Sarah, the downstairs maid, would help me become accustomed to my duties. But she ordered me to clean myself first, as if I enjoyed being a dirty, wrinkled, unwashed mess. I wished I had known how to tell her how badly I wanted to be clean, but I did not have the words.

"The servants' quarters had its own bathrooms, one for the women, one for the men, with showers so that I could wash. I washed and washed and washed until my skin was red, but I felt clean all over. Sarah, the downstairs maid, showed me how to put on the white cap and cuffs, the plain black dress that reached almost to my ankles and the white apron. Sara did not speak Finnish, but with gestures and my use of the few words at my disposal, we managed to get through that, and I was introduced to Mrs. Christopherson, who was in charge of handling the staff. I would not, Sarah said, see Mrs. Young again unless I broke something or misused my time or had to be disciplined in some way. None of those meanings came out clearly. I had to pick up words and try to figure out in Finnish what I was being told in English. But I think that's close to how my work began.

"Next came a tour of the whole house but especially the second and third floors of the mansion. For the first few days, Sarah helped me with the bedrooms, and I enjoyed cleaning them because they were so beautiful. I lemon oiled the mahogany bed posts, the dressers and tables and arms of the chairs. Every week I changed the doilies and the antimacassars. But I lifted the doilies every day to dust underneath and then replaced everything. If it were glass, like a picture or a knick-knack, I had to wash it—oh, and the windows, too—with ammonia and vinegar, and when the lace curtains began to look limp—they were crocheted underneath with heavy velvet pulls for cold weather or the evening—I sent them to the laundry.

"Mr. and Mrs. Young's room was a bed-sitting room where they often spent evenings together with her doing handwork or reading and him with some ledgers or business concerns. All through the second and third floors, I had to empty book cases periodically and wipe the books and shelves. Every week, I used the carpet sweeper on the floors where they were carpeted and scrubbed and waxed what were not.

"Both of the young gentlemen had similar rooms, but they were rarely home. Mr. Arthur was attending Oxford University in England, and Mr. Charles was at Bowdoin College in Maine. Charles . . . came home . . . quite often . . . for vacations and all through the summer."

When Ma paused, I waited for her to tell the story in her own time without interrupting, especially now when she paused because I was sure that Charles figured largely in the denouement, and suddenly I was frightened. It felt as if Ma needed a time out.

Although the morning was warm, Ma asked me to bring her a shawl that lay on a chair facing the swing, upholstered in colorful chinz materials.

"Mrs. Maki went to do some grocery shopping this morning. She wanted me to have this time alone with you."

I wrapped the shawl around her and took her hand again. I was amazed at how beautiful she looked, with her hair washed and carefully arranged in a pompadour. She had gained some weight, but it was not fat. She was still slender, but underneath I felt strength. I smiled to myself because she was wearing trousers, which she never did, with an exquisitely crocheted sweater on top. She had lost twenty years during these weeks, and she looked so lovely that the tears collected behind my eyes, and I reached over to hold her close again before she drew back, ready to continue.

"The girls' rooms—oh, I wish you could have seen them—were so beautiful that cleaning them was just joy. Miss Julia's was all in blue and white with small accents of pink; Miss Amelia's was pink and white with accents of blue. It took hours every day to do these rooms. Each girl had her own dressing room with a full-length mirror and two sides of hangers of clothes and drawers of underclothing and sweaters. Each had her own bathroom too. I had to clean the tub, wipe down the shower curtain, clean the toilet—Imagine. an inside toilet!—wash the sink and the mirror, and scrub the floor. Anything soiled was dropped down a chute that led to the laundry room in the basement.

"There was some jealousy because I was higher on the servant list than a scullery maid or an assistant in the kitchen or those who did the laundry, but I had looked so awful that Mr. Young's assistant had thought there would be no trouble with the boys playing around or anyone bothering me because I had looked like such a mess when he saw me on Ellis Island."

"Then the problem was one of the boys, Ma?"

She clasped her hands together tightly. "I rarely saw the girls. I hurried to do their rooms quickly while they were downstairs in the breakfast room and practicing their piano, voice, water-color, and harp lessons downstairs.

"The nursery was left for a superficial cleaning perhaps, once a week since it was not used. Mrs. Christopherson said that when the children married and came home, there would be a place for the grandchildren. Similarly, the small bedroom assigned to the nurse or governess was closed off and cleaned infrequently though it would be used at some time in the future. It was said that Miss Julia was keeping company with a young son of friends of the Youngs, but that Miss Amelia wanted to go to a School of Nursing, which was causing her parents a good deal of distress, Sarah told me. She loved to hear about the Youngs—where they were going and whom they entertained and what plans were being made for the children.

At that point, Ma's emotion overcame some of her coherence, and the words began to run together. "Charles, when he was home from college, used his own big room with a bath adjoining his and Arthur's rooms . . . he was . . . very kind to me . . . when I was cleaning . . . he asked about Finland and about the passage over . . . and about my dreams of opening a shop for women who wanted their dresses custom made . . . he would pull my apron strings or pick at my cap to see if he could get it loose.

"Once he followed me upstairs, and he put his hands . . . on my legs . . . and said . . . I shouldn't have to wear . . . a long dress . . . because my legs were so perfect.

"I didn't know what to do. I tried telling Sarah, but she said that if I told Mrs. Christopherson and she told Mrs. Young, I would be fired. That had happened with the last upstairs maid who was just too pretty. She was the reason Mr. Arthur was sent to Oxford. When I was washing the windows or the mirrors, Charles would come up behind me and put his hands around my waist and ask how I stayed so slim. Once when I was scrubbing the floor and waxing it with both hands at work, he pulled my small cap off and took all the pins from my hair and pulled it down to see how long it was. When I stood up, it fell below my hips, and he caressed it. Oh, it felt so good to have someone massage my temples and, taking his own brush, he brushed it down over and over again. It felt too good for me to make him stop.

"I knew, Ilmi Marianna. I knew that I should not have let him do those things, but I was so starved for friendship and for affection . . . for someone to pay attention to me. The rest of the staff spoke English, so even when we ate together, I felt like an outsider. And it did not help that as I ate well and worked hard and was able to keep myself clean, I came to look . . . more like myself. Some of the young men on staff wanted to become . . . more friendly than was appropriate, and I had to deal with that. The other maids did not appreciate how I looked, either. I had been given a job which many of them had wanted, and the reason for which I had been given the job had proved itself false."

I really didn't need to have her tell me the rest. I could put one and one together and make three. But I desperately needed to know how I could have been born in Port Arthur and Fort William and how and why she had married Pa.

Closing her eyes for a moment, she paused, saying, "And now we get to the hardest parts." She kept her eyes closed as she said, "It . . . seemed as if it became natural for Charles to pat me as I went about my work . . . I appreciated . . . being touched . . . with kindness . . . and then . . . it just seemed . . . natural . . . for him to kiss me . . . just light kisses . . . and I kissed him back . . . and we kissed more and more and then kissing wasn't enough.

"He told me that I was too pretty and too intelligent to have to do this kind of menial work. It was wonderful to know that someone believed in me and in my dreams. One day I was changing the bed. We changed both top and bottom sheets almost every day. Downstairs there was a room with a special drying system and a round machine called a mangle where the laundresses could iron a whole sheet one section at a time. Still, it was a lot of work, and I felt bad for them. But it was their job. And I had my job. I could hear the sheets as they slid down the laundry chute."

She rubbed her eyes and asked if I wanted some coffee. Again, there was a pause.

"That day he started to help me make the bed. But he was so inept at pulling it tightly and making square corners that I had to laugh, and he was laughing and suddenly it seemed natural for him to hold me and then the holding became serious . . . and we really kissed . . . and he rubbed my back and said again that I should not have to do this . . . and then he was taking off my cap and letting my hair down, and taking off my collar and cuffs and saying that once we were married I would never wear collars and cuffs again."

Houses were small in those years, and privacy a premium. Children grew up understanding the relationship between male and female animals . . . and humans.

"You don't have to go on, Ma. I can tell this is very hard for you, and you could finish some other time." Ma was shaking by this time, and I was terribly afraid of her falling back into dark days.

"Yes, I do," she answered fiercely, "because I don't want you to think your father didn't love me or want you.

"That was the first time. He always assured me that as soon as he graduated from college, we would be married, and I could have the shop I dreamed of, or we would hire our own maids to do the work, and I would be a lady of leisure.

"Then came a time when I did not get my period. When he came home late that July for summer vacation and I told him, he was so excited, he twirled me around and around and around until I was dizzy and said we were only a few months early.

"I will go straight down to father," he said, "and tell him that we need to be married now so our child would be born in wedlock."   " I ' l l soften him up and then come and get you," he said, squeezing my hands and looking as happy and excited as I had ever seen him. He kissed me on the cheek and said, "All will be well. Don't worry. And for heaven's sake stop cleaning!

"I sat down on a leather chair in his room to wait. Things were very quiet at first. Then I heard some shouting, and I couldn't wait upstairs.

"I heard Mr. Young's voice: 'WHAT? YOU INTEND TO MARRY OUR MAID? HAVE YOU LOST YOUR MIND? YOU HAVE ONE YEAR LEFT AT BOWDOIN, AND HOW EXACTLY HOW, PRAY TELL, DO YOU EXPECT TO SUPPORT YOURSELF AND A WIFE?'

"'I have mother's trust fund, which is solely mine,' Charles began.

"'That,' his father responded, 'comes into your hands when you have graduated from college OR when I believe you have reached the age of majority. Obviously you are still responding to life as if you were a White Knight saving the beautiful, and of course, willing damsel from distress. I want to see her.'

"By that time I had crept to the doorway of the library, and when I peeked in I could see Mr. Young's eyes. They reminded me of pictures I had seen of a snake's eyes—obsidian. Black.

"'IF YOU PUT ONE FOOT OUT OF THIS HOUSE WITH HER, YOU WILL NEVER SET FOOT IN THIS HOUSE AGAIN, NOR WILL YOU RECEIVE ONE CENT OF MONEY FROM ME OR FROM YOUR MOTHER'S TRUST OF WHICH I AM THE EXECUTOR, AND, IN ADDITION, YOU WILL BREAK YOUR MOTHER'S HEART.'

"Charles was sitting in the brown leather chair opposite his father's desk. He was white as a sheet with his hands over his eyes and his elbows on his knees.

"'GET HER IN HERE.' Then his father's voice softened. 'Son,' he said, 'that's what all of these young women dream of happening. They want to get a good job in a wealthy home, marry the son of the house, and live happily ever after on his money. Well, I'll tell you, this piece will not use you. You did wrong. But you cannot tell me you got her pregnant by force. She must have been very willing. She was, wasn't she? She went right along with you, didn't she?' His voice rose again. 'You are not going to ruin your whole life by marrying a . . . servant.'"

How that must have hurt! She had remembered that speech word for word for fourteen years.

When Charles saw her at the door, he had gone to take her hand, to tell her that his father was against their marriage, and to protect her if he could. He had drawn her into his father's study, intending to explain.

Instead, his father took over. "I'll make it easy for you to leave," his father said to Ma, pulling out his money pouch. "What's it worth, getting rid of you? I'm on the board of the Rutland Sanitarium. I can get you a job there so that you're able to support yourself and enough money so that you can care for you and the child once it is born. Perhaps five hundred dollars? A thousand?"

Feeling faint, Ma said she had leaned against Charles, hoping this was a bad dream that could still turn out for the best.

"I'll call for a drink of water for you," Charles had said, ringing a bell.

"You see," his father had told Ma, his eyes narrow as slits, "Charles - doesn't even know how to get water without help. How do you expect him to function in an apartment without a staff to wait on him? He doesn't know any other kind of life."

Ma, still reliving that scene, continued, "I have always been proud of what I did then. I threw the money back in Mr. Young's face and said I would leave for Rutland immediately, but I would take no money. 'I'm no whore!' I said. I don't think he even heard me. Or understood me. Under such stress, I'm afraid I reverted to Finnish. I think all he understood was the action and perhaps the word 'whore.'

"'That's up for debate,' his father had said sarcastically, and then, 'Charles, you will take the next ship to England where Arthur can watch over you until you come to your senses.'

"'Woman,' he said to me, 'I want you out of the house NOW! CHARLES,' as Charles began to get up, 'SIT DOWN AND DO NOT LOOK AT OR TOUCH HER AGAIN!'"

Ma said she stopped long enough to tell Charles with her hands and a touch of her lips that she loved him, and then she left forever.

"The work at Rutland Sanitarium was too heavy for a woman who was having a difficult pregnancy. Remember how it was with Baby Teddy?"

I nodded.

"So I wrote to the only relative I knew how to get a hold of, my cousin Betty in Port Arthur, Ontario. I told her exactly what had happened and asked her for help. What a woman she was! Do you remember her at all? She sent one of her brothers, Jack Wirtanen and a friend of his—Knute Brosi—to Rutland to make sure I was all right."

Ma swallowed hard and forced herself to continue, not looking at me but looking at a past that she had worked for almost fourteen years to forget. "When they came, I consciously seduced Knute. I was still very slender and," she paused, "attractive. Knute was susceptible to flattery. Jack was so overwhelmed by the size of the sanitarium and the complexity of the journey that he spent almost no time with us. I prayed I could convince Knute that the baby, to be born in March, was his.

"It was a foul act. I remember hating every touch. I just kept telling myself that my baby needed a father, that the alternative was that you would be born a 'bastard.' The Finnish community is small and irrevocable in its condemnation of those who act beyond the pale. Knute was my only hope. He and Jack wanted me to come to Port Arthur with them, but I refused.

"Deep inside I still thought that Charles would somehow come and spirit me away to the dream world we had created together. My hopes were dashed in December when I received a picture post card of a park in Worcester, Massachusetts. It was addressed to 'Mary Rajamaki, Rutland Sanitarium, Rutland, Massachusetts.' There was no message, no return address, but lightly in ink across the bottom of the picture were the words, 'How are you in Rutland tonight?' That was the only message I ever received from your real father. One of the matrons slipped it to me in a way that suggested that other letters had been destroyed. At any rate, it effectively shattered all of my hopes. Before it was too late, I had to leave, and by then I had set aside enough money to get to Port Arthur/Fort William."

This time Ma could not hold back her tears, and I was sobbing, too.

"But how and why Ma, did you marry Knute Brosi?"

"It was a terrible mistake. The cousin I had written to, Betty Wainio, lived in the Port Arthur/Fort William area of Ontario, Canada. I had just enough money to get to her. The Finnish community there had turned a boxcar into a sauna, and that's where you were born—in a boxcar on a railroad siding outside of Port Arthur."

"'Betty took a survey of the bachelors in the Finnish community there and chose Knute for me. She mistook a man of culture who loved music and literature as a good candidate for a husband. Neither of us got what we wanted. He wanted a wife who would cook his meals and keep his house clean and let him come and go as he pleased. I wanted a real home and was willing to work to get it. I was willing to try with all my heart to forget Charles and find a way to love Knute. He was a handsome man, well-spoken.

"But the vows I gave him were false. I've loved Charles all these years, and Knute knows that I was pregnant and had a three-month-old child when we married. He wanted the story I have never shared with him. But I had to marry. How would we have been treated—a single woman with a child? Think of that child we tried to help in Virginia. I could not take a chance on your being treated like that.

"And we both have loved you. You think your pa doesn't care about you, but he does, very much. That's why he's so critical. He wants you to be perfect. But he doesn't know how to love. I've loved you all your life, at first because every time I looked at you, I saw Charles and then for you yourself. If Charles's father had ever seen you, our lives would have been very different. But Charles was too young and too easily influenced, and I was too proud."

"And Pa has been too proud to let himself love me completely because he is sure that I am not really 'his.'"

"As a couple, we were doomed from the start. You were obviously, that March, a full-term baby. I've never told this story to any other living person."

I felt as limp and worn as Ma looked. She said, "I think we need some more lemonade, or perhaps some lunch. I think I hear Mrs. Maki in the kitchen."

She tried to stand up alone, but sank back down onto the swing, white and lost in memories that, as she recounted them, drained her of strength and energy.

At first, I blamed myself. I should have stopped her when I saw how difficult it was for her to go on.

Trying to make her laugh, I wondered, "What would happen if some day I went to Boston to the Young house and introduced myself as Mr. Young's granddaughter?"

I succeeded in making her smile. "That would be the confrontation of the century." Then she sobered. "I've always wished for a way to let Charles know about you." She touched my hair and my cheeks. "You are so like him—all black hair and green eyes, full of spunk, ready to look at society's rules which say, 'You may not,' and ask, 'Why?'

"Some day you'll tell your own daughter the truth." she whispered, the tears flowing again.

"Now, now," said Mrs. Maki, coming out of the house with a dish cloth in her hands. "Here I have a lunch all prepared for my guests, and they are busy watering the plants."

We stood up, hugged each other tightly, and went inside to make small talk with Mrs. Maki and eat a delicious chicken salad with homemade rolls and iced tea.

"Dr. Malmstrom gave me enough money to take the train home to Zim," I mentioned, as we were finishing the dessert of Danish kringle with almonds.

"Oh, dear," said Mrs. Maki. "I'm not sure when the last train leaves. Hurry, Ilmi. Leave the dishes. Your ma and I will worry about them, and she'll rest a bit this afternoon. Wait a few days. Then come back with Margie. Your ma may be ready to go home with you then. We'll consult with Dr. Malmstrom and see."

I kissed and hugged Ma and thanked her, assuring her that she had been right to tell me her story.

"There are no words to thank you adequately, Mrs. Maki," I said, as I lifted my carpet bag and ran out the door toward the depot.

"No thanks are necessary, child," she called after me. "It has been delightful to have a new friend and to help her find herself again."

I made it to the depot just as the train was pulling out. The ticket master said I could buy my ticket from the conductor and helped me climb aboard the last set of stairs.

It felt as if a part of my life had ended, and I knew I needed a respite. Our little half-house in Zim sounded like paradise, and believe it or not, I could not wait to see Margie.

CHAPTER TWENTY-FOUR
Winter Plans

Ma stayed with Mrs. Maki for about a month longer. The highlights of the weeks for Margie and me were our visits with her.

But it was amazing how well we got along when we were home together. One night when it was too hot to asleep, we discussed our relationship.

Margie admitted she had resented me. "You're the older one so I've had to obey you the way I do Ma and Pa. That doesn't seem fair. We're sisters."

"I haven't felt good about having to take care of you either. I've thought you were spoiled. I always hated it when I was disciplined when you had done something wrong. I bet I've heard Ma say, 'You should have been watching her because you're older' a thousand times."

We really didn't fall asleep that night until the coolness of dawn crept in through the window screens and a vague, hazy brush-stroke of pink touched the eastern sky. While we were talking, we started doing with each other what we so often did with Ma. When we were especially good or when Ma felt especially loving, she would untangle our hair and brush it gently from the scalp to the ends or she would tickle our backs. So we did the same thing. We took turns tickling each other's backs and brushing each other's hair. I couldn't find the words to express how restful and how loving it felt.

That night we turned the corner of our relationship and began the process of being soul-sisters even if we were only half-sisters. I explained to her what Ma had told me about her and Pa, leaving out those areas that needed to wait until she was older.

After that night, when we disagreed or threatened to be crabby, we penalized each other with five minutes less of hair brushing or back-tickling. If we worked together well or did something extra nice, the reward was five or ten minutes of extra.

Our days fell into a pattern with Margie doing the cooking and me doing the housework. In the late afternoon or evening, we sometimes went to Salins' or Aros' for sauna. Sometimes we went for a walk. Sometimes we just lay in bed and read aloud. I finished the last chapters of *Ivanhoe* which Kabe had been reading aloud to everyone who wanted to listen the previous summer in Kinney. Then Margie read to me, and we made flashcards of the words she didn't know. I didn't push her too hard because I wanted her to enjoy it too.

In short, we shared the household chores and reached a point, except for how much we missed Ma, that our little house stayed spotless. Meals were delightfully original, with breakfast sometimes at supper and supper at breakfast. My favorite suppers were *kropsua* or thin pancakes or bread dipped in egg and fried in butter. Mrs. Aro called it "French toast."

All in all, it was a Happy House. Only since it was only part of a house, Margie labeled it "Happy Corner." The label stuck.

At night after reading, we talked.

"Was it my fault that Baby Teddy died?" Margie asked. She hid her head under the pillow, fearing the answer.

"It was no one's fault," I told her. "It was one of those things that just happen."

We talked a lot about Pa, too—the things he did to hurt us and the beautiful sounds he could make—poetry with his pen and music with his fiddle. Neither of us understood him though we agreed that he preferred Margie.

"I'll make it up to you, Ilmi," Margie said. And I believed she'd try.

We were busiest of all during berry picking season, but we made picnic treats for our expeditions and, thanks to Mrs. Aro's directions, made jam out of part of the results and ate our fill of the extra. Margie made strawberry shortcake, blueberry pie and muffins, and pancakes. She made rhubarb pie with eggs like custard, and regular rhubarb pie.

My favorite was the raspberry season because they were so easy to pick and so abundant. We made glass after glass of raspberry jam, ate it on the homemade bread, combined it with chocolate to make the very best raspberry-rhubarb cake. And every night we tickled backs, brushed hair, and became more and more like sisters.

All we knew of Ma was what we observed when we visited her. The changes were subtle, but we could see them. We always had a lot to tell her, so much that she teased us that we didn't need her at home anymore.

"Oh, Ma, we do!" we said. "It isn't really home unless we're together. We bought a lock and a hook and eye so that no one can surprise us by coming in uninvited." Of course, we all knew we meant Pa.

And finally, the week came when Ma said she was coming home with us for good.

"I have a suggestion for this fall," she said. "But I want to find the right time to broach the subject. How you are doing with your lessons is a critical question."

She looked at Margie, but I answered for her. "At first I read to her every night. Now we take turns reading."

Margie burst out, excited, ". . . and I make flashcards of the words I don't know so I can study them."

"I've kept up with my reading lists from Miss Loney and Miss Heino, too, Ma. Flashcards and everything."

"And we count!" Margie's exuberance was infectious. "When I hang clothes pins on the line and take them down, I do addition and subtraction, and Ilmi promises to teach me to multiply and divide." Her voice was full of excitement and pride.

"Then, perhaps, oh, dear, I'm not sure . . ." Ma hesitated. "I have to give you credit, Margie, for being so responsible for continuing to learn, and to you, Ilmi, for continuing to help and encourage her. Margie," she asked gravely, "would you continue to study and work to learn even if Ilmi weren't there?"

"Yes. I think so. It's like a game. Ilmi has made it . . . almost fun. Well, sometimes, anyway."

We begged her to tell us right away, but she just murmured, "I need to think this through more. Please don't tease. I have to decide if it is right for me and then if it is right for all of us . . ."

But finally one morning she asked us to sit down and told us that she was ready to ask us a very important question: "Would you be willing to take off one full year of school, Margie?"

Margie's eyes sparkled, and she jumped up and down.

Was she going to ask the same thing of me? I feared, holding my breath. Ma continued to look at Margie.

"Let me explain. Mrs. Maki is distantly related to Jennie Johnson, Mrs. Alfred Johnson. Jennie lives in Alango with her husband and ten children. Willmar, the oldest, is going to enlarge his logging operation this winter near

Cusson, and he needs a cook. It is not a big camp. Perhaps ten to fifteen men. I don't know whether I could manage that all myself, but if you came with me, we could work together. That would divide the effort in half. Mrs. Maki said she would recommend us and suggested that Mr. Johnson stop here to see if he would approve of us as cooks during this winter's logging season. What do you think?"

Margie was virtually bouncing at the thought of having a year away from school. "Ilmi could send books with me and write down assignments, and I would work hard to learn, and I could help you, Ma, by making bread, and learn some of your recipes. Oh, it would be such fun, and we would will be together!"

"But . . . what about me?" I asked in a hollow voice. The words came from so deep in my soul that I feared to voice them. Ma wouldn't ask me to go to a logging camp instead of to school, would she? And if she did, could I refuse her? She might not be strong enough to do everything that would be asked of her.

With all my heart, I wanted to begin my high school years in September.

Ma looked at me sympathetically. "Ilmi," she said slowly, "I considered asking this of you, too, but I cannot. I know this is your time to begin the next step in your education, and not for the world would I stand in your way."

My relief was palpable. I almost melted into the bed.

"There are two things, however, that need to be done before we can make definite plans for the winter. First, I have to pass a test to see if Mr. Johnson and his father think me a good enough cook. And secondly, we need to find you a school and a place to work."

"I know it may seem selfish, but I don't know what I would do if I - couldn't go on to school."

She gave me a kiss. "Don't you think I know that, Ilmi? You have worked and sacrificed and in every way earned it. We'll address how we'll set that into action after we get this logging camp business settled."

"What do you have to do, Ma?" I worried that she wouldn't be strong enough.

"First of all, I'll tell you what Margie and I do not have to do. Mr. Johnson, the owner, has already hired a 'bull cook.' It's a funny name, but the bull cook doesn't cook at all. He just makes our work a lot easier. It's his job to keep the bunkhouse clean. He keeps the stoves going and the lamps clean and full, the bunkhouse lamps lighted in the morning and hot water brought to the men so they can wash. We don't have to wash the men's clothes either. He washes the towels and keeps the wash basins clean. Oh, and if we are hired, Mr. Johnson will build a new room off the kitchen for us."

"In other words, the bull cook is the one who takes care of the men, right, Ma?" Margie asked.

"Not only them. In the morning he hauls wood both for the bunkhouse and for the kitchen. It's part of his responsibility to get the kitchen stove going and to fill two large barrels of water, one hot and one cold."

"He has to work really hard," Margie commented, impressed.

"Yes, well, he also has to keep the paths shoveled, the wood carried, and the right kind of wood available so that the bunkhouse is warm and so we can have the best of our choice of wood for cooking."

"Maybe that's what's wrong with me, Margie. It's always the wrong kind of wood when I cook!"

Margie got serious then. Sometime she amazed me with her sensible practical view of life. Of course the primary concern we still had not addressed. "What do we do, Ma?"

"I have asked everyone I've met, everyone who has visited or worked at a lumber camp, and they all say about the same thing—Make 'good solid food.' Pies for sure, made from canned or dried berries or prunes or raisins, potatoes, lots of them, and gravy."

"My gravy doesn't lump," Margie asserted. It wasn't bragging. It was a fact.

"Oh, there are lots of jobs I can set aside for you." Ma smiled.

"Let's see. On hand we have to have prunes, raisins, peas, salt pork and beans, baking powder, dried apples, peaches and apricots, rice, barley, macaroni, and tapioca. Mr. Johnson said that he'll have them shipped in dried. He'll also be responsible for getting fresh rutabagas, potatoes, cabbage, and carrots. Oh! We'll also have canned milk, tomatoes, and maybe corned beef and sometimes bacon and ham. I think a lot will depend on what is available and what he can afford."

"But before we are hired, we have to go through a kind of test."

Margie and I waited, eyes wide.

"Mr. Johnson, that's Mr. Willmar Johnson, the owner of the logging camp, and his father, Mr. Alfred Johnson, are coming here tomorrow to see how we keep house and to sample our cooking."

Margie grinned. She obviously looked forward to baking and showing off the results.

"I'll make two loaves of bread and a pan of rolls and *pulla*. We have fresh jam," said Margie and got up to get going.

"I'll do the pastry. What kind of pie?" Ma asked.

Margie and I answered in unison—"Raisin because men like that."

"I can do a pound cake if you watch me and give me directions," I offered.

"Ilmi, you can also put the split peas on to soften overnight. Tomorrow morning you can add the potatoes and carrots and brown salt pork into a kind of *mojakka*."

The house was already in flawless shape so all we needed to do in the morning was to do a quick dusting, sweep, shake the rugs, and make the bed.

A little after noon the two Mr. Johnsons got out of their car (They owned a car!). Willmar looked like the kind of lumberman who worked for months without drinking a drop of liquor and then drank himself insensible. Heavy-set, his complexion was ruddy, his nose red, and he wore the standard work outfit from Sears & Roebuck—dark green pants and shirt, suspenders, and laced boots which he did wipe carefully on the outside rug.

The elder Mr. Johnson, who insisted that we call him Alfred, was no more than five feet tall. He looked like a pixie in a plaid shirt, work pants, carefully cleaned boots, and a dress hat with a wide brim. When he took off his hat, we could see that he was bald, but his baldness was far overshadowed by bright, sharp, blue eyes, and a big nose.

"Every man who is a man has a big nose," he informed us. Not until his father removed his hat did Willmar follow suit, and for perhaps Alfred's fifty words, one came from Willmar, who said we should call him Bill.

"I'd like you to meet my daughters Margie and—she paused—Marion."

Alfred told us that Bill was the oldest of ten children and that he had a son named Emil Cliffert, who was just my age. "But he'll be going to school this winter."

"I graduated from eighth grade this May," I explained, "and I'll be going to high school wherever I can find a place to work for my room and board."

Blushing, I stopped. He probably didn't even care. I always did that—talked too much and over-explained.

By then Ma had dinner ready and served them their choice of hot bread or rolls fresh from the oven, a thick *mojakka* with potatoes, rutabaga, onions, garlic, and chunks of canned venison. Margie had made a brown gravy of the sauce, which smelled delicious. The only thing we had borrowed for the dinner was buttermilk from the Salins. The dessert included my pound cake, raisin pie, and coffee.

When they had finished the last piece of pie, reached for a toothpick, and leaned back in their chairs, Bill said, "You're hired."

"Maybe you could just move in with us and do the cooking," teased Alfred. "My Jennie, she's prettier than Jesus' strawberries, but she doesn't like to cook, so the girls never learned."

"I hope you won't mind if Margie comes with me to the camp," Ma said, very firmly. The old Ma was definitely back again. "Margie made the bread and rolls. I only made the pie, the *mojakka*, and the coffee."

"You're both hired," said Bill.

"And, say, why don't you stop at our house and give my girls a lesson or two on your way to the camp? We live on Highway 22 right on the way to Highway 73, which leads through Orr to Cusson. The camp's maybe fifteen miles in toward Elephant Lake," Alfred offered. "Jennie'd pay you with a rug."

"We would enjoy cooking a meal even without the rug," Ma answered, "though I would much appreciate a new rug from a good loom. Are you sure she wouldn't resent our doing that?"

"Nope. She'd be too busy making rugs. We'll do an exchange," Alfred affirmed. "And bring Marion, too, so she can meet my girls. We can arrange to get her back to . . . wherever she is going to go to school."

"All right," Ma answered.

It was the funniest thing to listen to their conversation since both of them spoke and used a little English, sprinkled into a framework of Finnish.

Ma hugged both of us when they left. The winter would be full and busy . . . and safe for both her and Margie.

"Tomorrow we'll take your future in hand, Miss Marion Brosi," Ma teased.

I didn't smile. My tummy turned flip-flops and butterflies invaded my insides.

It would have been much easier just to go to the logging camp.

CHAPTER TWENTY-FIVE
Mt. Iron

he next day was my day. Ma made that clear from the beginning. By the time I woke up, she had already shipped Margie to Salin's, and she was donning her very best clothes and doing her hair in its most elaborate pompadour.

It was fun to lie quietly for a while and watch her because it was such a joy to have the old Ma back. The old Ma did everything efficiently and quickly. She never hurried, but she didn't dawdle, either.

This lady who was readying herself to help me approach my future was the mother I had always known until she became pregnant with Baby Teddy. This was the mother who swore equally fluently in Finnish and in English, although her use of English languished in other ways. This was the mother whose place I did not have to take.

Once again, I could lean on her. It was such a relief that when we finally walked out of our Happy Corner, dressed in our best, with Ma as the ocean liner, and me the tugboat bobbing along in its path, I could not find words to express my gratitude.

In addition to her purse, she was holding a package wrapped in brown paper and tied with twine. It had come in with the rest of her belongings when she came home from Mrs. Maki's. But she had simply set it aside, and then there had been all the furor of the discussion and preparation of the "test" for the logging camp, and my curiosity had been set in abeyance until now.

I have to admit, too, that it was so wonderful to have Ma to myself that everything else seemed extraneous. Right now I needed her strength and her support and her calming good sense. I needed her to believe in me so I could go back to believing in myself. Most of all, I needed to trust that however difficult the path I chose, I would find strength within myself to follow it.

We took the train to Virginia first. "To give ourselves time to think," Ma said. "And we are going to treat ourselves to a snowball and a cup of coffee at the White Pastry Shoppe. Then I will show you what is in the package."

It was a long walk to the White Pastry Shoppe on Second Avenue that late summer morning, but we didn't mind. We window shopped, pointing out the lovely displays and noting changes in styles. We just sauntered along, not hurrying. Ma and I had never done this before, so it was a very special gift for me.

When we were finally seated at a table for two by the window in an unspeakable extravagance, ordering coffee and a sweet treat and being waited on, for a time, I simply savored the chance to look out of the window and smell the delicious aromas coming from the kitchen. Ma acted as if she had done this every day of her life. Finally, after we had eaten every crumb of the chocolate snowball dipped in coconut and accepted a second cup of coffee, she pushed the package at me as if she couldn't wait one minute longer for me to open it.

Inside was a slender booklet entitled *The Mountaineer*—the first annual yearbook of the new Mt. Iron High School.

"While I was at Mrs. Maki's," Ma said, casually, "she wrote to the new principal of the Mt. Iron High School, Mr. Luther Vessel, asking him for any information he could send me about the school. He sent me this. It is the first try at a yearbook with some pictures of the school and the staff and the classes you'll enjoy if you pass the testing process."

Ma paused, remembering. "I know we had talked about your going to Roosevelt High School in Virginia, but once, when I was strong enough, Mrs. Maki and I visited the school and inquired about possible places you could work for your room and board. We even visited one house, and we talked about it for a long time afterward. It didn't seem right to either of us. The school is so large and the faculty and students are so well-entrenched, we wondered how you would fit in. On the other hand, this high school is relatively new. That means almost everyone will be a new student. It should make it much easier for you to fit in. Also, it is not as large, which means you would get more personal attention, and lastly, I've heard that a lot of Finnish students choose to go there. Not that I don't want you to make many different friends. But many of those Finnish students will also be working for their board and room so you'll have something in common."

Ma had obviously given this a lot of thought. And she was right. I had been intimidated by the very size of Virginia's Roosevelt High School with its adjacent buildings for the junior high and junior college students.

"Here," Ma pointed, opening the book, "is what the rooms are like. And this is the school itself."

It had been designed like an H with the major entry on the second story of the middle cross bar. In front of the legs of the H was the first set of three windows, exactly below, though not as large as the six flanking the white-pillared second floor main entrance and above them were three on each side of the third floor.

Later, I learned to call it a modified Georgian design because the entire building was perfectly symmetrical with a high flat roof over windows above themselves on the first, second, and third floors.

A wide view of the compass showed three small trees set in a triangle.

Sitting back, I started from the first page, and, Ma with me, went through the entire book, looking at all of the pictures.

"The original high school building," the introduction stated, "though built in 1911 at the cost of $100,000, proved inadequate and so a special election was called for in 1918, providing for the addition of the grade and athletic building at the cost of $305,000. Just recently, it was designated a Consolidated High School, which," the booklet concluded, "increased the district's state aid by $4,000."

If I proved myself worthy, I could be part of the class of 1928, the third class to graduate from this brand new school, I thought to myself, almost overcome by the difference between our little school in Zim and this imposing edifice (vocabulary word of the day).

Ma set the book aside, took both of my hands, looked me squarely in the eye, and said, "I would be so proud. Margie and I will come to your graduation, and we'll clap louder than anyone."

"I feel that this is the right place for you, Ilmi," Ma said. "Mrs. Maki says the whole town has the same sense of newness. Not far from the end of the main street, there are new open pit iron ore mines, as if the whole town is just beginning."

And so that night when we got home, in my very best Palmer Method Handwriting (it took me three tries), I wrote a letter to Superintendent J. F. Muench asking for an appointment to meet whoever would test me to determine whether I would be worthy to enter the class of 1928 as a sophomore.

In response we received a form letter inviting Ma and me to a meeting of all students who had attended schools other than those in Mt. Iron. We would have individual meetings with staff members, and our parents were welcome to accompany us. I was to meet with Mr. Luther Vessel, the high school principal, who would arrange a tour of the building and, with the other new students, discuss the necessary qualifications for enrollment.

We newcomers would take a series of tests to enable the staff to place us in areas which were to our best advantage.

That day again Ma wore her very best dress. Ma had finished the work on my graduation dress so I wore that, and I had light-colored hose and my white graduation shoes.

I shall never forget that morning as we approached the school. It seemed presumptuous for us to enter by the main doors on the second level, but other students and their parents were heading that way, so I held tightly to Ma's hand, and we followed them.

Awaiting us at the top of the stairs in front of a statue of Lincoln, sitting, with his hand outstretched, as if to offer us knowledge (later we put pennies into that hand for good luck), stood a young man with glasses who introduced himself to us as Principal Luther Vessel. Dividing us into two groups, he introduced the young women who would conduct us on our tour—Joy Carmen and Evelyn Swedman.

They both had bobbed hair.

As we followed Miss Swedman through the basement floor of auto and machine shops and domestic science rooms and, she adopted Mr. Vessel's tone of voice, "These are most suitable for our school's aim of providing training for the occupations for which most of our young ladies are best fitted."

I clenched my teeth to bite back an argument, vowing never to take a domestic science class if I could possibly avoid it.

Ma, following at a polite distance, understood only part of what Evelyn said, so she forbore from commenting other than, "Very nice. Very nice."

I thought Ma and I would have a discussion about domestic science when we got home.

I responded very differently when we reached the second floor with its huge assembly room and stage, laboratories, and recitation rooms. This was where I belonged. Miss Swedman smiled at me, "Wait until you see the entire school gathered in the assembly room, reciting the Pledge of Allegiance and singing the national anthem. It is very moving."

Few of the teachers stopped to talk at any length, obviously intent on their preparations for the first day of school, but Miss Swedman took time to introduce us to bespectacled Miss Angela Costigan, B.S.

I did not understand the "B.S." I'd heard the phrase used derogatorily by some men. Obviously it had another meaning here.

"I hope to see you in Latin during your junior and senior years," Miss Costigan told me in a sweet voice. She must have seen the excitement in my eyes because I earned a special smile. My body made an involuntary bob which almost turned into a curtsy because I was so impressed. Her eyes, her severely tailored suit, her hair marceled into exact waves, cut just at ear length, exemplified what I hoped some day to emulate.

Miss Swedman introduced the next teacher as the darkly romantic "Miss Isadora Duda," head of the English and Public Speaking Departments. Thick heavy black hair waved down to her shoulders as uncontrolled as my mop when Ma took it out of my braids before bedtime. Ma gave me a telling look. I had begged to have my hair bobbed. I knew my school wardrobe would be limited to two skirts, two blouses, and two sweaters.

I had told Ma, "If I have no choice in the matter of my clothes, may I please at least have the right hair style?" But looking at Miss Duda's heavy black lashes, thin aristocratic nose, and flowing flowered dress with its soft, white chiffon collar, I had to admit it wasn't just the hair that made the style.

Still . . . if I had my hair bobbed, I wouldn't feel quite so much like a farmer.

Finally, Miss Swedman led us to a classroom. She asked each of us to introduced ourselves and tell something about us so we would at least know someone on the first day of school.

I looked at everyone as carefully as they looked at me. We would be together for three years. We would be friends . . . and enemies. Some of us would be eligible for honors. Others would not make it through.

All of the last names were Finnish so I suspected that we were all doing the same thing—working for our room and board so we could go to high school.

All of the other girls had their hair bobbed.

I tried hard to memorize names and faces. Eino Wainio said he liked music. Arthur Saari asked us to call him "Art" and to cheer for him on any sports team he could make. I had to listen very hard to hear the name "Ellen Tuomiranta." She looked as frail and shy as she sounded. I vowed to make a point of greeting her on the first day. John Fiola, leaning over to shake hands with Art Saari, said his middle name was "football." I felt for Urho Perala, who was literally biting his nails. "I sure hope I make it," he said. I couldn't catch the first name of Mr. Marttila, who, like Ellen, seemed to be trying to make himself invisible. Kaarlo Otava told us he was bound to grow from his present size and joked about it as if he didn't mind at all that he looked as if he should be in junior high. His grin was so infectious we all grinned back.

The next two, I think, were Helmi Kauppila and Thelma Komulainen, but by that time I had lost my ability to absorb any more names.

All the while, I weighed the merits of 'Ilmi Marianna' and 'Marion' then with a glance at Ma I said, "I'm Marion Brosi, and I'm looking for somewhere to work for my board and room."

Thus ended the morning of my introduction to Mt. Iron High School.

That afternoon at twelve-thirty, those of us who were new to the district gathered together in the assembly room to be tested. One look at the examination, and I breathed a sigh of relief, because it was only a slightly more complicated version of the State Board Examination for graduation from eighth grade.

My sign must have been more audible than I intended because a young man two seats over and two to the front, turned around to give me a wink. He was grinning, too. When we were excused one by one as we finished the test, I made sure to check his name tag—Ero Wainio. We shook hands and laughed again.

We reconvened at three o'clock in the assembly room.

Superintendent Muench looked very pleased as he approached the lectern, his imposing bulk preceding him, and his hands holding his suspenders.

The wooden seats shook when we sat on them, and it was very difficult to maintain an attitude of absolute stillness when we were all jittery with fear.

"Our Mt. Iron teachers will have to go some to keep ahead of the class of 1928!"

At that we couldn't help it. Some of us cried. Some cheered. Some hugged, whether we knew each other or not. It was a moment of supreme joy, and we gloried in it.

Ma had waited patiently while we were testing, but I found her in Mr. Vessel's office. They were shaking hands on a verbal contract. He and his wife were newly married, and he was also new to this school. He sounded very pleased to have arranged for someone to come in to work for her room and board.

"Would you please come one week early, Miss Brosi?" he requested. "That will give you time for you and my wife to become acquainted and for you to work out what your responsibilities will be."

Ma nodded. "That means you will come here at about the same time as Margie and I leave for the logging camp."

I knew I should be happy. But suddenly the thought of being here in Mt. Iron so far away from Ma and Margie not just for weeks but for an entire school year sounded overwhelming.

Out of my mouth came one of those questions that surface unplanned. "Mr. Vessel, may I visit my mother and my sister during Christmas vacation? They will be working at a logging camp north of Orr, not far from Elephant Lake. A train leads to Cusson, and I believe we can arrange to have someone from the owner of the camp pick me up there. I would not be gone longer than two weeks."

Ma smiled at me. She approved of the request, her eyes said.

"Well," Mr. Vessel stopped to think it over. He had had no previous experience with this situation and thus had no base upon which to build his answer. "I will discuss it with my wife, but I believe it could be arranged. Perhaps not a full two weeks, but certainly enough so that you can have an adequate visit with your mother and sister."

My mind shouted *Hooray!* But my voice said a very calm thank you, as if the request were the most natural in the world.

I would be bound by the circumstances of school and the Vessels' needs. But I had had the fortitude to captain my own soul even if it were for only two weeks. Oh, it felt good!

CHAPTER TWENTY-SIX
Beginning

s Ma and Margie were packing to go to the logging camp, and I was examining the meager allotment of my wardrobe for the year of school, Margie had an idea.

"Ilmi, why don't you come with us when we visit the Johnson's house on the way to the camp? It would postpone our having to leave you, and I'm sure Mr. Alfred would arrange for you to be shipped back to Mr. Iron in time to get to the Vessels."

"Shipped. Like a package?" I teased.

We tried hard those last few days to keep our feelings hidden. We had been together just the three of us for such a short time that to be separated so soon was very difficult. We all understood without saying it why Ma had had to think over her idea very carefully before she raised the question to Margie and, I guess, to me because their moving far-away left me with no one to go home to for a long weekend or probably for Thanksgiving.

When I thought of that, my throat got very tight, and I had to fight the tears.

Of course, I wanted to go on to school and was willing to work for my board and room, but I had always envisioned Ma and Margie at Happy Corner, not that many miles away. If things got too rough, as they almost had at Reid's, I'd always have them to go back to. Now there would be nothing but a cold and empty house.

I knew I'd never give up and "run home to Mama," as Pa would have put it sarcastically. But it was just the idea that made the separation so . . . emphatic. Once I got to Mt. Iron and to the Vessels, no matter what I found there, it would be my home for nine full months.

The time between the opening of school and Christmas yawed like a chasm I must cross. And deep down, I feared that once there, I might not have the courage to leave Ma and Margie again to go back to . . . whatever I found.

My mind consoled my heart when I thought of all I would learn at school, at the excitement of meeting other students with the same goals as I had, at putting into action the dreams I had lived with since that day long ago when we entered the train in Malcolm and I realized that the only English word I knew was "toilet," and that would not get me far.

Still, my heart wept. Leaving Ma and Margie! They were all I had in the world. It was almost impossible not to find myself equivocating over a decision that I knew was the only one that was right for me.

Margie's suggestion, therefore, was an unadulterated blessing. It would give me one more day with Ma and Margie, and Mr. Alfred Johnson had seemed so . . . interesting in a clever and funny kind of way that I looked forward to meeting his other children.

It would be a little trip away from home, a kind of adventure. A day spent without anything being asked of me but my presence.

Ma seconded Margie's suggestion by saying, "Of course, Ilmi will come, too. I can't imagine her missing out on a day spent visiting some new and interesting people."

We continued our organizing and packing and buttoning up "Happy Corner" in silence. Then Ma put the whole question to rest.

"Besides," she said again, "this will give us one more day together."

And so it was arranged.

We were picked up at dawn by Mr. Willmar Johnson, who loaded our luggage into the trunk of his Model A Ford truck and us in the front and back seats, and drove us along the two-lane country roads to a long drive-way and a house that looked amazingly like the Salins'. I wondered if they could be ordered by the package from the catalog, like clothing and house-hold goods.

My sparse luggage was unloaded, and we walked past a well-house with a hexagonal roof through a yard edged with small pine trees on the north side and enveloped with flowers everywhere—underneath the pine trees, in front of the sun porch, and in a huge circle in the middle of the green lawn. Even in Virginia, I had never seen a lawn that beautiful. From the front door of the sun porch came a woman, no taller than five feet, round and pillowy, with a cotton house dress like Ma's and an apron upon which she was drying her hands.

"*Tervetuloa*," (welcome) she said, in Finnish. She spoke no English, which was fine with Ma, but she did not need to speak the welcome. It emanated from her as it did from her husband, who followed her out the door.

I had never met a family like that. Not that the families in Zim were unfriendly or standoffish. Experience had amply exemplified their kindness and generosity. But the Johnsons made us feel as if we were part of their family from the moment Ma and Mrs. Johnson, who said to call her "Jennie" and "Alfred" enveloped first Ma and then me and then Margie in embraces that said, "We are delighted to see you here."

And they were!

Jennie was not the housekeeper Ma was. But I liked the way their sun porch and living room looked. They were clean, but not immaculate. It was clear that someone had been reading a book, because it was turned upside down on an end table. A pile of records lay unsheathed by the first Victrola I had ever seen, and the seat of the player piano was pulled out, as if someone had just gotten up from it. One of the end tables held a wooden board with holes drilled into it, marbles set into the holes and dice lying on four sides. Some kind of competition had been in progress.

We met all of Alfred and Jennie's children, but not, as I had feared, in a rush. Ten is a large number.

"I'm sorry Wylma is not here to meet you, though you may see her before you leave," Jennie said. "She is already working at Lofgren's store in Angora, adding up figures and figuring out how much is paid and how much is owed. She likes that kind of work, but she doesn't like housework." She showed us a picture of Wylma. "Wow," I thought. She had scads of black curly hair, bobbed, big blue eyes, and a slender figure.

As we walked through the living room, heads poked over the stairway leading to the bedrooms.

"Boys," their father said, "come down here and be introduced like men instead of gawking like that."

There were so many that I remembered only a blur with maybe one distinctive characteristic. Walter's hair was parted in the middle and slicked back. He winked at me, and I blushed. Warren was dressed in slacks, a shirt and tie, and excused himself. He was on his way to work in a grocery store in Angora.

"Casey's real name was never mentioned. I could see him eyeing Margie, and I thought it would be a good idea to keep my eye on both of them or there would be mischief. When we sat down together to eat, he managed to keep us all laughing. Little Raymond was reminiscent of what Baby Teddy might have been like had he lived, and Ma asked right away if Jennie would mind if she held him. He climbed on her lap, put his thumb in his mouth, and was perfectly contented almost the whole time we were there.

Emil Cliffert, who said to call him "Cliff," was so handsome I blushed again when he looked at me. He was packing to go to school in Minneapolis to become a barber.

I think that took care of the boys.

But the girls. Oh, my. They were all . . . so very beautiful. I learned later that they had that reputation. They were called "the Johnson girls."

It was obvious from the start that the only one who had the knack of cooking or wanted to was a girl my age named Marie. Her hair was long and braided, and she had big dark eyes. I think, like Jenni Aro, she was a second mother to the younger children. She asked Ma if she could help her with the dinner, and Ma named her "second cook." Ma praised her highly when we finally sat down to eat. "She definitely has the feel for putting ingredients together—how much and how little and when." I don't think Marie got much praise because her eyes just got bigger and bigger. I thought she was going to cry.

Ma didn't let her do the dishes.

"I'll be right down!" a lovely voice called down from the register above the kitchen stove as we sat down for morning coffee. When she walked in, I did gasp. Jennie and Alfred introduced her as "Tyra," but she grinned at me and said, "Call me Doris." She slipped into the chair next to mine and said, "I hear you'll be in Mt. Iron next year."

"I'll be working for my board and room at the new principal's house and going to high school," I answered. It didn't sound very exciting.

"I'm going to beauty school," she fluffed her hair. "How do you like it?"

Her hair wasn't a bob. But it wasn't long either. It fell from a side part almost to her shoulder and then flipped up just above the shoulders of what I would call a "trouser suit," for want of a better word. I had never seen one like it before, not even in the catalog.

Doris noticed my studying her outfit, which made me feel ashamed, for it was none of my business, but she just laughed and smiled, "It's called a page boy. A really new cut. And Wylma, who prefers to be called 'Pat,' ordered me this from Minneapolis. I'd never seen anything like it either, but I love it."

"So do I!" My admiration was wholehearted.

Finally, just before dinner was ready, Jennie disappeared upstairs for a while and then called for Alfred, "Come and carry Faye!"

Doris explained quietly, "My youngest sister had polio and almost died. Now Ma massages and does special exercises on her legs three times a day, but she still has trouble walking."

I almost gasped again when I saw her. Alfred set her down gently. She was as exquisite, as beautiful, slender, and fragile as a lady slipper or a single arbutus hidden within the moss. It seemed to be taken for granted that she would be waited on and given what she wanted, no questions asked. But she was sweet and polite to Ma and Margie and me nonetheless, though we felt like Brobdingnags, way too big to live in the same world as one so delicate.

But too soon, too soon our visiting time was over. The dinner had been eaten, the kitchen cleaned, and Mr. Willmar Johnson was looking at his watch.

"I think you and Margie should stay here overnight," he told Ma. Jennie and Alfred said they would be most welcome. "We can start early and get to the camp in plenty of time for you to get settled."

"Marion, I have just enough time to get you on the train for Mt. Iron."

And so went our farewells. There was barely time for a hug and a kiss, and I was off, biting back tears.

But perhaps that was best. No matter how much time we took, it would never have been enough. "Write to us care of Willmar Johnson!" Ma called out as Willmar cranked the car and we set off, "and we will, too!"

"I will! I love you, Ma! Margie!" I waved until I could see them no more and then sat straight backed in the seat next to Mr. Willmar Johnson, who did not say a word but delivered me onto the train and left.

Never had I felt so alone. Never would I have guessed I had met the man I would someday marry.

CHAPTER TWENTY-SEVEN
Vessels

I tried to approach the Vessels' house with a willing heart and a positive attitude. It was a two-story "bungalow" with a third-floor attic room, which I supposed would be mine. Like the town itself, it had an air of newness. There was no real lawn or picket fence as so many of the houses coming up on the block were adding. Some of the older homes had gardens in the back and flowers in the front.

Unlike the Reids' house in Virginia, the neighborhood made me feel at home. And it was barely a block and a half from their house to the school. I imagined myself running that distance at least twice a day all year.

Mr. and Mrs. Vessel both met me at the door. Obviously newlyweds, they were still unpacking boxes of wedding presents, but what they had already done to the house was lovely. Freshly painted a light cream throughout with a living room, dining room, kitchen, and pantry downstairs, it looked like something out of a magazine. They showed me the two large bedrooms upstairs, and—I had been right—the small "apartment" on the third floor with plenty of room for my bed, a dresser, a table and chair, and a desk for my books. Mrs. Vessel had gone upstairs earlier to open the windows, one on each end of the room, so the stuffy closed-in feeling was gone. She had also laid out pretty rose-bud sheets, pillowcases, blankets, and a coverlet with rose-colored rugs on the floor.

The kitchen had a gas stove, and the back entry was large enough to hold not only the ice box but shelves of canned goods, many of which were donated by various church congregations and/or the wives of school board members.

They offered me coffee or iced tea, and we sat in the dining room to work our plan.

"We won't expect you to do heavy housework, like washing windows or moving furniture," Mrs. Vessel explained. "But I would like the living room and dining room dusted and the floors either dust mopped or a carpet sweeper used on the carpeting every morning. We will not expect you to do laundry. A neighbor lady, Mrs. Martilla, has been recommended to us. It really would be too much for you to keep up with, since you'll have schoolwork, too."

I appreciated that and said so.

But then they dropped the blow.

"We plan to dine together in the dining room, a full meal every evening at precisely six-thirty, right after we finish having 'aperitifs,'" Mr. Vessel said, mispronouncing the word I recognized as I proceeded through French!

Thus, every afternoon when I got home from school, the evening's menu would be written in white chalk on a blackboard just inside the kitchen door. Since Mrs. Vessel subscribed to *The Household Magazine*, a lot of the menus included dishes described in the magazine or in *The Minnesota Searchlight*, a recipe book that had been a wedding present.

Of all of the ironies fate had to bestow upon me, this was the most horrific. I, the kitchen klutz, was to become the chef for the high school principal and his wife.

I almost asked if they would consider hiring Mrs. Martilla to do the cooking and leave the laundry to me, but that would not have been suitable. The kitchen was to be my province and to the kitchen I went.

Most of the time I managed a fair rendition of whatever Mrs. Vessel ordered. But I had a lot to learn. I had never heard of a salad before I got to their house. Thus I was amazed to find not only that there was such a thing but also that there were so many kinds—fruit and vegetable, meat and fish and chicken salads, cheese and gelatin and frozen salads, and two full pages of "dressings," as if each salad required its own proper attire.

Every afternoon Mrs. Vessel sat down to plan the evening's menu.

It was a good thing that Mr. Vessel arranged that I be dismissed early from my last class, or the process would have defeated me altogether.

Getting up as surreptitiously as possible while the class had study time, I grabbed my school bag and hurried home to read the recipes and interpret them before I began to cook. Sometimes I gagged as I read, but truly the results rarely tasted quite as good or bad as the recipes sounded.

"Porcupine salad" was a good example. All I had to do was arrange lettuce leaves on a salad plate, cut blanched almonds lengthwise (That was no small task because they tended to shatter although the broken ones tasted just as good), stick them in halves of canned pears, place the pear on the lettuce, arrange salad dressing around the pears, and sprinkle the dressing with grated carrots. Difficulties emerged when I faced the last two steps. The boiled dressing should have been made first. Hurrying to combine two teaspoons of sugar, one of salt and one of mustard, I added a well-beaten egg and mixed them thoroughly. In went two tablespoons of butter, which I had to melt in a hurry, and quarter cup of mild vinegar, which I mixed thoroughly. But I had forgotten to fill the bottom of the double boiler so that the water over which I was to mix them was not boiling.

Waiting until it boiled and then cooking the dressing mixture over the hot water, stirring constantly until it was thick and smooth, took long past the prescribed 6:30. And then it had to cool. I cheated and put it into the ice box in the back porch, where it curdled.

Thank goodness, the wait had given the Vessels time for a second (and perhaps third) aperitif, so they were not critical of the salad. Mrs. Vessel's only comment was that I should have added more sugar.

I wanted to dump it on her head.

Awful as the salads were, however, they were nothing compared to game. "Game should not be cooked too soon after being killed," the *Household Searchlight* recipe insisted. "Nor should it hang too long. In autumn it can be kept from one to four days, depending on the temperature. Whether furred or feathered, game should be hung where it may have free circulation of air."

That meant the back porch. Mr. Vessel hunted in the fall, bagging and bringing home geese, wild ducks, and partridge. He killed them. He hung them. He left them to me to fix. The smell alone—a combination of open viscera, dripping gut, dried blood, and death—gagged me, and I had to endure it for every one of the prescribed one to four days Mr. Vessel demanded and the recipe said we had to wait before I could "dress" the bird.

I had not the slightest idea of what the word "dress" meant. Pa had never hunted. He was more inclined to feed partridge than to harm them, and the sight of wild ducks or geese flying south moved him to call us all outside to marvel at the perfection of their pattern, at the song of their farewells, at the whipping whirr of the wind on their wings. No, Pa never could bring himself to harm a living thing, which was in the last analysis one of the reasons why so often we went hungry.

Ma got so frustrated that she taught herself to use a slingshot. We didn't have the money to buy a gun. And she actually got us a partridge or two or sometimes more every fall. Ruthlessly pulling off feathers, she took issue with the whole concept of hanging, ordered us to fill a pail with fresh cold water from the well, washed the carcass well, threw it into fresh water, added a liberal palm full of salt, then cooked the bird for that evening's supper.

We never smelled a thing except the richness of onions and celery braising in butter, the salt and pepper spiciness of the flour-dipped pieces sizzling in the pan, and the fragrance of baked bird, covered with strips of bacon if we had any, roasting in an oven on a rich bread stuffing made of her own homemade bread and eggs and more onion and celery and boiled bits of the bird's heart and liver. (We didn't know that at the time, of course, or Margie would have said "Yuck!" and refused to eat it at all.) Ma added nutmeats or sausage also if we had any. Unlike many Finnish cooks, she was a great one for adding herbs, especially those familiar to our Italian neighbors in Virginia, who had shared parsley and sage and basil and thyme and oregano and rosemary, which at first caused us to ask Ma why a sauce or a roast tasted so funny. We adjusted and soon missed them when they were not included.

I could not adjust to the horror of those hanging dead birds. Moreover, the first words of every single recipe were the same: "Dress squirrel. Dress rabbit. Dress quail. Dress prairie chicken. Remove feathers. Dress."

Thank goodness for Mrs. Marttila, who came in with the laundry basket under her arm one Monday morning in late September when I was standing in the back entry staring at the birds in utter dismay. "Don't worry about what the book says," she told me in Finn. "Just take them down, pull off the feathers, soak them in water with salt until the water is clean, and bake them."

Just like Ma, I thought, until I attacked the feathers. They stuck to my hands and to my apron when I wiped it, then, loose feathers floated around the kitchen, adhering wherever they landed. Blood dripped onto the table, ran down the side, and pooled on the floor.

My stomach heaved, the bile rose into my mouth, and I barely made it out the back door before I threw up all over the flowers near the kitchen door.

The recipe said to "parboil them for fifteen minutes." The smell spread until it permeated every corner of the house, and I heard Mr. Vessel exclaim as he walked in the front door. "So, we are finally having duck for supper. Good. Good."

Poking his head into the kitchen, he warned, "Don't overcook them."

Filling the cavity with the prescribed apple stuffing, I baked the birds in a hot oven, holding my apron over my nose at the smell when I basted them with their own fat and almost threw up again when I watched Mr. Vessel carving them on the serving platter. The flesh inside was still red, and the juices looked more like blood than sauce.

Mrs. Vessel looked rather white, too. After all, they had been married less than a year.

But not even the horrors of the uncooked duck could compare with the trauma I faced the night of the angel food cake debacle.

It had been, of course, a long and very difficult day in school, as most days were, and I came home with a list of vocabulary words to memorize for French, a page of Latin to translate, and the culminating project of our study of the English pre-Romantic poets, the memorization of Thomas Gray's *Elegy Written in a Country Churchyard*.

I had known about the memorization assignment for weeks, of course, but with all there was to do, I had postponed it, certain that given a single quiet evening I could absorb it with relative ease. Often when Mrs. Martilla called me over for sauna and coffee, as she did most Saturday nights, I reciprocated by reading and reciting poetry.

Mrs. Martilla did not always grasp the words, but she loved the rhythm and the rhymes. Since she was strongly Evangelical Lutheran, she had no trouble at all answering the question Blake asked in "The Lamb"—"Little Lamb, who made thee? Dost thou know who made thee?"

But when I read "The Tiger" too with much expression, she said it reminded her of Hell and wanted nothing at all to do with that poem. Weeks later I heard her singing with a Finnish lilt the English words "Little Lamb, who made thee? Dost thou know who made thee?"

She also got a big kick out of my reading of Robert Burns' cottage poems with an accented Scots dialect. I'm sure mine was way off, but even if I did murder the dialect, both of us grinned all the way through "To a Mouse" and "To a Louse." I apologized to her for the fact that I had no idea how Scottish dialect would sound, but she didn't care.

"Have you ever seen a louse?" she asked.

I told her they had crawled around the braids of the girl who sat behind me in our school until Ma put a stop to it.

"I imagine she washed your hair with kerosene," she nodded, approvingly.

I had also picked them off and killed them with my fingers.

My English instructor, Miss Costigan, was always less enamoured than I of the content of the poems. Her focus was on relevant facts about the author's life, his—they were all men—birth and death dates, the correct titles of his works, and memorization of key lines. Every day she came into class with a ten-point quiz at the ready.

It behooved us also to be prepared, our notebooks snapped open as she barked, "Question One: In what English city was Samuel Johnson brought up?" Pause. "Question Two: With whom did he journey to London?" Pause. "Question Three . . . and she'd progress like this through all ten questions. The reading assignment had included the life of Samuel Johnson and definitions from his dictionary. As review questions, we were further requested to provide the title and author of the first novel, the titles of two newspapers written by Addison and Steele, and the author of *Gulliver's Travels*.

But the most challenging assignment she had ever given was that in order to earn an A, we must memorize "a significant amount" of Gray's "Elegy." Fewer than twenty-five pages of the section on the eighteenth century remained, and that day Miss Costigan assigned the dates when each of us were to present our memorized recitation for the edification of the class.

"Miss Brosi, you shall be first," she had announced just before the bell. "We shall begin right after tomorrow's quiz. One student shall recite every day until the entire class has completed his or her portion of the poem."

The fact that the last person to recite would have twenty-eight more days to study and prepare did not signify. Regardless, Charlie Beck was to be second.

It was a compliment. I knew that and appreciate it. Nonetheless, in order to fulfill Miss Costigan's faith in me and to complete the assignment to my own satisfaction, I had to memorize as much as possible of the 128 lines and thirty-two four-line stanzas of the poem. I wanted to be able to recite all of it.

Of course, the opening two stanzas I already knew because the class had recited them in unison every day for the last week with an appalling emphasis on the iambic beat, every line end stopped:

The CUR -FEW tolls the KNELL of PARTing Day - comma
The LOWing HERD wind SLOWly O'ER the LEA - comma
The PLOWman HOMEward PLODS his WEARY way - comma
And LEAVES the WORLD to DARKness And to ME - period

I had gritted my teeth, trying hard not to scream, as we plodded our own weary way through that darkness. Of course, I knew very well that were we not to approach the whole poem this way, fully a third of the class, from Kabe up, would fail miserably upon the altar of Miss Costigan's despair without some guidance.

Oh, yes, Kabe was in my life again. He, too, had moved to Mt. Iron to attend high school. Miss Costigan called him "Diodado." His mother still rattled the full "Diodado Carmen Joseph Vanucci" whenever she referred to him, which was usually when she wanted him home. The rest of us still called him "Kabe." The girls who were lucky enough to live where there were telephones called him frequently. Even the teachers, like the rest of us, swam in the warmth of his sultry brown-eyed curly-haired charm, calling on him late enough to guarantee that he would not be completely comatose. In fact, we were all certain that he would be number twenty-eight, thus able to recite quite a bit of it, making it into a song.

At any rate, it was no surprise to find that Kabe would recite last, thus almost guaranteeing him a passing grade, for he was quick to pick up the rhythm and words of any popular tune.

The issue was the final item on that night's menu. Angel food cake.

The recipe on page fifty-four of *The Household Searchlight* called for one cup of egg whites (eight to ten eggs), one and one-quarter cups of sugar, one cup cake flour, one teaspoon cream of tartar, one-eighth teaspoon salt, one-half teaspoon orange flavoring, one-half teaspoon vanilla flavoring and one tablespoon water.

Simple enough, I thought.

Nor were the directions daunting. I recited Gray while I sifted the flour and sugar separately four times and waited to measure each until after the first sifting. I whipped the egg whites lightly with a wire whisk, keeping an iambic pentameter beat and added salt, water, and flavorings when they seemed half

211

beaten. After sifting in the cream of tartar, I continued whipping until the whites held their shape, and I blessed the regularity of the eighteenth century beat which carried the memorization right along.

By that time, my right arm ached, and my hand was stiff.

Dividing the sugar into fourths, I folded in each fourth making ten strokes of the spatula, each as long as one ten-syllable single line. I divided the flour into fourths and folded each fourth in again, maintaining the pace of a steady stroke per line.

My right hand cramped. But I had ten more lines down solid.

Finally I poured the whole into the un-oiled tube pan. It did not ooze out the bottom as I had feared. While it baked in a slow oven (325 degrees) the prescribed fifty minutes and I had turned it upside down to cool, my hands prepared the rest of the dinner, but my mind went on over and over the earlier lines, adding a stanza each time.

> Let not ambition mock their useful toil
> Their homely joys, and destiny obscure,
> Nor grandeur hear with a disdainful smile,
> The short and simple annals of the poor.
>
> The boast of heraldry, the pomp of power
> And all that beauty, all that wealth e'er gave
> Awaits alike the inevitable hour.
> The paths of glory lead but to the grave.

I wholeheartedly agreed with and understood those lines. Lacking anyone to talk to about them, I talked to myself as I often did during the lonely days of that early high school year. I knew all about ambition. And I didn't ever mean to mock the hard work Ma did to keep Margie and me fed and clothed with a roof over our heads. I cherished every second of the homely joys of being at Happy Corner, of going to wedding dances and having company afterward, even hauling Margie.

And Mr. and Mrs. Vessel were living proof that neither power nor beauty nor wealth can withstand the onslaught of time. Mr. Vessel had power; in relation to most of the families of the students in school, they had wealth; and nothing would keep them from aging as Ma was aging and Mrs. Martilla. Of course it helped a good deal for Mrs. Vessel to remain sylph-like and slender, her hair bobbed in the newest style and curled with hot irons every morning before she came downstairs. She had me to do the work.

Ma had looked like that once, too. The early pictures of her show a Gibson-girl in white lawn blouse with tatted inserts and a long, dark skirt. Her abundant hair, coiled high and full in the back, rose in a roll above her forehead, and tendrils of curls framed her cheeks. Only the set of her mouth and chin anticipated that those warm gray eyes would see the world as it was and work to make it better for those she loved. With her aristocratic nose and her head held high, her hands clasped at the waist, she had looked . . . lovely enough for a wealthy man to give up everything he had to have her for his wife.

But the years had taken their toll. Every time Pa left, every time she faced a tenuous future, every time we endured a winter without wood, without adequate food, without warm clothes, her mouth and chin had tightened. Finally, that fall, she had cut her beautiful hair the length of her ears and let it hang straight so that it would be quick to wash during Wednesday and Saturday saunas and dry quickly over the huge black stoves she used at the camp. Cast iron kettles and frying pans weighted down her slender arms until muscles built up to strength them. Her letters made clear that a winter of lumber camp fare of pancakes and sausages, doughnuts for morning coffee, meat and potatoes and bread and beans at dinner, "appl-y" pie and cakes for dessert and coffee, thick, warm sandwiches of leftover meat and potatoes and gravy would have thickened Mrs. Vessel, too.

Had Ma not managed to meet the demands on her, she would have died, unable to bear the weight of the work.

Ah, Ma. And then there was the memory of Baby Teddy's heartbreaking death.

I tried hard not to think of her or of all that she had to do at the camp to survive. I hated the coarseness that surrounded her. I hated having Margie grow up playing cards with rough men and working like a small shadow to be Ma's extra hands.

At times I thought of quitting school. I remembered Mr. Aro's offer of the cow and forty acres. Ma and Margie could have lived with us. I remembered the Savolainens and what our lives would have been had fate stepped in with its tempting alternative.

But then I remembered Pa and swore to show him that I could do it. I could become an interpreter or a teacher. I would not go to school in order to learn to make apple crisp and aprons and wash diapers. I would make my own success and then take care of Ma and Margie the way they should be cared for.

Against those dreams were balanced times like the night of the angel food cake. Mrs. Vessel wanted a cream filling composed of butter, sugar, salt, flour, and beaten eggs with milk added slowly, the whole to be cooked over hot water until it was thick and smooth. I curdled the first batch. Mrs. Vessel wanted a seven-minute icing, which took me more than ten because the sugar, salt, boiling water, and unbeaten egg refused to thicken, no matter how I beat it with the egg beater.

It occurred to me too late that I might have forgotten the cream of tartar, but even when I added it, the filling languished.

Calling Mrs. Martilla in tears, I begged advice.

"Throw it out and do a quick butter icing," she said. "Or better yet, I'll come over and do it for you."

Oh, how I wanted her to do just that. Had Margie or Ma been the one challenged with cooking, I could not help but know, none of this would have been a challenge to them. I knew that, ironically, my fate was to be faced with recipes that challenged me when even the basic elemental tasks in the kitchen were more than I could bear. Thank goodness, I was good with the house. It shone. But in the kitchen, I continued to struggle. But pride stepped in and decreed that I tried a different tack. By the time the melted butter, lemon juice, salt, milk, and sugar were creamy, my arm was ready to drop off and I was so tired, I had to fight back the tears.

When I went into the dining room to remove the main course and reset the table for dessert, Mr. Vessel told me to help myself to all of the duck I wanted. The fat had congealed on the plate, surrounding the leftover pieces with grainy gray foam. The inside was still red.

I forced out the prescribed, "Thank you."

Mrs. Vessel frowned when she saw the butter icing, and I knew I was in for a scolding.

But the worst moment came when, dessert served, I returned to the kitchen. Stacked all across the table were the dinner dishes, the pots and pans, the beaters and spoons, a mish-mash of rejected or ruined ingredients, egg shells and canisters, salt shakers, a lemon still in the squeezer. And the angel food CAKE PAN.

I could hear Mr. and Mrs. Vessel talking in the dining room then caught the movement of chairs as they adjourned to the living room where she sat down at the piano, he beside her, to play and sing some of their newest sheet music.

And I took a good look at the kitchen.

For all her seeming largesse, Mrs. Vessel tended to be parsimonious with food, monitoring left-overs closely and making sure they were reintroduced into the next days' menus, much disguised, of course.

But precious little remained of that duck dinner once I was through. I disposed of the leftovers ruthlessly, just throwing it into the trash can, not even into the slop pail kept to feed the neighbors' pigs. The leavings of the boiled icing could have been reworked into candy. I scraped whatever I could skim out of the pan and added it to the slops. Normally I was careful to save bones and vegetables for soup stocks. That night, they disappeared in rolled up newspapers.

I would hear about it, of course. It was not uncommon for me to stop at the butcher's shop on my way home to pick up meat for dinner—four wieners—two for Mr. Vessel, one for Mrs. Vessel, one for me. That night food was so distasteful, I thought from then on I'd rely on Mrs. Martilla's *pulla* and my one wiener.

Dishes. Ma had ingrained in me the correct sequence for washing them: silver in the hottest water, delicate glassware, plates and cups next, serving dishes, and finally the pots and pans, which she had always warned me to soak just as soon as the food was removed from them. That night in my rush I had not only forgotten about the soaking but had failed to scrape them clean. Pans which had been left on the stove were encrusted with burned-on potato, duck, and gravy.

Taking a deep breath, I took off the frilled skirt of my serving apron, tied on a serviceable full-sized coverall, propped Thomas Gray's "Elegy" on the window sill above the sink and set to work.

I felt the "chill" of "penury" but it did not repress my "noble rage." The "genial current of (my) soul" was less frozen than it was flaming. I pounded pots and threw the silverware into the dishwater and would, had I dared, thrown a second plate to follow the one which dropped and cracked.

"Be very careful with this china, Marion," Mrs. Vessel had warned. "It is not our good Limoges, of course. Still, Haviland is a worthy name. Try not to break any."

It took all the strength I had not to smash the whole dishpan full.

By the time I had washed and wiped and put away all of the silver, glassware, and china, the dishwater was cold. Backing out into the entry, holding the dishwater pan in front of me, I slipped. Some water had drained from the ice box and frozen into a slick puddle that ran from the drain to the door.

I had to change clothes before I could scrub the floor. Otherwise, the entryway would be impassible come morning, and a big splurch of dishwater had splashed its way across a good half of the kitchen. Dirty dishwater.

Running up the servant's stairs to put on something warm and dry, I heard the grandfather clock strike ten. The Vessels called "Good night!" to me, and I could hear them closing the piano, turning down the gas lights, and locking doors and windows before heading up the stairs, arm in arm, it seemed, their day over.

I still had all the pots and pans to do. And the angel food cake pan.

While the pots and pans soaked, I dashed off a translation of the Latin passage. While the fresh dishwater boiled, I worked my way through the French vocabulary lesson, conjugating the irregular verb, changing first person sentences to third person, adding correct verb endings, making the definite articles masculine or feminine as the gender of the noun dictated, though the rationale of a book's being masculine and a table feminine continued to escape me.

Finally, I approached the angel food cake pan and concurrently the next passage of Gray's "Elegy."

Scraping the edges of the pan first with a spatula and then with my fingers to remove the heaviest layer of crumbs, I recited it to myself.

With exquisite clarity I remembered the day Alex Savolainen and I had found Uncle Charles' grave in the Ely cemetery. I remembered what I had said to him then, to his soul that was lost to us, about the dreams that had died with him. Sorrow, arriving unannounced, drowned me like a tidal wave on a deserted shore.

Oh, my, I thought and cried. Uncle Charles had been so generous. He had loved us so much, really loved us, even Pa, just as we were without stipulations about correct or proper demeanor.

There was no other recompense left, after Mr. Smith and Mrs. Juola got through with what was left of Uncle Charles' money. The tears escalated to sobs. I sobbed, hating them still in spite of the requital we had considered adequate and just—the demise of their social aspirations.

Standing at the sink, scraping and washing and scraping and washing that angel food cake pan, I sobbed, sobbed for Uncle Charles, gone from us forever before we really had a chance to know him; sobbed for Ma, lost from me because of distance and dreams, the latter, unfortunately, largely mine; sobbed for Pa, adrift in a world he accepted only in its most natural sense, where even his family were interlopers; sobbed for myself and for that cake pan, which never did come clean until Mrs. Martilla took it home with her the following morning. Coming in to pick up the laundry, she saw me asleep at the table, my hands still in the cake pan on my lap, my cheek on Gray's "Elegy."

Oh, I blundered my way through most of the poem when Miss Costigan called on me, but I know she was disappointed that I was not able to recite it beginning to end without a flaw.

Charlie Beck did the very next day.

I hated him and vowed not to go to any school festivity with him ever, no matter how many times he asked.

Little did I know what fate had in store for me along those lines.

CHAPTER TWENTY-EIGHT
School Woes

*I*n any school there are classes which meld together, encompassing everyone so no one feels left out. And then there are classes full of cliques. It is almost impossible to identify what qualities are necessary to belong. One just does or does not have them, is or is not one of them. So it was with the senior class the year I was a sophomore. None of us with Finnish names who were working for our room and board fit in, and there was no attempt to pretend the situation was different.

Most of the time I could ignore the "in" group because we were in different classes, because I was never in school before or after the school day, because I did not have the qualities they sought, and because my hair and my clothes were all wrong. But I was able to ignore my being an outcast because I was so busy. That is until the senior girls' tea.

Because Superintendent Muench was a bachelor, he asked Mrs. Vessel to host what he hoped would become a tradition—a senior girls' tea. The school was so new that there were not many traditions. There was, for example, no basketball or baseball team, and there were very few clubs. Except for the senior class play, the Glee Club, the orchestra, a declamatory contest, and the *Tell-Tale*, the newspaper, there were very few extra-curricular activities. He thought a tea would offer the senior girls a chance to dress up in their best, practice their social skills, and receive recognition as graduating seniors.

There were fewer than twenty girls in that first official graduating class, not too many for the Vessels' living room to handle, and thanks to Mrs. Martilla and the recipe books, I had some idea of what to serve. Thankfully, Mrs. Vessel ordered a cake from Mrs. Martilla. Mrs. Martilla and I laughed because it was to be an angel food cake. Thank goodness I didn't have that responsibility. Nor did I have to choose the rest of the foods. I just had to make them—finger sandwiches of cheese, pimento, cucumber, toasted cheese, and black walnut, deviled eggs, and "prize-winning delights" were some of the choices. I tried them all out one night for dinner, and we chose the ones that were tastiest and most attractive.

We found a recipe for "punch," and a variety of cookies and bars, recipes from Mrs. Martilla. Thank goodness there was a telephone in the Vessels' house and in Martillas' because when I got stuck I just called.

The sticking point for the tea was neither the food nor the arrangement of the table. (I was actually glad I had taken Domestic Science.) But what would I wear? I knew the senior girls and even liked a few of them. Ellen Mattson, known as "Broady," really did have "true friendship" written on her heart. She was class vice-president, secretary, on the newspaper staff, in the athletic club, in both junior and senior class plays, was vice-president of the student council and a representative to the girls' conference, some of which activities I had never heard of. I knew she would be kind.

Esther Young, called "Stubs," was sweet and pretty, and Margielian Mattila or "Margie" was even more shy than I had been even at the beginning of that year. Emelia Seppi or "Amulius," the brains of the Latin Class, knew my academic ability, so I could expect at least respect from her. Rose Scinto, like Ellen Mattson, would be kind. Some of the girls with Finnish first or last names like Lempi Saari, Lempi Jusela, and Lempi Staff had been very nice to me once they found out that I was Finnish, not Irish. And Mary Sassone, "Sass," though she had a sharp tongue and was quick with her comments, generally was kind, not cruel.

But I absolutely dreaded the rest of them.

It had been a downhill year, that second year—my sophomore year, but no day was worse than that Senior Tea. Of course, the "in group" were all invited—Esther Carlson, whom everyone called "Scottty'; Emelia A. Seppi, whose father owned Seppi's Lumber Yard; Mary Anderson, Edith Babbini, Julia Comparoni; Cecelia, whose pearl necklace, she insisted, was real; and Margherita Bianchi, "M," the prettiest, wittiest girl in school; Evelyn McGregor, "Patches," with marceled hair and pearls in the neckline of her dress and spit curls across her forehead, and Ellen Mattson, who truly meant it when she told me, at the end of that horrible day, "I'm sorry. I can't sit across from you in school anymore, but you'll always be sitting next to my heart."

Although that tea did not appear on any calendar of events, it was unquestionably the most elegant of the year's culminating activities, far outdoing the Baccalaureate service and even Class Night. Everyone pulled out all the stops. Since there wasn't a prom that year to show off spring clothes, everyone in the "in group" tried to outdo each other in what Miss Duda, in her languid drawl, called "Sartorial Elegance."

Mrs. Vessel discussed the prospect of inviting the women teachers with Mr. Vessel before the formal engraved invitations were sent out, but she decided against it. The dining and living rooms, though more than adequate to serve twenty, would have been stretched too far even had she included merely the senior high school faculty of nine and the three designated as the "Special Departments"—the school nurse, music supervisor, and physical director for girls.

Thus she and fate deprived me of the protective buffer which had made that second year bearable. I was on my own when the wolf pack arrived in twos and threes late that Friday afternoon, May 27th, three days before Baccalaureate, a week before Commencement, for afternoon tea.

Mrs. Vessel, being British, demanded that High Tea be served as it had been by her grandmother, she was wont to say. Guests who could afford them arrived wearing gloves and hats. Mrs. Vessel poured. Thin cucumber sandwiches were accompanied by hot scones, served with the closest approximation I could manage of clotted cream and fresh preserves. The Limoges was laid upon a spotless white damask cloth. The centerpiece of red carnations was trimmed in the class colors of crimson and gray, and in honor of the class motto "Out of the Harbor into Deep Channels," I had been directed to fold damask napkins into shapes approximating a ship with its sail held high.

It took me an entire week to prepare for the tea, a week when I was also preparing for examinations in Latin I, algebra, English, domestic science, biology, history, and French.

The raspberry preserves came from Mrs. Martilla, who was even more generous than usual, slipping me a goodly chunk of her homemade Finnish *pulla* to give me some sustenance among the sheets she knew I would put away.

For all of my hatred of *The Household Searchlight*, I have to admit I sighed with relief when I found a recipe for cucumber sandwiches on page 253.

The scones stumped me completely. I had no idea what they looked like or tasted like. Nor was Mrs. Vessel any help: "Scones?" she ejaculated when asked. "They look like scones. They taste like scones!"

Much as I had despised the prescribed one-year course in domestic science (i.e. cooking and sewing, Yuck), it was to Miss Ober that my final call of help was addressed. Ironically in spite of her B.S. (I knew then it meant a four-year college degree, Bachelor of Science), she too had to search recipe books for a clue and it was she who, in the last analysis, actually made them, swearing me to secrecy in the process.

By that time, I'd have sworn about anything to anyone.

When the day of the Senior Tea finally arrived, the house was immaculate, the table set, the napkins folded, the sandwiches at the ready, the scones secreted in the cupboard for immediate and surprising revelation, the teapot filled and covered by its cozy, and the cream, though more whipped than clotted, prepared.

It was then that Mrs. Vessel unleashed the final decree, in much the same form as she might have released guard dogs. I was to wear a maid's uniform—a black dress with black hose and shoes, a small frilled white cap, and a white frilled apron with black bows.

"How can I manage this?" I asked myself, in utter humiliation.

"How can I not?" the voice of realism answered. I donned the maid's uniform and answered the door, ushering the guests in with a face as blank as if I had never seen them in the halls at school. I stood behind the table to serve the initial round and walked through living and dining rooms to offer refills.

To give credit where credit is due, many of the senior girls were as dumbfounded and as ill-equipped as I to handle the situation. Should they greet me or ignore me? Was I supposed to hear their conversation or not? Was I a living being there in front of them, or was I merely the ghost of myself, in another guise so to speak, thus only marginally visible?

Yet the chains clanked regardless.

Esther, Evelyn, and Margielian ignored me completely. But then Evelyn always paid more attention to her own mirror image than to the world around her. Margielian's Gish curls swung down to and up from her eyebrows, her eyes were blackened, her lips reddened, and her collars dipped charmingly.

Esther Carlson giggled the same high, meaningless giggle which had stood her well in place of conversation. Rooter Queen of the senior class, she communicated primarily by running the gamut of laughs. A giggle of the kind that punctuated that entire afternoon meant clearly that the situation was too, too ridiculous, so ridiculous, in fact, that it decried any other communication.

The Lempi's, terrified, I'm sure, of being singled out, sat mute. Later, I received a note from Lempi Saari, whose "merriment and wit" usually made her "good company" according to the yearbook: "Roses may wither, Branches may die. Freinds may forget. But never will I."

Her intentions were good; only her spelling and her actions suffered.

Mostly the end result was the same. Mrs. Vessel had decreed my being obviated; thus, I was.

It had been that way, of course, all year, so that one afternoon should have been no surprise.

It was no surprise either that I spent a lot of that year talking to Laurence and Charlie Beck's mother. I had to talk to someone.

But that, too, was a horrible mistakes. Laurence, though short and unprepossessing, his eyes hidden by round dark glasses, his hair severely slicked above a high broad forehead, was a figure to be reckoned with in that senior class. Oh, he never made any class office, never made any key plays. He sang with the Glee Club and played small parts in the junior and senior class plays, but though under his picture in the annual were listed Hi-Y Club and T. N. T. Club, he was never an officer. In fact, no one was quite sure what either club did.

Based on my experiences with Kinney's good gang and bad gang, I had my doubts about the actions of any club named TNT.

The summer after my first year at MIHS, he appeared unannounced at Happy Corner one Saturday night, his brother in tow. Charlie was my nemesis, the only other candidate for Valedictorian in our senior year, the aim I had secretly set for myself.

How do I describe Charlie? If Laurence was thin, Charlie was scrawny. If Laurence was nearsighted, Charlie was virtually blind without glasses. If Laurence had two left feet on the dance floor, Charlie had four. And when Laurence made it clear that he venerated my being, Charlie made it worse by veritably groveling at my feet.

I abhorred him. He was Wilho Field personified.

No one who knew me at all could possibly have failed to know that Charlie Beck was an anathema to me, but in spite of the fact that I had lived with them for two full years, neither of the Vessels knew me at all.

Thus, when Charlie Beck appeared the afternoon of the tea at the front door, hat in hand, bow tie centered beneath prominent Adams' apple, suit well-pressed though glossy, Mr. Vessel ushered him in.

Still surrounded by the leftovers, dishes scraped but not washed, I had not been asked to answer the door. Nonetheless, when I heard Charlie Beck's voice, I cringed and shamelessly eavesdropped, terrified that the visit had something to do with me.

It did.

"Mr. Vessel," Charlie began, in excellent declamatory form, "since you act in *loco parentis* as it were to Ilmi Marianna Brosi, now also called 'Marion,' I come here with an urgent and heartfelt request."

Mr. Vessel waited, not altogether patiently, I knew. He had not yet sampled the sandwiches, scones, or tea.

"Because it is important to my life's plan that the arrangements by which I live be set in motion as early as possible . . ." Charlie began.

I cringed, "Oh, no, what now? Let it not be about me. Please let it not be about me."

Charlie had already invited me to be his "date" for Baccalaureate, for the graduation exercises, and for the picnic to follow our last day of school.

I had declined politely and, I hoped, with the adequate but absolute regret.

". . . before this school year ends, I wish to make sure that next year's events be so designed as to make efficacious use of qualities of natural compatibility, equal intelligence, and similar background."

Mr. Vessel nodded again, shifted in his chair, tried to look as if the message were clear, and leaning forward, did everything but motion with his hands for Charlie to get on with it.

"Miss Vera Carlstrom, faculty advisor, has already consented to assigning joint editors for next year's *Tell-Tale* staff to Marion and me."

"Ah, yes," Mr. Vessel responded, glancing at the table, "I did hear that the editors are to be equally divided between the sexes—one male, one female."

Charlie's color rose at the implications of such an explicit determination. The word "sex" clearly bothered him as much as did its connotations.

Hurrying on, he blurted out, "And before we depart to pursue our individual endeavors during the summer season, the solstice as it were," he paused.

Pushing the kitchen door open, I could hear every word.

"I wish to submit a sincere plea that this lowly penitent be granted the favor of," I thought I caught him looking at the kitchen door, just barely cracked open, and I shut it as quietly as I could, but not before I heard the conclusion, "your permission to squire Miss Ilmi Marianna Brosi, Miss Marion Brosi, as she prefers, to next year's promenade, or, should one not be held, the promenade of our senior year."

He blurted out the last words as if the hurry were necessary lest he forget.

"Lest he forget." I vaguely remembered a poem by a World War I poet with such a line. "Lest we forget."

I would have called down the worst of the German gas attacks could I have prevented Mr. Vessel's answer, "Why, yes, Mr. Beck," he smiled, happy to have the meeting come to a final fruition, "I think that may be arranged."

The two shook hands with masculine complacency, and I stood behind the door frozen and shaking, so angry I could have broken every plate in the kitchen, Limoges or not.

The ultimate indignity of that year of ultimate indignities was that if there were to be a promenade next year or during our senior year, and plans were already in the works, I would have to go with Charlie Beck.

CHAPTER TWENTY-NINE
Letters

Dearest Ilmi, When I suggested that I will be writing letters to you and asked him if he would mind delivering them, Mr. Johnson said he will not be leaving the camp regularly. He is so gruff sometimes that I hated to ask him again, so Margie and I have agreed to keep a journal, adding a bit more as something new happens. I shall write in Finnish, for which I apologize. But I know you read that as well as English, and I do not think I could put together English words into sentences yet, though I am trying.

Margie will add her own sentence or two.

The first week:

Margie has proved herself a great favorite with everyone in and out of the kitchen. I didn't realize how many songs she learned from Pa, and she has no compunction whatsoever about climbing up on one of the tables and singing and dancing to wild applause. The men consider her the best entertainment around.

I am very grateful that they watch their language around her and do not try to teach her anything we would be ashamed to have her learn. I hope all is well and that the Vessels are kind. All my love, Ma.

Dearest Ilmi, I am helping Ma to peel potatoes and rutabagas. It is a lot of work but fun, too. The men are very kind, and they like to be entertained a lot. One of them used to be a schoolteacher, and he is correcting my spelling and writing. Isn't that nice? I love you, and I miss you. Your sister, Margie Brosi.

Week Two:

Dearest Marion, This Sunday we had our first visit from the minister the men call the Sky Pilot. He ate and talked with the men and then had the tables and chairs rearranged so he could give a sermon. With so many languages here, he spoke a little bit of each, but mostly Finnish and English. You should have heard Margie's questions when he left. "Ma, what is God?" "Where does he live?" "Are there really angels?" "Where is hell?" "If I'm naughty, will I be sent there?" "Is it far away?" "Will you and Ilmi be there, too?" You would know just what to say. I have to make do with a lot of love and kisses, which I send to you in this envelope as I do from my heart every hour of every day. Your mother, Mary Brosi.

Dearest Ilmi, I won't ask you the questions I asked Ma about what the Sky Pilot said because the school teacher said he would lend me a book with all the answers in it. He called it the Bible. I tried to read it, but the words are awfully big. Before the Sky Pilot came, Ma let me play cards on Sundays. I learned to play poker and won a fiddle. Now Ma is having second thoughts about that game. The men seemed very surprised when I won. I wasn't. It was just a matter of holding the right cards. Someday let's try it together. If Ma says it is okay, that is. I love you even if you don't play poker. Your only sister, Margie Brosi

Third week:

My very dearest Marion, How I miss you! I have not been away from you as long as I was at Mrs. Maki's, but it seems much longer, and I feel so far away. Are you eating enough? Were your clothes acceptable? I promise we will bob your hair when this year is over. I feel sorry that we didn't do it before we left when I saw that all the other girls had bobbed hair. But yours is so lovely the way it is!

Mr. Johnson had some of the men help me rig up a sauna out of leftover boards with rocks and pieces of metal to make a kind of stove to hold them so we can throw water and have some steam. At first, just Margie and I used it, but now there is a line-up on Wednesday and Saturday nights.

One of the men, who smelled as if he needed one, told me, "Mrs. Brosi, I took a sauna last week!"

I don't suppose Vessels have a sauna. Perhaps Mrs. Martilla does and will allow you to use hers. Tell her I thank her for all she is doing to help and support you. Please remember how much your mother and sister love and miss you as every day goes by. Ma.

Dear Marion, Doesn't that sound grown up? You should see what Ma does before the men come to dinner. She makes them line up and show her their hands, front and back. If they are not absolutely clean, they have to wash them again. Tonight she gave Urho a whack with the wooden spoon.

I thought he would be mad, but he just went right back to the basin and washed all over again. I'm real careful to wash behind my ears and my *napa* because Ma checks me after sauna to make sure I hit every spot. You'd be surprised at how clean I am. I wish you were here to see it. Your little lonely sister, Margie.

Fourth Week:

Dearest Marion, Did we ever have a surprise this week. Willmar told me that before the weather gets bad, his whole family would like to come to the logging camp from Alango for Sunday dinner and to keep on coming, whoever is home, until the weather makes it too difficult. Wilmar says it is good for them, especially for Faye, to get out and see a bit of the world and for the boys to get a taste of what it's like to work in a lumber camp. This Sunday they came, almost all of them, except for Pat and Clifford, who were working. They must have left at dawn because they were here even for breakfast.

We served thin Finnish pancakes with maple syrup or molasses, sausages, bacon, doughnuts, and cinnamon rolls.

Margie and I cooked so hard and so fast that we sometimes had trouble keeping up with the dishes, and Jussi had to haul pail after pail of water. He helped after dinner. So did Mrs. Johnson. The others walked around and asked questions. I don't think any of them had ever been in a logging camp before, but Mrs. Johnson—Jennie—said that was how she and Alfred met—in a logging camp in Floodwood. It must have been a huge camp because all she did was the serving and the dishes.

Dear Marion, What a Sunday we had this week! Raymond Johnson and his family came to eat our breakfast and dinner with us, and Casey and I played all day. We made houses out of rocks and pieces of wood and plates and food out of mud and moss. We did get dirty, but Ma and Mrs. Johnson were so busy that they didn't seem to mind. We got so tired after dinner that they washed us off in the sauna and laid us down on the bed in Ma's and my bedroom just off the kitchen. I slept right through their leaving. Ma says they'll be coming again so we can play. He was lots more fun than Sarah Salin because he didn't brag a bit even if it is his brother's camp. I am still very sleepy so I will close now with all my love, your onliest sister, Margie.

Fifth Week:

Dearest Ilmi, I am not sure how much longer we shall be able to add to this journal and have you receive it. Mr. Johnson is going to leave the camp on an extended trip up from Elephant Lake and north to shoot ducks and, later, deer to stock our supply of winter meat. The weather has been so windy and cold that the men are predicting an early frost and an early snowstorm. Then we will be snowbound until it is time for you to come for Christmas. Somehow we must arrange for that to happen. I know there must be trains. Willmar will be going home to spend Christmas with his family.

You asked what we make for dinners here. Mr. Johnson likes a variety, but an organized variety. One Sunday we might have ham with a syrup glaze, scalloped potatoes with cheese, some kind of canned vegetable, dinner rolls, bread, and two kinds of pie.

Another week I'll make a big pork roast cooked with onions and carrots and rutabaga, soaked in one of Margie's sauces, which is so good it's becoming famous. It's better than just gravy. I have never told Mr. Johnson, but we add just a tiny bit of whiskey to the sauce before we boil it down. We hide the bottle in our room, and none of the men know it's there; and Margie caught on right away.

Then there are the venison roasts—the shoulder roasts, which are dry roasted with baked potatoes until they are almost black on the outside and well-done on the inside. That's the only way the men will eat it.

They love pork chops cut from a big slab of pork, sometimes breaded and fried, sometimes browned and baked in a gravy, sometimes cooked with sauerkraut.

And, of course, we always have bread and rolls and pies for dessert, with cinnamon rolls and caramel rolls and doughnuts always available for in-between-meal snacks.

Mr. Johnson just gave Margie and me a raise. He said the men have never been fed so well. I wonder every day what you are eating and how on earth you are managing the cooking. Oh, my dear girl, I worry every day about the decision we made and pray that it was the right one. I trust that you are finding the schoolwork, at least, all that you hoped it would be. How I wish there were a way to get your letters to us more easily!

We send ours with all the love that is always yours. Your mother.

Dear Marion, I thought you might get a kick out of this. When the Johnson family was here the last time, I heard one of our men bragging that "We always get at least two kinds of cake pieces—the appl-y pie and the do-nuts." Ma laughed, too, when she heard it. And now to serious things. I have set aside one hour in the morning after the chores are done to work on reading. I read aloud to myself, sounding out the words and then read the passage to the schoolteacher, who corrects me very gently when I am wrong.

My study time in the afternoon is devoted to arithmetic and penmanship. He is a great help with both of those things, too. He uses clothes pins and pieces of wood to help me with arithmetic, and he is even worse than Miss Heino was about the ups and downs and roundabouts of penmanship.

He has a book called *Children of Many Lands*, which he used to teach from. He reads me a chapter every night after supper and asks me questions about it.

Ma was worried about this arrangement for a while. But he took her aside and explained that he lost his teaching job because of his tendency to imbibe strong drink, and since there is none allowed in camp, he feels himself fortunate to be able to teach, which is the thing he most loves to do. If he could just keep from drinking, he said, he would be a happy man. He likes my full name and has taught me to write it. I am proud of that. Ma says we should pray for him. I do. But not as much as I pray for you, Ilmi. You are ever in the thoughts of your sister Margareta Brosi, who misses you every single day and is counting the days off and marking them on the calendar until we can be together for Christmas.

Dearest lmi, This will be the final entry. An ice storm has felled trees, and the season will begin in earnest now. Willmar Johnson will not be making any more trips out until the camp is operating at its full capacity and until he can be absolutely sure he is not needed and that our stocks are adequate as so far they seem to be. So we will hurry to tuck this into his pocket so he can bring it to the Johnson house, from which it will be sent to you with all of our love and devotion. Your mother and sister, Mary Rajamaki Brosi and Margareta Seraphina Brosi

Oh, how I waited for those letters. I read them over and over again, envisioning Ma's face as she wrote and Margie's as she bit the pencil and pressed down hard to make the words come out just right. My emotions were so mixed when one was delivered that I didn't know whether it was harder or easier to get one. On one hand, I wanted to cry because I missed them so much. On the other hand, I cherished every line and every nuance, capturing Ma's way of expressing herself—her love and caring—her renewed strength and the force with which she had taken over her role in

the camp—and Margie's exuberance and inimitable charm. They were infinitely precious to me and the only contact I would have with home. For
home is where the heart is. It is not a place. It is wherever you are with the
people you love.

Just before winter set in full blast, a car pulled up to the front of the
Vessels' bungalow one Sunday afternoon. Dinner had been served and dishes done so I was upstairs in my small apartment trying to keep concentrating with all my might on the next few French chapters, hoping to get ahead
of myself so that I could do other homework during the week. French came
easily to me. It kind of seeped in, like a gentle rain into the ground, and
held itself there, growing slowly until it became a part of me. I loved the
grammar and studied the pronunciation to myself where no one else could
hear me, trying for the uvula, until it became a natural part of the word,
uttered unforced. Also, when it came to French, it seemed, the faster the
better, so I constantly went back over the old chapters and conversations,
forcing myself to use two voices and speak as French people would, as
quickly as our teacher did when we had an "all French" day and she tried
not to slow down for us.

I heard the car stop and wondered who the Vessels had invited to visit.
They had not mentioned company, and I thought I had heard them settle
down for a nap. Glancing out the window, I saw a Model A Ford with a
rumble seat. Then the door knocker clanged twice, and I raced down the
stairs, trying to straighten my hair and my dress in the process.

The first drops of rain were falling as I opened the door to a young
man I thought was a stranger. He was nattily dressed—knickers, shirt and
tie, sweater, broad-brimmed hat, a jacket held over his head to keep out the
rain.

"You don't remember me." He was clearly disappointed.

I looked at the car and looked back at him again. "You're . . . (his hair
didn't seem to be parted in the middle), one of the Johnson boys!"

"I'm . . ."

"No. Don't tell me. You're . . . Emil Cliffert!" I cried triumphantly.
"For goodness sakes, come in out of the rain."

"Cliff, please," he said.

Mr. Vessel appeared right behind me. "Mr. Vessel," I said, "I would
like you to meet the younger brother of Mr. Willmar Johnson, who owns

the logging camp where my mother works—Cliff Johnson. He's . . . back from barbering school in Minneapolis?" I guessed.

"Right," Cliff said, smiling, holding out his hand, "and I assume you are Mr. Luther Vessel, principal of the high school Marion's attending. She is working here for her board and room, isn't she?"

"Yes, certainly, do come in. Marion, you might make your young friend some coffee. It's certainly the day for it. I will rejoin my wife. It was a pleasure to meet you, Mr. Johnson. Make yourself at home." And he left.

There we were left, neither knowing what to say.

Awkwardly, Cliff wiped his boots, took his hat off, and gave me the hat and jacket, which I shook out and hung in the entry closet.

He grinned. "I have a present for you." And out of his jacket pocket he drew a packet of letters from Ma and Margie.

"Oh, thank you!" I wanted to run right upstairs and read them, but I knew I had to be polite. "It was very kind of you to bring them. Surely not all the way from Alango!"

"No," he said. "I really am on my way back to Minneapolis. I don't like barbering, but my sister Pat paid the tuition for a full year so I have to get back to give her her money's worth."

"Didn't she ask you first?" I led the way into the kitchen and began making a fresh pot of coffee.

"Who, Pat? She doesn't ask. She orders. She figures out what jobs are available and what they pay and sends us on our way. Sometimes she's just right. Warren loves his job at the grocery store and is planning to work his way up with the Morrell Company, eventually selling meats to stores up and down northern Minnesota. He can't go to school to learn to do that. He'll have to learn on the job, but he's really giving it his all. And Doris, do you remember her?"

"Who could forget her? She is absolutely the most beautiful girl I have ever seen."

"Well, yes. But she loves knowing how just looking good can be made into looking glamorous and stunning with the right hair and clothes. She wants to open up her own shop after she finishes beauty school. Pat will finance her and will be repaid a hundred fold."

"And the others?"

"It's hard to tell. Walt . . . I'm not sure of. He might get a job in one of the steel mills in Duluth, but who knows. He's . . . kind of waiting things out right now. And Casey is still in school, driving my folks wild because he's always up to something. Then he makes everybody laugh, and gets out of whatever trouble he's in. That's why I've got the car. Dad said it would be safer with me in Minneapolis than available to Casey at home. Besides, I can come home more often."

He drank a cup of coffee with obvious gratitude. "I didn't realize how dark it was. That was a tough drive."

I sipped mine and tried to think of something intelligent to say. Here I was, me, Marion, sitting in the kitchen, entertaining a . . . man? I sure couldn't call him a boy! A beau? I was sure my face was beet red.

"How did you come to be 'Marion'?" he asked. "When you were introduced at our house I caught two names—'Ilmi Marianna' and 'Marion'? Is it like 'Tyra' and 'Doris'?"

"Actually, it was my elementary teacher in Kinney, Miss Loney. She was my idol. She and Miss Heino, who taught me in Zim. They helped me so much," I found myself explaining, "not just with lessons but with believing that I can go on to high school and college and make something of myself. That I can succeed in an English speaking world. They were strong advocates of the 'Speak English' campaign."

I found myself telling him about that silly episode on the train when we were traveling from Malcolm to Virginia, trying to find Pa, about the way the ticket master treated my Aunt Betty because she couldn't speak English, about the vow I made that I would learn to say "Tickets. One. Two. Three." And about the revelation that came when I realized that the one English word I could read and spell was "toilet." I was jolted into the realization of how much there was for me to learn.

"How did you learn to speak such good English, Cliff?" I dared use his name.

"You don't know my dad. He picks up languages like a sponge. I think a lot of that ability has been passed on to us. Mother refuses to learn English, sometimes I think just to spite him, but he just goes on, talking to whomever he meets, trying to learn what he can of their languages. It's amazing. When a gypsy caravan passed not far from our homestead, we couldn't find him for hours. Finally one of the kids spied him in the gypsy camp learning Romany."

I laughed.

He looked at his watch. "I've gotta go. Thanks a lot for the coffee. I hope I see you again." As I handed him his hat and jacket, he bent over as if he were going to kiss me then must have thought the better of it. But he did say, "Save me a dance every weekend next summer! I don't intend to miss a one!"

He opened the door to get into his car. Just before he closed it, he popped up again and said, "You take care of yourself, hear me?" And left.

Whew. That whirlwind visit had almost made me forget the letters, the final ones that came before the directions of how to get there for Christmas

I had never entertained a young gentleman caller before. Certainly never one as handsome as he was or one as easy to talk to.

I sighed. There was a big, wide wonderful world out there beyond Mt. Iron High School. For the first time I gave serious thought to those years, the years after I completed the big step which now enmeshed my every moment. What would that world bring? I ran back upstairs, climbed into my pajamas and into bed before I delved into the safety of Ma and Margie and the letters.

For now, my world was carefully circumscribed. I had not realized the safety there was in that knowledge.

CHAPTER THIRTY
Storm

*T*rue to their word the Vessels allowed me to go to the lumber camp for a part of Christmas vacation. The two weeks were pared down to a bit more than one—from early Christmas Eve to late on New Year's Day. But their Christmas gift to me was the cost of the train ride to Cusson, and Mr. Alfred Johnson said he would pick me up at the station there because he was bringing a new horse and dray to the camp that day. We should, he said, arrive in Cusson at about the same time since I would take the early train, and he would leave before dawn.

There he was, like a Finnish gnome, his beard and moustache white as snow, waiting as I stepped off the train, carpetbag in hand. I had struggled with what to get Ma and Margie, for I had no money. "To work for my room and board" meant exactly that. My "apartment" and my food were my payment for the honor of living in their house. But Mrs. Martilla taught me how to tat an edge on a lovely white lawn handkerchief for Ma. It had a delicate pansy embroidered in the corner. And for Margie, although I know she would have preferred a book, Mrs. Martilla gave me a wooden puzzle she had bought for one of her girls. It showed a little wear and would take a little work to figure out, but I thought it would be just enough of a challenge to be fun. I wished I had something for Mr. Willmar Johnson and for the Johnson family, too, because they had all been so kind to Ma. There was Mrs. Martilla again. When I mentioned it to her, not asking, not begging, she pulled out an assortment of preserves.

"Now don't get all teary and say I shouldn't do this, child. My own children have moved away, and my husband is dead and gone. Who do I have now to give presents to? It has been the light of my life this fall to have you as part of my world. I have come to love you like a daughter. Let me do this for you. It will make my heart happy," she said in such a kindly way

I could not refuse. But I vowed to bring her something back from camp. I hoped Ma would suggest something for me to bring back to the Vessels, too. In a sense, however, my agreeing to an abbreviated vacation was a gift to them. I would be there to mix and fix and serve and clean up after some of their holiday get-togethers.

Their house did look lovely when I left, the tree hung with new decorations and almost silvery with tinsel. Mrs. Vessel had brought with her exquisite ornaments she had been receiving from her family since she was a little girl. Mr. Vessel had gone into the woods and brought back boughs of balsam and spruce and pine, which Mrs. Vessel had arranged in artistic fashion, much as the magazines suggested, as centerpieces and on the mantel, and on end tables with countless red candles. She was very creative and clever with that sort of thing. She made the decorations look as natural as if they had simply grown there. Mr. Vessel made a wreath with a big red bow for the front door, and all in all, there wasn't a room in the house except mine that didn't look or smell like Christmas.

When I told Mrs. Vessel this in all sincerity, she blushed and said, "Thank you," as if she really did appreciate the compliment.

I thought to myself for the first time that it was not an easy year for her either. Since the superintendent did not have a wife, she was called upon to take up the social duties of the administrative element of the whole school system. That meant a lot of entertaining—of the administrators and their husbands and wives, if they were married. Of course, the women teachers were not, and most of the men were also young and unmarried, but still, that was a big contingent to have over for dinner or tea or cocktails. And she had to make the right choice of those alternatives.

In addition, she and her husband and the superintendent served an elaborate dinner to the members of the school board and their spouses. That big affair was scheduled upon my return. It was to be even more formal than the tea, requiring a long dress of Mrs. Vessel, a tuxedo of Mr. Vessel, and me there not just to prepare but to help with the setting up, cooking, and cleaning up of a multi-course dinner. I simply had to be back by New Year's Day night in order to have a few days to help with the preparation of the biggest evening's production Mrs. Vessel had ever attempted. She was nervous about it already, and I wish I had suggested that we do it before I left. But I was so eager to leave that I was not thinking of her worries, only of my excitement at seeing Ma and Margie.

The days sped by until the morning of New Year's Eve. I had counted on that one last day and night, but Mr. Willmar came in early that morning asking Ma how she was doing with the staples for the next few months. "The clouds and the wind are kicking up a storm," he said, "and the temperature is dropping fast. I don't want us stuck here without food."

Ma checked the pantry and the larder, which she had very well organized. They had used up a lot of food. They did need to do some replenishing. She had just not counted on it being done right now.

"I'll make a quick trip to Cusson to see if the road is passable," Mr. Willmar said. "If it is, Marion, pack your things and be ready; we'd better be on our way."

Our hearts just sank at losing those precious hours, but I did as I had been told. I didn't want to be stuck at the camp and not get back to Vessel's at all. That would be horrible in light of the Dinner Party of the Year. Yet I desperately wanted those last few hours with Ma and Margie. Ma appreciated the work I had put in on the tatting, and it had taken Margie a goodly amount of time to figure out the puzzle, but once she had, she wanted to do it over and over again.

Once I was ready, we clung to each other again and again, and made plans for what we would do once summer came and how wonderful it would be to have all that time together, and then he was here.

"The road is passable, but just barely. Hurry."

"I'll continue through Orr to the Sturgeon and Angora Co-ops, even to the Cook Co-op to get what we need. Give me the list. I'll drop Marion off at one of the railroad stations, wherever the schedule gets her to Mt. Iron at the best time. I'm going to stop at home, too. Don't expect me back until I have everything we need."

He had left the truck running so I just kissed Ma and Margie one last time and jumped in.

I confess I had qualms about going. When Willmar had opened the side door to the kitchen, which the men had protected with a rough side porch to keep out the wind, I had a hard time catching my breath because he smelled so strongly of spirits.

It was clear, too, when I got into the truck—a Model A—that he had had more to drink in Cusson. His nose was red, his face blotchy.

But it was early morning and he wanted to make the trip and get back the same day because he was worried about the ominous look of the dark sky and of the cold. I didn't think he would take a chance on drinking more.

Ma had braided my hair and stuffed it under the *tussu lakki*, which Mrs. Johnson had left on the rack near the stove. I had put on my heaviest dress, and the smallest of the men loaned me trousers, felt-lined boots, choppers with heavy linings, and a Mackinaw jacket. I was dressed so heavily I could hardly move. No one could tell whether I was a boy or a girl especially when we stopped at the garage in Orr. The men would never have talked like that if they had thought there was a lady present.

As we were leaving, one of the men called out that the temperature was hovering between ten and thirty degrees below zero by their reckoning. "Take care!" they repeated, to a man.

"Why don't you stay overnight at the Johnson's instead of chancing the drive back today?" Ma said I should suggest that to him, in case things did get worse.

But Willmar didn't listen. "This is nothing. The truck has a heater. The lanes are clear enough. I'll have no trouble getting you to a depot and get back probably by late tonight. Would you read me the list of what your ma needs?" he asked.

Ma's list was not extensive, but what she needed she really needed— the basics—flour, sugar, split peas, yeast, potatoes to replace the ones that had frozen, some canned goods, coffee.

"Well, let's be going about it," Willmar said. And off we went.

Just as we were heading out the door, Margie added one more: "Can you get something to get rid of the mice?" They had put her in the upper of two bunks, thinking she would be warmer there, but when she yelled and hit the ceiling to stop the mice from scrambling around so she could sleep, mouse droppings came tumbling down on her face. "Please get mouse traps . . . or a cat!" she begged.

Except for the discomfort of the frigid temperatures, the logging was going well. Willmar's father, Alfred, had brought a wagon pulled by two horses, King and Queen, to add to the sleighs. It was perfect weather for filling it since the tracks were iced from the storms, and the bull cook and the other men kept them iced. The sleighs and loaded wagon took little effort from the two horses. Once started, the sleighs just slid along behind them.

I wished the truck worked just as easily. It slipped and slid, and the heavy wagon we were returning to the Johnson place finally hit the ditch about halfway to Cusson. We tried shoveling it out, but I wasn't strong enough to be of much help and Willmar, suffering from a hangover, muttered under his breath until he decided to disconnect it from the truck and leave it.

At that time a man named Emil Metsa had a kind of bar or restaurant in Cusson. We stopped there to have a roll and coffee with a lot of sugar and cream for me. I'm not sure what extra was in Willmar's. Even with boiled woolen linings in my overshoes and the heavy jacket and linings in the mittens, I was frozen, cold to the marrow of my bones, as books describe it.

Willmar had to use the crank to start the truck again. It was a hand crank that he attached in front of the radiator. If it kicked, it could have broken his wrist. He tried again and again. No luck. He took a little rest then said, "We'll give it one more try." In Finnish, of course.

I was very happy when it did start because if my hands were cold, I could imagine how Willmar's were, holding a metal crank.

Between Cusson and Orr, about five miles, the truck started to steam. Willmar said, "The radiator is frozen. But don't worry. We can stop at Wally's garage in Orr. The only thing we can do is thaw it out."

When we got there, other men who were also waiting for their radiators to thaw told us it was at least thirty, maybe forty below in the middle of the day. Wally had plenty of business. Willmar talked to the other men clustered around a black pot-bellied stove. I tried not to listen and waited and warmed myself as near as I could get to the stove yet not close to them. I had never heard a group of men talking without a woman there, and I hope I will never have to listen to that kind of language again.

Once we got to Johnson's, I told the story of that ride. Doris ran downstairs in her pajamas and asked, "What happened to you? Your nose is all red, and your face is all white, as if it were frozen! Do you feel as bad as you look?"

More than anything I wanted to wrap myself in ten quilts and go to sleep, but I couldn't. I had to be ready to leave when Willmar was ready. And there was a lot more story to be told. Mrs. Johnson left the kitchen with a dish towel over her arm, and Faye made her way down the stairs slowly, bumping from stair to stair on her butt. I took up the refrain, swaddling myself in all the afghans and blankets I could find.

"When we left with twenty-five miles to go, it was already late afternoon, getting colder and dark already. The sun, had there been one, would have set about 4:15, and the entire day had been hazy, bleak, ominous. I suspect it was like that here, too."

They nodded.

"The radiator stayed thawed as we headed down Highway 73, but another problem erupted. We had trouble keeping the windshield clear. Willmar gave me a salt bag, a rag about ten by ten inches tied together with salt inside to keep the inside windshield clear of ice. My job was to rub it back and forth across the windshield so he could see.

"Then a second problem erupted. The light switch, which was on the steering wheel, flipped the lights off every time Willmar turned the wheel. That gave me two jobs. I had to keep on rubbing the salt bag fast enough to keep the windshield clear with one hand, and with the other hand I had to hold the switch on the steering wheel to keep the lights on.

"I should have been terrified, but there wasn't any time. I knew that if I didn't move the salt bag fast enough, our breath would freeze on the windshield; and if the lights went out, we could bounce off the ruts into the snow drifts. We could be stuck there until someone found us during the spring meltdown.

"We had to try some of the hills twice with Willmar backing down again, concentrating on not sliding into ditches that would have curled around us like the sides of a grave or a wolf's fangs.

"We made maybe five or ten miles an hour at best. Just about the time I thought nothing else could go wrong, something did.

"When we hit the Highway 73 cut-off to Linden Grove and Sturgeon, Willmar pressed on the clutch to shift down at a bad spot, and the clutch wouldn't come out again. It was frozen. I had to shake and jiggle it loose.

"From then on, every time Willmar pushed the clutch down to shift from high to second or second to low, I had a third job.

"So, I had to use the salt bag on the windshield. And, I had to keep the light switch on every time he turned the wheel. And then, I had to reach down and pull the clutch back out when it stuck and he had to shift down.

"What time was it when we got here?" I asked my audience, all of whom were in various stages of undress, indicating they had pulled on clothes over their pajamas when they heard us coming.

Just then the kitchen clock chimed two. "It must have been about one or one-thirty in the morning when we finally reached Highway 22 and made the left turn that led us the last four miles to the farm," I surmised. "It was actually the easiest part of the drive because the ice storm had not hit this area as heavily, and the overhanging trees had kept the road relatively clear. And here we are."

They clapped, both because they had liked the story and because we were safe.

All along the way I had wanted to jump out of the car and run back to the safety of Ma and the camp. But here I was stuck at the Johnson farm with Ma perhaps twelve hours away, completely inaccessible in weather like this. Moreover, I wasn't at all sure if any of the trains were running, or if the weather had halted their traffic, too.

The part of the story I didn't tell was what the men at Wally's garage had been discussing in lowered tones with significant glances—murder.

They had been talking half Finn-half English. I pretended I didn't understand, just kept concentrating on getting warm. But they were discussing a man they called "Tommy Simonson" or "Business Tom."

Mrs. Johnson said, "You aren't going anywhere else tonight. Go upstairs, get warmed up, put on a nightgown, and go to sleep. I'll get you up in plenty of time to get going with Willmar in the morning." And with a deep sigh of relief, so I did. After I had been rubbed dry and warm by Mrs. Johnson and Doris and ensconced in a nightgown large enough to go around me twice, long enough for me to tuck my legs inside, Mrs. Johnson tucked me into bed with Doris, whose real name was Tyra. We were about the same age, and neither of us wanted to go to sleep. I was still too keyed up and nervous from the harrowing drive. She was too excited about the story. She also sensed that I had left something out. Doris was like that. I think it came from living with such a large family. To survive, they learned to listen not just to what their brothers and sisters were saying but also to what they weren't saying.

"What were the men at Wally's garage talking about?" she asked, hitting the exact point that I had intentionally skipped.

Hesitating for a long moment, I took the plunge because I was curious too.

"They were talking about a man they called 'Tommy Simonson' or 'Simonsoni Tuppu' or 'Business Tom.'" Lowering my voice below a whisper and putting my mouth right up to her lips so no one else could possibly hear, I said, "They think he was murdered."

Doris pulled the covers over our heads and whispered, "I know a lot of stories about him. Pa used to get him to work for us.

"Casey could get him laughing so hard that he cried.

"One day Pa went to Tom's shop to get him to help with spreading manure. Tom had a twelve by twelve shack not far from Lake Vermilion, about a mile back in the woods. Willmar went along. Pa's a good storyteller so we heard all about it at supper time.

"Tom had asked, 'Would you like a drink?'

"Pa had said, 'That would be just fine. Say, can you come and help me with that manure?'

"Tom said, 'No, I'm too busy.'

"Pa drank some coffee *punna*—You know that means he added liquor to it. He asked Tom, 'You're sure you can't make it.'

"'No. No. No,' said Business Tom.

"'Well, then I've guess we've got to go. Okay, Tom. I'll pour you another drink before we go. If you could possibly find your way to come to help tomorrow morning, I'll pay you well.' And off they went.

"Sure enough, there was Business Tom the next morning, knowing that Pa would pay him not just with money but with moonshine, too, though that was always left unsaid because Ma belongs to the Women's Christian Temperance Union.

Doris paused, thinking aloud. "Strangely enough, though, Business Tom was very good to Ma, whom he called 'Yennie,' never drinking when she was around.

"When she knew he was coming, she set someone to start warming the sauna, made him wash up and gave him Pa's clean clothes to put on. He couldn't do enough for Yennie. 'She be a good voman,' he used to try to say.

"When we needed some help with haymaking, Pa asked Business Tom to come. Someone had seen him on Saturday night at the Good Luck Pavilion, a favorite watering spot where Highways 73 and 22 join, so Pa left word there. We waited and waited until Pa began to ask around. After that night, no one has seen him. There are lots of stories about how and why, but no one had an answer to why or how he had disappeared.

"Then, Pa heard someone had accidentally killed and buried him. Business Tom had been with three men. It was being said around that he'd been killed and thrown into a well because he had been playing around with one of those men's wives, but no one knew for sure."

I was almost asleep when Doris asked one more question: "Were you . . . comfortable riding with Willmar? Have your Ma and Margie been . . . comfortable with him at camp? He hasn't made himself . . . too friendly?"

I didn't know what I wanted to say to his sister, but I admitted finally, "No. I think he was drinking before he came to the camp and again in Cusson and maybe, though I didn't see it, in Orr. But though Ma can be beautiful when she sets her mind to it, she doesn't wear corsets or pretty dresses in camp, just shapeless cotton frocks that hang from her shoulders to her ankles with aprons over them almost as big. She just pulls her hair back in a bun. Honestly, no one would guess how she really looks. Then there's just Margie, the pet of the whole crew. I think they'd kill anyone who hurt her."

She yawned. I yawned. "How is school going?" we both asked.

"I'll bet you're having fun. You're very pretty and interesting, you know. You aren't just any old average girl," Doris whispered.

"Me? Pretty? You must be kidding."

"Honestly, I'm not. All that black hair and those huge eyes that show so clearly how you feel. You may think you're ugly. But there are gonna be a lot of guys who are gonna look at you very differently once you get your hair bobbed and some up-to-date clothes. You are still going on next year?"

"Yes," I yawned, almost too tired to answer another question. "I'm working toward it as hard as I can, reading and studying every day. I'll have to keep on working for my room and board, but I'm learning more every day. I'm even learning to cook . . . a little. But I'll never earn any money," the yawn widened, "with my culinary skills."

"But look at the words you know. I don't even know what 'culinary' means! We've both got a long way to go before we reach our dreams, but let's vow to stay friends."

"I'd like that." Those were the last words I remember saying before I drifted off to sleep."

"Friends?" she asked.

I think I answered, "Friends," but it may have been in a dream.

Except for Eino Salin, I had not had a close friend since Amalia Barone years ago when we lived in Virginia.

"Friends." It was a good word to fall asleep on.

CHAPTER THIRTY-ONE

Pa

I did make it back to Vessel's for the Dinner Party, and their attitude toward me changed after that. It was not that less was asked of me or that I was treated more as family. They were simply more relaxed, more . . . understanding, more . . . human. In that sense my second semester was a considerable improvement.

Scholastically, I continued to work with all my might to outshine Charlie Beck. I worked so hard, in fact, that except for Charlie, I really made no other friends. In May I bought a yearbook and wondered why I had bothered. It was full of pictures of the good times the students had had. In between classes, kids were passing their books around writing, writing, and writing about memories of all the activities, all the parties, all the fun they had had together.

The signatures in my book came from teachers. They were very complimentary, which was gratifying. But I felt like a butterfly trying to break out of a chrysalis, so ready to experience the joy of living that I was virtually bursting with desire to go home. When the Vessels asked if I could stay an extra two weeks to help with spring cleaning, I suggested that they begin their vacation right away because it had been such a strenuous year and that we return together two weeks early and do a thorough fall cleaning. I think Mrs. Vessel was as relieved as I. She had lost ten pounds that year and truly needed to get away from being Mt. Iron's most sought-after hostess. Being perfect had taken its toll. It had on Mr. Vessel, too. He had had a lot to learn, administering a large, new high school with few rules or traditions to fall back on. The rules and traditions he accepted or allowed would become ex facto laws for classes to come to follow. He had walked a narrow line with panache, but he too needed a vacation. We packed our belongings and left together, saying "Goodbye, house!" with enthusiasm. Part of the

Vessel's summer would be spent with her family at their beach house in Maine, part with his family on a large estate in Kentucky, and part just traveling alone wherever their little roadster took them.

I waved as they drove away, his arm around her shoulders, and hoped someday to have a future as secure as theirs.

But nothing ever stays the same! Of all the lessons I learned during those years of high school, the most important one, perhaps, was that life turns as the earth turns, in cycles of light and dark, joy and sorrow, hope and despair. It's particularly difficult to accept that truism when the world turns black as I believe it will for all of us in some way at some time in our lives.

The reunion for Ma and Margie and me came the next day.

We had all changed during that year. Ma, dressed in her best clothes, her hair done up in a pompadour, still bore the air of command that had lived within her all her life. It had been nurtured and grown to fruition at the lumber camp. She was, now, her own person, capable of making her own decisions, intent upon making her own way in the world.

No longer was she physically or emotionally dependent upon Pa. She had broken from her chrysalis and flown free. It showed in her walk, in her speech, in her demeanor.

I had my qualms about Margie. The adulation she had received at camp had two edges. She had seemed perfectly at home with the praise and murmurs of gratitude she heard from the Johnson kids. But though she had kept to her studies religiously, she had also strengthened what had seemed to be an innate belief that what she wanted, she should get and what she believed was right . . . was. I foresaw fireworks.

As for me, I was no longer the skinny, scrawny kid with too much hair. I had let it flow naturally in a halo of black. I had gained not weight but form. I'd have to ask Ma how to flatten down my breasts so they wouldn't show, as the new styles indicated. No one questioned my name anymore. I was Marion. And the only residue of Finnish was a slight lilt I could not control in times of stress.

We met, as we had parted, at the Johnson place in Alango. It was a Sunday so we went to church with Alfred and Jennie. I was entranced with the triptych above the semi-circular altar at their Unitarian Church. The left panel showed a homestead farm in the background with a farmer tilling the soil and the iron mines in the foreground. Central to the whole was a young girl, my age, holding books and setting out toward the panel on the right. It could have been a courthouse or a legal building of some sort, but I saw it as a school, the dividing line between those who accepted the farm and the iron mine from those who, with books in hand, traveled on into that new, difficult, and challenging world where they could achieve their dreams.

The speakers were Reverend Riisto Lappala and his wife, Milma Lappala. They both spoke of nature and the spirit or soul which pervades all things. I listened, rapt, for I had never heard anyone verbalize what I believed about the spirit world, which surrounds and encompasses us. After the service, I had a brief conversation with them. They did not serve congregations in Mt. Iron or in Zim, but they did have a church in Virginia. I vowed to get there whenever I could.

When Willmar paid Ma the money she and Margie had earned that winter—and a bit more, he offered us a ride home.

Ma thanked him but said, "No. It is time for our family to go together." So she once again thanked the Johnsons for their hospitality, promised we would return for a visit, and paid for our train rides back to Zim.

The first thing Ma did when we got there was to go to Salin's store where she paid them everything we owed and studied the fabric and patterns, planning for new winter coats, new winter dresses with buttons and piping, and looked for ideas for skirts and blouses that might be more up-to-date for me.

"We'll look at the yearbook to see what the girls are wearing," she said. "And we will bob your hair right now. Mrs. Salin," she asked, "you do such a good job with Sara's and Eino's hair, would you consider giving Marion a brand new bob?"

"Now?" asked Mrs. Salin.

"Now," affirmed Ma.

"Can you make these?" I asked, showing her the modern dresses in the catalogs. I had forgotten the old Ma.

"Of course," she said.

What a relief it was to return to a total belief in her ability to recreate any dress she saw! Why, she had done it for years!

Half an hour later, my head incredibly lighter, my hair still wavy, but under control, we left, our luggage in hand. Margie asked, "When can I get my hair bobbed, Ma?"

"When you are old enough" was Ma's firm answer.

It was about a mile from Salin's to our house, but all too soon we heard a voice singing. Pa.

Mr. Salin hurried after us. "Are you sure you want to go there right now?" he stammered, as he did when faced with an uncomfortable situation. "Knute is there, and . . . I'm afraid . . . he has been . . . imbibing."

"It's time we faced that, too," Ma answered, though her steps slowed. Margie and I moved behind her, forming a straight line. I was afraid. Margie grabbed my hand and held on viselike, as if she didn't want to fall away from its hold.

"Ah," slurred Pa, seeing us coming. "So, here is my family, 'home from the sea and the hunter home from the hill' except that I'm the one who is home from the hill."

Ma stopped several yards away from the doorway where he stood, brandishing a bottle.

"Nothing to say to your beloved husband, eh?" he asked. "Well, I've got a lot to say to you. Where have you been all winter? I see you coming home all spruced up with boxes and bags under your arms. You've been earning money, I gather. How?

"Did you find greener pastures again than old Knute Pietari Brosi?"

Ma struggled to keep her temper. "We worked at a logging camp in Cusson all winter. On our way home we stopped at Salin's to pay our bill. Marion went to high school in Mt. Iron, working for her room and board, and Margie has been at camp with me."

Ma tried to move past him on the stairs, but he sat on a step, set down the bottle, and begun rubbing a piece of rectangular steel against a whetstone. He wasn't about to move.

"I have to go to the outhouse, Margie," I said. "Want to come along?" It seemed a safe place for now.

Pa grabbed Ma and wrenched her arm so the luggage fell, and she was forced to sit down on the step below him. "I been here thinking for many days. And I realized that ever since we got married and even before, it was never what I wanted. We always had to do what was best for you and the kid. You never stopped to listen to me and my side of the story. Why did I quit jobs? What were my reasons? You never cared. All you ever cared about was that I brought in money. Well, now I've had a job that brings in lots of money, and where have you been? Gone. God knows where. No note. No message. No letter. So when I bring in the money, you're not happy with that either. You're only happy when you can control me, make me do what you want. You have never cared what made me happy. You didn't care what I needed . . . as a man. All you cared about is the money."

He had grabbed her around the waist.

"Well, let's go inside now and you can give me what I want, and I'll give you what you want."

He had not reckoned on Ma's new strength. She wrenched herself away and went inside. "Knute, the children!"

"They're big enough to know enough to stay outside. They know what happens between a husband and wife."

I could hear him tearing at her clothes, at that beautifully tatted lawn shirtwaist, at the belt on her skirt. I could imagine him pulling the pins from her hair.

"Ah," he said. "That's better. I've always liked your hair. Down like that."

Then his mood changed. "And could you take care of yourself when there was a chance that I would have a son to carry on the Brosi name, that I would know absolutely is my own? No. You were crawling up on the roof pounding boards and building with the men. I've heard the story. I'm no dummy. Men talk."

"That's not fair!" Ma cried. "You know Margie is your own!"

"She's not a son. And when you finally have a son to give me, you don't take care of yourself enough to give him life. All your strength went into cleaning house. Oh, yes, we had the cleanest house in Little Kinney. The floors and the windows were scrubbed every week. The sheets were changed every week. Our clothes were not only washed but ironed, even my long-johns. You'd stay up half the night so everyone would know you're the best. The cleanest. The neatest housekeeper. The best cook. And it's your kid who has to be the smartest. Not mine."

He slapped her hard. I could hear her falling to the floor.

"You adopted her, Knute. And she could have been yours. We'll never know."

"Bullshit. There was somebody fucking you before me, and I know it and you know it and God knows it. And sure I signed some papers. But what does she do when I come around? She goes somewhere else. Where are the daughters who supposedly love their Pa so much? I haven't seen them for months!"

"Maybe we should go in," whispered Margie.

"That's not true," Ma said with her old fire and spirit, not mincing any words. "When you're drunk like this, they're just afraid of you."

"You think I'm drunk? Just wait. I'll show you what drunk is. And it is true. Even when I'm talking to her, Ilmi goes somewhere else in her mind. I'm a Brosi. I'm no Finnlander farmer without any brains. Did I let her marry Toivo Aro? The stupid jerk. All he wanted was his piece inside her pants. Tell me I don't take care of her. And tell me," he slapped Ma again, harder this time, "why missing her eighth grade graduation was such a big deal. As if that's an accomplishment. Brosi's have gone through grammar school and on to special fields of study for hundreds of years. I have degrees in botany and zoology. But what good are they when they're in Finnish?"

"That's just the point, Knute. Her achievement was in English. The books she studied, the poems she memorized, the examinations she took—all were in English. She's preparing herself to accomplish something in the English world. That's our world now whether you like it or not. Why don't you take time to learn English? Then those degrees would mean something. Then you could get the kind of work you're capable of!"

Pa must have lifted her off the floor and shaken her because everything in the house rattled. It sounded then as if he threw her down on the bed.

"Oh, yes, my lady. I should go to school with a bunch of farmers, dolts who can't even read and write Finnish. They're illiterate numbskulls, and you want me to lower myself to associate with them? Especially in this swamp?"

He banged her against the head of the bed. "Why on God's green earth did you take it in your mind to move to this Godforsaken hole?"

Ma's answer was so quiet we could barely hear it, but she wasn't backing down one whit. "Because we had no money to pay the rent. All the land here is not like ours, Knute. If you had been home, you could have chosen a good plot. There is sandy loam soil all around us. But I was too sick by fall and too tired to do anything but take what there was and try to make the best of it."

"And you couldn't wait for me." His voice dripped venom.

So did hers. "I've gotten tired of waiting for you. We waited in Port Arthur, and we waited in Malcolm, and we waited in Kinney until the money ran out. Then we were the last ones to file a claim and this was all that was left."

"And you took it." Again he repeated, "Without waiting for me."

"That's not fair," she shouted. "You know full well that we waited as long as we could. Would you have preferred to have had Margie eat ashes from the stove to keep from starving?"

"And then," his voice rose and fell in ugly waves, "you made friends with the Savolainens. They could have helped you in many ways, if you hadn't let your pride get in the way."

"Or allowed our family to be broken up. I won't take charity any more than you will. I'm not listening to this any more," Ma said.

We could hear her getting up. I imagine she was trying to straighten her clothes and her hair. "Either you leave or we will. I've taken all I can stand. Once, it almost killed me to have you leave. Now, I'm strong. I can make it on my own. I don't need you any more, and I don't want you any-more. You're drunk. I'm asking you, in light of all we once meant to each other, please leave."

He must have grabbed her again because we could hear the slobbery kisses and Ma saying, "No, Knute. That used to work. All I wanted was for you to love me. I'd have given anything for you to love me. Now I know I can manage on my own, and I will, the girls and I will. Marion will get her high school education, and Margie will at least graduate from eighth grade, no matter how hard the work is at logging camps."

"I suppose there's plenty of extra money to be earned at logging camps, too, if you're willing. You're a hot-blooded woman." He was pulling her clothes off again. "I liked this. I've always liked this. Ever since that first time in Rutland. No one forced you to go to bed with me. No one forced you to like it. Tell me you still like it. Tell me you want it. Scream when I come into you like you used to."

She must have pushed him away again. "No. Now it's over."

"Sure," he said, "blame Knute Pietari Brosi. That's always the answer. That's always been the answer. Now I'll tell *you* something, Mary Brosi. I don't give a damn. You just quit trying to control me and my life. From now on I'm going to do what I please and to hell with trying to be a husband to a woman who doesn't appreciate me and a father to kids who wish I would leave."

Ma must have opened her mouth again, but he interrupted whatever she was going to say. "Don't protest. I can see the looks on their faces.

"Go ahead. Go to bed. Slam your head against the wall. Maybe you'll knock some sense into it. As for me, I'm gone."

Then there was a silence, and we heard a drawer open and close. "I'll just leave you something to remember me by."

Ma screamed, "No, Knute, NO! GIRLS, RUN TOWARD SALINS' AS FAST AS YOU CAN. DON'T LOOK BACK, JUST RUN. TELL MR. SALIN WE NEED HELP. I'LL BE RIGHT BEHIND YOU!"

"OH, NO, YOU WON'T."

I looked back to see Ma fall on the stairs with Pa behind her. In his hands were the knives he had made us over the years—the ladies' knives he had made for Margie and me and the kitchen knives and the machete he had made for Ma to use when cutting up game. He threw one at her, but he was so drunk his aim was poor, and it stuck on the stairway by her hand.

She ran, following us, crying to us to hurry, falling, running again, with Knute behind her, throwing the knives at random.

I heard Ma cry out as one hit her, and I turned back to help her, pushing Margie to keep going.

Then we heard a thud, and, looking back, realized that Pa had passed out in the field, still holding knives. There was blood all over. I think in the fall he had cut himself.

Mr. and Mrs. Salin and Eino came running. Mrs. Salin took Margie first, forbidding her to look back but repeating "Look toward our house. That's where you need to go to be safe. Run as fast as you can and then faster."

Eino reached me as I staggered and fell into his arms, not onto the ground. The next thing I remember is lying on the horse-hair couch in the Salins' parlor with a cool cloth on my head and Mrs. Aro next to me, berating herself. "I knew this would happen. I sensed it in my bones. I should have been there to warn you. Oh, my poor child, I am so so sorry."

"Ma," I cried.

"Your ma is all right. It was only a glancing blow. I cleaned it and stitched it up, and she will be good as new if she can put this behind her and stay strong. Knute will be back full of apologies. We must band together to help her hold onto the strength not to give in. Arguments are one thing. But when it comes to this, it has all gone too far."

I wanted to ask her what happened to Pa, but she gave me a soothing draught of something sweet and strong, and before the words could form themselves, I fell asleep.

At one point during the day, I wove a conversation into my dreams. Perhaps it was real. Perhaps it was a hope given form.

Mrs. Aro was asking Ma, "Why do you keep taking him back when he hurts you so? Especially now when he's drinking?"

"Because I truly came to care about him," Ma sobbed. "Because when I met him in Rutland, it was as if a light came on, as it has ever since when I see him come in the door. Because when he kisses me and touches me and is gentle and kind, I truly believe he will be that way forever, and I forget all of this and just ache with wanting him to come home. I thought I was over it when I left Mrs. Maki's house and when I talked to Dr. Raihala and to Dr. Malmstrom. But oh, the pain, the pain."

"In your arm?" Mrs. Aro asked.

"Of finally facing the fact that I will never see him again, that the family I dreamed of having will never be!" Ma sobbed.

Drifting in and out of consciousness, I listened to that conversation through ears blurred with sedation. And I called Mrs. Aro and told her what I had heard Ma say and asked her if she could help me to sleep again because I could not think of those things right now . . . or maybe ever.

She understood and helped me slip back into a welcoming gray pillow that held me as I fought to keep from remembering. The harder I fought, the more sleep eluded me, until someone lifted my head from the pillow and began to stroke my hair and utter the kinds of meaningless soothing sounds I used when Margie had trouble falling asleep.

When I finally woke up, my head was on a pillow on Eino's lap and he was sound asleep with his head on the back of a sofa pillow, his hands still stroking my hair, his voice still saying, "Shhh," like the sound of a wave washing onto the shore.

An overwhelming feeling of faith surrounded me, encompassing me in arms stronger and more profound in their origin than Eino's, and I fell asleep again, this time into a dreamless, healing rest.

I can't say I've ever forgotten that horrible time. I think Margie was young enough so that it faded from her memory, surfacing in nightmares now and again, but not in questions or discussions. I don't think she could articulate either what had happened or the feelings it aroused.

I had always known the blackness that lay there underneath Pa's relationship with us. There were two Pas—the gentle, loving, creative soul who wrote and dreamed and sang and held birds and chipmunks in gentle hands—and this Pa from whom hatred spewed like lava, often with no warning at all.

To Ma, it seemed, a family must be built upon two people who were married for better or for worse, keeping to each other in good times and in bad—a ma and a pa, in other words, and, if and as they came, children. She had been willing for years to play the "Nothing Ever Happened" game or to lose her temper so badly, Pa would leave, and we would go on as if nothing had happened.

To Pa, our family was a sham, a pretense, a play he sometimes entered into as one of the players but mostly denied, perhaps feeling it had been built upon lies and deceit. Who would ever know? Liquor had loosed the black underpinning of his beliefs in a fiercer way than we could ever have imagined. Before, he had simply left. This time, he wanted to take us with him . . . into that black oblivion.

Ma and I discussed this all over and over again until it became so old that, like a Victrola record, overplayed and scratched so the original sound was not clear.

I truly do not know what happened to Pa during those next years. Ma talked about filing divorce papers, but we never had the money to hire an attorney and go through the formal court process of legally separating him from us. Gradually, as time went on, we thought of him less and less. Someone, Mr. Salin or Mr. Aro, I don't know which, found an address to which they sent his mirror, his shaving supplies including the cup, brush, strap, and soap, his fiddle, and his extra clothing.

When he died, years and years later, and I, as his only surviving relative was informed, I received a trunk which contained all of those things, and, in addition, his birth certificate, his naturalization papers, never completed, his alien registration card, and two pictures of Ma, one sideways with her hair hanging to her hips, one full face in her white lawn waist with her hair in a pompadour.

Of all of the tragedies that life can offer, I think the relationship between Ma and Pa exemplified one of the most devastating. Both good people, they should never have married. Or, once married, they should have found time and space to talk through their differences. I read once that there is a very thin line between love and hate. In their case, the line was as thin as a piece of golden thread, strung until it is almost invisible, but not broken. Ma was never quite the same after that episode. There was a brittle edge to her that had not been there before. Like the sharp edge of a razor, it had cut so deep that no amount of bandaging could heal the wound. She gave us all the love she had to give, but something essential to her being was lost, irretrievably, and I grieved, not knowing what it was or why or what to do.

I had so looked forward to the summer, to the fun it would hold. But I was torn, too, in a way I didn't understand. A part of me vowed I would never allow myself to love a man so deeply that his loss would cause that deep a pain.

It took many years and much more experience for me to learn that love is an absolute, like truth and beauty. It exists beyond and above the conscious control of the most intelligent and well-educated mind, for it creeps in, unaware, and once there becomes so much a part of the whole that one who loves and the one who is loved are truly one, though, as John Donne put it, they stand alone as the pillars of a temple stand alone or as the strings of a lute spring apart though they quiver to the same music.

I did not hear the music that summer, thank goodness. It was, other than that one episode, a summer of innocence.

Chapter Thirty-Two
Summer Fun

It was so long since we had given ourselves up to pure pleasure—to what we wanted to do rather than we had to do—that both Ma and I had to spend a long time adjusting.

That must not sound like fun to anyone else, but to Ma and Margie and me, it was heaven. We had at least two months to ourselves to do as we wished, and the List included everything we could possibly cram into our allotted time.

Even what we had to do sounded like fun. I yearned to sleep between clean sheets that had blown dry on the lines and to hear the creak of the clothes pins as I fastened them down. I wanted to scrub and clean every inch of our Happy Corner—even the outhouse—until it shone, windows and walls and cupboards and shelves and books and everything. I yearned for Ma's *pulla* and *kropsua* and for hot saunas at Salins.

Of course, first on the list was what we all wanted most—to turn our little home until it was spic and span. We pounded the rugs and scoured the windows, starched the curtains, and aired the quilts. We even took the mattresses and springs outside for a good airing. Every shelf was emptied and washed and rearranged, and every bit of clothing, worn or unworn, was washed and dried outside and ironed and tried on for size, tucks and seams widened or narrowed preliminary to a remaking.

Ma scythed down the overgrown grass from around the house, and we asked Mr. Salin for a small plot of sandy soil so we could plant our own garden, which we tilled, weeded, and watered diligently. All of these workaday tasks set bulkheads between the ugliness of the confrontation with Pa and the beauty of a summer at home together. We gloried in everything we did.

When Margie woke up one morning, whining, "Can't I go and play with Sara?" we figured we had turned the corner into the natural world again, and we went back to the weekly routine of Monday washday, Tuesday ironing, Wednesday baking, Thursday cleaning, Friday shopping or mending or sewing, Saturday visiting with sauna and a dance, and Sunday relaxing with guests or books or long walks.

I knew we would be receiving a few visitors from Mt. Iron. Laurence Beck and Charlie for sure. Their dad had a car. And "Cliff" might stop to see us, too, once he was through with Barber College.

But more than anything else, we were sufficient unto ourselves.

Every Saturday night meant a dance at some town hall. The halls were just that—large buildings with a stage on one end and room for serving coffee and treats either behind the performers on the stage or in a kind of basement cellar built under the stage. During the winter, people in the community put on plays and performances, and a system of rolled backdrops had been painted to give an air of authenticity to the plays. Some were melodramas like "Little Nell," who needed to be saved from a dastardly villain. Others were musicals, depending on which community had the best choir. For performances, the chairs were arranged as in an auditorium. But when there was a dance, folding chairs were set around the edge of the hall, right under the windows, which could be opened on a hot night.

Every community had a hall. Sometimes the community was split between hall people and church people. Sometimes the hall people were considered Communists or atheists. But it didn't matter on Saturday night. Everyone went to the dances, from the tiniest baby to the oldest gramma and grampa, and everyone danced with everyone else.

Usually men would ask women to dance. The dance was divided into three sets. Then he would walk her back to her chair and ask someone else.

The men mostly stood at the back of the hall, maybe because it was easier to get outside to sip a shot of moon, maybe because they were shy, or maybe because it just was the custom.

But oh, we danced!

One night at Little Swan, a familiar looking face stopped me in the middle of a waltz and asked, "Are you Ilmi Brosi?"

I laughed. "Well, I used to be. Now that I'm in high school, I'm mostly called 'Marion.'"

"Don't you remember me?" she asked.

We moved over to the side of the circle of dancers, and I looked at her closely. I wanted her to be . . . but . . . "Are you . . . Java?"

"Yes!" she exclaimed, and we laughed and cried and ignored our partners completely until they disappeared. We sat down together, not knowing where to start.

"How do you happen to be here in Little Swan?" she asked. "I heard that you and your ma and Margie had moved to Zim, but the next summer when I asked, no one seemed to know what happened to you."

Whoo. How to explain what happened? I hardly knew how to start. "We did move to Zim, and I intended to go to high school in Virginia."

"Yes, and I wanted you to come to live with me in Evanston, Illinois, and go to school with me."

"Oh, Java, it was such a bad time. Even after we got the retribution money—and I have never forgotten that it was your idea!—and moved here, Pa was never here. Baby Teddy died."

"I am so sorry about the baby," she looked as if she would cry.

"It was a very bad year, too long a story to tell here." I gave her another hug.

She returned it, saying, "It is *so* good to see you. And I am very sorry about the baby. I know how much you all wanted it."

"It hit Ma the hardest. For a while . . . we just lost her . . . but I finished eighth grade in Zim and then got a job during the summer working for my room and board—but that's a story and a half. What about you? How do you happen to be in Little Swan? Aren't you staying in Kinney with your aunt? You look wonderful!"

She did. She always did. Although she spoke half Finnish and half English, her hair style and her clothes and shoes spoke Chicago. Her older brother had gone to the Chicago area first and started a small trucking company, raising vegetables and bringing them into town for sale. He had a green thumb, and very soon he had people working for him.

"You know there would have been room for you with us," I offered.

"Well," she paused, "I was supposed to stay with Aunt Mary in Kinney for the summer again, but it just didn't work out." She looked down at her beautifully manicured hands. "She pawned me off on a family called the Juntunens, who have to many children to have enough beds. Oh, Marion, they don't even have sheets on their beds! We sleep between army blankets. It's . . . not a nice place. I was just about to turn around and go back to Evanston when now tonight I've seen you, and I don't want to go back. How can we see each other?"

"I'm serious. Come live with us. We've only got one big room and two beds, but we can do two to a bed."

Jokingly she asked, "Do you have sheets?"

"Yes, and we wash and iron them, too!"

Arms around each other, we set off looking for Ma, who didn't hesitate for a minute. "The more the merrier," she said, in Finnish, of course. I don't know why what she said always sounded better that way. It was as if she were repeating old sayings or epigrams or aphorisms that just fit the situation. It made me wish that in my wholehearted desire to learn English I had not let my Finnish lapse.

And so, part of the fun of that summer was named Java.

I was too shy to accept anything that seemed like a date. But Java wasn't. She treated the boys who asked her to dance matter-of-factly as friends, and before we knew it, we each had a "special" friend. Hers was Leonard. Mine was Arnie. All four of us knew it was nothing serious. But they had a car and liked to dance, and, oh, we did have fun!

Ma welcomed everyone. If we got home at one o'clock in the morning, and Java said she needed to wash her hair, Leonard hauled water into the heater on the stove and washed it and brushed it dry into her naturally curly bob.

Arnie never came over without bringing something—a chicken, some fresh potatoes, corn just picked from the garden, a load of wood, which he chopped and piled.

They called Ma "Ma" and included her in all of the teasing. They treated Margie like a little sister, building her a swing from an old tire and rope on the one decent-size tree on our property.

It was, though we did not know it then, the last summer like that we would ever have—Margie and Ma and I. I remember every day of it, for it was a storybook summer—enough rain but never too much.

During June we picked strawberries and ate and picked and ate and picked and ate and picked and canned and canned and made jelly (which was an art I could not master, though Margie did), and jam until the strawberry season ended. Ma told us to be sure to come right home after the dance. She had a surprise for us—strawberry shortcake made with her own whipping cream and pound cake and rich with strawberries, fresh and mashed into sauce, so sweet they needed no sugar.

By late summer we were picking from our own garden of potatoes, carrots, rutabaga, onions, green beans, and a few experimental rows of corn.

We had had to work the soil well first before we could plant. Unfortunately, that was before we met Arnie and Leonard, but Ma and Margie and I had done pretty well for ourselves with one tilling and one weeding and one thinning, and we had kept it up every week.

It seemed as if we had no longer stripped every bush of blueberries than the raspberries ripened. That was the only stressful part of the whole summer—to find good picking spots with lunch and water along—and picking until every container we had was full. Then we had blueberry pie, blueberry muffins, blueberry pancakes, enough again, because it was a good year, to put up a goodly supply for the winter.

We tried not to think of the winter. We tried not to think of the fall. We took every summer day as it came, savoring the delights it offered.

We even coaxed Ma into going swimming in the St. Louis River, which was running high but not dangerously so. That became part of our daily routine, a part we looked forward to because it meant that every night we could go to bed fresh and clean.

Ma rigged up extra cheesecloth on the windows and door to keep out the bugs, and between that and our relentless battle against any other encroaching creatures, we kept the house comfortable.

And we continued to have company.

Cliff Johnson came.

But Ma made no bones about not liking him at all. "He's the dangerous kind. The 'happy-ever-after' kind. I've had plenty of experience with how long happy-ever-after lasts, and I don't want any of that for you. You have two years of high school left."

Nothing and no one would keep me from finishing high school. But Ma feared for me, and, based on her experience, I understood.

What she did not understand was that to survive, I needed more than a happy-ever-after promise—or even an offer.

All I asked for that summer was fun, just a little fun to offset the angel food cake night and the maid's outfit and Pa's drunken attack.

I deliberately sought it out and found that it was there, waiting. I just needed to be open to it.

No one can count on tomorrow, I knew. I wanted each day of summer to be "as rare as a day in June. Then heaven tries earth if it be in tune, and over it softly her warm ear lays. Whether we look or whether we listen, we hear life murmur or see it glisten." I knew the quote wasn't exact, but the feeling was.

Laurence and Charlie Beck drove until they found us, and I found to my surprise that they were not at all like Wilho Field. The three of us actually enjoyed going back over the year, reviewing classes and discussing the teachers. Moreover, they were very kind to Margie, which I appreciated.

I had not been aware of how much Margie had grown and matured during that last year, and deep inside I worried because I feared that neither Ma nor I was giving her adequate guidance. I hadn't needed much: it was thrust on me. But Margie had always been "the baby." Clearly, she was not the baby anymore. She danced as much as I did on Saturday nights, and I was not always sure of where she was during intermission.

But no one was as nice to her as Cliff. He treated her as he did his sisters, not putting up with any monkey business, but not ignoring her either. They played ball. He bought her the makings of a kite, which they put together and flew. They looked for pretty rocks and washed and displayed them in Ma's pink glass dishes.

When Laurence and Charlie came to visit, Ma served them homemade lemonade from the gold-trimmed glasses that had been her last gift from Uncle Charles.

When Cliff came, she served him leftover coffee in a stoneware cup.

If Laurence and Charlie came to visit, Ma made fresh *pulla*.

If Cliff made a date, he had to make do with left-over *kropsua*.

But when Laurence and Charlie left, only the dirty dishes or a book or two for me were left behind. When Cliff left, a chicken had been killed, its feathers picked, and it was soaking in cold water, ready to roast, the woodpile was taller, and more wood was split. When Cliff came, he bought staples—apples or crackers, or lime for the outside toilet. When he was there, Margie tended to be quieter and better behaved. She wanted to please him. So did I.

Eventually, though it took the whole summer, so did Ma.

He never promised what he did not fulfill. He lifted things that were too heavy for us. He mended things that needed fixing.

He came on Saturday night to drive us to a dance . . . but not every Saturday night.

Eventually, even Ma capitulated.

But August came, as it always does, too soon, too soon. Ma got a job at the Johnsons' boarding house in Winton, the center for logging in the Ely area, and Margie was enrolled in school there.

Fifty miles or more would separate us this year without a promise of Christmas vacation. It seemed like a million miles, a million years.

Ma packed all that we had harvested and all that we had preserved, which had increased her salary considerably.

But it left our Happy Corner empty.

My junior year began early with a letter from Mrs. Vessel reminding me that we were going to give the house a good fall cleaning before school started.

Ma and Margie left at the same time. Ma had written to the principal in Winton and asked if there would be someone willing to give Margie some extra early tutoring because she was so far behind.

During one of our last weekends, Doris Johnson came to stay overnight, and I told her about Pa. She said, "I think all men are like that. My dad had a girlfriend for a long time until Willmar actually brought Ma there to confront him. Ma threatened to divorce him, but what would she live on? Where would she go? Your ma has just Margie to worry about— and you, of course—but Ma has ten of us, though only eight are still at home, and Faye is so fragile. Ray, too, is too small for her to get a job. And what could she do to earn money? Make rugs?

"Last Christmas Dad had been in Cook drinking and carousing all day. We girls had prepared a really special dinner because, thanks to Pat and her good salary, there was a tree in the living room with presents on it. Two apiece for everyone from Pat. We got together to get Ma and Dad one big present—a Victrola. It was going to be a real Christmas. Marie had even invited Ed Lofgren, back from the war with a damaged lung—mustard gas—to join us. They had been seeing a lot of each other, even though she had had a kind of understanding with Hank Saari for a long time. But once Ed came home, there's been no one else for her. She always has had a kind heart for anyone hurt."

Ma and Margie were gone that weekend, one of the last ones in August, and Doris had come to spend the night with me. We had gone to a dance, of course, and Arnie and Leonard had driven us home. Java had left for Evanston, and it seemed as if the summer were already at its end.

"Anyway . . . what was I telling you? Oh, I remember. It was about Dad and Christmas. By the time Dad got home, all the food was overdone. He was so drunk, he couldn't make it up the back stairs. The boys were really mad at him. They took him into the sauna. That and a quart of coffee kind of sobered him up. Then all of the boys told him that if he ever came home drunk again or visited Sig Nora, the whore, they'd kick him out and never let him come home again.

"I'm sorry, Marion. I shouldn't have gotten going on this. But I feel like you do—as if I've *got* to get a job so I can help Ma."

We sat quietly for a while, tears mingling as we hugged each other.

"And your pa? Have you tried to track him down?"

"It wouldn't do any good. He'd stick around for a week or two and then off he'd go, leaving Ma hurt. He's hit her, once with a knife. Always with his cruel tongue. It's as sharp as his knives. It makes me afraid. Of caring for someone, you know?"

"Me, too," she added soberly. Then she bounced up and said, "Here we are worrying about September when it's still August. Isn't there a dance tonight?"

"I know there's one someplace, but no one has stopped to pick me up."

"Cliff can't. But what about your friends Arnie and Leonard?"

Sure enough, they did, thank goodness, and we danced until we dropped. Then Arnie wanted *pulla* and Leonard said he'd knead it so we stayed up all night, giggling and laughing and telling Doris about the summer and how much we missed Java and wished they had met each other.

"Maybe next year," we all said, hopefully.

It would be the last dance for Arnie and Leonard for a while. They had each picked up a job in Chisholm that had some promise of a future.

I had said I would not be kissed until I graduated, but after we had eaten the *pulla* and done the dishes and walked the boys to the door, I reached up to give each one of them a light peck on the cheek. Doris did the same. It felt right, somehow, like a period at the end of a sentence.

We knew we'd probably never see them again. And in every way, they had protected our innocence.

Our golden summer was over. It deserved the obeisance of a kiss.

CHAPTER THIRTY-THREE
Questions

*I*t was the first assembly of the school year, of our senior year, to be exact, and Superintendent Muench began with a
speech directed at all of the high school students.

He took the art of elocution seriously. It was obvious from the size
of the pieces of paper on the lectern that he had taken this opportunity to
elucidate very seriously.

He was well into what looked like the second page when he reached
what sounded like the key question of the entire lecture.

"Which," he emphasized, using his hand to indicate the choices, "has the
stronger effect on determining an individual's future? Is it the heart, the character and personality of the individual? Or, on the other hand, to what degree,
pundits question, is life governed, not by the decisions of the individual himself, but by an unknowable all-powerful happenstance, which one might refer
to as the hand of God or an inanimate First Cause or by the rules of, laws for,
and thence Powers of Nature, all of which are beyond the individual's control?

"To rephrase the question, does humankind in its temerity dare to suggest that it is we ourselves who control what our lives will be?"

Superintendent Muench coughed, took a drink of water, shuffled his
notes, glanced at his captive audience, the classes of 1928, 1929, 1930, and
1931—the seniors, juniors, sophomores, and freshmen—of the Mt. Iron
High School.

During his break, my best friend and alter-ego Ellen Kutsi whispered
to me, "It's the heart. No question. The heart has it first, foremost, coming and going, now and always."

I stifled a giggle. Trust Ellen to find something to laugh at even at this
first moment of what we should be considering seriously, the fundamental
question not only of our senior year but of our lives in general.

Since it was the first assembly of the year, the superintendent had vowed to begin on a serious note, "Ahem," he had stated to a general meeting of the school board, "I intend to deliver a lecture to set the year off on a suitable tone, centering upon thoughts which these young people need to consider as they begin this year in their pathway toward graduation and, in fact, toward their future."

Clearing his throat, he continued to the assembly, "Standing at the fork of the pathway of life, looking down the undergrowth at two roads, upon what basis is the decision made to take the first step down one particular trail and not the other?

"Is it we ourselves of our own volition who make the choices, so that the twistings and turnings of the pathways of our own lives are determined and governed by ourselves alone, by our own personalities, by our own character traits? Or are our lives governed by that unknowable, all-powerful happenstance, whether wielded by fate or God, or an inanimate First Cause, or immutably by the rules of, laws for, and thence Powers of Nature?"

Such was the question addressed to the student body in the presence of the members of the Mountain Iron School Board—Mr. C.A. Webb, clerk; Mr. Alexander Gill, chairman; and Mr. A.W. Saari, director; Mrs. Pearl M. Heath, director; Mr. R. Trevarthen, treasurer; and Mr. August Lostrom, director, on September the fifth, the day we began another step in our high school careers.

Ellen and I, dubbed as "The Gold-Dust Twins" because we looked so much alike, sat in the third and fourth seats of the back row, out of alphabetical order in honor of our status as seniors, trying not to give in to the impulse to jiggle so the folding chairs would squeak, avoiding each other's eyes, knowing we were thinking exactly the same thing about the erstwhile board members.

Had we ever discussed the board members, we would undoubtedly have nicknamed Mr. Webb "Duck" because of the size of his ears, which approached winged proportions. Mr. Gill would have become "Charlie" because of his small square Chaplin moustache. Mr. Trevarthen looked like "Grampa" because his eyes were kind, his hair gray, and his smile—directed right at us—real. Mr. Lostrom we'd term "Sniffles" because it looked as if he were breathing into his moustache. And Mrs. Heath had to be "Egdon" because we had just finished reading our summer assignment, Thomas Hardy's *The Return of the Native*.

At least I had. Miss Heino had assigned it as an extra-curricular project back when I was in eighth grade, but I had enjoyed rereading it in between dances and merriment the previous summer. I read the exciting parts aloud to Ellen so she could at least recognize the names of the characters.

I had been so moved by Eustacia Vye's regrettable demise in the weir that only severe disapprobation from Ma prevented me from acting out the scene in the blood-sucker-infested waters of Wiita's Creek, which ran through their forty acres in Little Swan, to the immense delight of Margie and all of her friends.

Considering Superintendent Muench's questions extremely profound, I weighed alternatives, decided upon my own personal response, then refocused my eyes and attention on the man behind the podium, who seemed totally oblivious not only of my attempt at attention, despite Ellen's quips, but of the corresponding inattention expressed with sighs all around me.

The high school students struggled to maintain a relatively adult demeanor. But feet, unused to shoes after a barefoot summer, wiggled. School dresses or skirts and middies or dress shirts and ties, chosen for a fall morning's chill rather than early September's unseasonable sultry heat, chafed. The morning was redolent of summer's warmth and freedom.

A vague squeaking began, as if a violin were being tuned, far to the right of the back row where our class sat in sacrosanct splendor. The unpadded wooden assembly seats, joined together in lines of ten, accompanied every movement up, down, or sideways, as if they needed rosin, like Pa's fiddle.

The squeaking escalated into the junior section.

Superintendent Muench, separated from the noise by the sophomores and freshmen in the front rows, remained oblivious. "Or, on the other hand," he pontificated, "does humankind in its temerity suggest that it is we ourselves who control what our lives will be?"

Clearly, the lower classmen agreed with the supposition that they were in control of their seats.

The members of the Board of Education, sitting in folding chairs flanking the superintendent, shifted also with obvious discomfort as the accompaniment began to move in unison.

Mr. Muench stepped to the side of the podium, spreading his legs apart like Colossus straddling the harbor of Rhodes. "Standing at a fork in the path of life, at the twists and turns ahead, at the undergrowth, upon what basis is the decision made to take the first step down one particular trail and not the other?"

Someone whispered, "Maybe one foot's asleep."

Another whisper said, "Maybe it's just time to take a leak." I was certain the voice was Kabe's.

Titters spread.

"Is it we ourselves of our own volition who make the initial and all subsequent choices," Mr. Muench continued to intone abstractedly, repeating himself endlessly, "so that the twistings and turnings of the pathways of our lives are determined and governed by ourselves alone, by our own personalities, by our own latent and active character traits?"

Turning back to the lectern to find his place, Mr. Muench glanced, by sheer chance, it seemed, to the right and caught the eyes of Mr. C.A. Webb, who was holding his breath. Mr. Webb's eyes flicked to the audience, signaled danger, flicked back to Mr. Muench, who turned.

Immediately, everyone in the lower classes focused on him. All eyes in the junior class refocused on him. All movement in the senior class ceased, all heads lifted, all eyes signaled attention.

Mr. Muench breathed again. So did the other members of the board.

So did I with heartfelt relief. I rather liked Mr. Muench, who always greeted me with a polite, "Good afternoon, Miss Brosi," when I passed him on my way out of school to begin dinner at the Vessels'.

During each of the four days since classes had convened, we had been the last two to enter the building, I to scurry up the steps to the lecture rooms on the second floor, he to continue his deliberate march toward his office behind one of the elaborately arched main-floor windows.

I knew deep down that he only remembered me because we had been introduced and reintroduced during the social occasions held at the Vessels.

So far I had made and served dinners for the members of the school board and for the administrators for three years in a row. I knew them better than I knew some of my own classmates.

The only real friend I had made was my seat-mate Ellen Kutsi. Both of us worked for our room and board. We snatched time to talk when we went grocery shopping for our respective households and tried to sit near each other during classes.

The difference between us was that I was much more serious about

265

my future than she was about hers. No one and nothing had interfered with my direction or my goal: it was straight ahead toward graduation with a perfect score so far and college in my future—the best that I could earn.

I really had thought about what Mr. Muench said, and I knew what my own answer had always been. I wanted to be and had been "the Master of my fate, the Captain of my soul."

It would have been much easier to give up and grant the Ghost of the Future—by whatever name he-she-or-it is called—total control, full power over my actions. How delightful it would be to languish in the hands of an unanswerable fate!

"It's not my fault!" I could then respond to criticism. "These things just seem to happen to me!"

HA! Nothing in my life, at least during the last four years had ever "just happened" without my making a conscious decision to act. As I looked back, every single effect had had a cause, the basis of which had been a decision I had made, mostly on my own. Like Marley's chains and the Ghost of Christmas Yet to Come, my own experiences reaffirmed that asseveration. With certainty it had been my own hands and my own mind that had controlled my own decisions, and my only real fate had been having to live with the consequences.

My own decisions had led me to high school in Mt. Iron and to that second floor assembly hall. My own decisions would lead me either to failure or to a successful graduation. My own decisions would make me a teacher or an interpreter.

Ignoring Mr. Muench's peroration—for he too was clearly bypassing the fickleness of fate in favor of laying the future in our own hands and setting our own feet firmly on The Right Path—I mused about the choices I had made during the last years and about the after-effects of those choices.

I had of my own volition left our rented home in Kinney alone to seek Uncle Charles in Ely. It had been my decision to beg the gypsies for aid, my appeal to the coroner that divulged the truth about Uncle Charles' fate, my willingness to enter the pest house to trace the path of his lost money, my vow added to Eino's and Kabe's and Fatso's and Java's that had sealed the fates of the evil Mrs. Juola and her pawns, the brothers Smith, my desire for retribution that had contributed to the ultimate denouement and their indignity at the Forrest Hotel.

In the last analysis I had been culpable.

Or, were the sequence of events to be surveyed from a different vantage, I was to blame—for leaving Ma alone when she had needed me and for causing her no end of anguish and worry. The possibility that my actions had contributed to Baby Teddy's death and Ma's depression will haunt me as long as I live. I was to blame for involving the gypsies and the Savolainens in deeds that bordered upon the nefarious. I didn't think that my actions had contributed to the widening rift between Ma and Pa, but something or someone lay at the root of their problems, and since neither of them seemed to have the same harsh words for Margie that were directed toward me . . . It hurt to pursue that thought.

I was to blame and ultimately accountable only to myself for the decision to go on to high school. With every waking moment it was I who would, by my own actions, had affirmed my commitment to work for my board and room and to do the studying that would lead me even farther into the land I had sought since that long-ago train ride that led us from Port Arthur, Canada, where it had been acceptable to talk Finnish to Malcolm, Minnesota, where the language of choice was English, and on to what I still thought of as "the land of the literate," an English land.

Moreover, I was once again fully aware of the moment in my life when I had articulated clearly and publicly what I wanted to do and where I wanted to go. It had happened the summer after my eighth-grade graduation when Pa was making one of his infrequent forays back to our lean-to house euphemistically then called "Happy Corner."

"Why didn't you send word? Why didn't you tell me?" he had shouted, accusatorily, blaming her.

"Why did I need to send word? Why didn't you just come home like most husbands and fathers do without having to be told?" Ma had shouted back.

As usual, neither had heard the other, either the words or the feelings that lay behind them. Was their relationship doomed by fate? Or by their own beings?

Ellen's nudge drew me back to the Mt. Iron high school assembly just in time for me to realize that the new creaks and shuffles indicated that everyone else was standing.

Mr. Vessel took the podium to thank Mr. Muench and initiate a round of applause as the superintendent bowed and followed the board members off the stage.

Classes were dismissed in inverse order, seniors first.

Was Pa the way he was . . . or Ma . . . or Margie . . . or I . . . as I grew even more that year, not just as a student, but as a person . . . were we what we were because of our own decisions? Or were we somehow following a path that was our "karma," a word which I had studied in a book on philosophy sent home for the summer for me by Miss Duda?

I had been so positive that I was in control. Were there forces at work that I could not control, other than Pa?

It was in many, many ways a year of revelation and deep and sincere reflection, a large part of which was dictated by a devilishly handsome, heartrendingly lovable junior named Gino Vanucci.

CHAPTER THIRTY-FOUR
Gino Vanucci

ino Vanucci. He was one year behind us in class ranking but a year ahead of me in age and decades in experience.

The most popular boy in school—tall, handsome, athletic, well-behaved—he was not much given to running around with any of the girls. Sometimes with a gang, but never with one special girl. I had never even presumed to say "hello" to him.

Ellen Kutsi and I were walking up together just on the edge of a group of seniors when I felt someone fall in next to me.

We had just finished watching the first football game that fall on a crisp, red and orange leafy day with a dazzlingly blue sky and just a hint of autumn in the air.

The team was walking behind us toward the showers, and suddenly there he was, holding onto his helmet, his hair all curly from sweat, wiping his face on the sleeve of his jersey.

Ellen quickly moved away, giving me The Eye.

"You're Marion Brosi, aren't you?" he asked.

I managed to croak, "Yes," and then my mind froze.

"Wanna go for a walk after supper?"

I wanted to say "I'd love to!" But reality intervened. "I work for the Vessels so I can't go anywhere or do anything until the supper dishes are done and then there's homework."

He shifted his helmet to his other hand and reached out to stop me so I wouldn't run away. "How about let's go to the library and do our homework together? You've taken Latin I? Maybe you could give me some help. I could use a tutor!"

"I'd be happy to," I managed, and he nodded as if it were settled before he ran to catch up with the rest of his team.

That was the beginning.

Just after I finished the dishes that night, there was a knock on the kitchen door.

"I think I'd better ask Mr. Vessel if it's okay," Gino said when I took my apron off and let him in. He waited there while I got Mr. Vessel from the living room.

"Good work this afternoon, Gino," Mr. Vessel said. "I think that last touchdown broke their willpower. It was nice to see us on the winning side again and good to see you in school. Can I do something for you?"

"I'd like to take Marion to the library. We could study together there, if that's all right with you."

"Fine. Just have her home before ten."

It was just that easy.

Pretty soon I came to trust that he would come, sometimes earlier, sometimes later, every night depending on the chores he had to do after school. He must have showered before he came because his hair was slicked back, though it was so curly it never stayed that way, and he had on a fresh shirt, usually with a V-necked sweater over it, sometimes slacks, sometimes knickers.

One night, I had actually come to the point of waiting for him, swinging on the gate, which opened from the picket fence into the steps toward the back door. He put his hands on top of mine and swung me back and forth a few times for good measure.

"Waiting for me, were you?"

I blushed. I shouldn't have been so obvious.

Lifting my chin, he said, "I'm glad. You're my girl, you know."

I had not known. My heart was pounding so hard I thought he would hear it.

"Do you have a lot of homework tonight?" he asked, continuing the swinging, but making sure it came closest to him when he drew it back.

"I do. But none of it's crucial. I can do it later." That was a real concession, the first time I had put him before the homework.

"Wanna go swinging on the kids' swings in the schoolyard?"

Of course I did. Gino, who was one of the "popular" kids, went there sometime during the week. I never had.

A lot of kids whose faces I recognized were there already, talking and laughing and playing as if they were in kindergarten. I didn't know all of

their names, but they all knew Gino. He introduced me casually, found a
swing, and up I went, reciting:

"Oh, how I love to go up in a swing
Up in the air so blue!"

"Did you just make that up?" Gino asked.

"No. It's from a children's book. But I've never really had a chance to
go on this kind of swing before, and it just came to my mind . . . how perfectly the poet captured the feeling."

"Do you like poetry?"

"I love it." Then I wanted to bite my tongue off. Here I was with the
captain of the football team, discussing poetry.

"My mother never had a chance to read to any of us, there were so
many." He drew the swing back to ground level again, put his hands over
mine and his chin on my head. "I've always thought that . . . if I ever got
married . . . I wouldn't want to have so many children . . . that I didn't have
time to spend with them . . . and I wouldn't want to get married until I
could support a wife . . . and a family . . . so she wouldn't have to work."

He didn't seem to want an answer, so I listened and for a brief time
we were alone in the midst of a crowd of kids clowning and goofing
around.

Then he grabbed my hand and we did the teeter-totter and laughed
because when we lost our balance, it fell with a bang.

Victor Lahti, one of the evening janitors responsible for keeping kids in
hand, came out about then. "Youse kids are always bounding and bounding,"
he told us. "Be quiet or go home where you belong now that it's getting dark."

It was hard not to laugh, but we didn't. No one talked back or made
fun of him. I was so glad. He was such a kind man. Once in a while when
I was really rushed, he had slipped me a dollar or two and told me to buy
myself some food. I think the word about four weiners had spread from the
butcher shop around town.

Gino held my hand as we went back to Vessels, and when we got to
the garden gate, he gave me a kiss—just a light, friendly peck on the cheek.
But a kiss nonetheless. I knew it was coming, and I didn't turn away.

I had wanted him to kiss me.

I didn't want to wash my face that night.

Suddenly, from being a nobody, I was somebody. I was Gino Vanucci's
girl. Kids I didn't know said, "Hi," to me in the halls.

Mr. Vessel drew me aside one night as I was waiting and asked if I were able to keep up with my homework, going out like this every evening.

It was ironic because although there were trips to the playground and long walks when we talked about school and the latest songs and shared gossip, we mostly did go to the library.

My grades, if anything, improved. I improved. I stood and sat straighter. I held my head up while walking the halls. I yelled for Gino at football games and waited for him, taking it for granted that we would walk up the hill together.

I found myself busy in other ways, too. Miss Duda named me editor-in-chief of the *Mountaineer*, our annual yearbook, with Ellen Hill as business manager.

We had no trouble with the dedication page—"To the Ideal of Education. We Climb though the Rocks Be Rugged" has led us through our high school days. May it serve as a shining star to light our pathways to our goal, "Success."

One night we walked to the front stairs of the school, built of solid granite on each side of the imposing central entrance, and Gino drew stick figures of MBGV 1927-1928 on a little piece of paper and left it sitting on the raised brick edges of that entry with its curved archway and windows with the balcony above.

It took him a long time to open up about his family and friends. I could tell that he adored his mother, and when he was not walking me to classes, he was somewhere in the vicinity of Kabe, who was in my class.

"Shouldn't you be a senior, too?" I ventured one night when he had been unusually quiet. We had met a couple of guys from my class, and Gino had reminisced with them about some stunt they had pulled in junior high.

He scuffed the dirt with his foot, then looked at me, made a decision, and started talking. We walked from the library to Vessels, and he talked. We walked past Vessels to the edge of the open pit mine, and he talked. He talked straight for two hours that night. About how hard it had been for him to drop out of school just when he would have been starting high school. About the financial problems his family faced and how hard his mother had worked to solve them. Finally he and his brother Rocci had taken over, gotten fairly good jobs, and/or enough jobs so they could survive. They had saved as much as they could.

I listened and made supportive sounds. I don't think he had ever talked about those years before. They had shaken him to the core and made him understand how much responsibility he had for his family's financial survival, now that he was as grown up as he was. School, to his dad, seemed to be a frivolous waste of time.

"I think the only reason he has agreed to let me come back is that he likes having a son who plays football . . . and wins." There was just a tinge of sarcasm, or was it hurt in his voice?

He had never asked much about my background either, so I shared some of my stories with him, especially about Pa and Baby Teddy and Ma's depression.

But that night subtly changed our relationship. It was less superficial, more intense. When we held hands, it was as if we were drawing strength from each other, and when he kissed me goodnight, I could feel it to my toes.

On the rare nights when someone could borrow a car, Harold Schur and Mildred Mitchell asked if we wanted to go for a drive. Mildred's parents refused to allow her to date Harold. They had plans for her to go out East to finishing school and to marry well someone out there.

So she developed a subterfuge, which I was not comfortable with, but given the way I felt about Gino and the little time we had together, I understood.

She told her parents, "I'm going to visit Marion. We might go to the library to do our homework."

Harold would pick up Gino and the two of us, and we would drive.

Then we began the "What If" game.

Gino started it. "What if instead of going to Illinois to college you went to teacher training in Virginia? We could see each other weekends, even if I had to walk into town."

We never mentioned the big "M" word.

One weekend we really took a chance. I told Vessels Ma needed me in Zim. Mildred told her parents she was going to stay with me. Harold and Mildred and Gino and I drove to Happy Corner. We took some food along and something cool to drink. Though it had been a hot day, the inside of the house was cool from being locked up all year. I opened the windows and door, and we played house. Mildred and I put a tablecloth on the table and laid out apples and cheese and bread as if they were a banquet. The boys swept the floor and shook the rugs and chopped some wood.

My only fear was that the Salins would rush over to see what was happening.

We were all in that category labeled "good kids" and it was all so very innocent. We held hands and watched the sun go down. Mildred and I slept on the bed. The boys took the trundle bed. We talked and talked and talked all night. Mildred cried about her parents' intractability. Harold tried to soothe her, but short of their running away . . . on nothing . . . he had nothing to offer her except years of grinding poverty.

I told Gino the whole story about the Quest to Ely. He asked lots of questions about every detail. I even told him about the Savolainens' desire to adopt me.

His only comment was, "If they had, I'd never have met you."

We sat together at all school events, but even that was difficult because so much was done "just for the seniors," and Gino wasn't one.

Prom night was especially hard. In spite of all of our entreaties, both Gino's and mine, I had to go with Charlie Beck, as Mr. Vessel had promised the day of that senior tea, which now seemed so long ago. Mrs. Vessel made over a pink chiffon dress of hers and painted the flounces with gold paint. It was the most beautiful dress I had ever had. She helped me with my hair and a tiny bit of makeup.

Gino waited up for me, walking the streets until I made Charlie take me home. When Charlie left, Gino and I sat on the front porch. The Vessels had a Victrola playing, and we danced on the sidewalk first to real music and then to the music within us until Mr. Vessel came out aghast and said, "Marion, haven't you come in yet? Gino, I have trusted you all this year to use good judgment, but this is going a bit too far."

Gino apologized, and I scrambled up the stairs, feeling like Cinderella when the clock struck twelve.

Mrs. Vessel refused to take the dress back. "It looks much nicer on you than it ever did on me," she said. Looking at me in that dress, she began to cry. "I remember the time I wore that to a dance at Wesleyan and how happy we were then."

CHAPTER THIRTY-FIVE
Senior Year

hanges were afoot in the school district. Superintendent Muench was replaced by N.J. Quickstand, and there were problems at the Vessels.

Under Mr. Quickstand's photo in the *Mountaineer*, "Stebbo" Gidas wrote, "I know Gino will eat good some day in the future in the little bungalow in Zim. Gino will milk the blonde cows and Marion the brunettes."

I was enough in the "in" crowd now to recognize and use nicknames, and my own annual was full of writing about silly jokes. One day our whole class skipped school and walked to Virginia, arm in arm, and Ellen wrote, "You and Gino surely make a happy pair. I adore you both!"

The kisses had deepened, but kept within clear boundaries. Ellen taught Gino to say *"Anna mulle sumppia"*—"Give me a kiss." Her Finnish was no better than her English. But that was all right. We pulled her though a senior year that was "supreme."

My list of activities ran half a page. The class prophecy said I would marry Charlie Beck, and every page of that yearbook was filled with notes in Finnish and English about trips with whoever had a car to wherever they could think of to go, especially to Happy Corner, which earned its place for posterity with a sketch including furnishings, car, and birds.

How bad things were at Vessels' just slipped by me. Luther Vessel had a Bachelor of Arts degree from Iowa's Wesleyn College. He had married his wife right after he graduated and she completed finishing school. The curriculum there had taught her very little about the practical day-to-day workings of the world. She wasn't ever cruel to me, just remarkably unaware. But during those years, she had made no attempt to learn. She could still decorate a table or decide upon exquisite-sounding menus but could neither cook nor bake beyond making a sandwich.

She never even learned how to make coffee.

She had been raised to have breakfast in bed, to keep an orderly household through the discussions with a housekeeper, to arrange flowers, to do exquisite handwork, to entertain, to plan a garden but not plant it. In short, she had not been raised to be the wife of a poorly paid small-town high school principal.

At some point during my senior year, Mr. Vessel began spending more and more time with Miss Isadora Duda, my drama coach and head of the English department.

One night when we were deeply involved in a student-faculty play, I saw the two of them together, looking at each other in the way Gino and I did, and I wondered if either Mr. or Mrs. Vessel was finding happiness in their marriage. I thought them sadly mismatched.

Soon after that they began to sleep in separate rooms, and the time for their "aperitif" lengthened still more. But I did not know how bad things were until I came back from Christmas break that year. They were packing to go to Washington, where Mr. Vessel had accepted another job.

I panicked. There was no way to get hold of Ma. I ran to tell Mrs. Martilla and ask for her advice. I cried all that day in school and got a lot of sympathy, but no help until the end of the day. Then just before classes ended, Mr. Radcliffe, director of the high school orchestra, knocked on the door to the classroom and invited me to come to his house after class instead of going to the Vessels'.

I did not know Mr. Radcliffe any better than I did any of the faculty members whom the Vessels entertained. I knew that he was the kind who said, "Hello," to everyone in the hall, and I had attended and enjoyed his orchestra concerts, but our relationship had never progressed beyond that.

Mystified but willing to do anything that offered hope, I went to the Radcliffes. Mt. Iron was small enough so everyone knew where everyone else lived, and I barely needed directions.

Mr. Radcliffe ushered me into their living room and introduced me to his wife, Pearl.

With no beating around the bush, he said, "Pearl and I would like to have you stay with us for the rest of your senior year. We want you to consider it your home. None of this 'room and board' stuff," he said. "You'll come to live with us as if we had another daughter. Our little girl, Carolyn, would love a big sister, and my Pearl and I would welcome you with open arms."

After a long pause, he added, "I don't mean to criticize. That's not my place. But several of us have felt that your situation at the Vessels has not been as it should have been." He paused. "We're aware of what it is fair to ask of one who works for her room and board, and . . ." again he paused. "I believe there have been times when the Vessels have exceeded their prerogatives. But let's say no more of that. Things will be very different here."

When I started to cry about how wonderful that would be, he put his arm around me and said, "No 'Mr. Radcliffe' either. Just call me 'Pa.'"

"Did she say yes, Pa? Did she say yes?" A face peeked from around the door, and I was introduced to Carolyn Radcliffe, who, in junior high school, considered it the greatest of all things to have a "big sister," who was a senior.

Mrs. Radcliffe concluded, "I will answer to 'Ma' or to 'Pearl,' whichever you are more comfortable with."

And so I it was arranged.

It was heaven. I was free to go out when someone had a car—once even a Studebaker—and we drank root beer floats—Heino and Myrtle, Robert and Ellen, Chas and Ruby, Gino and I. Once when Robert wanted to kiss Ellen, he said, "Get your face over here!"

That became the theme of our next few outings.

Although I didn't have a part in the senior class play, I went to rehearsals, gave a dramatic reading of "Ben Hur and the Chariot Race" in the declamatory contest, and—with Ellen—gave the prophecy on Senior Class Night. On Bums' Day, I dressed as a nurse, and Gino skipped school to come to the senior class picnic.

We sang "Girl of My Dreams" and "Kiss a Miss" and "Daddy Mine"and "Ramona"; and as we neared the end of the year, we cried a lot. Our class drew closer, the lines of demarcation that had been laid between nationalities disappeared, the feeling of sadness at having to part growing stronger with every day.

Yes, I was named valedictorian, and yes, Ma and Margie were there, sitting with Ma and Pa Radcliffe and Carolyn to clap me across the stage.

Gino didn't sit with them, though I did introduce him to Ma and Margie.

We—Harold and Myrtle and Gino and I—left after the festivities and gave that night to ourselves. We talked and drove and remembered, laughed and cried and knew that no matter how hard we tried, this time would never come again. Gino would have to finish high school. Myrtle's parents were sending her out East to college to get her away from Harold. They made no bones about it.

I had earned a scholarship to Macalester, but no matter how I tried, the money I would still need to go there far exceeded the amount we could raise.

I vowed not to worry about it that night, that graduation night, that night when I had to say good-bye to friends who had become like family, to a small Minnesota town that had become home, to a second family that had taken me in with love and kindness. And to Gino.

He had no access to a car. He said he'd try to get to Happy Corner. But I knew he'd be working to save money so he could finish school.

Ma knew right away that he wasn't Finnish. He was Italian. That was one strike against him. The way he looked at me was a second strike.

"Is it fate or is it your own decision that ordains your future?" Superintendent Muench had asked at the beginning of that year.

Through my life I had been so sure I knew the answer. I had vowed to follow the path I had set for myself and no one and nothing would stand in my way.

Suddenly, fate had thrown me a blow. I had not meant to fall in love. That was not part of my plan. But being with Gino was different from any relationship I had even had with a boy . . . or a man. Arnie and Leonard had just been dancing partners. Laurence and Charlie were friends, enjoyable participants in intellectual pursuits. But the feeling I had for Gino was not at all intellectual.

I felt safe when he held my hand, safer when I was in his arms, safest when he kissed me and told me that he had never felt toward anyone as he had toward me.

He played the "if only" game. If only he could have graduated with me and our friends. If only his family had the money for him to go to college, too. Wherever it was that I would go, he would go.

If only we could be patient and wait another four years . . . why, we had already waited almost one whole year . . . we would know each other even better and share our dreams and make plans that could come true because we would have good jobs that we could rely on.

If only we were both of the same nationality, his mother would make me part of their family and not resent the fact that I was Finnish, or if only he had been born Finnish, Ma wouldn't resent him.

And the final one—if only we had the courage just to realize that fate had thrown us together this last year. We had never intended it to.

"I never intended when I walked up that hill after the first football game to stop and talk to you, but you were there and something made me stop."

"I think back to what Superintendent Muench said at the first all-school assembly. Remember? He asked us to think deeply and consider what would govern our future—our own hearts, our character and personalities or some external force, like God or fate or something beyond our control."

"Is this beyond our control?" he asked and kissed me until I was ready to have the kiss never stop and forget control.

"I don't know," I cried miserably into his shoulder. "I know what my heart says. It says I want you desperately. I want to be yours in every way. And then my head says, 'That's what you've been working toward all these years?' And I don't know what is right."

Mildred and Harold didn't wrestle with that decision. They spent graduation night alone in Mildred's family's cabin on Sand Lake. They asked us not to interrupt them. They would come out in the morning.

We sat in the car and fought off the urge to do what we knew they were doing in the cabin.

We discussed it openly.

Gino made no bones about it. "I won't pretend that I wouldn't give up almost anything to spend one night with you, and the guys say there are ways so that you wouldn't become pregnant, but what if you did. That's the 'what if' neither one of us could live with."

So we held hands and kissed . . . discreetly . . . walked for miles . . . slept a bit . . . pretended we were married and built a house and decorated it, discussing colors and styles of furniture and where it should be built . . . had and named three children.

"Two would be better," Gino said. "There's always just so much money to go around, and we'd never have enough for a big family. Two would be just enough."

"A boy and a girl," I agreed.

Then we argued about names. Gino wanted something Italian; I wanted something Finnish.

And we went back to Superintendent Muench and the beginning of the school year because Gino had listened to him and thought about it, too.

"Fate . . . or circumstance . . . or events beyond my control . . . have taken over this last year," I admitted. "When I came back in August, I never would have dreamed that you would be there, as if you were waiting for me. And when Vessels left, I was sure I'd have to quit school until I could find another family to take me in. Then you were there. And Radcliffes were there. And neither was of my making."

"Well," Gino disagreed, "that's not quite true. I noticed you long before I did anything about it. I thought you were just too beautiful and too smart to want to hang around with a dumb Wop like me."

"I refuse to have you use that word!"

"Everyone does."

"No, they don't. That's a derogatory word, and it's wrong. It's like making jokes that make Finnish people sound dumb."

"Okay, okay. But I really wasn't sure what you'd say about going out with me. I was holding my breath, I tell you."

"Silly!" And I kissed him. "And you the most popular boy in school."

"It's easy to be popular if you're good in athletics. Nobody knows the real *you*. They just kowtow to the guy who makes the touchdown or throws the best pass. That's not *real* friends. And as far as the Radcliffes are concerned, there's not anybody in Mt. Iron who didn't know how the Vessels were treating you. Buying four wieners to feed three people for dinner! And making you serve tea to girls you went to school with. And on top of it making you wear a uniform. There may have been one or two girls who thought it was funny, but everyone else thought it was awful. Word gets around. I'm just surprised that something didn't happen earlier. I guess having the Vessels leave just left the door wide open for someone else to step in. And the kindest guy in town is "Pa" Radcliffe. He and his wife have done so many things I can't begin to count them. And they never want anyone to know. They just do it because they're good people. This time it so happens that it shows. Don't ever doubt that they've meant what they've said. I truly believe they've considered you another daughter."

I thought about it with great thankfulness. "They have certainly treated me like one. And Carolyn is an angel.

"But the Vessels did teach me something I really wasn't aware of before. For all that they demanded of me, they introduced me to a . . . different way of life. I don't want to speak English with a Finnish accent. I want to earn enough money so that I can buy a house with a living room and dining room. I want to learn to entertain . . . all kinds of people. Not the way they did, just the 'upper' class. It's just that . . . it's hard to find words for it without sounding . . . as if I'm dissatisfied with my place in life. And yet I am. I want . . . more. And I want someone to share it with, someone who cares for me, really cares. Who won't drink or gamble away our money but will want to come home after work . . . to me . . . and the children."

"Are you taking applications?"

"Oh, Gino." I wanted to throw a pillow at him. Instead I gave him a cuff on the arm.

He caught my hand and pulled me across him so that my head was on his other shoulder and my heart against his.

"So your dreams for the future require maids to do the laundry and the housework. If we wait until I can afford that, we won't be able to . . ."

I covered his mouth before he could say the "M" word. "I would appreciate having some help in the kitchen . . . maybe . . . someday. But that's not the point. I want to speak better English, how to live more . . . graciously, how to entertain . . . with poise and dignity." I struggled to find the right words.

"It's not that I want to be like them in other ways. It's more that I didn't even know there were people who lived like that! Part of it was the way that they talked and dressed. Part of it was the way their home looked. They—Mrs. Vessel especially—really made me aware of the line between people like them who are cultured and educated and those who are not, and I sure knew where she put me."

"She put you down. Everyone knew what she was doing, but no one knew how to stop it or what to do about it."

"I don't know, Gino. I don't believe they were being cruel. I belonged to the class of people who ate in the kitchen, not in the dining room. I'd like to be able to speak correctly and have a lovely home, too. But the other part was . . . awful."

"What a difference now, hey?"

"You'd better believe it. From the very beginning 'Pa' and 'Ma' Radcliffe drew a circle that took me in. Their circles include all kinds of people—not just administrators and teachers and board members. Why, Victor Lahti came for dinner one Sunday night and teased me about you and the noise we made that one night on the kids' playground. And one afternoon I came home to see Mrs. Martilla in the kitchen with Pearl, in the middle of shaping a braid of *pulla*. She had helped create a Finnish dinner and stayed to eat with us, including Carolyn, in the dining room."

"You like having a little sister?"

"Carolyn's an angel. But I have a real one—Margie!"

"I can't wait to see Margie! She must be a little spitfire!"

"Yes, well, she's not so little anymore. I worry . . . she's missed out on so much school, and she's too big to be considered cute and dance on the tables and sing for the loggers anymore. I'm anxious to see her and Ma and to be with them. But not tonight. Tomorrow."

"Tomorrow." He echoed the dreaded word.

Early, early in the morning, Harold and Mildred came out of the cabin, holding hands, their eyes red and puffy from tears. There was nothing we could say. They held each other tightly in the rumble seat until we neared Mt. Iron, then Harold took the wheel. Mildred and I had to be dropped off at Radcliffes' while it was still dark.

Harold's car was noisy, doubly so in that pre-dawn stillness. There was no time for more good-byes. Mildred and I jumped out as soon as Harold slowed the car as much as he could without stalling, and they were gone. We ran the last block and a half, gratefully opened and closed the unlocked back door, and collapsed on the living room couch, too exhausted to move. There was some cold coffee left on the stove, and I warmed it while Mildred sponged her eyes and face with cold water.

I'm not sure why I couldn't cry. Instead I felt dead inside. Leaving Mt. Iron and high school and the Radcliffes and all of my friends would have been a devastating loss had there been no Gino. But there was, and if I allowed myself to think about it at all, it was as if a part of my very being were being torn away.

At the same time, it didn't seem real. Of course there would be school next fall, and of course Gino would walk me to classes as he had all second semester.

I'd wear his letter jacket even when I wasn't cold, and Mildred and Harold would double date with us or go walking or study or just sit and talk as we always did. Of course, I'd be known as "Gino's girl" and because I was, everyone would ask, "Hi, Marion! Who's going to win tonight?"

Of course at first his parents wouldn't like me, but after they invited me to dinner a few times, they'd realize that I looked as Italian as they did, and that would help a lot. And I'd get Gino to start teaching me Italian, at least a phrase at a time.

Ma and Margie were always gone anyway so they didn't have to be consulted about Gino until . . . well . . . until we had our arguments all ready for them.

Of course, I would see Gino again. How could I not? How could I live if I didn't see him? I refused to consider that alternative. It simply was not acceptable.

So I gave all my sympathy to Mildred and listened to the story I had heard so many times I could have recited it myself. She was underage. Her parents were not only extremely strict, but they were wealthy and influential. To them Harold Schur from Mt. Iron was as unimportant as a flea on a dog. Pick it off, and it simply goes away. Or, get rid of the dog.

"I hope and pray that I'm pregnant," Mildred whispered to me. "If I am, they may have no choice but to let me marry Harold. Unless they send me away to one of those places where rich people send their daughters who have made 'mistakes' that need to be corrected. I could hide it and not tell them. But they still have control over me."

I was honestly afraid for her. She was so upset she was almost incoherent. One minute she clutched at me until my hands hurt. Then she threw herself into the pillows of the couch and sobbed. No one that I knew had committed suicide, and the only contact I had ever had with depression had been Ma's withdrawal, but I knew this was far more serious than anyone had guessed. Should I tell Harold? Should I talk to her parents and tell them honestly how she felt and plead with them to take her feelings into consideration? Would they listen to me? Or would they blame me for somehow bringing this on by helping her see Harold?

Double French doors led from the central hallway into the living room—I suppose it could have been considered a parlor—but everyone actually lived there, sitting on the davenport and chairs reading magazines and books and talking. I had closed the doors, but one opened very quietly, and Pearl Radcliffe slipped in, a robe over her nightgown and slippers on her feet.

She put her finger to her lips indicating, "Shhhh," and knelt on the floor by Mildred.

I went to the kitchen for more coffee, but when I came back with a tray, Mildred was sitting up facing Pearl, who was holding both of her hands. They were talking, Mildred first, then Pearl, then Mildred.

I went back to the kitchen and drank the coffee myself, too exhausted to stay up but too worried and worn to sleep. I finally dozed off with my head on the table.

I don't know what magic Mrs. Radcliffe wrought, but when the Mitchells came to pick Mildred up about noon, she had bathed and dressed and, although her face was still a bit puffy, she seemed self-contained, as if she had found some kind of peace.

We promised to write each other often, and she whispered to me that she had a plan that she could live with.

I was enormously grateful to Pearl. I struggled with what to call her. "Mrs. Radcliffe" seemed too formal, but "Ma" was not right since I had one, and "Pearl" put her at my own age, which seemed disrespectful.

But that was a minor concern.

Mildred gone, I knew it was time for me to turn the wheel of my own life. *I will not think of Gino*, I told myself over and over again. I put a rubber band around my wrist and told myself I would snap it every time my mind slipped into thoughts of him. I could not go there yet.

Moreover, I had sensed, as I had told Gino, that all this time when I had been so concerned with my own growing up, that Margie had been growing up, too, with Ma, of course, but largely in one lumber camp or another, one boarding house or another.

I worried about whether she had advanced in her studies. But that was only a minor concern. The other concerns took me to other places I was not sure I wanted to go.

Ma had suggested that this summer Margie and I stay at Happy Corner while she worked in Virginia and, hopefully, came home on weekends.

In a sense, she said, I would have a summer off. My job would be to take care of the house and of Margie. Ma had been offered an excellent salary if she would cook at Jukolas' boarding house for the summer. Their head cook had gotten married and left them high and dry with a houseful of men and no one to handle the kitchen. They had heard nothing but compliments from the camp bosses for whom Ma had worked and promised to make it worth her while if she would help them. "I can make more money than you could, taking care of children or cleaning houses," Ma said to me. "The offer is much too good to turn down and it may make a difference next fall."

The Radcliffes' graduation gift to me had been generous. A card and check from the Savolainens had been an even more generous and welcome surprise.

But the gulf between what I had in the bank, including a scholarship, and what I required in order to go to Macalester, my dream college, remained enormous.

We had to have a council of war, Ma and Margie and I, and it should take place soon.

I needed to have an alternative in place, just in case, and I thought I knew what it could be.

CHAPTER THIRTY-SIX
Margie

Pearl had written an invitation to Ma and Margie to stay with them during the graduation festivities, and Ma had responded in Finnish with her acceptance and appreciation.

The gulf between them and the Radcliffes was heartbreakingly evident. Not so much where Ma was concerned. She had stopped in Virginia to buy a new dress, and she had had that beautiful long hair cut, not really into a bob but straight across just above her ear lobes. Parted on the side, it was neat, and her dress with its white collar and bar pin was appropriate, but the winters at the logging camps had . . . coarsened her. She still spoke very little English, none of it grammatically sound, and I simply transferred to Finnish and translated what she said, sometimes rephrasing it so that it sounded more like the English I had grown used to. It shamed me to do this. I felt as if . . . the real Ma wasn't quite good enough. It was a horrible feeling. Otherwise, Ma had Boston to fall back on. She remembered those rules of etiquette and slipped into that old role naturally.

But Margie. She had escaped from under Ma's tutelage and was going her own way in as headstrong a fashion as she had when she was little. But she wasn't little anymore. She had matured early, too early, and lacked the underclothing that would have controlled her overripe body. Ma told me when we had a moment to ourselves that Margie had chosen the dress she wanted and thrown such a fit in the store when Ma dissuaded her that Ma, too embarrassed to argue any more, bought the dress and left. It was cut too low on top and too high on the bottom, making her look like what the kids in school called a "floozy." Girls like that at Mt. Iron High School were shunned by our crowd.

Her table manners were atrocious as were any attempts at English. It was not "May I please." It was "Gimme."

Thank goodness for Pearl, who seemed to understand. She went out of her way to be kind to Ma and to Margie. She never uttered a word of reproof, no matter how outrageously Margie looked and acted, but Margie was the only reason I was glad to leave, in fact, to leave as soon as I had kissed Mildred goodbye.

I did not look forward to a summer alone with Margie. There was a time when we had seemed to have bridged the gulf between us. But these four years had widened it almost immeasurably, and if, in fact, Margie were left in my care, I anticipated some battle royals because I was not going to give in either to what she considered an appropriate appearance or to her bad manners.

Thank goodness there was only a little time left before we took, not the elegant passenger car the Mitchells rode on, but the stop-and-go milk and baggage train that would still get us to Zim in plenty of time to open the house and get settled before nightfall.

Margie was very quiet when we left Radcliffes. It was another painful parting for me, and Ma understood, urging Margie along with her and giving me time alone with my "other family" to say good-bye.

It was one too many. I had managed to stay strong until I felt Pa Radcliffe's arms around me and Carolyn, her hands clutching my skirt, saying "Don't leave, M'rian. I will miss you something awful." Again it was Pearl who took charge, disentangling me from Carolyn and from Pa, whose eyes looked teary, too.

"When we offered you our home, we knew you would be welcome," she said gently. "But we didn't count on having you become such a part of us, or on loving you as much as we do. We know you need to go now to be with your own family. But never forget that we consider you a part of our family, too. Consider us a backup. We will always be here for you whenever you need us."

That broke me down completely, and I finally forced myself away in a whirl of hugs and tears and promises.

None of us—Ma, Margie or me—said an unnecessary word on the train or on the long walk home. It took three of us to carry my precious belongings, all of which had fit neatly into one carpetbag when I had left just a few short years ago.

But things erupted when we walked into the house.

Margie threw her load onto the bed and said, "That's the last time I'm going to carry anything for you, Miss High and Mighty. Don't think I didn't notice how you were buttering up to the Radcliffes and apologizing for Ma and me as if we're not good enough for you, now that you're a high school graduate and living with the upper class and talking like them and eating like them. I'm surprised you didn't feed us in the kitchen."

My quick temper, which I struggled mightily to control, flared right back. "The way you were dressed and the way you talked and the way you ate, that's exactly where you belonged. You behaved as if you were in a logging camp instead of a teacher's home. Why didn't you have the good sense just to sit quietly and watch what other people were doing and do the same? That's how I learned. That's how Ma learned. No one gave us a class.

"And that dress. How old are you? Twelve? That dress makes you look like a teenage streetwalker, ready to be picked up by some guy who wants a cheap date for a night."

"Well, at least I'd have some fun then. How would you like to be stuck at a lumber camp for months with nobody there but Ma, always yelling at me about something, and a bunch of dumb lumberjacks who have to be taught even to wash their hands? Do you think that was fun? And all the while, Ma's saving money for guess who? So guess who can go to college? And guess who is stuck washing and wiping dishes and scrubbing floors and baking and cooking until I was so sick of it I could die. How about a little fun for guess who?"

Margie was throwing things, pulling off the dress and tearing it, yanking clothes out of the carpet bags and throwing them on the floor and stamping on them. It was just like the temper tantrums she used to have. But she wasn't little anymore. And it wasn't cute anymore.

"Has she been like this all year?" I asked Ma quietly.

"It's gotten worse and worse since Christmas, when we didn't get out because of the snowstorms. She won't listen to anyone. If she were smaller, I'd say she needs a good strong bout with the razor strap, but she's stronger then I am. I couldn't hold her. And by now, I don't think it would do any good. I don't know what would. And I can't give up that job at Jukolas.' I've never gotten the kind of salary they've offered. I am sorry, Ilmi, but someone has to butt heads with Margie this summer, and there isn't anyone else but you."

Ma left the next morning.

There was a lot to do. We had done a lot of coming and going that spring, but we'd never stayed long enough to do more than pick up after ourselves. I decided to follow Ma's old pattern and start at the beginning.

Margie refused to get out of bed so I yanked the sheet from under her and set about doing the washing. I made coffee and cut bread, which Ma had brought from the camp, and ignored her. I left her dirty clothes in a pile next to the bed, finished the rest of the washing, hung everything on the line, and scrubbed the kitchen floor hard with lye soap.

Then I did the same thing to the outhouse seats and floor.

I ate a bit of cheese, also from the camp, with bread for lunch, but we needed some groceries. Without saying a word to Margie, I walked to Salins', bought enough to last me for a couple of days, stayed there long enough to take a quick sauna, and walked home in time to get everything off the line before it started to rain. Margie had evidently been up to go to the outhouse because there were wet footprints on the floor and a chunk of bread and cheese were gone.

I told her that I was going to sleep on the bed. If she wanted clean sheets on the trundle bed, she'd have to wash them herself. Folding and putting away the rest of the washing and dampening things that needed ironing took as much energy as I had left. I read for a while, but the fresh bed was so inviting and I felt so clean all over, I crawled in early and slept the night through.

Next morning, Margie was still on the trundle bed, her pile of dirty clothes a nightgown higher. At some point during the night she had washed her face, gone to the biff outside, and eaten something, but she played possum all that day, too.

I ignored her. Mrs. Aro sent Jenni over with an invitation to come to dinner to celebrate my graduation. I said that I would love to come but that Margie was evidently not feeling well enough to go out.

It was a delicious dinner, and they wanted to hear about all that had happened. I told them about everything . . . except Gino.

Wednesday should have been baking day, but I freshened up the house, washed the windows and began the long process of emptying and washing shelves and reorganizing them. That afternoon I spent at Salins'. When I asked if they would consider hiring me for some part-time work, they were enthusiastic. Eino was in Chisholm for the summer. Sara was spending most of the summer with a friend who lived in Hibbing. I think Salins were intending that the experience would teach her the kinds of things I had learned the hard way at the Vessels. At any rate, they said they could use a pair of extra hands, especially on the heavy shopping days. They couldn't pay me much, but I thought even if they paid me with groceries, we would be making some progress instead of falling behind.

In public, I maintained the fiction that Margie was suffering from some kind of flu. At home, I completely ignored her.

It became a case of who could out-wait whom.

That first Saturday night, Cliff Johnson, his sister Doris and her latest beau Bill Kaukonen from Virginia drove up in Bill's car.

"Marion!" they chorused. "We've missed you and missed you. But we guessed you'd be home by now. Come on, get dressed. There's a dance at Little Swan, and we're ready for some fun!"

"I'm really sorry," I said, motioning them to come away from the house so I could explain. "I can't come. Margie's carrying on a one-woman battle because I refuse to have her go anywhere dressing and looking the way she did during my graduation. She hasn't gotten out of bed all week other than to go to the outhouse and sneak some food, but I'm not giving in even if it takes all summer."

Of course, Margie heard every word as I intended her to. I hoped she would think long and hard about all the fun she was missing by being so stubborn, and I hope she remembered that when it came to stubbornness, I could outdo her any day without getting angry at all. For as long as it took, I'd wait it out.

It took two weeks.

Then she cracked. "How can you be so mean?" was her opening gambit.

I ignored her.

"We're missing out on all of the dances."

"That's right," I said, as I alphabetized the spices in the spice drawer.

"It's all because you're so stubborn and won't see my side of it."

"I see your side of it very clearly, and I sympathize. It must have been an awful year. But that's no excuse for looking and acting like a strumpet. If we're going to go anywhere as sisters, we're going to look and act like ladies, not ladies of the night."

She didn't bother to ask what I meant. She knew.

Heaving a deep sigh, she asked, "What do you want me to do?"

"You know the ropes as well as I do. Probably better. Just dig in. When you've spent a week doing your share of the work, we'll discuss what to do with your hair and your clothes and your manners."

"Then can we go to a dance next Saturday night?"

"That, my dear sister, all depends on you," I answered, looking her straight in the eye. I didn't blink an eyelash or indicate in any way what she needed to do. She knew.

She helped me wash on Monday, took her turn at ironing on Tuesday, did all of the baking on Wednesday, shopped with me on Thursday, and practiced table manners every time we sat down to eat.

If she used incorrect English, I corrected her. If she swore in English or in Finnish, I put a mark on a piece of paper, which I fastened to the recipe rack in the Hoosier cupboard.

"What do those marks mean?" she asked.

"Every time I have to correct you, I'll mark it down. If there are ten marks on Saturday night, we go to the sauna and go to bed early. No dance."

"That's not fair!"

I marked down a second line.

She opened her mouth again. I held the pencil over the paper.

She closed her mouth and stomped outside. But she didn't swear. At least, not within my hearing.

We took Margie with us as a matter of course. Once we got to the dance, I enlisted Cliff's help, and between the two of us, we kept an eye on Margie all during the first half of the dance.

Margie should have been sitting with the girls and women waiting to be invited to dance, but she danced every dance with Arnold Suomela. I knew him by reputation only, and it was not good. He was ten years older than Margie and ran with a much faster crowd than I was familiar with.

When they waltzed, he had his hand on her buttocks, and when they did the polka or schottische, I was afraid they would fly right off the floor. There was a looseness to her dancing that . . . worried me.

When the break finally came, the dance half over, we were up near the stage, and I couldn't see Margie anywhere.

We explained briefly to Bill and Doris and then went out on a search party.

We found them in the rumble seat of Arnie's car, half-dressed, passing a bottle back and forth.

She looked at least four years older than she was, maybe more, with makeup, now smeared.

"Margie!" I ejaculated.

She giggled, "Here, Sis, Arnie has some really good stuff tonight."

"Get out of that car right now. Margie, what are you doing?" I wanted to snatch her out myself.

"Arnie, she's under age. You could get into big trouble for this. You should know better."

He was too drunk to hear me much less connect with what I was saying. "She might be a little young, but she knows her way around, hey, babe," and he took a swig and handed it to Cliff. "Here, take a swig."

"Mur'rian, I don't feel so good." Margie's voice sounded strangled. Cliff and I hauled her out of the rumble seat, but she couldn't stand on her own feet. We braced her against the car, but she fell forward and began to throw up.

"Get out of the way. I know how to handle this," Cliff told me. He held her by the waist and leaned her hands against Arnie's roadster and she retched and threw up and retched some more until all that came out was bile.

Half carrying her, we got her to Bill's car.

I honestly did not know what to do other than bring her home and stay there myself.

We apologized to Doris and Bill. Cliff promised to bring the car back when the dance was over, and we headed for Happy Corner.

Along the way, Cliff stopped to help her throw up again and told me, once we got home, to make a strong pot of coffee.

She was a mess, the vomit all over her dress and shoes, even in her hair. Cliff went out to get some fresh cool water, and mixing it with hot water from the boiler, I set myself to cleaning her up. Cliff sat outside and smoked his Camels, throwing comments in the door every once in a while.

"Will the coffee sober her up?" I asked, because she was still like a limp doll in my arms.

"No, I'm afraid not. She'll just be a drunk who's had a lot of coffee. Time is the only thing to get her sober. We'll just have to wait it out."

I appreciated the "we." This was a problem I had never faced before, and it was daunting, especially because I felt culpable. I should have been taking care of her, watching what she was doing and where she was going.

"Remember, Marion," Cliff commented through the screen door. "She's spent a lot of time at logging camps with your Ma. No matter how strict your ma is, Margie was bound to learn about life much earlier than you'd have liked."

"Oh, and I thought she was so safe there!"

"Well, safe physically. But otherwise, who were the people she was in contact with? How did they talk? How did they treat her? Especially now, when she looks so grown-up? Your ma probably didn't notice the change as you did. It doesn't happen all at once."

"Ohhh . . ." Margie staggered out of the cabin and started crying all over Cliff's clean shirt. "Mur-rian, I'm so sorry. I just. It didn't seem so bad. It's the first time, honest. That I've had that much, and I never will again."

She cried for one reason, and I cried for another.

She threw up again, and I cleaned her up again.

Finally, Cliff said, "Just let her sit out here until she gets it all out of her system. Right now, there's no use trying to salvage anything. She'll just keep on until she passes out. Then you can clean her up and we'll get her into bed."

Cliff poured coffee for himself and for me, and we went inside to talk. Or not to talk.

"I feel terrible about this. Ma left her with me this summer, trusting me to be responsible, and I've done an awful job. All I've cared about is my own fun. It's been such a release from school that I've been giddy with the joy of it. And when we're home here together, we get through the everyday work just fine. I just never thought about what might be happening at the dances. I shouldn't have let her go."

"You couldn't keep her home. The minute you left, Arnie Suomela would have been here to pick her up, and they'd just have gone to a different dance hall and tried to be back here before you were."

"It's pretty clear she needs a firm hand. No sign of your dad?"

I shuddered. "None, thank God."

"And your ma?"

"She's trying to earn enough at that boarding house in Virginia so that she won't have to go to a logging camp this year. I'd give anything to have Margie finish eighth grade. There's a practical nursing course in Hibbing. She could go right there and into a fairly decent job. If she finishes eighth grade with any kind of decent marks. Oh, what a mess! I honestly do not know what to do."

Cliff had no answers. I sensed that he understood on a closer level than he was saying, but he kept quiet. This was our family's problem.

CHAPTER THIRTY-SEVEN
Still Margie

I may have won a battle, but I had a long way to go before winning the war.

That Margie had always resented my tutelage had been evident, to varying degrees, since we were old enough to talk. If she misbehaved, Ma said, it was my fault because I was older and should have been watching. I resented the ensuing spanking. Margie resented the watchful overseeing necessary to prevent the spanking.

No matter how I admonished Ma that it wasn't fair, and it wasn't, the situation never changed. If Margie erred, I was at fault. Of course, since Margie caught on to that situation as soon as awareness arose, she took advantage every time she had a chance. If she finished her ice cream cone first, she insisted she had dropped hers, and to keep the peace, I had to share mine.

Given the level of stress in our household whenever Ma and Pa were together, it's not surprising that Ma would do most anything to prevent another crossing of swords. The older I grew, the more I understood her desperate reasoning. But all Margie knew was that whenever she was crossed, a temper tantrum would be offset by a treat, and if she downright misbehaved, the error would be mine.

So it is no wonder that by the time she was old enough to need strict discipline, when her behavior was no longer cute, when her adorable appearance could no longer be used to justify her actions, it was too late.

She had been raised to get what she wanted, and she saw no reason to change that scenario. Our first two weeks together had constituted a mere minor skirmish. I was truly unprepared when the cavalry charged—in public, of course, at a Saturday night wedding dance.

Having granted me what she must have considered a minor concession, she played her cards perfectly. Those winters at the logging camps must have taught her to hold a straight flush as if it were two of a kind. She had mastered the art of the poker face. I didn't suspect a thing.

When we got word that Cliff Johnson, Doris, and her newest beau Bill Kaukonen, who drove a new Dodge, could pick both of us up for a dance at the Linden Grove Town Hall, I had no qualms about accepting the invitation.

There had not been even the shadow of a pencil mark on the recipe holder's paper for two full weeks, and I was overdue for a chance to relax and enjoy what summer was supposed to offer—FUN!

It was not unusual for us to take Margie along. Country dances were family affairs. Everyone went from the tiniest baby, who was passed from lap to lap, to the oldest Gramma and Grampa who twirled their way around the circle of the dance floor as smoothly as everyone else. It never occurred to me to leave Margie at home. Nor did I keep an eye on her during the dance. Everyone was free to dance with everyone else—women with women even, if no man came to get them. So I threw myself into the delicious luxury of a whole evening of going from one partner to another, reminding myself of Margie only when the band took a break and everyone went for refreshments—sometimes downstairs, sometimes behind the stage, at Linden Grove in an area set aside from the dance floor—for coffee and sweets or outside for something stronger.

Suddenly I realized I couldn't see Margie anywhere.

Although I had not spent the entire evening dancing with Cliff, it was usual to have coffee with whoever brought you to the dance, so I met him at the serving table and asked if he had seen Margie .

"No, I haven't," he answered, helping himself to a piece of chocolate cake and a cup of coffee. "Why?"

"I don't feel right about this. Will you come with me and look for her?"

He followed me around the hall. It was very easy to see who was and who wasn't there. First we checked the line of people waiting for coffee and a sweet. Then we studied the dance hall itself and the seats that surrounded it. They were virtually empty except for the little kids who were running and jumping and pretending to dance while the young mothers were nursing their babies and the grandparents were resting and fanning themselves and gossiping while they were waiting their turn to go for coffee.

No Margie.

We looked at each other, thinking the same thing. She had to be outside.

"Maybe she's just at the outhouse," I offered, hopefully.

"You check there. I'll start on this end and see who's in the cars."

It wasn't as if that were a secret. The car doors were open, and most of those who had come outside were sitting on the running board or leaning on the fender, talking. Some were drinking moonshine, of course, but others had gone outside just to cool off. It got mighty hot in the hall on a summer night as warm as this one.

There was a system to the way cars were parked. They formed a semicircle with an opening at one end for the hall and at the other end as an exit for those who wanted to leave early.

I could hear Cliff's bantering as he moved slowly from car to car. With another kind of girl at another time, I was sure he had had his evenings outside during intermission. He seemed to know everybody, and everybody seemed to know him. He didn't hurry, didn't act as if he were looking for anyone, just sauntered along as if he too, were enjoying the cool breeze.

"Who's the Rice River Romeo honoring with your presence tonight, Cliff?" The question came from more than one source. "Hey, Cliff, where's the lucky girl?"

He had a quick response for every question or a wave over toward the outside toilets, which also seemed to be a satisfactory answer.

But there was no reason for me to stay at the outside toilet. I waited to see who came out. It wasn't Margie, and she wasn't in the long line.

I joined Cliff, linked my arm with his, teased "so I'm the lucky one tonight, hey?" and we continued the casual stroll with him answering quips with quips just as clever, introducing me sometimes, sometimes not.

He told me later that he chose to make introductions when they were people he wanted me to meet.

"Some of what's goes on outside gets pretty rough," he explained.

"The voice of experience?"

"I'm not proud of it," he answered and drew my arm closer, protectively.

It was pretty clear that some of the loiterers would not make it back onto the dance floor. They'd stay outside and keep drinking, fall asleep, or drive away . . . wherever.

We had almost completed the end of the circle when we heard giggles from the rumble seat of a car parked farther back than most, under a tree with widely spreading branches.

I was sure I recognized that giggle, and my heart just froze.

"Margie?" I asked, throwing the question toward the rumble seat.

"Mur'rian," came a slurred answer, "Cum-on back here. Riisto has some (hiccup) really good lemonade. I drank a whole glass straight down, an' it made me feel so relaxed and cool. Here, you can have summa mine."

Riisto Salmela stood up, leaning over the top of his coupe. "Hey, Cliff, wanna little moon? I mixed it at home, and it's really good."

With a freezing glare, I told Margie, "Get out of that car right now."

And then, "Riisto, do you know how young she is? She is way under age. You had no business taking her out here."

"She may be unn'er age, but she knows her way aroun', hey babe?" And he reached over to give Margie a slobbery kiss.

"I do'n wanna go back to the dance. Do'n feel so good," she slurred.

Cliff didn't have to tell me we'd better act. He reached over and took her by one arm. I took the other, and we virtually dragged her out of the rumble seat. Riisto was no help. I don't think he even noticed she was gone. But he held a bottle out to Cliff, who brushed it aside. "Hey, how cum y'r so high an' mighty t'night? Y'r us'ally one f'r a good time."

"I'm sorry, Marion," Cliff managed to say, as between the two of us we tried to prop Margie up against the car. She couldn't stand up.

Suddenly, Cliff pushed me back and said, "Let me handle this." He grabbed her by the waist just as she was beginning to throw up and kept hold of her as best he could. I got the idea then, and it did take two of us to hold her as she threw up and retched and threw up some more.

No matter how we tried, however, she got it all over the front of her dress and her shoes.

Half-carrying her, we step-walked her over to Bill's car, then looked at each other in dismay. We had come in Bill's father's brand new Dodge.

There was absolutely no possibility of bringing her back home to Zim in that. Cliff said, "Wait here. I'll be right back."

Margie slumped to the ground crying, "Mur'ian, why'm I so sick?"

I stood over her, not sure whether to shake her into sensibility or burst into tears myself. Some big sister I had been. Too busy having a good time myself to watch over her.

It seemed forever before Cliff returned, and when he did, he was driving Riisto Salmela's car with Riisto passed out in the rumble seat.

"What do we do with him?" I asked.

"Leave him there. He's so far gone he'll probably stay passed out until morning or until he takes another drink of booze. He's got the bottle cradled in his arms like a baby."

"What if he falls out?"

"Good riddance," Cliff said at first. Then he mitigated it. "I took his pants off and tied him down with them. He'll never be so far gone that he'll get up half dressed."

"How do you know that?" I asked, not quite believing him.

"Trust me," he said grimly. "I know."

Along the way, every time Margie began to retch again, Cliff stopped the car, grabbed her from between us, and slung her over his lap with her head out the door. Of course, she messed all over his pants, but when I commented, he said, "It won't be the first time," with that same grim look on his face.

"Ohhhhh, I feel so sick." And then she started crying all over Cliff's clean shirt. "Oh, M'rian, I doan know what he gave me to make me so sick. He said it was lemonade, but I couldn't be this sick from lemonade. We make lemonade at home all the time and I never get sick from it."

"Shhhhh," I soothed, and finally drew her head onto my lap, disgusted with the vile smell that permeated her hair and her breath and her clothing, but sickeningly certain nonetheless that she truly had not known what she was getting into.

"I should have warned her," I told Cliff, crying by then myself.

"How were you to know?"

"I just should have. I didn't realize how grown-up she looks now. I should have talked to her about what to do and what not to do at a dance."

"Did you try?"

"Well, yes. I did tell her not to go outside during intermission. I told her to be sure to stay inside and to find us and we'd save her a seat with us and Doris and Bill, but I didn't tell her clearly enough about what would happen if she did go outside."

"Cut it out."

His voice was so sharp I felt like slapping him. "What do you mean 'cut it out'?"

"How many years has she been going to dances with your ma and pa and you? Since she was big enough to stand up, I bet. Don't give me that 'I'm to blame' business. She knew exactly what she was doing when she went outside, and she knew exactly what was in that bottle, and she knew damn well it wasn't lemonade. Don't let her get by with putting a guilt trip on you. It's not your fault. Do you hear me? Repeat after me: 'It's not my fault.'"

"It's not my fault." I said it, but I didn't believe it.

"That's better. But say it again as if you mean it. Or keep saying it until you do mean it. I like Margie. She can be a real sweetheart. But if there's a way she can twist a situation to her own advantage, even if she's drunk, she'll do it.

"Let's try it again. Who's to blame for this mess?"

I vacillated. "Well, I . . ."

"Dammit," he said, "I'm going to stop this car and shake you. There are ten kids in my family, and I know and love every one of them. But through the years I have learned one lesson the hard way. If they can get by with something by foisting the blame on someone else, they'll do it in a minute. It's human nature. Now let's try this once more. Say it ten times. *Who is to blame for the mess Margie got into tonight?*"

In a very small voice, I answered, "Not me."

"That's better. Now try it again. Who made the decision to go outside during intermission even though she'd been warned not to?"

"Margie," I whispered.

"Do you truly believe she thought that bottle was full of lemonade, given what all of us know about Riisto Salmela?"

In an even smaller voice, I answered, "No."

"So, on the basis of whose two facts, who made the decision not only to go outside but to go out with a fellow with a reputation like Riisto's and drink something from a bottle he offered her?"

I finally got it. "Margie."

"Good girl. Now, before you lose it, who's to blame for this whole fiasco? Is it the big sister Marion who dared to dance and have some good, clean fun for once?"

"No."

A whole lifetime of taking the blame hung in the balance. "It was Margie," I admitted, though I had to grab his hand and hold it so hard it hurt as I mouthed the words and finally said them out loud.

"Good girl. Now you're talkin'." He ruffled my hair with that hand and patted me on the shoulder. "That's a good start. She's completely passed out now, or we'd never have made it this far. Now. The next question. What do you intend to do when you get her home?"

"Why, clean her up and get her into bed."

"Don't—you—dare! You wash yourself and get into bed and lay her on the floor just the way she is and let her sleep it off and wake up looking just the way she looks now and smelling and feeling awful. Don't make her coffee or feel sorry for her or listen to her excuses. She brought this on herself. She made her own choices. Make her live with them. We all—except you—" and he reached out a hand to trace the curve of my hair and cheek, "have had to learn from our mistakes. If you make it easy for her, she'll just do it again and again.

"Be tough. There's a chance she'll remember tonight the next time we go to a dance and make a better decision. Can you trust me on this?"

It was impossible not to trust him. We had been friends on and off for—what was it? Three years? But this was the first time he had ever opened himself to me or talked to me seriously. Before, it had all been fun and monkey business, joking around like Arnie and Leonard and to a degree with Laurence and Charlie though their joking was more . . . intellectual.

I had never seen this side of Cliff before. This compassionate, caring, understanding yet . . . commanding . . . strong man who had taken charge of a horrible situation when I did not have the vaguest idea of what to do, who had taken care of Margie as if she had been his own sister, without getting angry or yelling at her, who had just gone ahead and done what needed to be done and just now had given me good advice. I had been so conditioned to taking responsibility for Margie that I would have done it again, without even thinking of whether it was right for her. I had not known what to do or where to turn, and he had taken over. I trusted his judgment implicitly. It could have been disaster for Margie's reputation . . . more than that . . . for Margie's whole future. Who knows what could have happened had we not found her?

I didn't know how to thank him.

And he still had to drive Riisto back to the dance and ride home with Bill and Doris! I had ruined his whole evening.

He stayed just long enough to help me get Margie settled on a rug on the floor with a basin next to her and a towel nearby.

300

Then I walked him out to the car, trying to think of how to say all that I felt.

Just before he opened the car door, he cupped my face in both his hands and asked me to remember what he had said about Margie's and my relationship.

"One more time?" he asked. "Who was to blame tonight?"

I was able to look him straight in his eyes. "Margie. Not me."

"Remember."

"I will," I promised, and he kissed me on the lips, a kiss so full of that same tenderness and strength that for a minute all I could do was lean on him as his arms went around me. I whispered, "Thank you, thank you."

He lifted my chin once more and said, looking into my eyes, "If you ever need me, I'll be there. Just call my name, and I'll be there for you. Always."

Then he was gone.

And I was left standing alone in front of Happy Corner, my fingers on my lips.

A door had opened between us that I had not been ready for. But I knew we would never return to the place we had been before.

CHAPTER THIRTY-EIGHT
Reality

hen we caught sight of Ma coming home from the depot next day, struggling to hold a package and her purse, every step labored, all thoughts of family conferences and problems with Margie melted away. We ran to meet her, Margie taking the package and her purse, I putting an arm under hers to steady her. Although it took her a few minutes before she could even talk, she reached out to both of us, her hands patting our cheeks. Tired tears streaked down hers, her hat askew, grayish strands of hair escaped from the usually immaculate chignon, her coat hung listlessly from a body too weak to support it.

Once she had caught her breath, she made light of her weakness, telling us she had not walked that far for a long time. "Remember, girls," she told us, her breath catching as she made the effort to speak normally, "I stand still in the kitchen."

Clearly, she did not intend that we comment on the change in her. But, looking at each other, we shared an awareness of the pallor of her cheeks, the darkness spreading beneath her eyes, the frightening slenderness of a body known for its stocky strength.

By the time we reached Happy Corner, she did not demur when we divested her of coat, hat, hose and shoes. Her ankles were so swollen it was difficult to untie the shoelaces, and Margie ran for a basin.

"Which would feel better on your feet?" she asked. "Hot or cold water?"

"I think just water. Plain water. Any temperature will feel wonderful."

"Ilmi," Ma took my hand, opening the package, "look at this pattern. Does it look like the style the girls in school were wearing?"

It was a versatile pattern that could be adjusted to make a muslin dress with long sleeves, a drop waist, also gathered, a separate skirt with a middy top, and a bow to tie under the collar.

"It's perfect, Ma." The dress and the variations in one step had potentially doubled the size of my wardrobe. She had bought enough muslin for a summer dress, which I desperately needed. The heavy skirts and tops, which had lasted me through the school year, were too warm and uncomfortable at home and inappropriate for dances. "I love the color." It was a soft peach, popular in the catalogs, thus, I assumed, very much in style that summer.

"Margie, next time it'll be your turn for some new outfits. But you have grown so much, I need to measure you. In the meantime, I think I can make over last year's blue summer dress of Ilmi's."

I threw in for good measure. "It'll look much nicer on you, Margie, than it ever did on me." Blue was always a good color for Margie.

"Wouldn't you like to get your dress clothes off and a house dress on?" Margie undid the decorative silvery bar pin we had bought her for Christmas to attach to her collar and began to unbutton the white collar itself and the front of Ma's good black dress.

Ma sighed with relief as we divested her of dress and girdle and garter belt, all of the appurtenances that should have fit her tightly but hung instead, even on the tightest fastening.

Moving the coffee pot to a front burner to heat faster, I removed the hair pins from her chignon and began to brush her hair.

"My goodness, girls, what have I done to deserve all of this attention?"

We answered vague variations of "We missed you, Ma," wondering how she could have come to this state without our noticing it before. Had we been so wrapped up in our own needs that we had ignored her appearance? Or had she put on such a good act that we had believed her when she had said she would enjoy working at Jukolas' rather than staying at home or spending the summer at another logging camp.

"Just think," she had told us. "When my work for the day is over, I can walk up and down Chestnut Street and window shop. Each time I come home, I'll know more about what is in fashion and what to buy when there are sales. How much easier it will be than having to order from the catalog and guess your sizes! And, Ilmi, every weekend we can count the amount of my pay and see if we are any closer to getting you to Macalester."

I had figured the required amount to the last penny, including the scholarship the college offered, the gifts of money I had received for graduation, and the distance between what we had amassed and what I would need for even one year spent at their campus. That afternoon I realized what I should have known all the time. It had seemed like a dream, and it was.

The first night Ma was home, I had wanted to hold what I had considered our first real family council meeting. The Radcliffes had held them weekly. Everyone, including Carolyn and me, had a chance to talk about the previous week and what about it had been good, what not so good. Then we all had a chance to offer suggestions or to make resolutions to make the following week better. I had wanted to ask Ma and Margie to sit down with me after supper with the same idea in mind. I would bring up two subjects. The first would be Riisto Salmela and last night's cavorting. The second would be the question of what Margie should do next year.

"I don't believe she should go back to any logging camp for another winter," I had intended to tell Ma. "And I don't think you should either."

But now, looking at Ma, I didn't think she was in any condition to deal with problems of any kind, much less major ones like that. The only thing I felt good about was that she did not have any work to do at Happy Corner. The washing and ironing, the cleaning and scrubbing, the window-washing and airing had all been completed even to her high standards before we had left for the dance the night before.

By the time Ma got home, it was almost noon, and Margie had bathed, washed her clothes and hung them on the line, cleaned up her own mess, and downed enough coffee so that although I was sure she still felt sick and nauseous, she no longer looked or smelled drunk. I did not think Ma could catch the smell of alcohol on her breath, but I had had her brush her teeth and wash out her mouth with baking soda over and over again just in case.

Serving Ma and Margie some coffee and *korppua*, I tried to hide the fear that made the hand holding the coffee pot shake until I needed two hands to steady itself. I moved a chair near the bed to serve as a table so Ma did not need to get up. When I sat down opposite Margie, the lump in my throat was too large to allow me to swallow even a sip of coffee. Catching Margie's eye, I saw my feelings echoed in the stiffness of her posture and the two-handed hold on a cup that didn't make it to her lips. We were terrified. Ma was our rock, our refuge, the center point around which our lives circled. And she was ill, obviously very ill. I reached a hand across the table to grasp the hand Margie reached out to me, and we clung together as if, by touching each other we could find strength.

Ma continued talking lightly, telling us about the men living at Jukolas, funny stories about their reactions to dinners she had made, a little about the Jukolas themselves, whom we did not know at all. She described the bedroom they had given her.

I did not hear a word she said, though I nodded and responded when she paused. I wanted to throw my arms around her and beg her, "Ma, don't be sick. Please, Ma, don't be sick. I can't bear to have you be sick."

Margie looked as if it were taking every ounce of her energy not to burst into tears.

Again and again I asked myself why I had not noticed this change in Ma before. How could I possibly not have seen it coming? Had I been so selfish, so blind? Or had the work at Jukolas simply taken the last of what little strength she had left to draw on?

What should we do?

Ma obviously did not want us to comment on her condition. She wanted us to act as if all were well. As if . . . this were the norm.

So, were we to pretend along with her?

How could we?

My attempts at pretense had worn themselves out already. Obviously, so had Margie's. But how were we to approach a truth that she did not want us to acknowledge?

"Excuse me, Ma. I have to go to the bathroom," I finally said, making a frantic rush for the door.

"Me, too," said Margie, following me in a similar mad rush.

We met each other outside and clung together in desperation.

"There must be absolutely no repeat of what happened last night," I told Margie fiercely, holding her by the arms and forcing her to look me in the eyes. "You can see how ill Ma is. If she heard what you did, it would be more than she could stand right now. We have to think of her first. In the meantime, no more dances for either one of us until we find out what's wrong with Ma. DO YOU HEAR ME?"

Margie's eyes turned a deep violet blue, and her skin, usually pink and ivory, looked mottled red and white. "I'm sorry, Ilmi. I'm truly sorry. I promise from the bottom of my heart I'll put Ma first until she's well again."

If she gets well again, I thought.

My heart sank as I watched Ma try to breathe normally. Her feet were so swollen that when we had rolled down her stockings and undid the ties, fixing a basin for her to soak them in and then insisting that she take off her good dress and lie down with her feet elevated, which seemed to ease her breathing, too, she had said, weakly, "You must not fuss like this, girls." But she did not refused any of our ministrations.

What I saw was equally clear to Margie, who had hung up Ma's dress and rinsed out her stockings without being asked. She had also set a bread dough rising and begun the preparations for dinner.

When I reached over to give Margie a hug, she repeated, "Please don't tell Ma about last night, Ilmi. Please!"

I did not. Not because I didn't think Ma should be told but because I didn't think that she could manage to handle any bad news. She looked so exhausted that we were both frightened.

Once she had slipped into a restful sleep, I took Margie outside where we held a mini-conference.

That was the beginning of a week of terror.

On Monday morning, Mr. Salin drove the three of us to Virginia even though it was not a day for him to go to the Co-op Creamery. First, he dropped me off at Jukolas, where I told them that Ma would not be able to return to cook until she was given permission from the doctor.

"We have been worried about her these last few weeks ourselves, but we have not known quite what to do," Mrs. Jukola said sympathetically. " I think you are doing the right thing, you and your sister. Let us know what the doctor says. In the meantime, we'll find someone to replace her. No one will cook as well, but we'll manage. Do not let her worry about us or her job. If and when she is able to come back, there will always be work for her here. But her health must come first."

I had to fight from crying because they had been so kind.

Margie had stayed in the truck with Mr. Salin, who then drove us straight to the hospital entrance. Dr. Malmstrom was busy, his nurse said, but when he saw us, he told her to arrange his schedule so that he could see Ma immediately.

"Dr. Malmstrom," I said, "I do not believe you have met my sister Margie."

Margie shook hands with him in her most mannerly way, and said, in English, "I am happy to meet you, Dr. Malmstrom." We had practiced so that she was able to say that with very little Finnish accent. He grasped Ma's hand and drew her into his office, murmuring words of reassurance.

He asked us to wait in the outer room while he checked Ma thoroughly. It seemed to take a long, long time, and when his nurse came out to usher us into his inner office so that he could talk to the three of us together, he did not exude his usual jovial self.

"Your mother has extremely high blood pressure," he explained. "You could bring her to Duluth to see a specialist, but I don't think any other doctor would suggest anything different from what I'm going to tell you. First, Mrs. Brosi, you must learn to be extremely patient with yourself, with your family, and with me, in the matter of obeying to the best of your ability our directions. Sometimes you will disagree with us, but if you wish to feel better, then you must listen."

"Girls," he told both of us, "your mother needs from six weeks to two months of complete rest. This means mental relaxation as well as physical quiet. She may go to the bathroom but not climb stairs. Most of all, she must stop worrying." Margie and I both nodded.

He paused, looking at Ma. "I am deeply sympathetic to the situation you are in. I'm particularly pleased with the nice daughters who have come with you to talk to me. If there's any other way I can help, please do not hesitate to come back. But for now, your prescription is very simple. I cannot give you pills to make you better. You must allow your daughters to pamper you. Do light handwork that gives you pleasure. Have the girls read to you. Allow neighbors to visit, but do not encourage them to stay long. Above all, listen to your body. When you feel tired, rest and sleep, not only all night but every afternoon and often in the morning, too."

I desperately wanted to ask him if she obeyed all of his instructions, would she get well, but I was afraid.

Hanging back after Ma and Margie began making their slow way out of the hospital toward Mr. Salin's truck, I did ask, haltingly, "Then will she be well again?"

"You are very strong, my young friend," he answered, reaching out one of his sturdy arms to give me a hug. "You'll need to call upon that strength and courage increasingly as the weeks go by. I had hoped that the stay with Mrs. Maki would make a lasting difference in her physical health as well as her emotional well-being. But I fear that she has pushed her physical strength as far as it will carry her. What kind of work has she been doing?"

"She has been cooking in logging camps for the last few years, mostly winters but sometimes summers, too. This summer she accepted a position as head cook for Jukolas' boarding house. When she came home yesterday, it was as if all of her strength had been leeched out of her. I can't understand why we hadn't noticed. She had seemed so . . . enthusiastic . . . so sure that she could earn enough over the summer so that I could go to Macalester next year."

"I assume you earned a scholarship."

"Yes. And friends were generous with graduation presents. But," I continued miserably, "I should have known. She insisted that she could earn much more at Jukolas than I could if I would just take care of Margie and work part time at Salins' so that there was a chance, just a small chance that I might be able to go there to college."

"You understand the situation now?" His question, though kind, was incisive.

"Of course." I was surprised that he even had to ask.

"I was sure you did. I just wanted to make sure." He paused for a long time. "I am very sorry, truly sorry, Marion."

I reasserted, "Ma comes first."

"Yes."

We shook hands. Or perhaps I should say he held my hand and patted it gently. "Life sometimes seems very unfair."

Fighting back the tears, I hurried after Ma and Margie, fully aware not only that the news about Ma was not good but that my dreams of attending Macalester College were not going to come true.

If Ma continued to work as hard as she had been, the money she earned would pay for her funeral, not for my tuition.

Just a few short weeks before, Ma had insisted and our joint figuring had supported that there was a slight possibility that if Ma earned the salary Jukolas had promised, and if I could get a job either on campus or, as I had during high school, off campus working for my room and board, we might make it, just barely make it. During the summer my task would be to care for the house and Margie and to earn extra money by working part time for Salins during their busy days. Ma could come home every other weekend or whenever the Jukolas arranged a substitute for her, and we would save every penny we could toward my expenses.

I was fully aware of how unfair this would seem to Margie and how much effort it would exact of Ma. My unselfish, caring self said I should forget the dream and sign up for the teacher training program, which was part of the Virginia Junior College curriculum. A limited number of 1928 graduates would be accepted into that program, based upon their high school class rank. Mine would place me on top of the list. I could not spend time feeling bad for whoever was going to be discharged from the program because her class rank was the lowest of those who had applied. The one-year program would enable me to teach in a country school and earn money to support Ma and Margie.

On the other hand, my selfish . . . and not uncaring self . . . insisted that if I were to attend college winter and summer, carrying an overload of classes straight through, that I would be able to teach in a graded school, earn a much improved salary, and support Ma and Margie.

But that would take at least three years.

Ma had assured me that she could manage three more years of winters cooking in logging camps or in boarding houses, taking Margie with her.

Saturday night had proved her wrong. Margie could no longer be dragged with Ma from pillar to post, as the old saying went. She needed stability and discipline, a school that would require her attendance on a regular basis and the company of young people her own age, preferably young people whose families mandated that their daughters dress and behave according to what was appropriate for their age. That meant no more rumble seats with Riisto Salmela. No more unchaperoned country dances. No more life among rough, largely untutored loggers whose life-style and language were no pattern for Margie to emulate.

And now it was obvious that it was not only Margie's future which was at risk. Much more seriously, it was Ma herself.

I wanted to crawl into a corner and hide, to go into the sauna and scream and take steam until I was dizzy and my spirit was cleansed of selfishness.

But there was no sense in bemoaning what had to be. Someday I would go to college. But next year was not going to be the year. Now was not going to be the time.

"I'll be there for you. Just call my name, and I'll be there. Always."

On our way back to Zim and all during the next few days I remembered those words. It seemed as if I had heard them years ago instead of a few days, and I wondered if he had meant them. But the look on his face and the sound of his voice and the touch of his hand had made me believe him.

So I wrote a short note to "Clifford Johnson, Angora, Minnesota," hoping there were not so many Clifford Johnson's that this short address would find its mark.

Dear Cliff,

Little did I know on Saturday night that I would be writing, barely three days later to ask for your help. Ma is very ill, and I will definitely not be able to go to Macalester. Thank goodness before I left Mt. Iron I asked for a letter of recommendation from Mr. Quicksted and an official copy of my class rank and my letter grades, intending to send them to St. Paul with my application.

But they will not, now, go to St. Paul. I desperately need to talk to someone about my choices for next year. Part of me says that I should just stay home, take care of Ma and Margie and forget my dreams of furthering my education.

The problem is, of course, that should I do that, then we'd have no income at all. There is another alternative: I could go to Virginia to apply to their Teacher Training Program. It begins in September and ends with actual student teaching. Those who pass both the academic program, which is extremely rigorous, and the actual work done under the supervision of an experienced teacher are certified to teach in a country school.

If I were to use all of the money Ma and I have saved for my dream of going to Macalester, Ma and Margie would be able to survive here. Just barely. But they would survive. And I would work for my room and board while I prepared myself for the second semester, during which I would work full time at teaching.

I am torn between two alternatives, neither one of which seems workable. Have you any suggestions? Although I know you are not much older than I am, it was very clear Saturday night that you are far ahead of me in terms of experience. I do not mean that badly. I simply mean that you have been out in the real world far longer than I.

Last Saturday night you saved Margie from an experience that could have ruined her future forever. I trusted you implicitly then to know what to do, that I can trust you to help me . . . at least to give me advice. Could you drive to Zim so that we could talk? If not, would you write?

Awaiting your insights, I sign myself, affectionately,
Marion

Clenching my teeth to keep myself from crying, I walked to the depot, bought the stamp necessary to send the letter, and left it with the postmaster there.

In the meantime, I wrote another letter addressed to the director of the Teacher Training Program, Virginia Junior College, Virginia, Minnesota, requesting a copy of the application form and including the letter of recommendation, my class rank, and a copy of the classes I had taken with the letter grades appended. I sent that one the next day, just in case. I reasoned that an application was not an acceptance. Should they accept me, then I would have to make the decision of whether to go or not.

Margie and I moved through the rest of that week doing what the day required, trying to be cheerful and happy. I entertained Ma with my yearbook, reading aloud the messages teachers and friends had written, expurgating those that dwelt too directly with Gino and explaining what we had done to prompt the reminiscences that were referred to.

It all seemed as if it had happened to someone else in some other world.

The night of my eighth grade graduation when I walked across the bridge over the St. Louis River, tore up and threw away my valedictory speech, and thought briefly of floating with those pieces into nothingness, I thought that life could deal me no harder blow.

How childish that all seemed now! I had dreamed and set myself to making those dreams come true. But I had never considered the price Ma and Margie had paid for my dreams. Oh, of course, I had done my part. I knew that. I had worked hard at Vessels and even at Radcliffs. I had driven myself to excel in school and won the laurels that I had sought.

And all that time Ma had been working in logging camps, doing heavy, unceasing work. And Margie had missed out on critical years of her own growth and development.

A letter arrived from Virginia by return mail requesting me to appear at the office of the director the following Friday at eleven o'clock for an important interview.

Cliff didn't write. He had borrowed his dad's car and simply appeared on Thursday morning.

When I heard the car coming, I ran out to meet him.

He gave me a quick hug, looked me square in the eyes, said, "Always," asked if Ma were presentable and if he could see her.

She was and he did.

This was the first time he and Margie had met since that dreadful Saturday night, and I could tell by the look in her eyes and the way she shied away that she was terrified he would bring up her misbehavior.

He simply said, "Hi, Margie. It's good to see you."

She went back to kneading dough, and he pulled up a chair so he could sit next to Ma. He took hold of her hand and asked if she remembered him.

Ma still had her doubts, and she was never shy about voicing them. "It's Cliff, the Rice River Romeo, right?"

"Right guy, outdated nickname," he answered. "I've been there and done that. It's not my style anymore."

"So . . ." a fit of coughing interrupted Ma's question. He reached back and held her until the coughing ceased then doubled the pillows until she seemed more comfortable.

"My sister Faye has taught the rest of us . . . a lot," he commented apropos of nothing, it seemed. Then he answered the unspoken question. "I finished school in Minneapolis and have a barber shop in Angora now. I thought I'd have to move to Virginia to get enough business, but the appointment book seems to fill up faster than I can get the work done. I think it helps that I can talk Finn and joke around with the old bachelors. And I know the latest styles for the younger guys."

Ma nodded and grasped the hand he had been holding with her own hand.

"You took Marion to the dance last Saturday night?"

"Yes, and Margie, too."

"You don't mind taking her little sister along?"

"Remember I have four sisters of my own. I'm used to a big family."

"That's good." Ma leaned back on the pillows, looking gray, her breathing heavy.

"I came to see how you are and to visit with Marion, too. Would you mind if I took her for a ride?"

Ma smiled and shook her head.

Margie said, "Go ahead. I have to keep an eye on the bread."

And so we went. Not far. Just far enough to be able to talk.

As soon as we were out of sight of the house, he stopped the car and held out his arms for me. It was such a relief to have a shoulder to cry on, not to have to be the strong one, that everything I had been holding in poured out.

He waited until I had gone over all of it again and again, and then he said, "There's a new song out I'd like you to think about: "I'll be loving you, always." I'm not sure about the words, but I know it has the right feeling."

"I . . . I . . . I'm not ready . . . to make that kind of commitment," I had to say. "I wrote to you because right now, you're my best friend. You seem to understand."

"I'm not asking you for anything more than you are ready for. But I want you to know that those words capture how I feel about you and how I will probably feel about you forever. I've talked to my mother and dad about your problem. I hope you don't mind. But since Dad has quit drinking, he seems to have very good sense about problems. And Ma cares deeply about people.

"I don't know if anyone has ever told you the story. How could you know? But when our neighbor, Mrs. Hakala, my aunt, was too sick to nurse her baby at the same time Raymond was born, my mother took both babies, nursed and cared for them both. She's like that.

"One of our neighbors is losing her eyesight. I can't tell you how many times my mother has gone there for an afternoon or taken the girls to her house, sometimes the boys, too, for a day, to clean and wash clothes and iron. Then they will sit on the porch and knit and tell stories and laugh. Mother is like that. When someone needs help, she's there. I'm telling you this because I want you to know that what she is offering comes from the heart."

"I don't know what you mean." I leaned back against his arm, which rested behind me along the edge of the seat.

"We would like to have your mother and Margie come to live with us this fall while you go to Virginia's teacher-training program."

Silence. I honestly did not know what to say. I took the route of the least important first. "What if they don't accept me?"

Cliff hooted. "From everything I've read, the applicants are chosen based on their class rank and grade point average in high school. Have you written to them or heard anything?"

"Yes," I admitted. "I'm to go for an interview on Friday—oh, my goodness, that's tomorrow!"

Then I tackled the more serious question. "Ma will never accept charity. She's too ill to do anything. If she were well enough to cook or to clean or in some way to contribute to the upkeep of the house, that'd be different. But she can't even climb stairs, and all of your bedrooms are upstairs."

"One of the downstairs davenports opens up into a bed. It can be closed during the day so that she can lie down and still feel part of whatever's going on. On warm days, the boys will help her into the sun room. On cloudy days, someone will read to her or use the Victrola or the player piano, or Mother will just sit down and talk with her."

"Margie could help with the cooking." I was desperately trying to think of ways to offset the incredible offer with equivalent work.

"No. Or perhaps on weekends. She is Casey's age, and she'll go to Alango, School 45 with him."

"But she's not prepared for school at all."

"Don't worry. Faye is over-prepared. All she's been able to do for most of her life is read. She can work with Margie until school starts. It'll be a wonderful way to build Faye's self-esteem—she always thinks of herself as being useless because of the polio and her weak legs—and Margie is so full of fun, she'll help Faye to see that there's more to life than pain and problems."

"We'd have to talk to Ma about this."

"I know. And I know that it won't be easy to convince her. But if we gang up on her, I think we can prevail. After all, there's Mother and Dad, Marie and Pat and Doris and Faye, Brother Bill, Walter and Warren and Casey and Raymond and me, not to mention you and Margie. She'll just be out-gunned."

"But Margie, I don't know . . ."

"I'll put this to you straight. My mother is a wonderful woman in many ways, but she does not have the driving force that your mother has. I think Margie will find life a lot more comfortable when there is a little less expected of her. You and your mother are a tough act to follow. The teachers at Alango won't have any built-in expectations of Margie. They'll just see her as another new student, one who happens to be staying with us for a year or so. It'd be a lot easier than sending her to school here, where the teacher would expect her to be the kind of student you were."

I thought about what he was saying, and it did make sense. It made good sense. I could work for my room and board in Virginia first semester. We would have to set aside money for me to live with a family while I did my student teaching second semester. But there would be nine other girls in the same boat. "I think the program takes in nine students each fall. Or maybe it's eleven. I know there is a very limited number. And in the meantime, some of the money we had set aside for me to go to Macalester could be used to help pay for Ma's and Margie's expenses at your house."

Cliff started to argue but thought better of it. "Your mother and my folks can fight that one out."

And so it was arranged.

The next day, the brief interview complete, the director of the Teacher Training program stood up, held out his hand, and congratulated me. "You have the highest class rank of any of the candidates I have interviewed thus far for a position in our program. My secretary will give you information about what the program entails as you leave since you have only a brief time to prepare. You'll have to find your own place to stay, but you may find someone else to share those expenses. Otherwise," his left hand covered mine, "I'm extremely pleased to have a student of your caliber enter our program and shall look forward to seeing you at our opening convocation very soon."

And that was that.

I never did find out who was at the bottom of the list and was, therefore, dropped from the program.

We spent one last weekend together at Happy Corner, and then, suddenly, Ma and Margie were whisked away, and I was left packing my clothes to move to another third floor room where, until January, I would be a housekeeper.

But even that was a source of joy, for the Savolainens had returned from their extended trip out East, bringing Anna's mother with them. My chief task would be to spend time with her, reading aloud from Finnish and English newspapers, magazines, and books. The Savolainens had hired a nurse to be responsible for her physical care, and they spent a good deal of time with her, also. But I was to be her companion. I listened to her stories and, unbeknownst to her or to Alex and Anna, encouraged her to be as specific as she could be. Each night before I began my homework, I wrote down her memories. They came to be a source of constant joy when, as the year progressed, she gradually slipped away. But while I had been there, I had captured a treasured moment which I was able to give to Alex and Anna when I left.

It was a small recompense for all that they had done for me, but they seemed to find in that act an enormous solace.

I had read once and never forgotten a verse that said:

> All things to nothingness descend.
> Grow old and die and meet their end;
> Man dies, iron rusts, wood goes decayed;
> Towers fall, walls crumble, roses fade . . .
>
> Nor long shall any name resound
> Beyond the grave, unless it be found
> In some clerk's book; IT IS THE PEN
> GIVES IMMORTALITY TO MEN.

It was a message I was to remember all of my life.

CHAPTER THIRTY-NINE
Cliff

I awoke surrounded by white. But unlike fog, I sensed shape and form. I could feel the crispness of a sheet under my hands. And a curtain swayed in the breeze from an open window. But when I tried to turn my head to the window, hearing thunder and seeing flashes of lightning, I gasped at the echoing thunder and lightning within me. When I tried to open my eyes more than a crack, my world turned into splinters of pain.

Shaking, physically aware that my head was covered with a cloth of some sort, I sensed a shadowy presence near me and felt someone holding my hand.

"Lie still," a gentle voice ordered. Squeezing my hand, it answered the questions I simply could not ask. When I tried to ask "Where . . ." I became nauseated. The shadowy form held a basin. Nothing much came, but the thunder and lightning reverberated inside me from one ear to the other, and I would have fallen backward had the figure not caught me.

Tears seeped from under my eyelids, and slowly the worst of the storm within me abated.

"Squeeze my hand if you want the window closed."

I kept my hand immobile, feeling somewhat akin to the storm outside. Droplets of rain—just a few—touched the bed. My hand explored the crisp sheets, blankets, and a gown that wasn't mine.

"We've forgotten the question. You are in the hospital in Virginia. I brought you here. You were in bed in the teacherage, obviously very sick." Just then the figure moved. I grasped for the familiar hand, my link with the world and reality.

A cool woman's hand replaced it. "I am Dr. Malmstrom's nurse, here to give you some relief from the pain. You will sleep then, and soon he will be in to explain everything to you. In the meantime, try to let the medication allow you to relax." The hand patted mine comfortingly and disappeared. Her crisp dress sounded as if it had just been stiff starched and ironed.

I felt myself being carried away like the wind and cried until I felt the firm masculine hand linking me to the earth and life.

A bright light pierced the darkness, but I was not of this earth, nor was the tunnel leading me there. A place of darkness yawed, too. It frightened me.

The hand seemed to know. It tightened, and a voice began to hum. The tune was familiar, and my mind provided the words to it, though where I had heard it before I could not remember:

"I'll be loving you always, with a love that's true always. When the things you've planned need a helping hand, I will understand always, always. Days may not be fair always; that's when I'll be there always—not for just an hour, not for just a day, not for just a year, but always." And with the song, the lights disappeared, and I fell into a heavy, sedated sleep.

As I awoke, I heard Dr. Malmstrom right by the bed. "I'm sorry I didn't get here earlier. I had a very difficult birth that turned into a C-section. The mother is fine, but we lost the baby." He sounded tired and dis-spirited, not his usual ebullient self. "Fill me in."

"I was on my way to Duluth. We had heard that the Coolerator plant was hiring. But I stopped at the school in Peyla where she taught to drop off letters from her mother and sister who are staying at our house. The school was dark and empty though it was the middle of the day. The teacherage was dark too, and at first I thought she had left. I knocked and finally went in anyway. The whole room smelled of vomit, and she must have tried to make it into the slop pail. She was lying behind the curtain on her bed. It's a one-room school with a teacherage adjoining," the voice explained. "She was thrashing on the bed, crying from the pain. I think she was unconscious because she didn't open her eyes to see me. She was just limp, holding her head, sometimes screaming. I wrapped her in a quilt and drove straight here."

"It's a good thing you had a car and were wise enough to bring her in." I recognized Dr. Malmstrom's voice again.

"Well," the voice paused, unwilling to accept a compliment he felt unworthy of. "It's my dad's car. And I care for her . . . a lot . . . though I don't think she knows it . . . or even wishes to acknowledge it right now. But if I can comfort her . . . even a little . . . I'll stay as long as I can do that."

"Hyvasti," Dr. Malmstrom said, clasping the shadow on the shoulder. Trying to modify his normal booming voice, he added, "You did well."

"What is wrong with her, sir?"

"If you step outside, I'll answer your questions and then have you come in when I explain. She will need the comfort."

I heard the conversation as if it were through a haze, dealing with someone else. Then I felt Dr. Malmstrom sitting near the bed, telling me what he was going to do: "Well, what have we now, my grown-up Miss Ilmi Marianna, now Marion?"

His experienced hands tried to lift me with pillows, propping me up, but the minute I was raised from a prone position, I gasped and gagged and cried and shook with the force of the rain pattering against the window.

"I will be as quick as I can." Dr. Malmstrom was as good as his word. But by the time he reached the layer closest to my head, I could not hold back the scream. Lowering me, he moved, and I reached for the comforting hand. It appeared willy-nilly, no doubt in response to my scream.

"This will hurt so hold tightly."

He took a small black shape of some kind from a pocket of his white jacket, turned my head to the left, where it lay an entity of its own, separate from me, or I would not have been able to bear it.

"Relax if you can and let me do the work."

The hand that somehow was there for me squeezed.

The instrument neared my ear. I pushed it away with all of the strength I had and fainted.

When I awoke, a nurse was cleaning me up. I had thrown up again.

I wanted to ask if I were going to die, but Dr. Malmstrom forestalled me. "I suspect that you have had an earache for some time. Correct me if I'm right by squeezing my hand."

I realized that I had received some kind of painkiller again. I had been moved from my "bad" side to my "good" side with my bad side up.

"In simplest terms, that earache has gotten worse and worse. The infection has spread from the outer ear into the bone behind the ear called the 'mastoid.' It has nowhere to go from there except into the brain, into a kind of meningitis. Thank God in spite of all of the pain you are experiencing, you were brought in just in time to forestall that.

"As soon as I'm through explaining this to you, we will bring you into the operating room, where we will put you to sleep. I will drill a hole in that mastoid bone, allowing the infection to drain out. It will not happen quickly or easily, but it will happen, Miss Marion. Do you trust me?"

I tried to nod.

"Your friend will make arrangements to be here while the anesthetic wears off. The nurse is ready now to give you an injection to relax you. Do you understand and accept what I'm going to do? Squeeze your friend's hand if you do."

I tried to nod and clung to the hand as hard as I could and managed two words in a whisper: "Please sing."

The last sounds I heard were "Carolina Moon, keep shining, shining on the one who waits for me . . ."

They were also the first sounds I heard when I came back from the operating room.

The pain had not really abated, but it now grew, peaked, dissipated, and began again in a cycle radiating from my mastoid bone. Several times a day Dr. Malmstrom came in to irrigate it. I dreaded those moments.

The shadow held my hand, sharing his strength with me. Of course he was no longer a shadow, although my room was kept dark.

"Do you still have your dad's car?" I asked when it was possible for me to phrase a full sentence without vomiting or push the pain beyond bearing.

"Pa and Casey came to get it. It's okay."

"But where are you staying?"

"Dr. Malmstrom is lending me a bed upstairs in his garage and providing me with dinner. He's arranged for me to get all of the good food you're not ready to eat yet."

"You were the shadow."

"Yes."

"Would you mind singing again?"

"I'll do anything you want. Would you like me to brush your hair? As soon as Dr. Malmstrom gives the okay, I'll wash and fix it for you."

"That would be lovely," I sighed. In the dim world where I slept and dozed and fought the tears and fell into a false sleep, it didn't signify. Having it brushed slowly was comforting though. I liked "Always" and "Carolina Moon" best and never tired of hearing them sung in his deep baritone voice.

320

And so we went on forever, it seemed, the days slipping into weeks, the weeks into a month with no appreciable change, the nurses changing linens, giving me bed baths, providing relief from pain; and in between, Cliff, my shadow, by my side, sometimes singing, sometimes just sitting and talking quietly, always holding my hand.

A letter arrived from Ma:

"Dearest Ilmi," it began, "I still can't get used to calling you 'Marion.' I am doing much better, and Margie is, too. She enjoys going to the Alango school. No one there compares her with you. The big surprise is that I got a letter from Knute, your pa. He finally has a job that he likes. He was chosen to be the caretaker of Mesaba Park, which is on the way to Hibbing on a lake. He has a small house there with a dog he calls Babe. He said that he will be sending us a small check every month, and I believe that he means it. That will help when you are well again and I am, too, so we can go back to our house in Zim. Please know that we are thinking of you every day and wishing you well. Cliff keeps us informed about how you are doing, and Dr. Malmstrom sent me a letter also, for which I was very grateful. Margie sends all of her love, as do I. Your mother, Mary Rajamaki Brosi"

It was written in Finnish, of course, but that was the gist of the contents. I was enormously grateful to hear from her, yet I was equally grateful that she could not come to visit me. Somehow, seeing her would remind me of all of the responsibilities I could not assume right then.

One day, the nurse came in to tell me I had company. Cliff left quietly, saying he would have a smoke.

In came Arnie and Leonard, Java's and my dancing partners from summer days in Zim. They brought me a gold metal box with an eighteenth-century man and lady engraved on top and filled with candy. They had come to entertain me and make me laugh. I enjoyed the candy, but it hurt to laugh. Clearly, they were uncomfortable with the hospital room— its quiet, white simplicity. Still, it was nice of them to come.

An even more important visitor followed them perhaps a week later— a representative of the St. Louis County Board of Education of the Unorganized Territory, informing me that they had found a replacement to finish the year in Peyla and probably would not have a job for me next year. It was unlikely that I would be strong enough anyway, Dr, Malmstrom had told them.

I should have been upset. But when he left, I felt relief. How long had it been since I had not been responsible? Forever, it seemed. I had long since considered it up to me to care for Ma and for Margie. Way back when we lived in Kinney and Pa left. Even more when I had worked frantically to finish eighth grade so that I could go on to high school. All the time I was working for my board and room, striving for a better life for myself, yes, but for them, too. Ma had pulled my hair when Margie had misbehaved because I was older and should, therefore, have been responsible.

I had barely finished one year of teacher training before I had become responsible for eight grades in the one-room school in Peyla.

But I had not been responsible for the need of a mastoid operation. I was only partly responsible for making myself well. I was to do as I was told. Other people were taking care of me.

In spite of the pain that would still have been excruciating were it not for the medicine, my sole responsibility was—wasn't. Gradually as the weeks went on, I began to accept the freedom that had been granted me. No one expected anything of me except to do what I was told—gradually a bit more as I slowly improved.

And Cliff was always there, the package of Camels in his shirt pocket, staying relatively free, for he rarely went outside to light up.

We never talked of the future. We lived in the "now." That pleased Dr. Malmstrom. He said Cliff was making me stronger and helping me in my recovery.

One evening, Gino Vanucci came. I had already been prepared for bed and was floating on a lavender cloud, looking at the sunset, when there was a knock on the door. Holding a bunch of wild flowers, still in his mining clothes, unwashed, unchanged, he came.

"I am sorry to see you like this. But I had to see you. I had to talk to you before anyone else. I'm getting married. I don't want to, but I have to. Do you understand?"

My heart lurched from joy at seeing him to disbelief. "Then why?"

He just sat there, looking miserable. "I want you to know that you are the love of my life."

"But your plans to go to college? What happened?"

"One of us had to stay home and work. Kabe and I flipped a coin, and I lost. I lost all around," he said bitterly.

Then he left, and despite my tries, some bit of me went with him.

But when he left, Cliff came back into the room. Without asking any questions, he took hold of my hand again, patting it gently, as if he understood without any explanation how I felt.

Cliff had, unwittingly, turned into the most important person in my life, the one I turned to when I was in pain, the one who seemed to understand without my telling him exactly how I felt and what I needed. I did not need to worry about Ma or Margie. They were both being taken care of. I did not need to worry about myself. He and Dr. Malmstrom were doing that. All I had to do was to be, to let go, to allow them to take care of me. It was such a heady feeling that I began to feel light again, as if a weight had been lifted off of me. I did not need to worry about my teaching job or my students or the teacherage at Peyla—whether there was enough wood to last the rest of the winter, whether the people would come to accept me as Finnish, even though I had been foisted on them as being Italian so that they would have no choice but to speak English when I was around, whether I would find another job after I was released from the hospital, when I would be released. It was all out of my hands now, and my hands felt as light as gossamer. The pain was going away, bit by bit, and soon I would be able to return to Happy Corner. Perhaps Ma would be well enough, too, to join me there. And Margie . . . she would have to make her own decisions about her own life, I realized, with great joy and a sense of incredible relief, that she was no longer under my tutelage, that she would finish eighth grade . . . or not . . . as she decided herself. I could not make her into a practical nurse or, in fact, change her at all. She was . . . what she made of herself. Just as I would continue to be what I made of myself. But I would never again be alone. Cliff, my shadow, would always be there to hold my hand, whether I was in pain physically or emotionally. I knew I could count on him . . . always, just as the song said.

And on that thought, I let myself float away again into the land beyond pain, still an English land, where I could work as my body allowed me to work, on becoming a literate person, a writer, a teacher perhaps, one who was beloved and would be . . . always.